ROUGH
&DIRTY

The Coyote Ridge Universe

Alluring Indulgence

Kaleb
Zane
Travis
Holidays with The Walker Brothers
Ethan
Braydon
Sawyer
Brendon

The Walkers Of Coyote Ridge

Curtis
Jared
Hard to Hold
Hard to Handle
Beau
Rex
A Coyote Ridge Christmas
Mack
Kaden & Keegan
Alibi (a crossover novel)
Trey
Rafe

Brantley Walker: Off The Books

All In
Without A Trace
Hide & Seek
Deadly Coincidence
Alibi
Secrets
Confessions
Bounty
Off Course
Chain Reaction
To Have and To Hold

THE JAMESONS OF COYOTE RIDGE

Hot Chocolate Wishes
Rough & Dirty

AUSTIN ARROWS

Rush
Kaufman

CLUB DESTINY

Conviction
Temptation
Addicted
Seduction
Infatuation
Captivated
Devotion
Perception
Entrusted
Adored
Distraction
Forevermore

DEAD HEAT RANCH

Boots Optional
Betting on Grace
Overnight Love
Jared *(a crossover novel)*

DEVIL'S BEND

Chasing Dreams
Vanishing Dreams

MISPLACED HALOS

Protected in Darkness
Salvation in Darkness
Bound in Darkness

NAUGHTY HOLIDAY EDITIONS
2015
2016
2021

ROUGH & DIRTY

The Jamesons of Coyote Ridge, 2

NICOLE EDWARDS

NICOLE EDWARDS LIMITED

A dba of SL Independent Publishing, LLC
PO Box 1086
Pflugerville, Texas 78691

ROUGH & DIRTY

The Jamesons of Coyote Ridge, 2

COVER DETAILS:

Image: © ivantsov (52684348) | 123rf.com ; © primopiano (197155613) | 123rf.com

Design: © Nicole Edwards Limited

INTERIOR DETAILS:

Formatting: Nicole Edwards Limited

AUDIO DETAILS:

Narrators: TBD

ISBN: (ebook) 9781644181003 | (paperback) 9781644181010 | (audio) 9781644181027

BISAC: FICTION/ROMANCE/General | FICTION/LGBTQ

PART
ONE

ONE

Fifteen years ago...
Friday, May 15, 2009

"YOU HUNGRY?" STONE JAMESON ASKED HIS GIRLFRIEND as they walked into his mother's bright and airy kitchen.

Stephanie Shepherd, whom everyone lovingly referred to as Stevie, had texted him as she was leaving school, just as she'd done every day since they started dating exclusively in July of last year. And just as *he* always did, Stone shot back a message, asking her to come over.

It was a phenomenon he'd never experienced before, but he found if he went a few days without seeing her, he started jonesing like an addict seeking a fix. It was so intense sometimes that he figured he could likely find satisfaction by sitting across the street and staring at her from afar. Not that he'd resorted to stalking—that was insane—but he would admit he'd come damn close a few times.

He didn't have to worry about that tonight because she was there. They didn't have any formal plans, yet she'd come over anyway.

That was another surprising marvel about his relationship with Stevie: he didn't even care if they spent the evening watching movies on the couch while his mom and dad stood over them. Spending time with her, being in the same room, smelling her sweet strawberries-and-cream scent, was enough for him.

And when the hell that had become a thing, he honestly didn't know. Stone might've believed it was because Stevie was his first real girlfriend, but his lack of relationship—the sort that had a name and defined parameters—had always been his choice. Until her, he'd never had the desire to be monogamous, always worried he would find himself tied down and something better would come along. With Stevie, he didn't worry about that. He was convinced there was no such thing as something better than her.

"I won't say no to food," she said, her stomach rumbling in agreement.

"Did you skip lunch again?" He smiled down at her, trying to sound stern.

"I had an orange," she said succinctly, a hint of pride ringing in her tone.

He'd bet money that was all she'd had that day, too. "That's not lunch, baby. That's a snack."

She smiled so sweetly he had to fight the urge to wrap her in his arms and kiss her to see if she tasted the same. He would have if his mother weren't in the next room.

"Anything sound good?"

"I really hope you aren't plannin' to cook for that girl," his mother called, her voice growing closer with each word.

Stone turned to see her coming into the kitchen, a wide grin on her face.

"Hi, Stevie," she said, walking over and hugging Stone's girlfriend as though she'd been a member of the family her whole life rather than only having been introduced a few short months ago.

"Hi, Mrs. Jameson." Stevie hugged her back. "I love what you've done with your hair."

Stone stared at his mother, trying to figure out what was different. *Did she cut it? Dye it?* He had no idea. She looked the same to him. As she always did. Like a mom.

Stevie fluffed imaginary hair near her cheek. "Very hot."

His mother giggled.

She actually fucking giggled.

And were her cheeks turning pink?

Confused by what was happening, Stone said, "You don't hug *me* every time I see you."

"You got plenty of hugs growin' up." She laughed as she came around the island, her attention shifting to Stevie. "I fear for your health if you let this boy cook you anything."

"Hey," he said, feigning insult. "I can cook."

"You can." His mother nodded slowly. "Provided it comes in a can, and you can pour it in a bowl and pop it in the microwave."

Stone winked at Stevie. "It counts."

Stevie's eyes lit up with amusement. Damn, the girl was so fucking cute. Especially when she had her long blonde hair pulled back in a ponytail, her bangs sweeping across her forehead. Her little bow-shaped lips and those big brown eyes ... God, he loved looking at her.

"What's the plan for tonight?" his mother asked, opening the cabinet beneath the stove to get whatever pan she needed to make a meal.

"We don't know yet," he told her. "We thought we might just hang out here."

Behind his mother's back, Stone quirked an eyebrow at Stevie. He knew what he *wanted* to do.

"Well, I'll make somethin' simple. That way, you can have some now and more later if you're up late. Dad took Reilly and Tate to a birthday party at the skatin' rink. Won't be home until after nine. How about soft tacos? They can heat 'em up when they get home."

"Perfect." Stone honestly didn't care. The only thing he was hungry for was Stevie. "And while you do that, we'll—"

"Goddamn you, Nico Daugherty! You are *such* an asshole!"

Stone looked at his mother as Chelsea's high-pitched scream echoed through the house, followed by her stomping down the stairs.

Deborah shook her head. "I don't know what's goin' on with those two. Chels left for school pissed off at him. Came home in the same state."

Stevie was staring toward the front of the house. A second later, the front screen door slammed. Chelsea continued to shout obscenities, but now she'd taken it outside.

Stone walked around to Stevie. He leaned down and kissed her lightly on the temple. "Give me a minute."

He could feel her staring after him as he headed for the back door, choosing to walk around the house so he could keep an eye on Chelsea without interrupting. His sister was capable of fighting her own battles—she'd told him as much—but according to what his father told him and his brothers, their job was to keep an eye on her. According to Owen Jameson, that was what big brothers were for.

So that was what he would do.

"I fuckin' hate you, you stupid bastard!" Chelsea shouted at Nico, the guy she'd been dating for the past few years.

That was the term Chelsea used, anyway. Stone wasn't sure it could really be called dating. Those two broke up more times than Chelsea changed clothes in a week. And that girl thought she needed a different outfit for every damn thing—sleeping, breakfast, school, homework. He swore she changed at least five times a day.

And socks. Jesus. His sister paired her socks to match her freaking clothes, and if they didn't, she flipped her shit. Hell, Stone was content to wear the same socks until the damn things stood up on their own. Or he had right up until he met Stevie. These days he was paying a little more attention to detail. But as God was his witness, he would never match his socks to his fucking shirt, thank you very much.

"It's not what you think," Nico told her, holding his hands up in front of him.

Nico Daugherty. High school senior, star tight end for the Coyote Ridge Roughriders. One of two Coyote Ridge natives scouted by colleges in the past few years—the other being Beau Bennett, a quarterback whose plays had become standard in the coach's playbook. Unlike Beau, who'd shattered his arm in a car crash and ended his possible career in the NFL, Nico was still trying to determine whether he wanted to go to UT or LSU on a full ride. That was the rumor, anyway. Stone didn't understand what the hold-up was, but according to Chelsea, he was "being an idiot" because no one passed up the opportunity to go to the NFL one day.

Then again, Chelsea was pissed at Nico because he was entertaining colleges that she wasn't going to. Among other things.

Chelsea threw something at him. "You can take back that stupid bracelet."

Nico huffed. "Come on, Chels. Don't do this."

"Fuck you."

She threw something else. "And there's that stupid pin you gave me."

A second later, a small (probably stupid, too) teddy bear went flying across the yard next.

Obviously, Nico had done *something* wrong if she was giving back everything he'd given her. Too bad, honestly. Stone liked Nico. He didn't know the guy well, but he knew a hell of a lot about him. Not only because Nico was dating Chelsea but also because Stevie was Nico's sister's best friend. What he hadn't picked up on from Chelsea, he'd learned from Stevie.

As he stared at Chelsea, Nico made no effort to pick anything up off the ground.

"And your stupid jacket!" Chelsea squealed, making dramatic movements as she threw it on the ground, where it joined everything else.

Nico sighed.

Stone laughed. Thankfully, he was out of sight and earshot. Otherwise, his sister would've turned her wrath on him, and Stone had far better things to do than get a dressing down from his sister. He'd had more than his fair share, so he was content to let her focus her outrage on someone else.

With that said, he found it amusing as fuck that Nico wasn't placating her with bullshit. It would've only added fuel to the fire, and based on Chelsea's animated hand gestures, the flames were already hot enough.

"You're a jackass. A stupid. Fucking. Jackass."

The girl had a mouth like a sailor.

"You and Jenny deserve each other!"

Hold up. Stone stood taller, his sister's words registering. Jenny? As in Chelsea's best friend? No fuckin' way.

"Nothin' happened, Chels," Nico drawled. "I swear to God."

"Swear all you want. You're a fuckin' liar."

Since Nico continued to back up with each step Chelsea took, Stone figured it was safe to let them hash this out alone, so he headed back into the house. As fun as it was to watch, he had a girl waiting for him inside, and he already spent far too little time with her.

Since she was still in high school—only a few weeks away from graduating—Stevie's schedule and his rarely meshed. Not to mention, her parents weren't exactly keen on the idea of their eighteen-year-old daughter dating a twenty-one-year-old who was filling in at his parents' store until he could figure out what he wanted to do with his life. If the rumors were true, Stevie's father thought Stone was a deadbeat without a future and had no business preying on his little girl.

Unfortunately, the deadbeat part was spot on. Yes, it was true. He hadn't yet figured his shit out, but he was working on it. As for the preying part, well, that part of the rumor wasn't accurate. Stone had done right by Stevie, keeping his hands to himself—mostly—until she turned eighteen back in August. They'd spent almost a month in each other's company before he even kissed her.

But Stevie's folks were the only ones who seemed to have a problem. Stone's parents didn't seem to mind that Stevie was eighteen or that she was still in high school. Then again, they'd always trusted his judgment. The same went for his brothers and sisters. Deborah and Owen Jameson were lenient right up until their kids gave them a reason not to be. Stone did his best to straddle the line between right and wrong, never deviating too far in either direction.

"She's in the living room," his mother told him when he walked inside. "Dad won't be home for a while, so I'll give you two some privacy. I'll put the food in Tupperware so you can get it when you're ready."

"Thanks, Mom."

Stone went to the living room and joined Stevie on the couch, where she sat, remote in hand, flipping through channels. He sat beside her, stretching his arm out, teasing the end of her ponytail with his fingers. Her hair was silky soft and smelled like strawberries.

"Miss me?"

She giggled, leaning into him.

He loved that she did that. Loved that she was always touching him somewhere. Holding his hand, rubbing his back. What he loved the most was the way her hand slid over his thigh, the edge of her pinky grazing his dick every so often. As he said, he'd never once preyed on the girl, but Stone wasn't sure the reverse was true. Stephanie Shepherd knew what she wanted and wasn't afraid to go after it.

"You better be careful with that hand, little girl," he whispered, nipping her earlobe.

A shiver rocked her small body.

"Payback's a bitch," he promised, pressing his fingertips to her chin so he could turn her head toward him. "Is that what you want?"

Her expression was one of sweet innocence. The little minx. She knew exactly what she was doing to him.

"Kiss me, Stevie," he whispered against her mouth. "Show me how much you missed me."

Her lips met his, lingering in a sweet caress for a brief moment before he tilted his head and claimed her. Instantly, she was pliant in his arms, her hand cupping his cheek, her tongue slashing his in barely restrained hunger. This always happened when they were together. Didn't matter if he'd seen her that morning. His hunger for her simmered in anticipation, threatening to boil over as soon as he saw her again.

"God, baby," he mumbled. "Keep that up, and we'll have to take this somewhere else."

"Lead the way," she whispered, her eyes sparking with the same burning desire that threatened to incinerate him.

The girl was a handful. A tiny, sexy fucking handful.

Back when they'd first started talking—sometime in June of last year—she'd been a little shy. A friendship grew organically from their conversations whenever he saw her at one function or another. Then, one night, he asked her to grab a milkshake at the diner. She said yes, and that was all she wrote. They started dating exclusively shortly after that, taking things slow. She was the first girl he'd been with who'd captured more than just his dick's attention.

He wasn't sure if it was because she'd been seventeen at the time or what, but their relationship had started off platonic for the most part. Talking at first, then holding hands. They progressed from there. A little kissing, some light petting, but nothing more than that. Right up until she turned eighteen. That was the night she'd given *him* a birthday present when she asked him to screw her. Her exact words: "I'm tired of waitin', Stone. Screw me already."

Stone hadn't been able to tell the sweet little virgin no. He was incapable. And yeah, his ego had wanted to claim her virginity because it thrilled him that he was her first. He'd been given something no other man on the planet would ever have. He would admit he didn't cherish much, but from the moment he slid inside her, he knew what a gift it was.

Since then, he'd been doing his best to keep up and loving every second. Whatever she wanted, he was bound and determined to get it for her. And if that involved certain parts of his anatomy, so be it. The girl was kinky as fuck, and the more he introduced her to, the more she wanted.

It was safe to say he'd never met a girl like Stevie. And he seriously doubted he ever would.

"I hate you!" Chelsea screamed from the front porch.

"Shit," Stone muttered.

Please don't come in expectin' to chat.

"Go fuck yourself, Nico. I never wanna see you again!"

The screen door flew open, and Chelsea stormed inside. He looked up and saw tears in her eyes. As soon as he did, he patted Stevie's thigh and shot to his feet, heading out the door. He didn't think twice. The fucker had made his sister cry, and he was going to get a beat down for that. It was one thing to piss her off, but to break her heart … the bastard didn't get to just walk away.

Nico was grabbing the things Chelsea had thrown on the ground as Stone walked up to him. As soon as the guy was upright, Stone reared back and punched him, throwing a right hook that got him in the mouth.

Nico stumbled back, dropping the shit in his hands. "What the hell'd you do that for?"

It took everything in him not to punch the guy again. "You're a shithead, Nico."

"What the fuck did *I* do?" Nico popped off. "Your sister's fuckin' crazy."

Stone kept a firm grip on his control right up until the asshole licked the blood on his lip and grinned.

"You bastard," Stone snapped as he threw another right hook, this one harder than the first.

Nico tripped but caught himself before he hit the ground. "Goddammit, Stone. What the fuck?"

"You broke her heart, you fucker. You deserve worse."

Nico's laugh lacked humor. "Have you *met* your sister? No one breaks Chelsea's heart."

Stone watched as Nico gently touched his lip with his finger and then his tongue. He didn't smile this time. No one said he wasn't smart.

"Talk shit about her. I'm itchin' to hit you again."

"I ain't talkin' shit. She's the one tellin' everybody—" Nico rolled his eyes. "Fuck this shit."

Nico pivoted on his heel and made a beeline for his truck. Stone followed, not letting him put any distance between them. Just as Nico reached for the door handle, Stone shoved him. Nico stumbled, putting his hands up to break the fall. He rebounded back, spinning around.

"What the fuck is your problem?"

Stone didn't stop, barreling into Nico's personal space, getting right up in his face.

Nico stumbled, his back hitting the truck. Stone took advantage of his surprise, leaning in, glaring at the man. He had plenty of time to throw another punch or two, but something stopped him. Maybe it was the hint of fear in Nico's ocean-blue eyes or the gleam in his eye. Hell, it could've been the trickle of blood on his lip.

Whatever it was, his desire to break and maim turned into something else entirely.

"Seriously, man. I didn't break—"

Stone gripped Nico by the throat, careful not to apply too much pressure. He wasn't interested in killing him. He wanted to prove to the man who was in charge here.

As soon as he felt the prickle of stubble on Nico's jaw, Stone's dick kicked in his jeans. He was already rock hard from being around his girl, then add in the adrenaline rush from the fight. But every drop of blood in his body detoured right to his dick the moment Nico surrendered.

Stone remained there, holding him in place as he skimmed every inch of his face.

Nico Daugherty was, for lack of a better word, hot. There was something about the chiseled lines of his narrow face, the aristocratic nose, the high arch of his eyebrows. From the first time Chelsea introduced him to her boyfriend years ago, Stone had dropped Nico into the "I'd do him" category. And thanks to the rigorous football regimen, he was ripped. It was about the only thing Chelsea ever talked about because, according to her, being a tight end wasn't nearly as cool as being quarterback, which was why Chelsea was always harping on Nico to be better.

Then again, nothing and no one was ever really good enough for Chelsea. Stone loved her, but Jesus, was she a spoiled bitch.

But bitch or not, she was still his sister.

"What was Chelsea tellin' everybody?" Stone asked, wanting the complete story—Nico's version, at least.

"She gave me an ultimatum," Nico said, holding Stone's gaze, his chest still heaving. "If I don't go to Texas Tech, she's not interested in me anymore."

That sounded like Chelsea. She was annoyingly self-centered. Never mind that Nico had a scholarship opportunity, Stone could see her insisting he follow her around like a puppy.

What Nico probably didn't know was that Chelsea's view on relationships wasn't much different than Stone's. He figured that was partly why she'd dated Nico on and off for the past few years. She had someone to fall back on when she needed him, and when she didn't, she could push him aside, knowing he would always come back.

"What about Jenny?" Stone prompted. "You fuck her?"

Nico's eyebrows slammed down. "Hell no. She's Chelsea's best friend. I'm not a complete asshole."

"So what happened?"

Nico's blue eyes skimmed his face, but he still didn't attempt to shove Stone away. "I flirted with her. Figured it would get back to Chelsea, and she'd have a reason to dump me without feelin' bad about it."

Well, hell. Maybe Nico wasn't as clueless as Stone thought he was.

"You *want* her to break up with you."

"It's what's best for her," Nico said, his voice lowering. "Above all else, we're friends. It's easier for her to hate me now than to lose that."

Stone's ire dissipated, replaced by a new respect for the guy. It sounded like he genuinely cared about Chelsea. Enough to sacrifice his pride.

"You two done? For good?"

Nico nodded. "It's been over for a while. This just makes it official."

"Good."

"Why?"

Stone smirked. "Because I said so."

He let his gaze slide to Nico's mouth, and he imagined all the wicked things the guy could do with it. It didn't matter that Nico's lip was split, he still wanted to know how good those lips would feel wrapped around his cock.

When he looked up, Nico was still watching him. Only now, he was breathing harder despite not having moved an inch.

"Where's Stevie?" Nico asked, obviously bringing her up because he thought Stone had forgotten about her.

He hadn't.

Rather than tell Nico that Stevie was standing only a few feet away on the other side of his truck, listening to every word, he said, "Where do you want her to be?"

Stone's gaze shifted to his girl. Her eyes were wide, but the way she nibbled her lower lip told him she wasn't worried. She was watching them with intrigue glittering in her pretty brown eyes.

He held her stare for another second, and that was when he saw it. Her left eyebrow rose slowly. He swore he heard her silent question: *Is he the one?*

Their last intimate conversation replayed in his head. The one where Stone told her he was bisexual and asked if she'd one day be up for bringing another guy into the mix. A one-night-only kinda thing. An experiment. For both of them. Granted, he'd only been partially serious, but Stevie hadn't hesitated to agree when he asked.

Not only that, but Stevie had talked about Nico more than once in the past several months. Since Nico was Stevie's best friend's brother, she was around him a lot. More than Stone had been comfortable with back in the beginning. At least until Stevie assured him she simply thought Nico was hot. She wasn't interested in being with him.

So, was she suggesting Nico as their plus-one?

Stone kept his eyes on her as he tilted his head toward Nico and raised an eyebrow.

Her response was a slow nod.

Damn, but the girl never ceased to amaze him.

Stone remained where he was, keeping Nico pinned to the truck, neither of them speaking. The guy should've been shoving him away, trying to free himself, but he wasn't. No, he was standing there like a deer trapped in the headlights of a speeding truck, those big blue eyes wide as he anticipated the inevitable crash. But the flash of heat Stone saw in them intrigued him.

Nico was turned on.

That acknowledgment had a groan rumbling up from his chest. Tempted to see how far Nico would let him push, Stone kicked the man's feet, forcing him to widen his stance so Stone could move closer. He kept his hand on Nico's neck as he pressed their bodies together, maintaining control.

Nico could've easily shoved him off. He wasn't a lightweight. But he wasn't moving. The only thing he did was glance over his shoulder toward the house.

"She can't see us," Stone assured him. They were hidden from view of the house. Even if Chelsea were looking out the kitchen window, she would only see the top of Stone's head over the roof of the truck.

Stone let Nico hold some of his weight, testing the waters, seeing how far he would let him go. Again, Nico made no attempt to fight him off.

"Push me away, Nico."

Nico's hands shifted to Stone's hips, but he didn't push.

Stone lowered his voice. "That's all you hafta do. Push. Me. Away."

He was so close now he could feel Nico's breath. Tilting his head, he leaned in, letting his lips brush Nico's ever so slightly.

"Say no, Nico."

Nico didn't make a sound.

"Tell me to stop."

Stone ground his hips forward, feeling the hard ridge of Nico's dick against his own. As he did, he scanned their surroundings, ensuring no one else was out there. Convinced they were safe, he turned his attention back to Nico.

"I didn't realize you played for both teams," he taunted.

"I don't."

"No?" Stone reached down with his free hand, grinding his palm along the outline of Nico's dick. He was hard as fucking steel.

A rough groan escaped the man, spurring Stone to continue.

"Coulda fooled me."

Nico grunted again when Stone continued to rub.

"You like this. You like it rough."

He hadn't phrased it as a question, but Nico gave an almost imperceptible nod.

"You want me to do dirty fuckin' things to you, don't you?"

Another groan, and this time Nico pressed his hips forward, grinding against Stone's hand.

Stone shifted his hand off Nico's throat, sliding his thumb along his lower lip, gently caressing the injury. "You ever had a cock in your mouth?"

"No."

When Nico's mouth opened, he pushed his thumb inside. "Suck."

There was only a brief flash of hesitance before Nico's lips closed around his thumb, and he sucked. His eyes were flinty, his expression one of defiance, but there wasn't an ounce of resistance in the action.

"Fuck." Stone leaned more of his weight on him. "I want those lips wrapped around my cock."

He pulled his thumb from Nico's mouth and pushed two fingers in. His gaze shot to Stevie's again. She'd moved closer, watching Nico as Stone's fingers hooked on his lower teeth.

"I wanna fuck your face. Bury my cock in your throat until you can't breathe." He lowered his voice. "Then I wanna bend you over and drive my dick in your ass."

Nico hummed softly, but he didn't stop sucking Stone's fingers. His eyes glittered, his coiled muscles loosened. Oh, yeah. He was turned on by the picture Stone painted.

"I'm not sure you can handle me, though. Rough and dirty are the only way I know how to fuck. Ain't that right, Stevie?"

"Yes," she said, her voice trembling.

Nico's eyes darted left toward Stevie, but Stone held him in place, making it impossible for him to turn his head.

"My girl likes rough and dirty," Stone told him. " What about you? You wanna try rough and dirty, Nico?"

There was a brief hesitation, but then his surrender was complete. This time, Nico's nod was clear as day.

"Say it." He pulled his fingers out of Nico's mouth so he could respond. "Tell me how you want it."

His dark blue eyes flashed with definite heat. "Rough. And dirty."

Stone leaned in, his lips lightly brushing Nico's. "Good. Because that's what you're gonna get."

TWO

STEVIE HAD COME OUTSIDE TO CHECK ON Stone. Not because she'd sensed Stone's fury when he bounded off the couch, although that was true. Not because she'd heard raised voices, although that was also true. And not because she feared they would throw down in the front yard, although that *definitely* was true.

No, she'd come outside because it was that or potentially end up becoming Chelsea's sounding board. While she had nothing against Stone's sister, Stevie wasn't interested in hearing her talk shit about Nico. She'd heard more than her share during her previous visits to the Jamesons' home and a couple of times in the cafeteria at school. Evidently, when you were dating Chelsea's brother, you were automatically dropped into the bucket labeled: *likes to listen to Chelsea rant*.

Again, Stevie had nothing against the girl, but it wasn't easy pretending she was okay when Chelsea berated her best friend's brother.

So, yeah, she'd slipped outside before that could happen.

When she didn't find Stone in the front yard, she headed for the side of the house. She heard voices, so she moved toward them.

NICOLE EDWARDS

The first thing she noticed was the stuff strode over the ground—a teddy bear, a jacket, something gold that glittered as she passed. As soon as she rounded the end of Nico's truck, she came to an abrupt halt. She was expecting to see confrontation, but she didn't anticipate finding Stone pressed against Nico, a firestorm of electricity pulsing in the air around them.

More than that, she didn't expect the reaction she had to seeing them like that. Especially not the reaction she had when she realized they weren't fighting but rather … well, she wasn't sure *what* they were doing, but she recognized sexual dominance on Stone's face when she saw it. It was something she would likely see in all her fantasies for the foreseeable future.

Was she surprised Stone was directing all that heat and energy at Nico? No. She knew Stone was bisexual. His reputation preceded him. As soon as word got out that she was dating Stone Jameson, she'd been inundated with warnings.

Stone has no experience being someone's boyfriend.
Stone doesn't know the meaning of monogamy.
Stone likes playing the field too much.
Stone prefers guys to girls.
Stone prefers girls to guys.
Stone prefers both at the same time.
Stone prefers orgies in the gym.

Okay, so the last one was definitely bullshit because her best friend Niyah was the one who used the retort when someone else was going on about what a horrible choice Stone Jameson would be for any girl. Niyah always had her back.

As for the rest… It was endless the amount of crap people spewed in this town, but she'd grown up here, so she expected it. Because of that, she'd taken it all in stride, choosing to use Stone's actions as a guide rather than all the bullshit people said. And yeah, being the type who wanted to know the truth, she'd confronted him about it. Namely, the part about him preferring guys to girls. Stone hadn't been offended by her curiosity. In fact, they'd talked about it at length which had helped her understand. To a degree. According to him, it wasn't a switch he flipped. He was attracted to *people*, not necessarily gender. He didn't crave one over the other.

17

And yes, she might've pushed the issue a time or two when they were intimate because Stone Jameson turned her on like no one else. When it came to dirty talk, Stone knew just the right words to say and the right scenes to set to get her engine revving. The first time he mentioned bringing another guy into the mix, she'd gone up in flames. She'd even added it to her bucket list, and she'd told him as much.

But that had been foreplay. That had been a way to fan the flames.

This ... this was on a whole other level. Not once had Stevie considered that it might one day become a reality. It was sex talk. People said shit in the heat of the moment, right? She damn sure hadn't expected how hot it would be to witness an intimate moment between two guys. The *idea* of it was one thing, but no one told her how this scenario might make her break into a sweat.

Stone and Nico.

Wow.

It was a scene pulled right out of one of her wildest, dirtiest fantasies.

Here she was with a front-row seat, and her body was screaming for her to encourage them to do more. Stevie couldn't explain it. Did that mean she was broken? Was it wrong that her insides went from simmer to boil instantly? Did it make her a pervert that she had this overwhelming urge to watch them?

She figured the answers could go either way, depending on who you asked. But if it made her a freak, she didn't care—not at the moment, anyway. She'd always thought Nico was sexy and not just on the outside. He was smart and funny, and ... okay, yeah, he was definitely easy on the eyes. But he was her best friend's brother, and everyone knew that meant she never had a shot with him.

"Come here, Stevie," Stone said, his gaze sweeping over to her.

She didn't hesitate. She came around the truck, approaching slowly, taking it all in. The way Stone's big body was pressed intimately against Nico's. It was such a dominant position to be in. The way he was holding Nico down, not allowing him to move. That was one thing she loved about Stone. He was the aggressor, and though she hadn't realized she enjoyed that sort of thing until she started dating him, he'd certainly shown her how good it could be.

"Give me your keys," Stone told Nico.

Nico's eyebrows slammed down. "For what?"

"So I can go get some ice cream," he retorted snidely. "What the fuck do you think I want 'em for? To pull your truck in the barn. You want Chelsea comin' out and seein' that you're still here?"

Nico dug in his pocket and pulled out his keys, passing them to Stone.

Palming them, Stone turned to her. He moved closer, tipping her chin up with one finger so she was forced to look into his eyes.

Even that move turned her on.

"You good with this?"

Although she wasn't exactly sure what *this* was, Stevie nodded. She was too curious not to.

He leaned in and kissed her. Lightly at first, but as was usually the case, he didn't stop there. That sexy rumble sounded in his throat as his tongue slipped into her mouth. His hand moved to her ass, his fingers teasing under the hem of her shorts. She kissed him back, her nipples pebbling as warmth spread throughout her body.

"Anytime you wanna stop this, we can."

She smiled, feeling empowered because he was seeking her approval. "I'm good."

And oddly enough, that was true. She was turned on and curious about where this might lead.

"Take him up to the hay loft. I'll be up in just a second." Stone turned back to Nico. "Unless you're havin' second thoughts."

Nico looked at her, and Stevie knew she couldn't hide how hot this was making her. His eyes narrowed only slightly before he looked at Stone.

Nico shook his head. "No second thoughts."

"Good. Then go."

When Stone started picking up the stuff on the ground and tossing it into the bed of Nico's truck, Nico started walking. Stevie followed, pretending it wasn't weird that Nico kept glancing over his shoulder. Once looking at her. Another at the house. Again, at her.

"Is this some kinda game he's playin'?" Nico asked when they were inside the cool interior of what used to be a barn. Now it was merely a bunch of mostly rotted wood that still managed to remain upright. The Jamesons used it as extra storage and a place for Stone and his siblings to park their vehicles.

"Stone doesn't play games," she told Nico, taking the lead and going toward the ladder to the hay loft.

She didn't hesitate. As she climbed, her body warmed even more. She wouldn't pretend she didn't know what was going to happen. She might've been a virgin when she met Stone, but that didn't mean she was clueless. Stone Jameson was responsible for every orgasm she'd ever had, and he was the first guy she'd been physically intimate with, but she had plenty of guy friends and they liked to talk, so she knew all about desires such as this.

Granted, most of her guy friends talked about getting it on with two girls at the same time. Apparently, that was every teenage boy's fantasy. Because of that, she was a little uncertain about the logistics, especially since she was pretty sure Nico was only into girls. Or at least that was what she'd thought before she saw him and Stone all but kissing. Whatever his preference, she figured she could go with the flow. Especially if it meant she could be with the untamed bad boy who'd captured her heart so completely and her best friend's brother, whom she'd been secretly crushing on for the past few years.

Only two people knew about Stevie's crush. Nico's sister, Niyah, because best friends shared everything. And Stone because he'd pried all her dirty secrets out one by one, promising and delivering orgasms with each one she told him. Since she happened to be quite fond of orgasms, she didn't stand a chance against Stone's interrogation techniques.

Stevie slipped through the square opening, using her arms to heft herself, then pulling her legs up. She backed up, giving Nico room to do the same.

He gracefully followed, making it look effortless to lift his body like that.

God, he was hot. He wasn't as big as Stone, not as tall or as broad, but he was packed with muscle, and she loved to watch the way his body flexed beneath the soft cotton of his T-shirt.

"You two done this before?" Nico asked when he reached the loft.

Stevie moved back, keeping away from the boards along the edge. The rest of the loft was sturdy, and she figured that was Stone's doing. Or maybe CJ's or even Chelsea's. They all used this loft to hang out with their friends. It was no secret that they came up here to make out. Stone had admitted as much the first time he brought her up here, on her birthday last year.

He'd told her that at one point, the loft had been open to the space below—which was why they called it a loft—but Donovan had put up plywood walls for privacy. There was a single window, but the glass was so grimy that not much light filtered through. A string of multi-colored Christmas lights had been secured along the ceiling, which lit the space enough to see and added a bit of ambiance.

"Do *what* before?" she asked, crawling over to sit on one of the foam mattresses covering the floor.

There were three, each wrapped in those waterproof covers that zipped around them, the crinkly plastic concealed by colorful fitted sheets. Stone said his mother did that to ensure nothing crawled inside them. It seemed odd that Deborah Jameson was okay with them hanging out up there, especially with mattresses and pillows, but Stevie figured that was because she didn't know what they *actually* did while in this space.

As for the potential rodents … that had freaked her out a little, but Stone assured her there weren't mice in the barn—at least not that he knew of. She'd never seen any, thank God.

Because the hay loft was the official Jameson hangout, it had gained a few items over the years: a television and a stand to hold it, a DVD player, several movies, most of which were no longer in their cases, and even a lava lamp that didn't work. It needed a new bulb, and no one cared enough to get one.

"Whatever he's about to do," Nico answered.

Stevie smiled.

Nico's eyebrows lowered. "Tell me he doesn't make you—"

"*Make me?*" She snorted, meeting his gaze so he would know she was telling the truth. "Stone doesn't *make me* do anything."

"And you're okay with this?"

Again, she didn't know what *this* was. Not exactly. But she nodded.

"Prove it."

The directive didn't come from Nico. It came from Stone as he pulled himself up into the loft. He reached for the square board they used to cover the hole, pulling it toward him until they were sealed in.

"How do I do that?" she asked, smiling as he crawled over to her.

Every time she looked at Stone, Stevie fought the urge to drool. She'd never met a sexier guy in her life. Everything about Stone got her hot and bothered. His dark hair, those hazel eyes that glimmered with mischief. She loved that he was so freaking tall and the layers of muscle that covered his enormous frame. But it was that sexy drawl that made her heart beat harder.

"Strip," he told her.

Stevie giggled because there was a gleam in his eye. He wasn't serious, but he wanted Nico to think he was. Before she could say anything, Stone started laughing as he looked at Nico's wide eyes and unhinged jaw.

"Jesus, man. What? Did you think I was just gonna bring you both up here and fuck you blind?"

Nico's eyebrows pinched, his gaze shifting between them.

Stevie sat cross-legged on one of the mattresses, grabbing a small pillow and putting it in her lap.

Stone jerked his chin toward the television that sat on an old wooden crate. "We're gonna watch a movie, dude."

"Seriously?"

"Don't tell me you and Chelsea never came up here just to hang out."

Nico's eyes widened.

"Really? Y'all never just chilled?"

Nico shook his head.

Stone laughed. "Well, that's what we're gonna do. For now."

Nico looked at her, then back at Stone. "Okay."

"Unless you want me to whip out my dick and shove it in your mouth right now?"

Nico's eyes flashed hot. Stevie's breath caught in her throat.

"Didn't think so." Stone moved behind her. "Come here, baby."

Stone took a couple of pillows and propped them behind him before he leaned back and pulled her between his legs. She relaxed against him, watching Nico as Stone wrapped his arms around her.

"Get comfy, Daugherty. You'll get yours. I promise."

It took about two hours before Nico lost that shocked look. Stone had flipped through the cable channels, watching bits and pieces of several movies, never settling on one. He'd also snuck down to the house and returned with tacos and soft drinks, which they'd devoured. He brought popcorn, too, and Jägermeister, which he'd stolen from his parents' liquor cabinet. The single, unpopped bag of microwave popcorn sat in a bowl on top of the microwave in the corner in case they wanted it later, but they'd cracked open the liquor and took turns taking shots. It was the grossest thing Stevie had ever tasted, but after the first two shots, it went down smoothly and gave her the liquid courage she needed.

Stevie was once again sitting in front of Stone, her back to his chest as she reclined against him. Nico had finally joined them, propped with his back against the wall beside Stone. He was close enough that Stevie could touch his leg but she didn't. At least, she hadn't meant to. That was Stone's doing.

His big hand covered hers, their fingers linking. The next thing she knew, he was moving her hand, sliding it over Nico's rock-hard thigh. She watched the movement at first, then looked at Nico. He was doing the same, his hooded eyes pinned on the point where she was touching him.

"You two ever … do anything?" Stone asked.

Stevie tilted her head, trying to look at him, but she couldn't in her position.

"No," Nico answered.

"You ever want to?" His question was directed at Nico.

Nico didn't answer.

"She's the sexiest woman in Coyote Ridge, man," Stone told him, his voice low and seductive, yet casual. Like he was making small talk. "Don't tell me you never thought about it."

Stone's chin brushed her temple when he looked back at her. "It was all I could think about the first time I saw you."

Her heart thumped hard in her chest.

"The first time I heard your voice, I knew it wouldn't be the last."

Again, his voice was low, with a hint of reverence. If she hadn't already been in love with him, she would be now.

"Any guy in this town would give his left nut just for a few minutes of your time, baby."

God, she loved it when he called her baby. It made her warm in naughty places.

Stone looked at Nico. "Tell me you don't want her."

"She's my sister's best friend."

"Yeah. And?"

"And nothin'," Nico grumbled, his gaze sliding to her briefly before dropping.

"Does he know you've had a crush on him for years?" Stone asked her.

Stevie felt her cheeks grow warm. She shook her head.

Stone chuckled. "He does now."

She felt Nico's eyes on her, but she couldn't look at him, choosing instead to keep her gaze fixed on the television.

They were silent for a bit as they watched TV. Stevie wasn't paying any attention to what was on the screen. She was more focused on the way Stone's fingers dragged across the bare skin of her side beneath her shirt, his other hand guiding hers on Nico's leg, moving it every so often. Nico was wearing shorts, so every now and then the crisp hair on his legs would tease her fingertips, causing tingles to race up her arm.

"You want me to change the channel?" Stone whispered in her ear.

Her eyes slid to the television, and she realized he had the menu open. Highlighted was one of the pornographic channels they'd watched before.

Stevie had seen porn before, both on screen and in magazines. She and Niyah had found Nico's stash in his room a couple of years ago. Every day for a month, they went into his room and flipped through the images while he wasn't home. As soon as they heard his truck pull up, they would shove the contraband back under his mattress and run to Niyah's room, giggling uncontrollably.

But those images didn't hold a candle to the hardcore stuff she'd watched on this television with Stone. His interests went far beyond naked women in provocative poses.

"Yes," she whispered, her chest beginning to rise and fall more rapidly.

"You haven't seen this one yet," Stone told her, his breath fanning her ear. "It's got two guys and one girl. You sure?"

Her pussy clenched with anticipation because she knew what she would see. "Yes," she repeated.

Stone clicked the button on the remote and started the movie. Granted, *movie* was a loose term for what played on the screen. There was zero plot, but she figured the viewer didn't much care. She certainly didn't.

"You good?" Stone asked Nico.

"Yeah," he said gruffly, his leg twitching.

Stevie didn't mean to do it, but she moved her hand along the inner part of his knee without Stone guiding her.

"It's okay, baby." Stone unlinked their fingers. "Touch him."

She kept her eyes glued to the television while her hand wandered along the inside of Nico's leg. She was nervous, but she didn't pull away. That being said, she exhaled her relief when Nico's hand covered hers. He didn't guide her; he just kept his palm over hers as she grew bolder, moving higher along his inner thigh, her pinky teasing the edge of his boxer briefs.

She didn't rush, listening to the way his breaths became more labored the higher she went. When the edge of her pinky glided along the hard ridge pressing against the cotton, he sucked in a heavy breath.

Stone swept her hair back, his mouth gliding along the shell of her ear. "You sure about this?" he whispered, his voice barely audible.

"Yes."

"If at any point you wanna stop, I want you to tell me."

She nodded.

"Promise me, baby."

She sensed his hesitation, but she wanted to reassure him. This was what she wanted.

Stevie sat up, then turned in his arms, getting to her knees. His legs shifted together so she could straddle his thighs, her arms wreathing his neck.

"I promise," she whispered against his lips.

Stone growled low in his throat as he kissed her, his hand pressing against her lower back, holding her, allowing her to grind her pussy against his erection. She wished they were naked because she wanted to feel him moving inside her. She couldn't seem to get enough of him. Whenever she was around him, she was turned on. She'd never had this overwhelming, all-consuming reaction to any guy before, but Stone assured her it was normal.

His fingers tickled along her side, moving higher, across her back, her shoulder, along her arm. He took her wrist, unlinking her arms from his neck and guiding her hand back to Nico's leg.

"You're in control right now."

"I don't wanna be," she told him.

"No?"

She shook her head.

His hazel eyes shimmered with heat. "What do you want, baby?"

Her lips brushed his again as she rocked her hips, trying to get friction on her clit. She wanted him to take control, to dictate her pleasure, as he liked to say. As much as she wished she was bold enough to say it aloud, the words wouldn't come.

She loved every single second of every single encounter, but it was the times when Stone took complete control of her that she craved the most. Her favorite were the times when he was rough with her. She enjoyed play-fighting with him, allowing him to overpower her. Which he did easily. Those times were by far the most incredible. There was something freeing about giving him control, letting him own her.

His mouth moved closer to her ear. "You want me to control you."

It wasn't a question, but she nodded, a gasp slipping past her lips. She was going up in flames and he had barely touched her.

Stone pulled back, meeting her gaze. His eyes bounced over her face, and she knew he was gauging her response, ensuring he was understanding correctly. And that right there was the reason Nico's question earlier had been preposterous. The thought of Stone *making* her do anything was ridiculous. There was a big difference between *force* and *dominate*. Stone had taught her that. He'd promised her he would never force her to do anything, but if she were willing to give up control, he would definitely dominate.

He leaned in and kissed her chin, nudging her head back. His lips glided down her neck, then back up, along her jaw toward her ear again.

"Do you want to kiss him, Stevie?" he whispered.

She nodded.

"Then do it. Kiss him while I watch."

His cock was hard as steel between her legs, but she swore she felt it harden more. The idea that it turned him on only made her hotter.

Pulling back, Stevie looked at Nico. He was watching her, his eyes glazed. She'd known him a long time. Not once had she ever seen that look on his face. Pure lust glittered in his blue eyes.

Once again, that rush of empowerment flooded her veins, and she found herself wanting to take charge, to make the first move.

She shifted her legs so that she was straddling one of Stone's thighs and one of Nico's, then kept going, moving over so that she was on Nico's lap, straddling his thighs. His hands shifted to her hips. She felt the strength in them even as he kept his touch gentle. Like he was holding himself back. That thrilled her. The idea he wanted her ... it caused her blood to heat to boiling.

Thank God for Jägermeister. It was giving her the courage she needed to take what they were offering.

Stevie cupped Nico's face, holding his stare as she leaned in. His eyes never left hers as his breath fanned her lips. For only a brief moment did she feel guilty, concerned that Chelsea was going to be pissed if she ever found out. Which she would, no doubt. Stevie knew she should care, but at the moment, she couldn't bring herself to.

She could feel Stone watching them, and the thrill of that ricocheted off her nerve endings, causing her skin to tingle.

Leaning in, Stevie went slow, holding Nico's stare, wondering if he would kiss her first or even at all. This man was not a stranger to her. She knew Nico better than she knew Stone. He'd been in her life since the fourth grade, ever since she became BFFs with Niyah. Stevie had been to the Daugherty's house, spent the night so many times. She'd had a crush on Nico for the longest time, but aside from those brief, erotic conversations she had with Stone about him, she rarely thought about him. Not since the day she met Stone. She had no room for any other man because Stone was the only one for her. And until this moment, he'd been the only one she wanted to kiss for the rest of her life.

"Stevie," Nico whispered, his hand sliding up her back, beneath her T-shirt. Warm, firm, confident.

She tilted her head, angling her lips so they covered his. The kiss was a light brush of their mouths, nothing more for several seconds. She felt the slightly swollen corner where Stone had hit him and tried to pull back, not wanting to hurt him. Nico had other ideas because his warm hand tightened across her back, his lips parting, the tip of his tongue sliding along her lower lip. Hesitantly, she greeted his tongue with her own, exploring this new endeavor. And then he was kissing her, the hand on her back pressing her closer, his other hand sliding up her thigh, his fingertips slipping beneath her shorts, his tongue dancing with hers as though they'd been doing this for a long time.

A soft groan sounded. She wasn't sure whether it was Nico or Stone or both. It didn't matter because she was floating on a wave of intense pleasure as Nico's hands moved, pulling her closer until her breasts were crushed to his chest. As with Stone, she fit perfectly, like she'd been made for him.

Stone moved, but she didn't stop kissing Nico. She didn't want to. The feelings that washed over her were intense. An emotional and physical rush that made her lightheaded.

And then there was warmth at her back. She was aware of the hardness of Stone's thighs as they pressed against her butt. He was behind her, straddling Nico's legs, molding himself to her as his arms came around her, his hands sliding beneath her T-shirt. His callused fingers scraped sensually against her belly, and her nipples tightened.

She felt Stone's lips on her neck, and she gasped, pulling back from Nico as the pleasure doubled. It was almost too much, the two of them touching her like this.

Nico was no longer a placeholder. He lifted the hem of her shirt, raising it, forcing her to lift her arms so he could remove it. She did, and before her arms lowered, Stone had unhooked her bra and was letting it slide down her arms.

A soft gasp escaped Nico as he stared at her breasts, licking his lips as though he couldn't wait to taste her.

Stone's hands grazed her ribs as they moved upward before cupping her breasts. Her breasts didn't come close to filling his hands, but Stone told her he loved her tits. Not because of their size but because of how sensitive they were. She leaned into him when he pinched her nipples, plucking them until they were so tight she felt an invisible tug on her clit.

"Tell me you haven't thought about what she tastes like," Stone told Nico.

Nico's eyes lifted, his gaze finding Stone over her shoulder. He didn't respond, but he leaned forward. When Stone stopped pinching her nipples, Nico licked the pebbled nub once, then drew circles with the tip of his tongue.

Stevie whimpered. "Oh, God."

"Feel good?" Stone whispered, his words directed toward her ear.

"Yes."

"It's so fuckin' hot to see his mouth on you. To watch him suck your tits."

Stevie gasped, his dirty words adding to the sensation.

That seemed to spur Nico because he took her into his mouth, sucking more firmly, his tongue flicking over her nipple. When he released her, it was so he could do the same with her other breast. Stone was still cupping her, offering her to Nico.

The eroticism of it made her pussy clench tightly. Nothing had ever felt this good. The intensity of it scared her. More so, her desire for it to never stop.

Somewhere in the back of her mind, she knew this wasn't normal. A man who loved you wasn't supposed to share you. And vice versa. If you loved someone, you weren't supposed to want someone else.

Yet here she was, aching for them to give her more. Desperate for them to ease the throbbing that was growing stronger by the second. And she didn't care about right or wrong. She couldn't.

Surely nothing that felt this good could be that bad, right?

THREE

NICO COULDN'T BELIEVE HE WAS HERE, THAT he was sucking Stevie's tits while Stone watched.

Little Stephanie Shepherd wasn't so little anymore.

Not that he'd ever really thought about her like that. Since the day his sister invited her for their first sleepover when he was in the fifth grade, he'd had a crush on her. In the beginning, he had teased and tormented them simply so he could be around Stevie. At one point, he'd even entertained the idea of asking her to be his girlfriend.

He refused to admit that he'd fantasized about her more than once. It was easier to keep her in the friend category for his sister's benefit. He refused to cross that line, fearful that when things ended, it might affect Stevie's relationship with Niyah. Nico didn't want to be responsible for that, so he'd limited himself to fantasies.

Stevie was part of the reason Nico hadn't dated anyone but Chelsea for the past few years. Whenever Chelsea would break up with him, his thoughts always returned to this girl. He spent most of his time hanging around the house when she was there simply so he could be around her. Then, when Chelsea decided he was worthy again, Nico would let her lead him around like a puppy because he genuinely liked her. He just didn't love her. And he'd never felt like this when he was with her.

Then again, he wasn't sure Stevie deserved all the credit for what he was feeling. Stone was responsible for a lot of it. He'd triggered something inside Nico with his dominance in the driveway. Nico had been all but ready to beg him to finish him off with his scorching looks and suggestive promises. The fact that Stone was straddling Nico's legs, offering his girlfriend on a silver platter ... *that* was doing it for him in ways he'd never expected.

Nico released Stevie's breast, sliding his lips up her chest, over her collarbone. He wanted to kiss her again. He wanted to feel her tongue in his mouth, her soft, cool hands on his skin.

As though he could read Nico's mind, Stone reached around Stevie to grip his shirt. Nico sat forward, allowing him to pull it up and over his head. Then Stevie was leaning into him, skin to skin, her breasts crushed to his chest, her lips sealed to his. He kissed her, gliding his hands over her smooth, warm skin. She was so fucking soft and so damn small. He wasn't used to being with petite women. Chelsea was bigger, sturdier. Not dainty and petite like Stevie.

Although he liked girls who wouldn't get hurt if he played rough with them, Stevie felt right in his arms. As though she was meant to be there.

Suddenly, she jerked back, a sharp cry escaping her. When she leaned against Stone, Nico looked down. Stone had his hand down her shorts, his fingers hidden by the denim.

"Stone!" Stevie was rolling her hips, riding Stone's hand.

She was a wet dream come to life.

"You're so fuckin' wet," Stone groaned against her neck. "God, baby. Did Nico do this to you?"

Her gaze met his. "Yes."

His cock jerked at the heat that flashed in her big brown eyes.

She whimpered. "Don't stop. Please ... don't stop."

"Me?" Stone asked, his eyes glittering with triumph. "Or Nico?"

"Both ... *uhnn* ... God, yes."

"Oh, yeah. You love when I finger your little pussy."

She nodded, although it wasn't a question.

The muscles in Stone's arm flexed and bunched as he fingered her. Nico couldn't see beneath the denim, but he could imagine Stone's fingers sliding into her, glistening with her silky heat.

"Tell me," Stone urged.

"Yes." Stevie whimpered again. "I love ... oh, God, I love when you finger me."

Nico's entire body flashed hot. Never had he been with anyone who was vocal during sex. Granted, he was nineteen years old, and he'd been with exactly three girls. No one but Chelsea in the past two years. Usually, his encounters were in the dark, he and Chelsea kissing while he did his best to give her pleasure before she pulled him on top of her.

This was so not that. This was both of them participating, and it was fucking hot.

"You want more, baby?"

Stevie nodded, her eyes closed, lips parted.

"Tell Nico to take your shorts off."

Her eyes opened. "Take them off," she demanded.

Nico couldn't move much in his position, but Stevie fixed that. She repositioned so she was sitting on his thighs, her legs straight. She moved again, sliding both legs to one side of him. Nico didn't hesitate, tugging on her shorts and her panties, dragging them down her legs. She kicked them away and spread her legs.

If she cared that Nico was seeing her naked for the first time, she didn't show it. Stone was still fingering her pussy, two fingers curled deep inside.

Damn, she was beautiful. Long, silky blonde hair. Even pulled back in a ponytail, it hung halfway down her back. That toned little body with curves that made his mouth water. She had pert tits with little pink nipples that darkened when she was aroused. Soft, smooth skin that was naturally golden.

"Look at him," Stone said. "He wants to taste your pussy, Stevie. His mouth's waterin'."

He wasn't wrong.

She moaned.

"Can he lick your pussy?"

Stevie nodded, her eyes once again locked with Nico's. "Lick me. Please, Nico. Put your tongue on my clit."

He'd never known a girl so blunt about what she wanted. Certainly not when it came to sex. But Stevie … she knew what she wanted.

It shouldn't have surprised him because Stevie was like that. She said what she was thinking. He'd always found that entertaining. But here … now…

Stone banded his free arm around her torso as he shifted backward, freeing Nico's legs. Stevie crab-walked with him, holding his arm as he got them onto the other mattress.

"Lift your knees and spread those sexy legs wide," Stone instructed Stevie, his fingers still buried in her pussy.

Nico got to his knees and crawled toward them, transfixed by Stone's fingers still fucking her. When she spread her legs, he took that as an invitation, lying on his stomach, settling between them. He didn't need instruction because he wanted to taste her. He wanted to lick her until she came on his face. Chelsea never let him do this. Not as often as he wanted, anyway.

Stevie dropped her bent knees open. Stone's fingers slid out, separating her pussy lips and exposing the tiny swollen nub at the top of her sex.

Jesus. She was completely bare, shaved smooth. It thrilled him in a way he didn't expect. Nico blew air across her silky flesh, and Stevie's hips bucked.

He leaned in, his broad shoulders forcing her legs apart even more, using the tip of his tongue to tease the little nub the same way he'd done with her nipple. Stevie whimpered. He did it again. She moaned. He licked her from entrance to clit, and she groaned low in her throat.

The sounds were so sexy he kept licking her. Along the seam of her pussy, sucking her labia into his mouth, then teasing her hole. He got lost in her taste, mesmerized by the sounds she was making. He took every cue from her, learning what she enjoyed based on the soft mewls and desperate moans.

He wasn't aware that Stone had moved until the guy was straddling his thighs, his big hands moving over his back, the hard ridge of his cock pressed against Nico's ass. They were both dressed, but the thrill was the same. He imagined Stone sliding his cock along the crack of his ass, pressing the tip to his hole, pushing inside him.

Nico groaned. It was a fantasy he'd indulged in since he hit puberty, although he never quite understood it. He could never rationalize how this exact scenario could ever be a reality because while he had gay urges, the female body got him off, too. How could he possibly have both? And if he couldn't, would he eventually prefer one over the other? So many questions. Never any answers.

Until now.

"Ahh!" Stevie cried out, fisting Nico's hair as she held him where she wanted him.

He focused on licking her, suckling her clit, tonguing her hole. She rocked against his face as though she was fucking him. When he sucked her clit between his lips and flicked it with his tongue, her back arched.

"Yes! Nico, yes! Don't stop!"

Stone shifted, grinding his cock against Nico's ass as he leaned over him. "I'm so gonna enjoy fuckin' this ass."

Nico's ass clenched.

Stone palmed the back of his head, forcing his face between Stevie's legs. "She tastes so fuckin' good, doesn't she?"

Nico hummed, but he didn't stop feasting on her. His body flooded with heat, his blood pumping faster than it ever had. He was pinned down by Stone's weight, his hand roughly holding his head. And God help him, he liked the roughness, the forcefulness. He liked that Stone was taking control.

"Fuck, you look good like that, baby," Stone said. "His head between your legs. Are you gonna come, Stevie? You gonna flood his mouth with your sweetness?"

"Nico!" Stevie's hand tightened in his hair, and her legs stiffened. "I'm comin'."

He pushed his finger inside her, wanting to feel the walls of her pussy tighten. They did as her clit pulsed against his tongue.

Suddenly, Stone's weight disappeared, so Nico got to his knees, sitting on his heels as he watched Stevie's chest heave, her smile so bright it nearly blinded him.

She was even more beautiful after she orgasmed. Her blonde hair slipping out of her ponytail, her pink lips glossy, eyes glazed. He wanted to kiss her again, but before he could move toward her, Stone grabbed his hair, jerking his head hard. Then Stone's mouth was on his. Nico was confused for only a second, but then he kissed Stone back, turning to face him, gripping his hip. He ignored the throb in his lip from where Stone had hit him. The kiss dulled the pain even as it intensified it.

Stone had discarded his shirt, and Nico didn't hesitate, running his hand over his torso, around to his back as he scooted closer. Where Stevie's kiss was soft and sweet, Stone's was rough and demanding. An intense contradiction that had him reeling. Nico couldn't figure out which he preferred. Both were capable of twisting him in knots, adding layers to the confusion already there.

Stone yanked his head back, their lips separating. Nico was breathing hard.

"Kiss me like you fuckin' mean it," Stone growled before loosening his grip.

Not wanting to risk Stone stopping, Nico kissed him again, this time putting effort into it. Stone let him lead, but he knew it was a facade. Nico was no more in charge than he had been a moment ago. He was still following, but he was participating, and that seemed to be what Stone wanted.

He was aware of the stubble on Stone's jaw abrading his face, the firmness of his lips, the musky scent of his skin. But it was the relentless thrust of his tongue that undid him. The pleasure was exhilarating. The way Stone dominated his mouth, his hand gripping his hair tightly, keeping him right where he wanted him.

Nico'd fantasized about this, too. Not that he was kissing Stone, but a man. His fantasy man had never had a face because Nico hadn't understood the desires that plagued him. He couldn't rationalize how he could be turned on by the thought of being with a guy when he was attracted to girls.

Stone pulled back again, still not releasing Nico's hair.

Nico forced his eyes open, looking at the man who'd rocked his world with only his mouth.

"Her pussy tastes good on your lips," Stone rasped.

Something shifted under his hand, and Nico realized he was cupping Stevie's knee, caressing with his thumb. He hadn't stopped touching her even as he kissed Stone.

Stone's hand was on her other knee, the three of them somehow linked through this intimate encounter.

"We're not done with you yet, sexy girl," Stone said, his smoldering gaze shifting to Stevie.

She giggled sweetly. "I would hope not."

"But I think Nico deserves a turn, don't you?"

Stevie's eyebrows arched as she sat up. Her smile was mischievous. She was no longer the shy, giggling girl he'd known for so long. She was a hot-blooded woman who knew what she wanted. Regardless of what happened tonight, he would never look at her the same. She would no longer be his sister's best friend. She was now the woman who had weaved a path deep into his soul.

Nico wasn't sure what the plan was, but he went with it, lying down when Stevie moved toward him. She cupped his face and kissed him, stretching out beside him, her knee resting on his thigh. He twisted his torso so he could hold her, cupping the back of her head as she kissed him. He expected her to pull back once she tasted herself on his lips, but she didn't. The one time he'd tried to kiss Chelsea after he went down on her, she'd pushed him away. Not Stevie. She shocked him when she licked his lips before kissing him again.

Nico's stomach muscles tensed when deft fingers dipped into the waistband of his shorts. He pulled back to watch as Stone worked his shorts and underwear down. Nico assisted, lifting his hips, a hint of fear trickling into his veins. It was one thing to eat Stevie's pussy while Stone watched. It was something else entirely to be naked and vulnerable to this guy. Stone was the one who'd punched Nico in the face—twice—just a short time ago. He still wasn't certain that this wasn't some sort of trick.

His muscles coiled, preparing to defend himself in case Stone went on the attack.

"Nervous?" Stone asked, moving between Nico's thighs.

"Yeah," he admitted. No reason not to be honest.

"Don't worry. It won't hurt." Stone smirked. "Much."

Nico prepared to get away, pressing his foot down, ready to shove away from Stone. But it was Stevie's gentle touch that held him in place. Her soft, cool fingers slid down his chest, his stomach, before curling around his dick.

He grunted, jerking his gaze to hers. She was watching his face as she lovingly caressed his cock. He gasped for air as her delicate hand delivered mind-numbing pleasure.

He was so focused on her that he cried out when something warm and wet circled the head of his dick. He looked down to find Stone leaning over, his tongue teasing his slit.

Beside him, Stevie inhaled sharply, her hand still curled around the base of his shaft. "Oh, my God. That's…"

"That's what?" Nico asked, still unsure what to expect.

"That's hot."

Stone's eyes snapped up to her face, and he smiled around Nico's cock before releasing it.

"Fuck, baby. Does that pussy need some attention, too?"

The direction of Stone's eyes drew Nico's gaze. Stevie released his cock and tilted her hips. She had propped her knee up, her pussy on display.

"Play with it," Stone instructed her, his hand curling around the base of Nico's cock.

It was too difficult to focus with Stone touching him like that, his warm breath fanning the sensitive head of his cock.

"You want my mouth on you," Stone said, meeting his gaze.

It wasn't a question, but Nico nodded anyway.

Stone leaned in again, swirling his tongue around the crown. He teased for only a moment before taking him into his mouth. The wet rasp of his tongue had every muscle in Nico's body drawing taut. He couldn't look away. He wanted to remember this moment forever because it was exactly like every fantasy he'd ever had.

Beside him, Stevie moaned, her fingers rubbing furiously on her clit. When she whimpered, Stone stopped, releasing Nico's dick with a dramatic *pop*.

"Come here, baby." Stone patted the mattress beside Nico's hip. "I want him to feel the difference between you givin' him head and me doin' it."

Stevie got to her knees, her hand trailing over his chest as she shifted so she was kneeling by his shoulder, bent over him.

"Finger her pussy while she sucks you," Stone commanded.

Nico slipped his hand between her legs when she spread her knees wider, giving him access. He teased her clit with the pad of his thumb as she pressed a kiss to the head of his cock. He couldn't see because her head was blocking his view, so he settled for watching Stone as he watched her. He must've realized Nico was watching because he glanced over at him, then shifted, straddling Nico's left leg as he began unbuttoning his jeans.

He was mesmerized by the sight of Stone freeing his cock. It was all he could do to finger Stevie's pussy. She didn't let him stop for long. Whenever he paused, she would shift her hips back, fucking herself on his hand.

Stone looked at Nico as he pushed his jeans down his hips. Nico didn't look away, waiting for Stone to push his underwear down. When he did, Nico swallowed hard and licked his lips.

Stone's words from earlier played in his head.

I wanna fuck your face. Bury my cock in your throat until you can't breathe. Then I wanna bend you over and drive my dick in your ass.

"You want my dick in your mouth."

Like all the words that came out of Stone's mouth, it wasn't a question. Nico didn't respond; he simply watched as Stone stroked his thick length. Nico's cock was bigger, but Stone's was certainly impressive.

Nico gasped when Stevie sucked him deep into her mouth, sliding down until the head bumped the back of her throat.

"She's really fuckin' good at that," Stone said, his voice raw with lust. He moved back, dragging his jeans down his legs and tossing them away. Finally naked, Stone got to his knees again. "Now, let's see how good *you* are."

Stone didn't immediately shove his cock in Nico's mouth, though. He leaned forward instead, his lips hovering over Nico's.

"You've never had a dick in your mouth."

Nico shook his head.

"Mine's gonna be the first."

Again, it wasn't a question, so Nico wasn't sure what he was telling him. It sounded almost as though Stone was seeking permission without actually verbalizing it.

Nico held his stare and dared to provoke the beast. "Do your worst."

FOUR

STONE TOOK THOSE WORDS AS THE CHALLENGE he suspected they were. He bit Nico's bottom lip—hard—careful not to split the already damaged part, but eager to show Nico what was in store for him.

Nico hissed.

Every cell in Stone's body flared hot at the reaction. He hadn't been lying when he told Nico the only way he fucked was rough and dirty. The fact Nico expected that spurred him to fulfill Nico's taunt and to do his worst.

He sat up, gripping Nico's hair enough to lift his head. He manhandled Nico without worry, tilting his head at the optimum angle, and brought his cock to Nico's lips.

"Open," he snarled.

Nico didn't hesitate, so Stone pushed his throbbing dick inside his mouth. The wet heat sent sparks dancing along his spine.

"No teeth," Stone warned.

Nico's tongue caressed his length, his lips curving over his teeth.

"Good boy," he crooned, watching Nico's reaction to his words.

More heat flashed in his eyes, and Stone had to grit his teeth against the pleasure that assaulted him.

He switched hands, keeping Nico's head elevated by fisting his hair, then reached back for Stevie.

"Come here, baby."

She sat upright, her knees still spread, Nico's fingers buried inside her cunt.

"His fingers fillin' that little pussy?"

She nodded.

"Fuck his hand while you watch him suck my dick."

Stevie moaned, her eyes glued to where his cock was tunneling in and out of Nico's mouth. Stone didn't go easy on him, pushing deep into his throat, blocking his airway before pulling out and thrusting in again.

"You sure you've never done this before?"

Nico's eyes were watering, but he didn't stop sucking, allowing Stone to control the depth and speed of his thrusts. It felt so good.

Stone alternated between watching Nico and watching Stevie. She was steadily lifting and lowering on Nico's fingers, chewing on her bottom lip as she watched them.

"Don't think you'll get a pass if you make me come." Stone waited until Nico met his gaze. "Because I *am* gonna fuck that virgin ass tonight."

Nico's moan sent vibrations straight to Stone's balls. He didn't want to come yet, but it felt too good. And the fact that Nico admitted he was a virgin when it came to sex with a man only made it hotter. But it was how hot Nico was for Stevie that truly did it for him. Stone had been with guys before. And he'd been with girls. He'd even been with two girls at the same time. And they had touched each other. But he'd never done *this*. Sharing Stevie's body with Nico would go down in history as one of the best nights of his life. As for whether it could ever happen again, he didn't know, but for now, he was going to milk every drop of erotic pleasure out of it as he could.

Stone pulled his cock from between Nico's lips. "Move down."

Nico shifted.

"Farther."

When he had moved enough for Stone to straddle his head, he did. Staring straight down at him, he angled his dick and pushed it into Nico's mouth again.

"That's perfect right there," he said, pumping his hips, pushing deep into Nico's throat and pulling out. He didn't rush, enjoying the wet suction of his mouth.

"Easy," he warned Nico when the man's eyes widened as Stone held himself in his throat longer each time. "Breathe through your nose."

He pulled out, allowing Nico to drag air into his lungs. When he looked calmer, Stone pressed his palm to the wall to hold himself up. He twined his fingers in Nico's hair, lifting his head for optimum penetration, and began fucking his mouth again.

"Relax your throat," he commanded, aware of Stevie moving so she could get a better view.

Stone meant to engage with her while he did this, but he could only focus on the pleasure that assaulted him. He wanted more. And he wanted to see just how far Nico was willing to go.

When Nico's throat opened, Stone pushed in deeper, groaning as the tight passage strangled his cock. He retreated.

"This is my mouth to fuck," he told Nico, the words gravel rough. "Just like that ass is gonna belong to me, too."

Tears were streaming out of Nico's eyes, and Stone fought the urge to pull back. It was instinct. He didn't want to hurt Nico, but he wanted to push his boundaries, see how far he was willing to go.

"My girl takes me better than you do," he taunted. "Stevie's mouth is fuckin' perfect. I could fuck it all damn night."

Nico's eyes were hard now.

"Do better," Stone hissed. "Suck me, Nico. Make me come down your throat."

Something clicked in his eyes, and then Nico was lifting his head to meet each of Stone's thrusts, his cheeks hollowed, taking him all the way in his throat each time. Stone tried to hold on, he tried to fight the inevitable.

"Goddamn," he roared. "That's it. Oh, fuck. I'm comin'. Swallow, Nico. Goddammit, swallow."

He groaned as he drained his balls in Nico's mouth.

Lightheaded and gasping for air, Stone fell to the side and rolled onto his back, grabbing Stevie and bringing her with him. She kissed him, her mouth hot and hungry. It surprised him at first, but he wasn't about to leave her out.

"Did you enjoy that?" he asked, brushing her hair back from her face as he stared up at her.

"Yes. So hot."

He slid his hand between their bodies. "Are you wet?"

She nodded.

"Show me."

She canted her pelvis, allowing him to push a finger inside her. She wasn't just wet. She was drenched.

"Does this pussy need to be fucked?"

"Yes," she whimpered.

"Can Nico's big cock fuck this pussy?"

She gasped and nodded. "Yes."

"He's big, baby. Can that little pussy take him?"

She nodded again.

"I want you to do somethin' for me," he whispered.

"Anything."

"Lift up." He cupped her ass with both hands and guided her until she was up on her hands and knees, hovering above him. If he wanted, he could've pulled her onto his cock and kept that sweet pussy all to himself.

"Stay right where you are."

He turned his head to find Nico. He was lying beside them, watching them intently.

"Grab a condom. If you don't have one, get one outta the TV stand."

Nico slowly rose, disappearing from view.

"Once you're suited up, kneel behind her." Stone met Stevie's gaze. "I want him to fuck you while you look at me."

Her lips parted.

"And I want you to tell me how it feels."

She swallowed.

Stone felt the brush of Nico's legs against his own. He spread his legs, making room for him as he lightly dragged his fingers along Stevie's hips.

"Tell him what you need, baby."

Stevie twisted, looking over her shoulder. "Fuck me, Nico."

A rough growl sounded behind her, and then Nico shifted, his knees touching the inside of Stone's thighs.

Stevie sighed. "Yes. Oh, God, yes."

"What's he doin', baby?"

"He's … He's pushin' his cock inside me."

Stone reached down, wanting to feel Nico's shaft as it slipped inside her. Nico grunted when Stone touched him.

"You want it slow or fast?" Nico asked.

"Slow," Stevie answered without hesitation. "I want to feel all of you."

Stone loved that she was so into sex. From the first time they were together, he'd known she wasn't like some of the other girls who thought sex was all about the guy's pleasure. They'd spent hours together, just touching each other, finding what they liked. Not once did she shy away from anything he'd done to her. The only thing they hadn't done at this point was anal sex. Stone didn't want to hurt her, and he knew he would if he tried to shove his cock in her ass. He was rough by nature, but he knew his limitations.

"Nico…" Stevie's head tipped back. "Oh, God, yes. That feels nice."

"How does *she* feel?" Stone asked, continuing to watch Stevie.

"Tight," he said through gritted teeth. "So fuckin' tight."

"He's so big," Stevie noted.

Stone remained silent, caressing her thighs and hips as she rocked over him, letting Nico fuck her from behind.

"He's stretchin' me."

"Fuck, Stevie," Nico said. "Your pussy feels good."

She rocked back against him, her head tilting down. Her eyes were open, and she was watching him. A smile curled the corner of her mouth.

"Oh, shit," Nico hissed. "Do that again."

Stone grinned when he realized what she was doing. Stevie did this thing with her hips, where she circled them when he was inside her. It changed the angle, making her even tighter.

"Holy fuck. Stevie … yes. Squeeze my cock."

Stone's dick was already hard again. He loved listening to them. Stevie moaned.

"What's he doin'?" Stone prompted.

"He's grippin' my ass. Tilting my hips." Her lips parted in a silent sigh. "He's fuckin' me so deep."

She began rocking faster, her tits swaying beautifully above his face.

"Fuck me, Nico," she whimpered softly. "Yes ... *unnhh*... Fuck me hard."

Her body jerked. Then it jerked again as Nico impaled her. Stone remained still, watching her face as Nico pounded inside her.

"You're so beautiful," Stone whispered. "Let it feel good, baby. Let his cock fill your cunt. I wanna watch you come."

He knew she liked it when he was vocal, so he continued, chiming in alongside Nico as they took their pleasure from one another while Stone watched.

"Oh, Jesus ... Stevie ... oh, fuck ... your pussy's tight."

"Are you comin', Stevie?"

"Almost." Her eyes squeezed closed. "God, yes ... Nico ... harder!"

Nico was slamming into her so hard the floor was shaking.

"Yes!" Her eyes opened, and she met Stone's stare. Her mouth opened as she gasped, a smile forming. "Oh, yeah. I ... Nico ... oh, fuck. I'm comin' on his cock! I'm comin'!"

Nico growled roughly and slammed into her one more time. They both stilled, their combined shouts echoing through the rafters.

Stone smiled, lifting his head so he could press a kiss to Stevie's perfect lips.

She went limp, dropping onto him. He wrapped his arms around her, holding her to him. Nico was on his feet, disposing of the condom. When he joined them, he had a Dr. Pepper in his hand and a bewildered expression on his face.

"Good?"

"So much better than good."

"Change your mind about me fuckin' your ass?"

Nico turned his head and met his gaze. "No."

Stone grinned. "Me neither."

STEVIE WOKE WARM AND COMFORTABLE. IT TOOK a moment to realize where she was.

They were still in the loft. She remembered passing out from exhaustion after Nico fucked her, but she didn't remember being moved. Someone—likely Stone—had given her a pillow and a blanket. He was always doing little things like that. Taking care of her. He was the first guy she'd ever dated, who didn't make her feel as though sex was all he wanted. Granted, he was the only one she'd actually had sex with, so maybe guys changed when they were getting laid on the regular.

She had no idea how long she'd been asleep, but she could tell it was dark outside because the little window above was black. Also, the television was off, but the small strand of lights was still on, casting everything in a festive hue.

She turned her head, peering around to see if they had abandoned her.

That was when she saw them. Stone and Nico were about three feet away from her on one of the other mattresses.

Nico was on his back, one leg angled to the side, Stone hovering over him. Stone had his forearm across Nico's throat even as they kissed. But it was the placement of Stone's other hand that had her curious. From where she was, she could only make out the way he was pumping his arm. Like he was fingering him.

"That's only one finger," Stone told Nico. "You want two?"

Nico nodded.

Stone shifted forward, kissing Nico roughly, his arm moving faster.

Nico pulled his leg toward his chest. It allowed her to see that Stone was thrusting two fingers into his ass.

Her pussy fluttered, her muscles clenching with arousal.

"Relax," Stone crooned, removing his arm from his neck and propping himself up. "Let me stretch you."

Nico whispered something, and then Stone was on his knees, reaching toward the television stand. The light glinted off something in Stone's hand, and a second later, she heard the click of a bottle cap opening. It was followed by a *slurp* as Stone squeezed it between Nico's legs. Lube? Stone watched Nico as he began fingering him again. This time, Nico relaxed, his chest heaving.

"Better?"

Nico nodded.

Stone tossed the bottle and leaned forward again, propping himself on one arm as he kissed Nico while he continued to finger him.

Stevie's entire body was hot. Too hot for the blanket, but she didn't want to move. She didn't want them to stop. Stone and Nico were by far the sexiest men she'd ever seen, and this ... the two of them doing this to each other ... it made her wet. It turned her on more than any vibrator ever had.

"Did you enjoy fuckin' Stevie?"

Nico's expression morphed into something that looked like confusion.

"Tell me you haven't thought about it before? Your sister's smokin' hot best friend."

"Yeah," Nico whispered. "I've fantasized about it."

"Of course you have. She's amazing."

Stevie wished he would say more, but Stone's eyebrows lifted as he peered down at Nico. "Three fingers."

Nico grunted, pulling his leg back again. "Fuck me."

"Not yet."

"I want your dick inside me."

"You have to earn it first." Stone began ramming his fingers inside Nico. The more aggressive he was, the louder Nico's moans became. Clearly, they weren't worried about waking her up.

"You ready to earn it?" Stone asked, his hand stilling, fingers buried deep inside him.

"Yeah."

Stone pulled his hand away and grabbed something from the floor. A towel. He wiped his hand, then leaned over and opened the cabinet beneath the television. He came back with a condom, and like she'd seen him do so many times, he made quick work of covering himself.

Rather than move between Nico's legs, Stone stretched out beside him, their lips sealing. The kiss heated until they were holding onto one another. Only then did Stone roll to his back, bringing Nico with him.

"Straddle me," he instructed, relaxing on the pillow.

Nico moved over him.

"Now take my cock and put it inside you. I want you to sit on me. Take me as deep as you can. Go slow. We're not in a hurry." Stone grinned. "Not yet, anyway."

Nico gripped Stone's cock, guiding it between his legs. He grunted as he lowered himself slowly, impaling himself on Stone's cock.

Stevie didn't move. She didn't want to make a sound. She just wanted to *watch*.

Not that she'd ever fantasized about two men having sex, but she never expected to see … *that*. She'd seen some porn before, and usually, one guy was behind the other. Not like this. They were face-to-face. No different than the times Stevie had sat on Stone's cock and fucked him. It wasn't her favorite position because her legs tended to start hurting. She preferred when Stone was fucking her, but she knew Stone loved when she fucked him.

Stone planted one hand squarely in the center of Nico's chest, the other wrapping firmly around Nico's cock. They were staring at each other while Nico rocked forward and back.

"Relax," Stone told him. "You can take more of me if you relax."

Nico's head tipped, and his chest expanded as he drew in a deep breath. He exhaled slowly, his hips lowering. He was now sitting on Stone's cock.

"Let it feel good, Nico. Fuck me. Right now, it's all you. Take it."

Nico grunted, his thigh muscle flexing as he lifted and then lowered. Again and again. He was moving slowly, as though it hurt. Stevie had no experience with anal sex. Not like that, anyway. Stone had introduced her to the idea of it by using his tongue and his fingers, but he'd never fucked her there. She'd thought about asking him to because she was curious, but she was still hesitant. She'd heard it wasn't the same for women as it was for men. Niyah had told her that men had a pleasure spot inside them. Kinda like a woman's G-spot.

Stevie wasn't sure that was true since Nico did not appear to be enjoying it.

"Lean forward," Stone instructed.

Nico shifted only as much as Stone's extended arm would allow. The muscles in Nico's jaw relaxed. "Oh, fuck."

"Better?"

Nico nodded.

Stone stroked Nico's cock, pumping it in rhythm to Nico's movements. It went on for what felt like forever, Stone whispering commands until Nico was groaning, his head tipped back. No doubt he was enjoying it now.

"You're ready for me to ride you, huh?"

"Yeah."

"You want me to split that ass open with my cock."

Nico groaned.

Stevie had to stifle a shocked squeal when Stone abruptly sat up, shoving Nico backward until he was flat on his back. A second later, Stone was pressing down on the back of Nico's thighs, folding him in half as he shoved his cock inside him.

Now, nothing was blocking her view of Stone impaling Nico. Rough, hard. He drove in deep, leaning on Nico's legs.

"Fuck ... oh, fuck ... Stone!"

"Jerk yourself off," Stone commanded.

Nico grabbed his cock, yanking on it as Stone drilled him with lightning speed.

"So tight." Stone gasped for breath. "So hot." He rammed in harder. "God, you're fuckin' perfect."

Nico's eyes widened as he stared up at Stone.

Stevie gasped when Nico's cock erupted, cum spraying over his stomach.

A second later, Stone roared, his hips slamming against Nico's ass, his muscles contracting violently.

"Relax," Stone whispered to Nico. "Let me pull out slowly."

He was the same way with Nico that he was with her. Underneath all that roughness was a man who genuinely cared. Her chest pinched, and her heart swelled.

"I'm gonna go in and clean up," Stone told him as he pulled free from his body. "I'll bring back some wet washcloths."

Nico nodded, his arm sliding over his eyes.

Stone leaned over him. "Regret it already?"

Nico peeked out from under his arm. "No."

That sexy smirk was back on Stone's face. "Good. Don't leave Stevie. I mean it, Nico. Don't let me come back and find you gone. If you are, I'll hunt you down and kick your ass."

"I won't."

Stevie closed her eyes when Stone got to his feet. She slowed her breathing, hoping they would think she'd been asleep the whole time.

As she lay there waiting for Stone to leave, she realized she was overcome by a sense of relief. Although she was fully on board with everything they'd done, she thought for sure this was going to be a night she would want to forget, one that would result in her seeing Stone differently.

She didn't want to forget, but she did see him differently.

If it were even possible, Stevie realized she loved him even more than she had.

WHEN STONE DISAPPEARED DOWN THE LADDER, NICO grabbed the towel that was on the floor and wiped the jizz off his stomach. He grabbed one of the open cans of Dr. Pepper, downed what was left, and then returned to the mattress. He eased down to his knees, moving closer to Stevie, doing his best not to groan. He hurt. It wasn't necessarily a bad thing, and there for several minutes, there'd been no pain whatsoever, only mind-blowing ecstasy.

Now that the adrenaline rush was receding, he felt like he was coming down from an intense high. Not that he'd ever done drugs, but he'd heard enough to know that it didn't last forever.

Exhausted and sated, he spooned behind Stevie, sharing her blanket and sliding his arm under her head. He probably should've kept his distance since she was technically Stone's girl, but he couldn't help himself.

"You okay?"

He went rigid when he heard her voice. He thought she was asleep.

"I couldn't bring myself to interrupt," she said, leaning into him.

Nico put his arm over her, pulling her naked body against him. She was so soft and warm. He knew he shouldn't be touching her. It was only going to fuck him up in the head later. He didn't have a chance in hell of being with her, so this was only prolonging the torture.

Still, he couldn't help himself.

"Are you mad?" she asked.

"That you watched?"

"Yeah. And ... everything else."

"Why would I be mad?"

She shrugged.

He kissed her shoulder. "Best night of my life. Swear to God."

Stevie twisted, rolling to her back. He gave her room but didn't move away.

"Mine, too," she whispered, meeting his gaze in the dim space.

Nico stared into her pretty brown eyes, wishing he could tell her that he'd had feelings for her for a long time.

"Niyah's gonna have questions."

He frowned. "Niyah doesn't need to know about this. No one does."

Her eyes searched his. "She's my best friend. I tell her everything."

Nico swallowed hard. "Please, Stevie."

"You have nothin' to be ashamed of."

"I'm not ashamed." And that much was true. What he and Stone did ... it had been incredible. And it cleared up all the confusion he'd had. Stone Jameson had allowed him to see that being bisexual wasn't abnormal. In fact, in one night, he'd opened Nico's eyes to a lot of things.

Stevie smiled.

"What?"

Her smile widened. "So you like guys, huh?"

Nico laughed. It bubbled up and out of him and made him feel lighter than before. "I like girls, too."

She tapped his nose. "Lucky us."

"Why's that?"

Her voice lowered to a whisper. "Because it would be a waste of incredible talent if you didn't."

His eyebrows shot to his hairline. "Sweet little Stevie Shepherd, are you sayin' you enjoyed me eatin' your pussy?"

She gasped, and her eyes glittered with renewed heat. "So much."

"Enough to let me do it again?"

Stevie nodded.

"Right now?"

Her answer came by way of her spreading her legs.

Nico reached down, cupping her, teasing her. Her legs spread wider when he pressed his finger on her clit.

"You want my tongue here?" He drew small circles on the little nub.

Her hips lifted. "Yes."

"Take the blanket off. Show me what I get."

Stevie pulled the blanket away, revealing her hot, wet cunt. Nico wasn't sure what Stone's reaction would be when he returned to find Nico eating his girlfriend's pussy again, but he decided he would deal with the repercussions. He had a feeling this was the last time he would get a chance, and he wasn't about to pass up the opportunity.

He moved, repositioning her so he wouldn't have to lie on the floor. He kneeled between her legs first, pushing her knees back and spreading her wide.

"You have such a pretty pussy." He dragged his fingertips over her mound. "So soft. So wet."

Stevie whimpered, and he knew he would never be able to hear that sound and not think about this night.

Nico lowered himself so his head was between her legs. He didn't hesitate, licking every inch of her, fucking her with his tongue, lapping up her juices. He alternated between flicking her clit and tonguing her hole, making her whimper and moan.

When she grabbed for his hair, he stopped.

"Put your hands above your head."

She stared at him, then slowly did as he asked.

When she was still, he slid his hands under her ass and lifted her pussy to his mouth. He feasted like a starving man. He was devouring her when Stone returned a little while later—verbally announcing his presence a second before he slid the wood over the opening in the floor.

Nico's first reaction was to stop, but he forced himself not to. He wasn't ready yet. He figured if Stone was one of those guys who didn't mind screwing someone when he thought his girlfriend was asleep, he deserved to find his girlfriend getting her pussy eaten by another man.

"Holy shit, baby." Stone crouched beside them, dropping several washcloths on the floor. "Did you ask him to eat your pussy, or did he offer?"

Nico lifted his head, prepared to take the heat, but Stevie beat him to it.

"A little of both."

Stone chuckled. "Did you ask nicely?"

He should've known Stone wouldn't be offended.

"Kinda," she said sweetly.

Nico resumed licking, this time teasing her clit with slow, gentle flicks.

"He's got a talented mouth; I'll give him that."

"Yes." Stevie sighed. "Yes, he does."

"But you know what happens to bad girls who don't ask permission first?"

Nico lifted his head, looking at Stevie. Her eyes were wide, her lips parted. "They get spanked."

"They do," he agreed.

Stone looked at Nico and cocked an eyebrow as though daring him to say something. Nico didn't say a word, curious what was happening.

Stone peered over at Stevie. "What do you have to do, baby?"

"Ask nicely," she whispered, her eyes wide, but this time she had a smile on her face. "Please. Will you spank me?"

Jesus Christ. The girl was going to be the death of him. Of all the things he'd thought would come from Stevie's mouth, that certainly wasn't one of them.

Since it was clear his meal was over, Nico moved out of the way. He thought Stevie would get up, figuring she needed to be across Stone's lap for a spanking, but she didn't move. Nico sat beside her, wondering what was about to happen.

He didn't have to wonder long because Stone lowered to his knees on her other side. He planted one hand on her knee, pulling it wide, his other hand hovering over her pussy.

His hair was wet, and he'd changed clothes. Since he smelled good, Nico assumed he'd taken a shower.

"How many?" he asked her.

"Seven."

They locked eyes, and a second later, Stone slapped her pussy. Stevie cried out, her back arching. Stone did it again. And then again. Nico counted seven swats. By the time he was finished, Stevie was gasping, her back arching.

But they weren't done.

Stone sat down, leaning against the wall. He patted his thighs. Stevie hurried to drape herself across his lap.

"When I'm done spankin' her pretty little ass, I'm gonna fuck her," Stone said, looking at Nico. "And she's gonna suck your dick. You good with that?"

"If she is."

Stevie lifted her head, peering over at him from behind the curtain of her hair. "I am."

She lowered her head again while Stone ran his hand over her bare ass.

"My girl loves gettin' her ass spanked. Don't you, baby?"

"Yes." The word was muffled because she kept her head down.

"It makes her wet. She likes havin' her wet pussy fucked."

As soon as she moaned, Stone spanked her.

Stevie whimpered.

He did the same to her ass that he did to her pussy, spanking her in rapid succession. The only difference was he delivered the swats in different locations. It was too dark in the room to see if her ass was red, but based on the delivery, Nico couldn't imagine it wasn't.

"On your hands and knees," Stone barked.

Stevie crawled off of him, moving away, closer to Nico. He didn't realize what she was doing until she pushed on his chest, urging him to lie back. He did, and before he could take a breath, his cock was in her mouth.

"You don't come in her mouth," Stone barked as he shoved his shorts down and got behind her. "You come in mine."

Without warning, Stone shoved his dick inside her, ramming in deep. Without a condom.

Stevie moaned around Nico's cock, the vibrations sending shards of pleasure down his legs.

Stone fucked her. He was wild and untethered, as though punishing her for some indiscretion. Perhaps because Nico had been eating her pussy? Maybe he wasn't as okay with it as he appeared.

"Fuck, Stevie." Stone slapped her ass. "Squeeze my dick. Goddamn, you're so tight."

He pounded into her while Nico endured her wicked mouth sucking him. When her movements became jerky and uncoordinated, Nico pulled out of her mouth and got to his feet so he could stand in front of her.

"Oh, fuck, yeah," Stone said when Nico fisted her hair and pushed his dick into her mouth.

Stone's momentum drove her forward and back.

"Don't you come in her mouth," Stone snapped, slapping Stevie's ass again.

Nico gritted his teeth, hoping he could live up to Stone's expectations.

It became easier when Stevie's mouth was yanked off his dick. Stone had grabbed her by her ponytail, wrenching her head back. Stevie stared up at Nico with glassy eyes, her breaths racing in and out of her lungs. She was moaning and whimpering, begging Stone to fuck her harder.

"Put your dick in her mouth," Stone bit out. "She gets what I wanna give her."

Nico moved closer, angling his cock down and pushing it into her mouth. It was erotic as fuck, although he was terrified that Stone was going to hurt her. She didn't look like she was in any pain, but he hadn't expected him to be quite this rough. Not with her.

"She likes it," Stone said, as though reading Nico's mind. "I told you, I only know how to do it rough and dirty, and my sexy girl likes both."

Nico stared into Stevie's eyes and saw her approval. She did like this. And that made Nico's task even more difficult because he did what he could to contribute, fucking his cock deep into her throat. Her eyes watered, and she was moaning. It was too hot. It felt too good.

"Oh, yeah," Stone growled. "That pussy's gonna come. I feel it, baby. Come for me. Come all over my dick."

Stevie screamed, the sound muffled by Nico's cock. He pulled out immediately, watching her eyes roll back. He looked up in time to meet Stone's gaze, and a second later, Stone slammed into her, his mouth slack as he came.

"Lay down," Stone shouted as he pulled out of her.

Nico was on his ass, and Stone was shoving him back before he took him in his mouth. Nico choked on the pleasure, remembering what Stone had said earlier about the difference between Stevie's mouth and his. Stone knew exactly what to do with his tongue, knew just how far to take him in his throat to blow Nico's mind. It took only seconds before he felt that electrical charge at the base of his spine.

"Fuuuuck," he groaned, driving his hips up and burying himself in Stone's throat as he came.

Several minutes later, after they'd cleaned up again, the three of them were on the mattresses, the blanket covering them. Stone was on one side of Stevie, Nico on the other. She had her eyes closed.

"The night's not over yet," Stone whispered. "But you can rest for a little while."

"Okay."

"Then we're gonna make the most of the hours we have left."

She didn't open her eyes, but she smiled. "As long as it's rough and dirty, I'm game if y'all are."

Stone chuckled, his eyes closing.

Nico was too wired to close his eyes, so he settled for staring at them. He knew then, as the dawn approached, that life as he knew it was over. Everything that had transpired in this hay loft had altered his chemical makeup. He would never look at Stevie the same way. It wasn't an option because she'd shifted something inside him the same way Stone had.

Sure, most of it was based on sex, but not all. They'd touched distinct parts of him without using any part of their bodies.

He wouldn't call it love because he hadn't felt that before, so he had nothing to compare this feeling to.

For that same reason, he had a terrible feeling that it was.

Unfortunately, two days later, Nico realized none of it mattered. The moment Stone Jameson drove out of Coyote Ridge, leaving Stevie behind, all hopes of a perfect existence faded almost as quickly as his friendship with Stevie.

PART
TWO

ALMOST FIFTEEN YEARS LATER...

FIVE

Friday, January 12, 2024

"OH, FOR THE LOVE OF—" STONE JAMESON rolled over and covered his head with a pillow.

It didn't help. Not even *two* pillows could drown out his sister's voice when she was excited. And heaven help them all, Reilly was evidently really excited about whatever the hell she just found. On a good day—and the jury was out on whether this one would be—Stone was a steadfast member of the *Reilly is adorable* fan club. At the moment, he wanted to cover *her* head with the damn pillow.

For fuck's sake.

"There better be coffee," he grumbled, tossing off the blankets and sitting up. He dropped his feet to the floor and wiped the sleep from his eyes so he could glance at his watch.

"Seven fucking thirty. Seriously, Reilly?"

Pushing to his feet, Stone took a single step and tripped over his damn boots. He fell against the desk, knocking his hip on the corner.

"Fuuuuck!" he hissed through gritted teeth.

Nope. Uh-uh. Not how his day was gonna go.

Stone turned around, stepped over his boots, crawled back into bed, yanked the blankets up to his neck, and covered his head one more time. He took a deep breath and exhaled slowly. He listened for a moment and heard ... nothing.

Maybe she left.

He took another deep breath and continued to hear blessed silence.

"Good girl, Reilly," he mumbled as his eyes closed. "Go to Mom's ... have some breakfast ... let me..." He yawned and instantly drifted off.

A delighted squeal jolted him out of that lingering hazy bliss. He shot up, grabbed the pillow with both hands and twisted hard, clenching his teeth to keep from shouting.

Deep breath in through his nose, out through his mouth.

"Sleep's overrated anyway," he muttered as he got to his feet again. This time, he managed to remain upright, kicking his boots aside with a grunt and ignoring the tightness in his back.

This was not how he saw the first day of the rest of his life going. Considering he'd pulled into town at the ass-crack of dawn, he should still be asleep. That had been the plan. Sleep for a few hours, then unload the trailer he'd hauled up from Houston. Only as soon as he walked inside, he realized the latter would have to wait until he helped Reilly and Tate move their shit out. Now it looked like sleep was out of the question, too, which meant the only thing left to do was to start moving shit. At least then he'd be able to sleep in his own damn bed. King-sized. With a pillow top. And pillows that weren't made of fucking air.

What grown man thought it was normal to sleep in a full-size bed? Yeah, Tate was smaller than the average man, but seriously? Stone's damn feet had hung off the end. And that was when he laid on his side and bent his damn knees. Anyone over six feet needed a mattress at least as long as they were.

Tonight would be better. He'd have his bed set up and all his—

He was about to open the bedroom door when he realized he was naked.

Well, hell.

If it'd been a regular day—one that didn't involve waking up with other people in his house—he would've wandered out with his dick swinging. He didn't give a shit.

But that was not cool when his baby sister was there. And not because he thought it would embarrass Reilly. Oh, no. It took far more than naked bits to make his sassy kid sister's cheeks turn red. No, it was for his own protection because, with his luck, Reilly would start calling him by some stupid nickname like Buck or Whitey or whatever else her crazy mind could dream up to make fun of his pasty white ass.

Turning back, Stone grabbed his jeans off the back of the chair he'd tossed them on less than two hours ago. He tugged them on, zipped them up. He didn't bother with the button since he was only going a short distance to the bathroom to take care of business. He snagged a shirt at the last second, figuring it was in everyone's best interest if he didn't have to answer unnecessary questions. No doubt, if his sister saw his tattoos, she would have them.

"Mornin', Stone!" Reilly called when he came out of the room that still contained everything Tate owned in it.

Stone grunted in response and kept going. There was no time for pleasantries. He had to take a piss.

He made it to the bathroom, kicking the door closed behind him. He scoped the room, shaking his head at all the shit that was supposed to be gone before today. Toothbrushes, curling irons, hair products. He glanced over his shoulder at the enormous walk-in shower. There was a damn pink puff hanging from the shower knob. Reilly's or Tate's?

The thought made him grin.

So much for them being moved out before he got to town.

Stone sauntered to the toilet, lifted the seat. He'd hoped that giving them three weeks' notice would've been enough to ensure he didn't have any obstacles to contend with when he arrived. Of course, when he originally thought he would have to move back, he'd expected to have to stay in the house with Mom and Dad. It was pure luck that Reilly and Tate were moving out, giving him a place of his own. At least until he could figure what to do next.

He should've known Reilly would procrastinate. She was good at that.

After flushing, he moved to the sink and looked in the mirror for the first time. Damn. He looked like shit. He needed a haircut in the worst way. He rubbed the dark scruff on his jaw. It needed a trim, too.

For all of three seconds he considered grabbing his toiletries bag but decided against it. He could deal with that this afternoon. *After* he was moved in and he wouldn't have to rearrange everyone else's shit just to shave his face.

A few minutes later, after he washed his hands, brushed his teeth with one of the new, unopened toothbrushes he found in the drawer, and splashed cold water on his face, Stone came out to find Reilly in the kitchen, a steaming cup of coffee in front of her. She flashed a smile and slowly pushed it toward him using the tip of one finger. She looked so sweet and so utterly innocent, but he knew better.

"A little sugar and a splash of milk," she said, her long lashes fluttering.

Okay, maybe she wasn't so bad. "Have I ever told you you're my favorite?"

"I'm everyone's favorite." Reilly gave him that *what-can-you-do?* shrug. "But I like hearin' it, so feel free to say it whenever I'm around."

Stone chuckled. He'd missed his kid sister. Hell, he'd missed this entire town. A month ago, if anyone asked him if he had plans to return to Coyote Ridge, he would've said no. Then the shit hit the fan, and here he was, back in the small town he was born and raised in. Thirty-six years old, and he was starting over. From scratch.

"Did we wake you?"

Stone cocked an eyebrow as he sipped his coffee.

"Okay, fine. I know we woke you. It's the least I could do on your first day back."

"You realize I got in about two hours ago."

Reilly flashed a guileless grin. "Well *that* was silly of you."

Yes, apparently, it was. "It's a day that ends in Y. Shouldn't you be at work?"

"Probably."

Stone waited for her to elaborate or possibly realize that no one was running the Jameson General Store if she was standing here in what used to be her kitchen but now belonged to him.

Reilly stared, those big green eyes glittering with mischief.

Fine. He'd bite. "So why aren't you?"

"That's my fault," Tate announced, joining them in the kitchen. "I have today off, and I thought you weren't gettin' in until next week."

Yeah, that had been the plan. But again, the shit hit the fan, and he'd put tires to asphalt.

"I wanted to get an early start," Tate explained. "Thought we could have it cleared out before you got here."

"Maybe if y'all'd started three weeks ago…"

They both looked at him as though they couldn't fathom what that meant. Whatever. It was too damn early to debate this. Until he filled his tank with some high octane, he'd only go down swinging.

Stone shrugged. "Hope you don't mind I slept in your bed."

"Hope you changed the sheets," Reilly said, mocking his tone.

Stone frowned.

Tate's eyes widened, and he shook his head at Reilly, then looked his way. "Don't listen to her. They're clean."

"So he says," she drawled.

"Rye," Tate admonished.

"What?" She'd certainly perfected that wide-eyed, innocent look. "You and D *were* gettin' busy in that bed the last—"

"No!" Stone held up a hand. "No, no." He shook his head and carried his coffee into the living room. "I don't wanna hear about how *anyone* was gettin' freaky in that bed with Donovan."

"Oh, but they were," Reilly said with far too much enthusiasm. "My noise-cancelin' headphones couldn't drown 'em out."

Stone took a seat on the couch and glanced at Tate. The kid's face was beet red. If he had to guess, Donovan thought that shit was adorable.

Never in his life would Stone have imagined his big brother settling down with Reilly's best friend from childhood, yet that was exactly what they were doing. Not only were they shacking up together, they were getting married. Provided Tate accepted D's proposal. According to Reilly, he would. One day. Probably.

Stone sipped his coffee and studied Tate. He would say yes eventually. Right?

His sleep-deprived brain decided that yes, Tate would get around to saying yes and walking down the aisle because, although Stone hadn't been around much these past few years, something told him they were going to get their happily ever after. Donovan deserved it. They were an interesting pair, that was for damn sure.

Almost as interesting as Reilly and Brady. Stone *never* saw that one coming. Then again, he'd never thought of his sister as being old enough to settle down and get trapped in domesticated bliss.

"So, you think we could borrow your trailer?" Reilly asked, practically skipping into the living room.

"Sure," he said, staring at her over his coffee mug. "Just as soon as you unload it."

"What's in there?"

"All my shit."

"Oh."

Yeah. *Oh* was right.

"What do ya need it for?" he inquired, still sipping coffee.

"To move our stuff."

"D's not springin' for movers?" Stone asked Tate.

"He offered. I declined."

"Well, that's not fair," Reilly said, hooking her hands on her hips. "Brady didn't offer to move *my* stuff."

"Probably figured you needed to earn your keep." Stone gave her a mocking grin.

Reilly looked at him, her innocence shining brightly in her big green eyes. "No. I pretty much paid my dues last night when—"

"Nope!" Stone shouted, shooting to his feet. He sloshed coffee on his hand but ignored the sting from the heat. "Do *not* even *think* about finishin' that sentence."

Reilly giggled. "What? Will it offend your delicate sensibilities?"

"Yes," he insisted, setting the coffee mug on the kitchen island and wiping his hand on his jeans. "Yes, it will."

He heard them both laughing as he stomped toward the bedroom. It took him two minutes to pull on his belt and boots. Another minute to tuck his cell phone in his pocket and shrug on his coat.

When he returned, he found Tate and Reilly still laughing.

Stone pointed toward the door. "Out."

"But—"

"Outside. You two pains in the ass are gonna help me unload that trailer. Then I'm gonna help you load it back up."

"Really?" Reilly squealed with delight. "You're the best."

Stone rolled his eyes and grabbed the trailer key off the counter.

Three hours later, everything was unloaded from the trailer, and at least a quarter of Reilly's furniture had been loaded into it.

Stone had been doing most of the work himself for a while since Reilly and Tate had made the excuse that they needed to pack the rest of their things. Somehow, they managed to avoid any *actual* work, choosing to wrap each individual item in enough bubble wrap to protect a small child. Then they ran into issues trying to fit everything into boxes meant more for shipping packages than packing houses. They looked like they were playing a complicated game of Tetris as they tried to get it to fit.

To put it simply, they weren't making a dent, leaving Stone with barely enough room to move his own shit into the house.

To keep them motivated, he'd started piling their crap in corners. It was only fair, considering they'd promised they would be moved out before he moved in. Since Tate already confessed they'd planned to take care of it today—rather than three weeks ago when they learned that he was moving back—Stone didn't feel bad about it.

Not that he needed their shit out of the barn. He didn't have enough to fill the place. Mostly bedroom furniture. If they took the couch and the dining room table, he would be left to sit on bar stools. Unless they took those, too.

"Looks like I got here just in time."

Stone glanced over his shoulder as he set down a box. Donovan walked into the house with a grin the size of Texas plastered on his face. Strangely, it grew even wider when he locked onto Tate, who was in the process of wrapping a fucking metal spatula in bubble wrap.

"Not if you planned to do the heavy liftin'," Stone told his brother.

Donovan smirked. "Like I said, just in time."

"I hope you brought pizza," Reilly called from the bathroom, where she was probably wrapping toothpaste in bubble wrap.

"Nope, but I could run and get some," Donovan offered, walking over to Tate.

Was it lunchtime already? He glanced at his watch. Damn. Almost eleven.

Stone stared with amusement as his brother tipped Tate's chin with one finger and leaned down to kiss him. Tate kissed him back, his cheeks his own personal mood ring, turning pink to signify what he was feeling.

Stone cleared his throat, reminding them they weren't alone.

"Is he gettin' pizza?" Reilly shouted.

"Hold your horses," Donovan said, glancing over at Stone. "You hungry?"

Stone wiped his dusty hands on his jeans and glanced at his watch. "I could eat."

"You look like you could use a beer, too."

"And a nap," he admitted. "Not necessarily in that order."

"Hey, Rye!" Donovan hollered.

Reilly stuck her head out of the bathroom. "Yeah?"

"Place the order. I'll run and pick it up. I need about twenty minutes."

"What for?" she asked.

"For you to mind your own damn business," he called back.

"But I'm starvin'," she whined, disappearing into the bathroom again.

"And I'm busy!"

Stone laughed. Not much had changed around here. "Somethin' I can help with?"

Donovan grabbed one of the boxes with Tate's name on it and stacked it on another. "Mom's got a landscaper comin' by. She asked me to meet with him."

"Ain't it a little cold to be worryin' about plants?" Stone asked, following Donovan when he hefted the two boxes and carried them outside.

"Yeah. But he's booked solid most of the year. She's hopin' to get on his calendar for March. This was the only time he had free to meet."

It figured. Especially since their folks took a quick trip to Dallas to see Chelsea and Paul.

"What're they lookin' to do?" Stone asked.

Donovan nodded toward the house. "Walk with me."

Because it gave him a break from moving furniture and boxes, Stone followed his brother toward the house. They reached the fence surrounding the backyard just as a white Dodge truck with a black and gold landscaper logo on the side pulled into the driveway.

"Perfect timin'," Donovan said with a grin that seemed a little too gleeful in Stone's opinion.

A few minutes later, he realized why.

NICO DAUGHERTY PARKED HIS TRUCK IN FRONT of Owen and Deborah Jameson's house, smiling to himself as he got out.

It'd been years since he'd been here. About fifteen, in fact. Not since his senior year of high school. More specifically, the night Chelsea Jameson broke up with him, accusing him of hitting on her best friend. Which, okay, fine. Maybe he had. But not because he was truly interested in Julie ... or was it Jenny? Something with a J, he was sure. Regardless, he hadn't been interested, just bored.

God, he remembered how pissed off Chelsea'd been. Ranting and throwing shit, cursing a blue streak. She'd put a ship full of sailors to shame that night.

Funny thing was, he was pretty sure Chelsea hadn't cared. She merely had a flair for the dramatic back then. After all, his behavior had given her the excuse she needed to end things. She never did own up to it, but before he'd come up with the grand plan to piss her off enough to break up with him, he'd caught a rumor that she had no intention of being in a relationship when she left for college. By doing it that way, Nico made it easier for her.

Not that it'd been a benevolent move on his part. Oh, no. He'd been far too self-serving back in high school.

But the most memorable part about the last time he'd been here had nothing to do with that fight and everything to do with—

"Hey, Nico!" Donovan Jameson called as he came around from the side of the house with another man walking beside him.

Not just *any* man. That was Stone Jameson. What the hell was he doing here? He was supposed to be in Houston. Forever.

Fuck.

This was so not good.

As Nico watched them approach, he realized something. Turned out that *stunned speechless* wasn't merely a figure of speech. It was real. And he knew because that was exactly what he was as the man who'd altered his world in the span of only a few hours quickly closed the gap that was separating them.

Both men were walking with their heads held high, backs straight. Every Jameson Nico had ever met was like that, proud of who they were, what they'd made of themselves. Another trait that held true was their dark hair, which these two showed off with thick stubble lining their jaws. Donovan, the oldest of Owen and Deborah's five kids, was a massive man. Six feet four inches and built like a Mack truck, the guy could intimidate with just a look.

Then there was Stone, the second oldest, who, at one point, Nico had thought was the best-looking of all of them. Eh. Maybe he still thought that.

Back in the day, Stone had been smaller than his brother, not quite as intimidating. That wasn't the case anymore. He was about an inch shorter than Donovan and just as broad. If the thick muscles that connected his neck to his shoulders—trapezius, he thought they were called—were any indication, the guy wasn't lacking in the muscle department. In fact, he looked as though he spent every waking hour doing biceps curls.

Not that Nico was admiring the man. Not even a little.

Okay. Maybe a little.

Where Donovan held an air of professionalism, Stone exuded a bad-boy charm. That swagger, the smirk, and the way he wore his ball cap backward were just a few things that hadn't changed.

"Nico, I'm not sure if you remember my brother, Stone. He's in the process of movin' back. Stone, Nico Daugherty."

Oh, yeah. Nico definitely remembered him. If he lived to be two hundred, he wouldn't forget Stone Jameson.

"You used to date Chelsea," Stone said in that raspy grumble that Nico found eerily sexy.

Used to date Chelsea? *That* was the memory he was going to draw from?

Stone looked at Donovan. "Or am I thinkin' of someone else?"

"No, same one," Donovan said.

That was how they were gonna play it, huh? All right then. Nico would play. "And you punched me in the face because she broke up with me."

Donovan glanced between them and barked a laugh. "Priceless."

"I punched him for makin' her cry," Stone countered.

Donovan's head tilted. "In that case, you probably deserved it."

"Probably," Nico agreed, grinning from the memory. At the time, he damn sure hadn't been smiling because Stone Jameson had a mean right hook back then. Looking at him now, there was a good chance he'd perfected those punches.

"Semantics," Stone muttered, glancing around him toward his truck. "You're a landscaper now?"

"You could say that." Nico figured it would come across as arrogant if he told the guy he was a landscape architect and that, technically, he owned the company and employed people who did the hard work. Based on the moue of Stone's lips, he found landscaping beneath him.

Nico turned his attention to Donovan. "Deborah left me a message last night. Said she'd be out of town, but to give you what I've come up with. Have time for me to walk you through it?"

"Actually..." Donovan pulled out his phone and frowned. "I've got somethin' I need to take care of." He looked at Stone, then back to Nico. "Mind walkin' my brother through it?"

Nico might've spent a good majority of his life playing in the dirt, but he wasn't an idiot. He knew a set-up when he heard one.

"I can do that," he said, keeping his tone professional. He was here on official business, after all. It didn't matter to him who he gave the information to. As long as it made it back to Owen and Deborah, he could outline it for the family dog for all he cared.

"I'll be back in a bit," Donovan told Stone.

"I want pepperoni on mine," Stone grumbled.

Nico wasn't sure if that was an inside joke, but he plowed right over it by pulling out the iPad he had tucked under his arm. He tapped the screen and brought up the design he'd created for Deborah when she first approached him to redesign her front yard. Due to the amount of work he'd been doing in some of the neighboring towns, Nico hadn't had much time to spend in Coyote Ridge.

Standing beside Stone, Nico showed him the 3D design he'd created that displayed all the work he intended to do. He'd been going on for about five minutes when he realized Stone wasn't listening to a word he said.

"You know, maybe it'd be best if I try to get by here when Deborah's back."

Stone glanced over, his hazel eyes rimmed in red, as though he was either hungover or running on little to no sleep.

"You told me you and my sister were done," Stone said.

Well, apparently, his brain was functioning even if he wasn't paying attention.

"She dumped me," he corrected.

Stone took a step closer, eyes narrowed, voice low. "I heard y'all were back together a week later."

So he did remember.

Nico glared back. "What the fuck did you care? You were *gone*, Stone."

Stone's gaze bounced over his face, but Nico wasn't sure what he saw. He knew it wasn't the same horny nineteen-year-old he'd been the last time they were face to face.

"Would it've changed anything?" Nico said when it was clear Stone didn't have a retort.

He thought for sure Stone would blast him with an adamant "no" but he didn't say a word.

"I didn't think so." Nico tucked his iPad under his arm.

"You could've told me," Stone finally said, his eyes imploring as they raked over Nico's face.

"If I recall correctly, you didn't give me a chance to say much of anything. One minute you were here, the next you were gone."

Stone's chin lifted, his massive shoulders squaring.

Nico shook his head and took a step back. "I'll send what I have to Deborah and get with her on the rest."

It wasn't surprising that Stone didn't try to stop him from leaving.

After all, it was no less than what he'd done the last time Nico walked away.

SIX

STONE STARED AT NICO AS HE WALKED away.

Images flashed in his mind's eye, some flickering brighter than others. All of them comprised of naked, sweaty bodies moving together.

One night.

That was all it had been. One single night that had forever altered Stone's existence. Wild. Rough. And so fucking hot it was a wonder they hadn't burned the fucking barn down with the heat they generated. It had been by far the most intense encounter of Stone's life. One he'd spent months trying to forget and years refusing to remember. But seeing Nico again brought it all flooding back.

Stone had learned a lot about himself that night.

Fifteen years ago, at the ripe young age of twenty-one, he'd had quite a few sexual encounters under his belt. None that tripped him up the way that one did, and it wasn't because he'd been with a man. Definitely not that. As with just about anything in his life, Stone didn't discriminate. It wasn't in his nature.

Growing up, Stone had created and nurtured a reputation of being the wild one, the unpredictable one. No one knew what to expect from him, and he'd liked it that way. He'd been a playboy all through high school. His only requirement was that they had to be willing, and he had to be interested. He'd never run out of options, and not once did he choose to have a steady partner.

He'd been around the block so many times that when his high school class was coming up with superlative awards, they'd chosen *Least Likely To Settle Down* as his. They weren't wrong.

It wasn't until he was a few years out of high school that a woman truly caught his eye, and he'd indulged in something that resembled a relationship. He'd never questioned how it happened because whenever he thought about Stevie Shepherd, he had only good memories. To this day, she was by far the sexiest woman he'd ever met. Not because she was gorgeous, although she certainly was that. Or at least she had been back then. He couldn't attest to it now because he hadn't seen her in fifteen years. But, yeah, she'd been hot enough to catch fire. Long blonde hair and big brown eyes, that elfish chin, and that perfect little ass, Stevie had caught his attention immediately. But her chipper personality and never-met-a-stranger attitude had turned him on like nothing else.

To sum it up, he'd been head over heels in love with her.

Stone wouldn't deny that the events of that night had sent him running. He'd pretended it was a job that had lured him away, but the truth was, he'd run. Fast. And he'd forced himself not to look back.

His reputation followed him even after he left for bigger and better things. He'd floated for a few years, moving from ranch to ranch, learning the ropes, sleeping in shitty bunkhouses with assholes who thought he was all hat and no cattle. He'd proven them wrong, working his way up to foreman twice. The first time had resulted from a rather heated affair he'd had with the ranch owner's wife. She'd been particularly fond of him, and he'd been working too hard to give a shit about whether he was crossing lines. He'd held the role for six months before her husband found out and fired him on the spot.

The second time he'd worked his way up had been on merit. That was about the time he'd realized he wasn't getting any younger, and fucking for the sake of fucking was getting in the way of his career growth. He'd lasted four years in a role that taught him so many things before finally getting a job offer he couldn't refuse. He'd hated to leave, but his boss had outright told him he'd reached the proverbial ceiling. He couldn't go any further.

So when Doug Johnson approached him to manage the Double J—known for producing high-performing cattle with a focus on champion bucking bulls—Stone had finally realized there was a dream to be had. He wasn't interested in being the hired help for the rest of his damn life. He wanted to run things. So for the past five years, he'd made it his mission to learn everything he needed to know about operating a ranch with the Double J's prestige.

He wasn't oblivious to the hard work and the ridiculous amount of money that went into a goal of that magnitude, but he was determined. Stone had secured his spot as Doug's right hand in all things and was on track to one day take over since Doug's daughter had no desire to take the reins.

It wasn't until about two years ago that Stone learned the real reason his boss had poached him, and it had nothing to do with his ability to make the man money, although he figured that had been at least part of it. No, the reason Doug Johnson hired him was because he thought Stone was gay—something Stone never refuted—and Doug figured that was the best way to ensure his daughter's virtue remained intact. Never mind that Stone was only one of dozens of men working on the Double J.

Too bad ol' Doug hadn't shared that little nugget with him from the beginning. Maybe then Stone would've made better choices.

No, Stone hadn't set out to get tangled up with Leah Johnson, but not because he wasn't attracted to her. She was certainly fuckable if you were into spoiled, smart-mouthed, overeducated women. She wasn't exactly his type, but he'd learned that pickings were slim when you lived on a ranch.

When he'd first started, Leah had been twenty-three, living at home without a plan for her future. According to her, it wasn't necessary because Daddy was going to take care of her. A few years passed, and he'd developed something of a friendship with her. She didn't have many friends because she thought she was better than most people, but Stone had looked past that. To be honest, he hadn't intended to screw her, but resisting her became damn near impossible when she set her sights on him. He eventually caved, insisting it was only sex. They'd kept their liaisons on the down-low for nearly two years. Then, a month ago, Doug walked in to find Stone and Leah in a rather compromising position. In the main barn.

Doug had been livid, insisting Stone man up and do the right thing, which, according to Doug, involved a wedding ring and a minister. When Stone told him he had no intention of marrying his daughter, the shit hit the fan. And when that declaration reached Leah's ears, Doug wasn't the only one chasing Stone off the property. Unbeknownst to him, Leah thought things were moving toward a walk down the aisle, too, and his rejection resulted in him peering down the business end of a double-barrel shotgun.

Needless to say, he'd high-tailed it.

Now, as he watched Nico's truck turn and head back the way he'd come, Stone was reminded why he'd never even considered settling down with anyone.

That night with Nico and Stevie had been eye-opening for him. He'd gotten his first taste of hardcore, *ride 'em till they beg* sex, which for many years was what he told himself it was. Deep down, he knew better. In the coldest recesses of his soul, Stone could admit something else happened that night. A connection had been established. One he'd refused to acknowledge because of how potent it had felt. But the timing couldn't have been worse. At that point, none of them had even begun to live their lives, so he'd done the only thing he could do. He'd run like hell.

Seemed he'd gotten really good at doing that.

Stone started toward the barn, wondering whether Nico was married. Had he settled down, gotten himself a wife? Maybe a horde of kids? And what about Stevie? Was there some lucky bastard she went home to every night? They were both a few years younger than him. Most people who intended to settle down likely did so before then. At least, that seemed to be the case for the people Stone knew.

Didn't necessarily mean it had happened for Nico or Stevie.

"Who were you talkin' to?" Reilly asked when Stone reached the barn's porch.

"Nico Daugherty."

"Really?" A huge grin flashed on her face. "He's the one you punched when you thought he dumped Chelsea, right?"

"Yeah."

"It's cool that he's a big-shot landscapin' architect now, right?"

Really? Architect? Why hadn't he made that clear when Stone asked?

"He owns his own business," Reilly continued. "D and S Landscape Solutions. Got an office out by Uncle Curtis's ranch. His sister Niyah just got married to some super smart tech nerd. Adam's his name. Adam Takahashi. They're movin' to California."

Where the hell did this girl store all this information? Jesus.

"He sniffin' 'round Chelsea again?" Reilly asked.

"Who?"

"Nico." She laughed. "The guy we're talkin' about."

Right.

Stone cocked his head. "Why would you think he's interested in Chelsea?"

She shrugged and spun on her boot heel before walking back inside. "He's single now. He was engaged to a girl he dated for a long time. Melanie somethin'. She's not from here."

Stone assumed she meant specifically from Coyote Ridge.

"They were together for like two years before he popped the question. The engagement didn't last all that long. Rumor is he called it off."

He followed her, trying to pretend he wasn't hanging on every fucking word.

"But I guess he wouldn't be sniffin' 'round Chelsea."

"Why's that?"

"I heard he broke things off 'cause he's gay," she chattered on as she grabbed one of her boxes.

Stone helped, taking the two beside it and following her. "He's gay?"

"That's what I heard. He broke up with Melanie 'cause he was ready to come outta the closet."

"Did he?"

"What?"

"Come outta the closet?"

Reilly shrugged again. "I haven't seen him hangin' on some guy's arm or nothin'. So maybe. Maybe not."

Stone kept his expression flat as he put the boxes in the trailer.

"Then again, that coulda been an excuse. Maybe he just didn't like her. Or he could be playin' for *both* teams now." She shrugged. "It happens."

He nearly plowed into her when she stopped suddenly and turned to face him. "You're a switch hitter, aren't you?"

"I don't discriminate," he admitted.

Reilly flashed another smile. "I like that about you."

"Thanks."

She pointed to a stack of boxes. "Help me with those?"

He grabbed the heaviest one and carried it outside. She was only a few steps behind him.

"So why'd you get bounced from the job?"

"Who said I got bounced?"

Reilly chuckled. "You're back here, aren't ya? Seems like a logical explanation."

"Fine. Yeah, I got fired."

"Were you boinkin' the boss's wife again?"

Evidently, there was no mystery left.

"Daughter."

Reilly spun around, grinning like an idiot. "Seriously?"

"Seriously."

"Was she hot?"

"You could say that." Provided she didn't open her mouth and let her idiocy come flying out.

Reilly laughed. "Spoiled, rich-brat hot?"

"Exactly."

"You got caught, huh?"

"Not on purpose."

She laughed again and headed into the house.

"Tell me D went to pick up the pizza," he said before she could interrogate him more. At this rate, he'd have no secrets left.

"He did. Took Tate with him, though. Might be a while. Those two..." Reilly shook her head and laughed again. "I think—"

Stone planted his palm over her mouth, cutting her off before she could tell him something he couldn't unhear.

"You're Tate's best friend," he told her. "So you're obligated to listen to his stories. I'm not. I don't wanna hear it."

She smiled, her eyes crinkling. She said something, but it was too muffled to make out.

He dropped his hand. "What's that?"

"You sure?"

"More than I've ever been."

"Fine. But only 'cause you're just gettin' your sea legs. Once you're settled, I make no promises."

With that, she skipped off to get more of her stuff.

WHEN THE PHONE RANG, STEVIE GRABBED THE small remote and clicked *stop* to silence the music.

She ensured she had a smile so it reflected in her voice when she said, "D and S Landscape Solutions."

"Hey, Stevie. It's me."

Since Nico was well aware she blasted music when she was alone, she pressed play, and Christian Kane's sexy voice came pouring through the speakers again.

"Aren't you supposed to be somewhere right now?" she asked, snatching her iPad off the counter so she could pull up the calendar. "At the ... uh ... the place ... with the ... uh..." She stalled as she flipped to Friday's appointments. There shouldn't be any since, technically, they didn't take appointments on Friday. But Stevie had learned a long time ago that the customer was always right, and if they wanted something done on a Friday, Nico would make it happen.

"The Jamesons," Nico supplied.

As soon as he said the words, she saw the calendar details. Deborah and Owen Jameson. Yep. That was the one.

"So? What'd Deborah say? Did she like the design?" Although Nico's designs were just short of brilliant, Stevie always added a few touches to make them a little more unique—to give them some flair, if you would. She'd been quite proud of the idea she'd come up with for the Jamesons.

"She asked me to give the info to Donovan."

Well, that was disappointing. "Did you?"

"No."

Putting her hand on her hip, Stevie turned to look out the window, pursing her lips. She hated it when Nico got all cryptic on her. Which he did. All the damn time. She tolerated it for several reasons. One, Nico was her business partner and had been since they opened D & S Landscape Solutions eight years ago. Two, Nico was Niyah's brother, and since Niyah had been Stevie's best friend since fourth grade, it was part of the BFF code. And three ... well, the third reason was something that Stevie and Nico never, ever, *ever* talked about. At least not when they were sober.

So.

"Should I move the appointment to another day?" Stevie asked before she set down the iPad.

"No. I'll get with Deborah later."

"Okay. Where're you headed now?"

"Anywhere but here," he muttered.

Stevie detected something odd in his tone. "You okay?"

"Not really, no."

"Why?"

He was silent for a moment. Long enough, Stevie glanced at the phone to see if the call had disconnected. It hadn't.

"Nico?"

"Did you know Stone's back?"

Every cell in her body flashed hot. Like nuclear reactor hot. At least a dozen snapshots flashed in her brain, memories from long ago. It happened anytime anyone mentioned the man's name and was usually followed by profound rage. This was part of the reason Stone Jameson was off-limits in terms of conversation topics.

"What do you mean *back*?" she asked, stepping out onto the porch where it was significantly cooler. It was the middle of January, and they were finally seeing some seasonal temperatures. She tugged at the collar of her sweater, urging the frigid air to get to her skin faster.

"As in, back for good."

Stevie didn't know what to say to that. No, she hadn't known. Now that she did, she wasn't sure why a swarm of intoxicated butterflies was taking up residence in her belly.

"Stevie?"

"Hmm?"

His tone was rife with concern. "You gonna be okay with this?"

"Of course I am," she lied, forcing a smile and tacking on a giggle for good measure.

She had to be, right?

Plus, it wasn't like she was going to see Stone. Sure, Coyote Ridge was a small town, but she didn't venture out much. When she did, she opted for the neighboring towns. And work kept her out and about more often than not. She would simply insist on taking all the clients who didn't live in Coyote Ridge. And for the times she couldn't avoid going into town, she would figure out what Stone drove and scour the parking lots before she stopped. If he were there, she would make herself scarce. It could be done.

"Stevie?"

The sky was overcast, but the day was unusually bright. She stared into the distance, not seeing anything thanks to the mental images still flashing in her head.

"I'm here." She sighed. "How's he look? Let me guess. He got fat."

"Not fat."

"Tell me he's bald." *Please, God, let him be bald.*

"Nope."

Damn it.

"But he looks old and scraggly, right? Rode hard, put away wet?"

"Sorry. No."

"Does he look … good?"

"Yeah," Nico said, and Stevie could tell it pained him to admit that.

She expected no less. The universe was clearly out to get her.

Then again, this could be a good thing. She hadn't seen Stone in nearly fifteen years. Not since he hightailed it outta town with a promise to call her the next time he dropped in. That call never came, and she knew he'd been back because, as she said, Coyote Ridge was a small town. Hell, the grapevine lit up when Old Man Thompson's tabby cat got Mrs. Devenmore's sweet little Persian pregnant. Of course it went haywire when people came back, even if it were for a quick visit, which Stone had done for many holidays over the years.

"I'm fine," she assured Nico before he could ask her again. "What about you? Did you talk to him?"

"Yeah. For a minute."

"And?"

"And nothin'."

Stevie knew better than to dig deeper. They'd made a pact not to talk about Stone, and they'd done pretty well over the years. A couple of times, they'd indulged, but those nights generally involved significant amounts of alcohol followed by deep regrets to go along with hellish hangovers the next morning. They tried to keep those to a minimum.

"Well, I'm gonna lock up here in a few minutes," Stevie told Nico. "You're headin' home, right?"

"Unless you need me to come in."

"Nope. Nothin' doin' here. Mike and Carlos are finishin' up their jobs."

"Okay. You want me to cook dinner? We can talk."

They both knew she wouldn't say yes because Stevie didn't like to overstep, and she couldn't even count how many times she'd called Nico up over the years, getting him to go out to grab a beer or dinner simply so she didn't sit at home and do something ridiculously stupid. Problem was, she usually did whatever stupid thing she was avoiding anyway.

But tonight, she had a different reason. "It's Friday. I'm havin' dinner with my dad."

"All right. See you when you get home."

"Yep," she said before disconnecting the call.

Taking a deep breath, Stevie went back inside.

SEVEN

AFTER HANGING UP WITH STEVIE, NICO HEADED home.

It was still early, and he was hoping to settle in his office for a couple of hours and take care of a few things he'd been putting off. He had several quotes to finalize and a few designs he was eager to start. It was difficult to get those things done in the office due to the constant coming and going and/or questions that arose throughout the day. He could find peace and quiet at home.

As soon as he pulled into his driveway, he knew his plan for a productive evening was about as hopeful as a bonfire in a hurricane. And it had nothing to do with the fact Stone Jameson was back in town or that he knew Stevie wasn't as okay with it as she pretended. Nope. His productive day was about to get quashed by five feet, eight inches of smiling sister.

It wasn't necessarily a bad thing. It was his fault. He'd completely forgotten that Niyah was coming over today.

That was a lie.

He hadn't forgotten.

The truth was, he'd been putting off thinking about it because he didn't want to.

He parked the truck and got out, wondering if it would've been worth his while to stick around and let Stone pretend he didn't remember that night all those years ago instead of coming home to find his sister waiting because she wanted to say goodbye. Nico would've much rather put up with Stone's blank stare than have to say goodbye to the only family he had left. He was going to miss her.

"I knew you forgot," Niyah said with a wide smile.

Nico's attention shifted to the wiggly puppy in her arms.

"Is that a—"

"Yellow Lab? Yep." She held him up like he was a sacrifice to the sun gods. "Ain't he cute?"

"Adorable," he said, giving the puppy's head a scratch.

"I was hopin' you'd say that. He's yours."

Always joking that one.

At least he prayed she was joking.

"Whatever," he shook his head and frowned at the little dog. "You know I don't have the time or patience for a puppy."

"Seriously? There's no way anyone can be that hard-hearted," she teased, shifting the puppy so he was cradled like a baby in her arms. "He's not a mean man. Just grumpy."

"You and Stevie have fun last night?" he asked as he spared the dog another glance.

"We did. That girl can hold her liquor better'n people twice her size."

Nico laughed. That she could.

"Speakin' of…" Niyah glanced back at the driveway. "I thought she'd be here."

He shook his head. "She's at the office."

"You mean she's avoidin' me because she knows we'll both cry again if we have to say goodbye twice?"

Nico figured that *was* what prompted Stevie to get up early and head to the office, although it was her day off. Their house was set up so they could work from here as easily and as comfortably as they could there. That was due to Stevie's persistence. From the day she became his roommate—shortly after Niyah got engaged to Adam— she'd been slowly but surely transforming his space into something that resembled a home rather than a structure that contained his furniture.

Although he hadn't been thrilled with the idea back when he'd made the initial offer—the result of a night of too much booze—turned out Nico enjoyed having a roommate. Especially one as low-key as Stevie. She was the polar opposite of Melanie, his ex-fiancée. Stevie was about as laid-back as they came, while Melanie had been high-strung and needy. Not that Stevie was perfect. She was a complete and utter slob. Since Nico had gotten used to Melanie's obsessive-compulsive housekeeping, it was taking some time to get used to.

Despite the mess Stevie left in her wake, Nico wouldn't change anything if he had to do it all over again. Stevie was his sister's best friend, but he'd forged a pretty good friendship with her over the years, too. Granted, it took several years for Stevie to get over her complete hatred for him—she'd blamed him for the events that transpired after *that night*. When she finally cooled enough for them to discuss what happened, she decided neither of them was at fault but made him promise they would never discuss it again.

For the most part, he obliged. As long as they didn't overindulge, they were capable of keeping *that night* in the past where it belonged. It was those other times that—

"I'm gonna miss her," Niyah said, interrupting his thoughts. "But she promised to come visit. The two of you can come together."

Shaking off thoughts of Stevie, Nico unlocked the front door and changed the subject. "Where's Adam?"

"He went to put gas in the Range Rover."

Frowning, Nico turned with his key still in the door lock. "You're really doin' it? You're really lettin' some random guy drag you across the country?"

Niyah barked a laugh. "I've been with that *random guy* for a year and a half."

"Irrelevant," he teased.

Her smile reflected more melancholy than excitement, but she was suppressing it for his benefit. Thanks to Stevie, Nico knew that Niyah was thrilled with the idea of a new life in California. And to be fair, he was happy for her. Adam was a good guy, and he genuinely loved Niyah. He would take care of her.

Nico sighed, pushing the door open and walking inside. Acknowledging that didn't make this any easier. He already missed Niyah and she hadn't left yet.

Doing his best to mask his expression, he forced a smile. "What's with Scrappy-Do there?" He nodded toward the puppy. "You thought you'd pick up a puppy on the way outta town?"

"Yep. Only this sweet little baby's not goin' with us."

Nico dropped his keys and his cell phone on the table. "Where's he goin'?"

Niyah mumbled nonsensical baby talk to the puppy before setting him on the floor. When she stood, she wildly gestured at the four-legged creature as though he'd specifically asked for one.

"He's yours."

For fuck's sake. She was serious.

His eyebrows shot up to his hairline. "What am I supposed to do with a dog, Niyah?"

"Love him and give him lots of smooches."

"Might I remind you, I'm not a smoochin' kinda guy."

"But you could be."

"No," he said adamantly, shaking his head for emphasis. "I do not need a dog, Sis. I don't have time for one."

"But he's so cute."

"Then you keep him."

"I can't."

He headed for the kitchen. "Why not?"

"Because I'm movin' to California."

"They don't let you have dogs in California?" he asked as he pulled the loaf of bread from the cabinet. "That's just another reason you should stay here."

Clearly, she was onto him because Niyah cocked her head and lifted one perfectly arched eyebrow. The expression was one she'd given him many times in his life. And though she was a year younger, she acted like she was the big sister.

To avoid that look, Nico glanced down at the puppy, watching as he sniffed around the chairs at the small table in the breakfast nook. He really was cute. Almost too cute. Like one of those stuffed animals his sister used to keep on her bed when they were kids.

Niyah cleared her throat. "You're in love with him already."

Nico rolled his eyes. "No. And I won't be because I'm sure it's only a matter of time before—" He pointed toward the dog, drawing his sister's attention.

"No, no!" Niyah squealed, scurrying toward the puppy. "Not in the house."

Nico laughed.

"I'm so sorry," she said as she picked him up in that sun-god-sacrifice hold again and carried him toward the back door. "I'll clean it up. Just a minute."

"I've got it," he assured her, grabbing some paper towels to clean up the little puddle on the floor.

He took care of the pee, tossing the paper towels in the trash, then grabbed a bottle of all-purpose cleaner to wipe it again. He was still bent over when the puppy came bounding into the house, ears flopping, tongue hanging out. If Nico didn't know better, he would've sworn that was a smile.

Before he could stand upright, the puppy practically launched himself at him, wiggling to get his attention.

Nico knew that as soon as he petted him, he would be doomed. He refrained as long as he could, refusing to give in.

Don't do it. Don't you dare do it.

"Come on," Niyah said. "You can do it."

He laughed, setting the cleaner and the towel on the table so he could give the dog some attention.

Sure enough, all it took was one puppy lick to the face, and he was in love. It was inevitable, he figured, and his sister knew that. Nico had wanted a dog when they were kids, but their mother was too busy raising them as a single mom with two jobs to handle anything more. And while he had assured her he would be responsible for the dog, she was smarter than him. She knew he was all talk.

Once he was old enough to get one of his own, life had conveniently gotten in the way. First college, followed by a job that he loved. Life moved seamlessly by for about three years, then one day, Stevie came to him with a business proposal. She wanted to do something with the inheritance she'd received from her grandfather, and for whatever reason, she thought opening a landscaping business was the best thing to do with it.

After weeks of trying to talk her out of it, Nico realized she couldn't be swayed. She'd punctuated the argument with an emphatic, "I'm gonna do it with or without you. You pick."

She was a master manipulator, among other things.

Luckily, Stevie only used her powers for good. Or so she claimed. Together, they'd created a company they could be proud of, building it from the ground up and keeping it afloat for the past eight years. A company that took up so much of his time he had too little to dedicate to anyone or anything else.

A horn honked out front.

"That's Adam," she said with a sad smile. "We have to get on the road."

Nico rubbed the dog's head again before getting to his feet. "I hate that y'all are movin' so far away."

"Well, the good news is, there's always FaceTime. And it's not like we won't come back to visit. Or you, Stevie, and that little guy"— she pointed at the puppy—"can come visit whenever you want."

He knew that, but it wasn't the same. He'd been close to his sister all his life, but they'd formed a deeper bond after their mother passed away five years ago. He was going to have a vast void without Niyah around for him to talk to and harass whenever he saw fit. Nico couldn't even imagine what Stevie was going through—Niyah and Stevie were thick as thieves—but as always, the woman radiated happiness at her best friend's good fortune. That was what Stevie did.

Nico held out his arms as his sister walked toward him. She was crying, something she swore she wouldn't do when she came to say goodbye.

"I want pictures," she told him when she pulled away, wiping her eyes. "Lots and lots of pictures."

Nico rolled his eyes. "Maybe."

She started toward the door, so he followed.

"Oh, I meant to tell you. I heard Stone Jameson's back in town."

Nico failed to school his expression in time. His sister knew him better than anyone, so there was no doubt she'd seen a spark of interest flash before he could hide it.

"You already knew that, huh?"

"Yeah."

"Maybe this is your chance to finally talk to him."

Niyah was the only person who knew about the events that happened all those years ago. Nico had never told a soul, but Stevie had broken down and shared the deets with her best friend. Evidently, that was part of the BFF code. Rules his sister and Stevie lived by. And much to his dismay, they disclosed everything. As in every dirty detail, including the ones he wished Niyah didn't know about. Specifically those that involved him and Stevie these past few months.

He shook his head. "I'm takin' the puppy. That's far more than I can handle."

Niyah laughed. "Just do me one favor?"

"If it's anything other than potty trainin' that little guy…"

"Keep an eye on Stevie. Make sure she's okay."

"You know I will," he promised and meant it.

"Maybe this is the opportunity y'all've been waitin' for. The three of you."

He didn't bother telling her there was no opportunity to be had. By leaving town, Stone Jameson had been relegated to the darkest recesses of Nico's mind. He'd put that night behind him and moved on. And because the guy had shattered Stevie's heart, Nico had no desire to ever forgive him.

"At the very least, you need to encourage Stevie to talk to him."

He would do no such thing. How Stevie chose to handle Stone was up to her, but he wanted no part of it.

"I love you," Niyah said, giving him another quick hug.

"I love you, too. Call me when y'all get there so I know you made it."

She nodded. "We're takin' the scenic route, so it'll be a few days."

Nico followed her onto the porch and waved at Adam.

He stood there staring after them as they backed out of the drive. Behind him, there was a whimper and a thump. When he turned around, he saw the puppy inside the house, trying desperately to open the screen door with his nose.

Laughing, Nico opened the door and picked him up. It earned him puppy kisses.

"You're gonna need a name."

That got him a lick on the nose.

"And some food. We're gonna have to go into town for that."

So much for getting any work done.

STEVIE WAS LOCKING THE OFFICE DOOR WHEN she heard tires crunching gravel as a car approached.

Since they weren't anticipating any clients coming in today, she didn't immediately go into professional mode. Because they opened the office for business on Saturdays to accommodate folks who worked the Monday through Friday, nine-to-five gig, they generally didn't come in on Fridays. Today was an exception because Stevie was avoiding having to say goodbye to her best friend again. Last night had been difficult enough. She knew there was a good chance she would hogtie Niyah and insist she not go to California if she was forced to watch her walk away. That or fold herself into Niyah's luggage and go with them.

She sighed. She already missed her.

Stevie pulled her hood over her head, holding the strings at her neck to keep it from blowing off, and turned toward the parking area. Before she reached the end of the deck, she heard footsteps. She lifted her head to look, figuring Mike or Carlos were coming inside to grab a coffee to warm up. But it wasn't Mike or Carlos now standing four steps down, staring up at her with a cocky grin.

"Hey, beautiful. I was hopin' I'd find you here."

Hadn't she had enough surprises for one day?

"What do you want, Oscar?"

"You wanna grab dinner?"

"No."

"Dessert?"

"No."

Because she knew this wasn't going to be a brief conversation, she tied the strings to keep her hood in place, then tucked her hands in her pocket.

Oscar suggestively raised and lowered his eyebrows. "How about breakfast tomorrow mornin'?"

She ensured he saw the lack of amusement on her face. "No."

"Come on, baby. When—"

Stevie jerked her hand out of her pocket and stabbed a finger in his direction. "Do *not* call me that."

"Sorry."

No, he wasn't. Oscar knew it pissed her off. Only one man had ever gotten away with calling her that, and she would forever hate the word. As far as she was concerned, Stone Jameson could shove that endearment where the sun don't shine.

"When are you gonna forgive me?"

Oh, man. This again?

"There's nothin' to forgive, Oscar. I told you. It's not you, it's me."

That was mostly true. Stevie had dated Oscar on and off for three years. They officially broke up a year ago, shortly after Stevie moved in with Nico. Her decision to end things with Oscar had nothing to do with Nico and everything to do with Oscar's inability to grow up. For six months now, they'd been doing the same dance they were doing now. Oscar would seek her out, he would ask her out, she would say no, and she wouldn't hear from him for another few weeks. Probably when he was bored and needed someone to hang out with.

What made it difficult was that she liked Oscar. As a friend, he was cool. But he was a bad influence on her, and though Stevie held no one but herself accountable for her actions, she knew she was better off without him. Since she didn't see a future with him, not even back when they'd first started dating and she'd actually liked having sex with him, their relationship had played out exactly as she'd anticipated: quick and painless.

Unfortunately, Oscar did not seem as content with the end as she was.

"Well, if you don't wanna go on a date, maybe I could swing by your place tonight. I'll crash in the guest room if you want."

"No." Stevie frowned. There was only one reason Oscar would ask to sleep in the guest room. "Wait. What happened to your place?"

His gaze cut away from her face. "Greg and I got in a fight."

"Because you didn't pay rent?"

"It's his *mom's* house," Oscar said defensively. "He's got no right chargin' me rent to stay there. *He* doesn't pay rent. Why should I?"

And there you have it, folks. Oscar was homeless. Again. And when he was homeless, he tended to lean on her. Back when she lived with Niyah, she hadn't minded him staying over for a few nights while he looked for another place to crash. But things were different now that she lived with Nico. She wasn't about to subject either man to that awkwardness. And, like it or not, it would be awkward.

"Oscar, you're thirty-two years old. Don't you think it's time you grew up and got your own place?"

"You wanna help me out with a job?" he countered hotly.

"No." She'd tried that already. Shortly after they first started dating, back before she knew he had a long history of getting fired for not showing up to work, Stevie had given him a job. He'd worked on Carlos's crew for three days before he just didn't show up. When she called to find out what happened, he told her he'd gotten a different job. She'd started noticing the pattern after that. Hence the reason Stevie had stopped thinking of him as relationship material and satisfied herself with the fact he was decent in bed.

Then, a little over a year ago, she'd learned he was living with a woman he met at a bar. She decided that was the perfect punctuation mark, using it to signify the end of a good run. Sadly, that woman had come to her senses, too, kicking Oscar out and inadvertently sending him running back in Stevie's direction.

"Come on, Stevie. Give me another chance."

"A chance? For what? A job? A place to live? Or a night in my bed?"

His smile was flirtatious. "Why not all three?"

"What's in it for me?"

"An orgasm?"

She huffed a laugh and started down the steps. Her patience had run out. "No thanks. I'm quite capable of givin' myself orgasms."

Oscar stepped back, letting her pass. He knew better than to stand in her way. The last time he'd tried that, she'd punched him in the nose.

"Fine. But don't come crawlin' to me when you get tired of hand deliverin' those orgasms."

"I won't," she promised, not bothering to tell him that she'd gotten quite a few that had been delivered by her sexy roommate. Not recently, but still.

"Come on, Stevie. I was kiddin'. Please, baby."

She spun around. "Do *not* call me that!"

His eyes widened, and he held his hands up, palms forward. "Okay, okay. *Gawd.* Why does that word piss you off so bad?"

She ignored the question. "I gotta go, Oscar. Have a good life."

Before he could say anything more, Stevie hopped in her Ford Bronco, grateful she'd already started the engine. She sank into the heated seat and clicked the button to lock the door.

She waited until Oscar got in his car and left. As she shifted into *reverse*, she found herself smiling.

Nico would be proud of her for standing up to Oscar. Especially since she'd been on a dry spell for the past six weeks. Stevie would be the first to admit she enjoyed having a healthy sex life. And despite his flaws, Oscar had been decent in bed. Good enough to hold her attention for years. Granted, she also preferred monogamy, which limited her options. She didn't hop from bed to bed by choice, which was the only reason she'd dangled the hook in front of Oscar for so long.

Perhaps she should consider giving him another chance. At the very least, it would relieve some of the pressure and reduce the risk of her making another bad decision. One that could potentially cost her everything she'd built for herself.

EIGHT

BY 5:30 P.M., STONE WAS READY to pass out.

Unfortunately, before he could do that, he needed to run into town and pick up his truck and trailer. Reilly had driven it with the promise to bring it back. Only she called to tell him she had to take care of something at the store and she wouldn't be able to come back until after eight.

Stone intended to be horizontal and well into his first REM cycle by eight.

So he offered to make the swap.

As he drove through town, he took it all in, letting the memories swarm him. He'd been back many times since he left fifteen years ago, but most of those visits involved him dropping in at his parents' house and slipping out just as quickly. He wasn't even sure he'd stopped by the General Store at all. Maybe once since Reilly took over, but if so, he couldn't remember.

While the town looked different, it still had the same feel. Small-town living in the middle of areas that were booming. Coyote Ridge had defied the odds, maintaining its country charm while cookie-cutter subdivisions, fast food joints, and emergency clinics grew at a rapid pace all around them. Coyote Ridge wasn't quite as rustic as the areas Stone had resided in over the years. Not anymore, anyway. Although large parcels of land were still used for farming and ranching, it was slowly being divided up, making it impossible to build something like the Double J. There simply wasn't enough room.

Despite that, it was good to be back. And though he wasn't sure what his plans were going forward, he knew whatever he decided to do, it would be here. In his hometown. He hadn't run out of here because he wanted to get away. He loved Coyote Ridge, but it couldn't offer him what he'd been looking for at the time. Stone wasn't sure it could now, but as had been the case when he left, he was once again running. Only this time, he hoped to run toward something rather than away.

Once he reached downtown, he pulled around to the small lot behind the shopping center and parked Reilly's truck beside his. She'd blocked half the lot with the trailer, but he squeezed into one of the open spots.

The sun was getting lower in the sky, the days still short. Winter and all. According to the weather report, they were about to feel the full brunt of it in the coming weeks. A chance for ice and possible snow was in the five-day forecast. Stone wasn't looking forward to it.

When he came around the side of the building, the cold wind that had picked up since that morning blasted him. He tucked his head down and headed for the door. The bells overhead jingled when he walked in.

He shook off the chill as the door closed, his eyes on the scene before him.

"I don't think these things are workin'," Stone said, jingling the bells with his hand to get Brady and Reilly to stop making out like teenagers behind the register counter.

"We knew it was you," Brady said, not bothering to look over.

Stone shook his head as he watched the pair. No, he never would've predicted those two would end up together, but based on the look on Brady's face, it wasn't surprising that they were. Now that he thought about it, Stone recognized that look. He merely hadn't ever connected the dots. Brady was head over heels for Reilly and wasn't bothering to hide it.

Good for him.

"Here's your keys," Stone said, placing Reilly's set on the counter.

She planted one more loud, smacking kiss on Brady's mouth, giggled, then shifted so she could hop down from the counter. Her cheeks were flushed, her eyes bright. Love looked good on her.

"I like what you've done with the place," he told her as she reached under the counter.

Stone hadn't been sure what to expect since Reilly had boasted proudly that she was updating the store to be more like its original design. That had been about the time Donovan and Brady started renovating the barn for Reilly and Tate. Since there'd been a significant amount of rotted wood, they'd all but taken the thing down in order to build it back up. Reilly had insisted she could put that old wood to good use. Looked as though she'd used it to practically wallpaper the interior of the store, and though it looked rustic and worn, there was still a clean, airy feel to it all.

Reilly placed his keys down. "You're welcome to work here anytime."

Stone laughed. "Why in the world would I do that?"

Reilly shrugged. "Boredom?"

"Who said I'm bored?"

"You wouldn't be here if you weren't."

Maybe she was right. "Well, if it's any consolation, I'm headin' home to pass out. I don't plan to get up for at least ten hours, so don't stop by."

She smiled. "I make no promises."

He cocked an eyebrow.

"Kidding." She took her keys from the counter and tucked them underneath. "All you gotta do is clear the biometrics on the lock. The instruction manual's in the kitchen somewhere."

"Good to know."

"We left a few things up in the loft, but we can get 'em next week sometime."

"I can always drop 'em off this—"

The sound of the bells clanging cut him off as all eyes, including his, shifted to the person walking in.

"Oh, my God!" Reilly squealed, dancing out from behind the counter. "Is that a yellow Lab?"

Stone stared at Nico, watching as he braced himself for Reilly's approach.

She didn't give Nico a chance to answer when she said, "Boy or girl?"

"Boy," he answered, his gaze shifting to Stone briefly.

"He's so cute!"

"Thank God for that," Nico grumbled, holding the dog toward her. "He peed in my truck."

Reilly laughed, taking him into her arms as gently as she would a newborn baby. "I've got some paper towels behind the counter if you need 'em."

"That'd be great. Thanks."

Stone heard movement behind him, then grunted when Brady smacked him with the roll of paper towels. He turned to find Brady thrusting them in his direction.

"I don't work here," Stone said deadpan.

"You don't work, period, from what I hear," he whispered, grinning.

"Touché." Stone took the roll of paper towels. "Catch," he told Nico before launching them in his direction.

"I have the cutest little collar for you," Reilly said, talking in that silly way people do with dogs.

Nico's gaze slid over Stone once more before he turned and walked out.

"I thought it was cold *outside*," Brady said. "But an arctic wind just blew through here. What's up with that?"

"What're you talkin' about?"

"He still holdin' a grudge?"

Stone tried not to react to that question. "For what?"

"For you punchin' him when he dumped Chelsea."

"You talked to Reilly."

"She couldn't get it out fast enough."

97

Yeah, his little sister certainly made a vast contribution to the town's rumor mill.

From the back of the store, Stone heard Reilly giggling.

"Might have to get her one of those," Stone told Brady.

"I'll get her a dozen if it'll make her happy," he mumbled, staring toward the back as though he could see her.

"You're whipped."

"Completely," Brady agreed.

Stone laughed. "Have y'all picked a date for the weddin' yet?"

"Sometime in June. That's all she told me."

Stone had gotten a call from Reilly on New Year's Day. She'd apparently been running through her contacts, telling everyone that Brady had asked her to marry him. He'd asked her then if they had a date. She'd said sometime in the summer. Good to know Brady was able to get her to narrow it down a little.

The bells chimed again, and a chilly breeze accompanied Nico into the store.

Stone did his best not to stare, but it wasn't easy. Seeing the man brought back memories of that night, and while he'd been attracted to Nico then, it was nothing compared to his body's reaction to him now.

He was still staring when Reilly came racing to the front, chasing the puppy despite him wearing a collar and leash, neither of which he'd had on when he came into the store.

"I found a few things," Reilly said cheerfully, passing over one of the small baskets that some customers carried through the store. "Collar, leash, some dog food. I don't have a huge selection."

"That's okay," Nico said, but his words were drowned out when Reilly kept going.

"There's a toy in there and some bells. I hear if you hang 'em on the back door, you can teach him to alert you when he needs to go out."

Nico nodded, his gaze sliding to Stone once more.

"You'll have to get him some bowls. Oh, and the collar and leash won't last him long," Reilly continued. "Based on his paws, he's gonna be big. But it'll work for now."

"That's per—"

"Oh, wait!" Reilly shouted as she spun around and raced through the aisles.

"Maybe you wanna get a line of credit," Stone suggested.

Nico laughed, and the sound was so sexy he had to shift because his jeans were becoming more uncomfortable by the second.

"Where'd you get the dog, anyway?" Brady asked.

"My sister."

"Niyah's still here?" Stone asked before he could think better of it.

"She left for California today." His eyes narrowed. "With her husband."

Stone figured it was safe to say Nico was aware that his sister'd had a crush on him back in the day. Nothing ever happened because she'd been too young when that revelation came to light, but Stone wouldn't deny he'd entertained the notion for a bit. But that was before he'd gotten his hands on Stevie. After that, no other female in Coyote Ridge had appealed.

And though he tried to tell himself otherwise, Stevie was a big part of why he'd left. What he'd felt for her had defied logic. It had been a whirlwind from the start, and it only picked up speed the longer they were together. If he had stayed, there was no doubt he would've disrupted her life, and the last thing he'd wanted was for her to look back and hate him for it.

Reilly came racing to the front again, holding out a bag of—

"Here's the gummy watermelon things Stevie likes," Reilly said, dropping the package into the basket. "What else?"

Nico said something back, but Stone couldn't process words because his thoughts were on Stevie now that his sister said her name.

"What does Stevie think of the puppy?" Reilly asked.

"She hasn't been home yet to see him."

"Home?" Stone asked. As in, they *lived* together?

He could feel all eyes on him.

"They live together," Brady said from behind him.

Stone frowned. Were they *together*? Thankfully, the question didn't fall out of his mouth.

"What do I owe you?" Nico asked Reilly.

"I'll tally it up and let you know."

"Here's a bag," Brady said, bringing one from behind the counter.

Stone stared, unable to speak. His thoughts were muddied by images of that night so long ago.

Stevie and Nico? Seriously?

"ALL RIGHT, LITTLE GUY. WE'RE GONNA HAVE to call it good. At least for tonight," Nico told the puppy, who was curling into a blanket he'd laid out on the front seat. "We'll figure out the rest tomorrow."

Nico put on his seat belt and started the truck, adjusting the vents so the heat would blow on the dog. Did dogs even get cold if they weren't out in the elements? He didn't know but decided he wouldn't take a chance. He would take his cues from the puppy.

For a brief moment, as the heat blew directly on him, the little dog lifted his head toward the air and closed his eyes. Again, Nico was pretty sure there was a smile on his face.

How was it that Niyah always seemed to know exactly what he needed? He was pretty sure this was the first time he'd slowed down in months. Slowed down long enough to appreciate something other than the hard work they all put into the business, anyway.

"Ready to go home?" Just as he turned to put the truck in reverse, Stone appeared, rapping his knuckles on the window.

The puppy's head popped up.

"It's cool," Nico assured him with a scratch on the head as he pressed the button to lower the window.

Stone held up a brown paper bag. "Reilly said to give you this, too."

Nico laughed. "Your sister's somethin' else, you know that?"

"Truly one of a kind."

Nico took the bag and reached back to put it in the back seat.

"You're not gonna look to see what's in it?"

"I like surprises," Nico told him.

When he turned back, he found Stone staring at him.

"What?"

"How is she?"

There was a wealth of emotion in Stone's voice. Enough that Nico couldn't bring himself to tell the man to fuck off because he didn't have the right to ask that question.

"She's good."

Stone nodded, his eyes seeming to search for something.

"What?"

Stone shook his head. "Nothin'." He backed up a step. "See you around."

Nico let him get a few feet away before he called after him. "You back for good?"

Stone turned around but continued to walk backward. "That's the plan for now. Who knows what tomorrow brings."

Nico nodded. "Maybe we could grab coffee or somethin' sometime."

"Maybe."

Nico cocked an eyebrow. "That didn't sound like an answer."

Stone smirked, and damn if it wasn't sexy. "That didn't sound like a question."

Before Nico could decide whether he wanted to ask him officially, Stone climbed into his big F350.

"I'm an idiot," he told the dog, closing the window.

The dog yipped, then burrowed into the blanket once again.

Half an hour later, after they got home and Nico convinced the dog to go to the bathroom—which evidently was inconvenient when there were so many things to sniff—he went to work putting up the supplies. He also went through the house and closed all the doors, ensuring the dog didn't wander away and get into something he shouldn't. When he returned, the little ball of fluff was lying on the floor, gnawing on the laces of one of Nico's work boots.

"No," he said firmly, reaching down and taking the boot.

He grabbed the other for good measure and set both on the bar stool before retrieving the toy Reilly had found for him.

"This is yours."

The dog pawed at it a few times, then rested his head on it, staring up at Nico with big, sad eyes.

"We'll get you somethin' to chew on tomorrow. Somethin' that doesn't belong on my feet."

His nose twitched.

"What? You want dinner?"

His eyes widened.

Nico took that as a yes and went to work digging slop out of a can and dumping it into a cereal bowl.

"Surely they make somethin' better than this." He set the bowl on the floor beside the counter and stood back, waiting to see if the dog was interested.

He was.

Very.

He scarfed down the entire bowl in a handful of bites.

Nico chuckled, filled another bowl with water, and placed it on the floor. The dog then went to work cleaning it out, too.

"I take that to mean you'll have to go out again in a little while?"

Something told Nico this was going to be a really long night.

Speaking of night...

He thought for sure Stevie would've been home by now. It was Friday, so she spent the evening at her dad's house. A tradition they'd been carrying on since Stevie's mother divorced her dad and moved to Buffalo to marry some guy she met on the internet. Stevie claimed she hung out with Stan so he didn't get lonely, but Nico knew she worried about him. Not that he saw the appeal of hanging out with a man who had no desire to converse with anyone. Nico had gone with her once but declined the offer the next time to avoid the awkward silence. Stevie and her dad had always been close, but Stan hadn't been the same since his wife left him.

Nico grabbed his phone and looked to see if he'd missed any texts from her. There were none.

He went to the window over the sink to look outside, checking to see if maybe he'd missed her Bronco parked in the driveway. It wasn't there.

Had she run into Stone? Were they in town right now talking about old times? Reminiscing?

Nico's chest clenched, and it felt a hell of a lot like jealousy that coursed through him. Why would he be jealous? It wasn't like he had a claim on Stevie. She was his roommate, nothing more. Sure, they'd … well, they'd scratched an itch a time or two, but never when they were sober. And after each encounter, they both agreed it would never happen again. For the most part, they managed to abide by that agreement. Until the next time.

He took a deep breath and turned around, leaning against the counter, watching the puppy gnawing on his toy.

"Where're you gonna sleep?"

The dog turned those big brown eyes on him, and Nico knew this little guy was gonna be trouble with a capital T.

"Maybe that's what we should call you. Trouble."

The dog tilted his head as though waiting for him to repeat it.

"Trouble? You like that name?"

His head tilted the other way.

"Maybe not. I'm sure I'll come up with somethin'."

Nico laughed, pushing off the counter and heading to the refrigerator to find something to eat. The sandwich he had earlier had long since burned off, and he was starving.

He opened the fridge and glanced at the contents, then looked in the pantry, tallying up what he would need. When he noted he had all the ingredients for chicken fajitas, he went to work preparing the chicken.

As he worked, his mind drifted to that night so long ago.

"What was Chelsea tellin' everybody?" Stone demanded, glaring daggers at Nico.

"She gave me an ultimatum. If I don't go to Texas Tech, she's not interested in me anymore."

"What about Jenny?" Stone asked. "You fuck her?"

"Hell no. She's Chelsea's best friend. I'm not a complete asshole."

"So what happened?"

"I flirted with her. Figured it would get back to Chelsea, and she'd have a reason to dump me without feelin' bad about it."

Stone continued to stare. "You want *her to break up with you."*

"It's what's best for her." Some of his frustration drained out. "Above all else, we're friends. It's easier for her to hate me now than to lose that."

"You two done? For good?"

Nico nodded. "It's been over for a while. This just makes it official."

"Good."

"Why?"

Stone smirked. "Because I said so."

"Where's Stevie?" Nico asked, more so to remind Stone that whatever was happening here shouldn't be happening.

"Where do you want her to be?" Stone taunted.

He felt a rush of unexpected heat as he stood there, pinned between Stone and his truck. He wasn't sure what the hell was happening or why he wasn't fighting Stone off. He couldn't move because he was mesmerized by the gleam in Stone's eyes.

For as long as he'd known Stone Jameson, Nico'd had a crush on the guy. Not the gay kind because … well, because he didn't swing that way. At least he didn't think he did. There'd been a few moments of confusion these past couple of years, but nothing Nico couldn't shove down deep and ignore.

But he wouldn't deny he was completely enthralled with Stone. Nico wanted to be him. The guy everyone wanted to be friends with. The guy the chicks wanted to be with, even though until recently, Stone had never let anyone stake a claim on him. Nico remembered his first day of ninth grade. Stone had been a junior that year, and there was no disputing he was the big man on campus. Even the seniors gravitated toward him. That entire year, Nico had attempted to emulate the guy. It hadn't worked, but it had gotten him on Chelsea's radar.

Not much had changed. Stone was still wild, untamable and Nico still admired that in him. He even admired the fact that Stone had succumbed to Stevie Shepherd's charms, turning over a new leaf. Not that Nico was thrilled with the idea of his sister's best friend hooking up with Stone Jameson. Those two were like oil and water, incompatible in every way. Yet, somehow, they'd managed to ride it out for nine or ten months already.

A soft groan rumbled in Stone's chest. The next thing Nico knew, Stone kicked his feet apart, moving closer. Closer still. The firm grip on his throat remained a steady pressure, reminding him that he wasn't in control here.

Not that Nico was a lightweight. He wasn't. His brain, however, didn't seem to be aware of that as he surrendered to the dominance.

Stone leaned in, eliminating the gap between their bodies. Nico was shocked by the heat of the man against him. The rock-hard plane of his chest, the steel in his thighs.

Instinct had him looking over his shoulder, attempting to make sure Chelsea wasn't watching them.

"She can't see us."

He hoped not. The last thing he needed was Chelsea thinking he'd done something to provoke this.

"Push me away, Nico," Stone insisted, taunting him again.

His brain flickered with the instruction, and his hands moved to Stone's hips, gripping as though he might do just that. Only he didn't push.

Stone's voice lowered. "That's all you hafta do. Push. Me. Away."

His warm breath fanned Nico's lips, and again, he was locked in a trance, completely at this man's mercy.

Stone tilted his head, leaning closer until their lips were so close Nico could feel the whisper-softness when Stone spoke.

"Say no, Nico."

He couldn't. Words wouldn't form.

"Tell me to stop."

Did he even want to? He wasn't sure what was happening here, but Nico didn't want to shove Stone away. He didn't want to tell him no. He wanted ... fuck. Possibly, for the first time in his life, he wanted.

The arousal was so potent it robbed him of breath and sense at the same time. There was no way Stone couldn't feel the steely length of his erection because they were pressed together from chest to groin.

"I didn't realize you played for both teams," Stone taunted.

"I don't."

"No?"

Nico hissed when Stone reached down with his free hand, grinding his palm along the outline of Nico's dick.

Yeah, you fuckhead, I'm hard. So fuckin' what?

"You like this. You like it rough."

Damn him. He wasn't asking for confirmation. He was telling him, and since Nico couldn't very well deny it, he gave a very slight nod.

"You want me to do dirty fuckin' things to you, don't you?"

Because he refused to be completely mowed down by this guy, Nico pressed his hips forward, grinding against Stone's hand as his official answer.

The sound of Stevie's excited squeal broke through the memory, drawing Nico to the present. He stepped back from the stove, remembering what he'd been doing before that memory had consumed him.

"You got a puppy! He's adorable. When did you get him?"

Nico didn't answer her, too focused on the smoke filling the kitchen.

"Shit," he hissed when he realized he was burning the chicken.

Just like *that night*, it looked like Stone could still drive him to distraction.

NINE

STEVIE WAS IN LOVE.

Completely.

Irrevocably.

She'd never seen anything as adorable as this puppy in her entire life.

"What's his name?" she asked Nico, aware of him banging around in the kitchen.

"Didn't give him one," he grumbled.

Stevie lay on the floor, knees toward the ceiling, letting the dog sniff her neck and face. She inhaled his sweet puppy breath, unable to stop smiling.

"Well, you gotta have a name," she whispered, then raised her voice to talk to Nico. "What were you makin'?"

"Fajitas."

Her stomach rumbled. She shouldn't have been hungry because she'd gone to her dad's for dinner. Unfortunately, Stan Shepherd hadn't made his famous fried spaghetti like he promised. He lost track of time, or so he said. When she got there, she found him on the computer in his office talking to some woman he'd met online. At that point, thoughts of food had evaded her, replaced by the overwhelming need to warn her father that he couldn't trust everyone he met on the internet.

"I'm not an idiot, Stevie," he'd told her.

He wasn't. She knew that. However, she also knew he'd finally moved on from his intense rage stage and was descending right into loneliness, and people do stupid things when they're lonely. She should know. She'd done plenty of them. Most memorably, having sex with Nico Daugherty. That seemed to be her favorite *stupid* pastime, hence the reason she'd repeated it so many times.

But who could blame her? Seriously. The guy was sexy in a humble, understated way. Not like Stone Jameson, who commanded attention simply by being in the room. Nico was the opposite of that. People paid attention because they were drawn to the mystery he exuded. He was also sweet and kind and generous. He cared about the people in his life. Genuinely.

And she couldn't forget the guy had a body built for sin. Beneath those loose-fitting clothes, every inch of him was rock-hard, finely honed by manual labor, not time in a gym. On top of that, he was talented and gifted in the pleasure department. He was seriously skilled when it came to giving orgasms with his hands, mouth, and, yes, with that generously endowed cock of his. And his cock was as beautiful as it was bountiful. Just thinking about it made her pussy clench and her mouth water.

Not that she would ever admit it to Nico, but she was as completely, irrevocably in love with him as she was with the puppy. And she had been since *that night*. Even through the few years when she hated his guts, she'd been nursing a broken heart because *that night* changed her. The crush she'd been nursing at the time had turned into a full-blown case of love in a matter of hours. The years that followed had been painful, but she'd gotten over it thanks to Nico and his insistence that they talk it out. And yes, she'd gone right back to loving him.

Secretly.

As far as he was concerned, she was only using him for sex. Stevie did her best to keep it only to those out-of-control moments when she was intoxicated. She wasn't to blame for those few times she'd done her I'm-drunk-let's-get-it-on routine on purpose. Suggesting a night of drinking simply so she could spend it in his bed. Her manipulation came from a good place because deep down, she had feelings for him. Feelings she refused to tell him about because that shit was what fucked up friendships. The last thing she wanted was to screw up theirs. At the same time, she couldn't imagine giving up those wicked nights spent with him rasping dirty words in her ear as he did dirty things to her body.

"I burned 'em," Nico said, his voice closer.

Burned 'em? What was he—? Oh, right. The fajitas. Yes. Yes, that smell was a definite sign that he burned 'em.

He appeared, leaning a shoulder on the wall that blocked the unsightly side of the refrigerator from anyone who was in the living room. The entire entertainment area was one giant room that spanned the front half of the house. With the kitchen bleeding into the living room, dining room, kitchen nook, and the front foyer. The back part of the house was dedicated to the sleeping spaces: four bedrooms with three and a half baths to go with them. Like Nico, she had her own bedroom with a dedicated bathroom. One bedroom was used as extra storage, with quite a bit of her crap still boxed up from the move stowed in there. The smallest room could pass for a guest room, although they'd never had a guest since she'd moved in. The second floor, which consisted of one enormous room and a full bath, was used as their secondary office, complete with two desks and a large drafting table that Nico used often.

Stevie tried to wrangle the little dog as she turned her head to peer up at him. She knew it was ridiculous that she still got that weird, wobbly feeling in her belly whenever she saw him, but it'd been the case for so long that she'd stopped questioning it.

Nico Daugherty was a beautiful man. Almost perfectly so, with his narrow face and angled jawline, perfect nose, and ears that she wanted to nibble on. His eyebrows were thin slashes across his pretty blue eyes, usually because he was deep in thought. His dark hair was longer than normal. What was typically shaved close on the sides and back now rested perfectly against the collar of his shirt and was haphazardly tousled on the top of his head. By mid-February, he would break down and get it cut, trimmed back to its usual short length. His jaw and upper lip were purposely dark with stubble, giving his youthful face a slight edge.

His eyes blazed with heat, and she knew it had nothing to do with the blackened strips of chicken in the skillet or her lying on the floor playing with the dog. She'd seen that look before, and it was almost always associated with the memory of *that night*. In fact, the first time she'd seen it had been *that* night.

The puppy started chewing on her ponytail, so she gently pulled the strands from between his tiny little teeth and sat up.

Because she could tell Nico needed a distraction, Stevie said, "Oscar came by the office today."

The heat in his eyes diminished instantly, a frown pulling at his mouth.

She smiled. "Don't worry. I sent him on his way."

His eyebrows locked down over his eyes, and that frown curved even more. "Did you have sex with him, Stevie?"

There was so much accusation in his tone that she took offense to it.

"Why do you fuckin' care?" she snapped, hopping to her feet.

Nico sighed. "I'm sorry."

"No, you're not." She spun on her heel and stomped toward her bedroom. "But that's okay. I forgive you."

Although she wasn't overly chipper about it, she meant it. She probably had every right to be mad at him but couldn't bring herself to be. Not after years of hating his guts, blaming him for something that was as much out of his control as it was hers. They'd moved past that, moved on. These days, her relationship with Nico was complicated.

So. Freaking. Complicated.

He was her best friend's brother.

He was her roommate.

Stevie kicked off her shoes when she walked into her bedroom. She hopped on one foot, pulling one sock off and dropping it on the floor, making her way to the bathroom. She did the same with the other sock when she reached the shower, opening the door to turn on the water.

Where was she? Oh, right. Nico and their complications.

He was her business partner.

He was her friend.

He was her orgasm delivery guy—on occasion.

But those weren't the complicated parts. That had to do with him being the man Stone Jameson had shared her with. The man who'd awoken her to things she hadn't known existed. And yes, the man who'd stolen a piece of her heart *that night*.

She started shoving her jeans down as she walked to the towel closet. She stripped them off completely and left them on the floor before grabbing a towel.

That night ... what happened between the three of them hadn't been planned. It couldn't have been because it had come right out of a fantasy. She'd never discussed anything quite like that with Stone, despite their scorching encounters. And Lord have mercy, they'd had some doozies. Stone Jameson had taught her things about herself that she wasn't sure she ever would've figured out without him. He'd taught her what true sexual freedom was and made her realize that her erotic desires were nothing to be ashamed of.

Stevie pulled her sweater off and tossed it in the direction of the dirty clothes hamper. It almost made it, one sleeve hanging haphazardly down the side. She unhooked her bra, slid it down her arms, and flung it in the same direction. Missed.

Nico also played a big part in that self-realization, even as Stone was teaching him the same thing about himself. She knew Nico had never been with a man before that night. He'd told her as much. Later. Much later. More specifically, he'd admitted it the night she was sloppy drunk, waxing apologetic about coaxing him into the situation. It was true. She'd played a huge role, considering she was the one who'd given Stone the nod of encouragement after she'd come outside to find Stone and Nico swapping air beside Nico's truck. Nico hadn't known she was there at first, but Stone had. He'd met her gaze over the bed of Nico's truck, and in his glittering hazel eyes, she'd seen the wild, untamed boy she'd fallen in love with. One nod of her head, encouraging him to take what he wanted, had started the ball rolling.

Oh, man. That night… She would honestly give about anything for a repeat of that smoldering encounter. For just a few hours with Nico and Stone, their skilled hands playing her body like a finely tuned violin. Sometimes, she would wake up drenched in sweat, her entire body charged and aching for release. It pissed her off every time because she knew there would never be another night like that.

By the time she was stripping her panties down her legs, her body temperature had risen, the memories scorching her as they always did.

She opened the bottom drawer in the vanity and retrieved her waterproof vibrator before marching naked into the shower.

There was only one way to stifle the heat from those memories.

NICO KNEW HE SHOULDN'T FOLLOW STEVIE.

It was reckless and stupid, and… Well, it was apparently inevitable because his feet were already moving.

Since Stevie never stormed out, he was compelled to go after her. He hadn't meant to ask her such a targeted question. And he certainly hadn't intended to accuse her of doing something she could do if she wanted. He blamed it on the memories. On seeing Stone today after all these years. When he'd looked into those hazel eyes, he'd been reminded of everything he'd had for that one single moment in time. Everything he'd lost when Stone left town because try as he might, Nico had never been able to replicate what he'd felt that night.

Not a single encounter had lived up to that one. Only a handful had ever come close, but those involved him and Stevie giving in to the lust that still sizzled between them despite their efforts to pretend otherwise. But Nico knew even those hot, dirty encounters would never quite quench that need because, although she came pretty damn close, Stevie wasn't capable of giving Nico everything he desired.

He marched into her bedroom, nearly tripping on her shoes. He spotted one sock and followed the sound of running water. The puppy was hot on his tail, but he got distracted by the sock, flopping down on his belly to chew on it.

Served Stevie right because Nico knew exactly where she was and what she was doing. Usually, he would turn around and head the other way at a quick clip. Not today.

The bathroom door was open, so he walked in. Her jeans were on the floor by the towel closet, and another sock was directly in front of the shower. It blew his mind that she was so organized at work but a complete and total slob at home.

He turned and leaned against the vanity, crossing his arms over his chest and pretending that seeing this woman naked didn't drive him absolutely insane. She was by far the most gorgeous creature he'd ever had the pleasure of looking at.

Stephanie Shepherd, whom everyone lovingly referred to as Stevie, insisted she was as masculine as she claimed her nickname was. Nico wholeheartedly disagreed. She was petite and toned from the endless manual labor their job entailed, but there was nothing masculine about her. She had curves where she was meant to have curves. And she was so goddamn soft, so perfectly sleek. She was so perfect—despite the many flaws she was amused to point out at times—Nico could get distracted staring at her.

Which he was doing now.

"I told you I forgive you," she said, leaning her head back to get her hair wet.

Stevie wasn't indignant. She didn't attempt to cover herself, didn't gasp or squawk about him being uninvited into her personal space. The woman didn't have a modest bone in her entire body. In instances like this, he found it sexy as hell. Others, when she was merely wandering through the house, usually streaking to the laundry room because she forgot to get her clothes out of the dryer, he found it frustrating. Wanting her and not being able to have her was enough to drive him mad.

"I have no right talkin' to you like that," he told her, trying to keep his gaze at eye level, but it was damn near impossible.

"We're in agreement there." She grabbed the shampoo bottle and poured a generous amount into her hand. "But I know it comes from a good place."

Yeah, maybe it did, but that didn't make it okay.

The steam carried the scent of strawberries through the room.

"What did Oscar want?"

"What he always wants." She kneaded her scalp, working the shampoo into a lather. "For me to do somethin' for him. Sex. A job. A place to stay. Today, it was all three."

Nico didn't care for Oscar. He was a mooch. Worse than that, he was a mooch with a warped sense of entitlement. The only reason Nico hadn't warned him off Stevie long ago was because, while he was relentless in his pursuit of her, he wasn't pushy. He didn't intimidate or use fear tactics to persuade her. He would ask for what he wanted. When she said no, Oscar respected that. Which, in Nico's book, put him one step up from total douche status.

Not to mention, it wasn't Nico's place to monitor or approve of who Stevie had sex with. If it were up to him, she would not be having sex with anyone but him. But wanting that and telling her that were two very different things. Stevie insisted their friendship was something special. She wasn't wrong. According to her, sex tended to complicate things. She wasn't wrong about that, either. So Nico kept his feelings to himself and let her believe their encounters were spontaneous, occurring solely because they'd had too much to drink and didn't have the common sense to do anything about it.

For the record, Nico had been drunk the first time. Every time after, he'd indulged, sure, but never too much. He preferred to remember every single touch, every kiss.

"Where'd you get the puppy?" she asked, rinsing the last of the shampoo from her hair.

"Niyah."

Stevie grinned, grabbing the conditioner. "She said she was gonna get you somethin' to ensure you didn't get lonely when she was gone."

Nico lifted an eyebrow. "She already gave me you. What else could I possibly need?"

"Aww." She giggled. "You say the sweetest things."

While she worked the conditioner into her hair, Nico's gaze shifted to the small neon green toy sitting on the shelf in the shower. As soon as he saw it, he knew he should've left. There were times when he was positive Stevie purposely pushed his buttons. The last time he'd seen that thing, she had whipped it out right in front of him. In the living room. While they were watching a movie. Yeah, she'd had a blanket covering her while she fondled herself with that damn toy, but it didn't matter. He'd heard it, and he'd seen the satisfaction on her face when she brought herself to orgasm.

The time before that, she had invited him to watch, which he had politely declined, hating himself as he did. But then Stevie dared him, and they both knew he wouldn't back down from a dare. So he had watched.

That was two months ago. To this day, he used that memory to get himself off in the shower.

"I've got a name for the puppy if you can't think of anything," she said casually, as though she wasn't soaping her perky tits and watching him while she did.

"What?"

She flashed a grin. "Jägermeister. We can call him Jäger for short."

A handful of memories flashed behind his eyes. Only once in his life had he drunk Jägermeister, and it happened to be *that night*. He'd hated it instantly, but by the third swig, it hadn't been so bad. Plus, it had done its job of easing the tension and lowering his inhibitions.

Speaking of *that night*.

"I saw Stone tonight," he admitted, tearing his gaze away from the vibrator and doing his best not to watch while she ran that soapy puff thing over every one of her lovely curves.

Her gaze cut to him briefly. "Tonight? I thought you saw him earlier in the day."

"I went to the General Store to pick up some dog food. He was there."

Stevie's movements slowed as she turned to look at him through the glass. "What did he have to say for himself?"

"Nothin' much."

She nodded, then turned the knob to a warmer setting. He wasn't sure why. It was already hot enough to smoke meat in the bathroom.

Or maybe that was just him.

"Reilly asked what you thought of the puppy. I told her you … hadn't been home yet."

Nico waited for her to say something. She didn't.

"He was surprised to learn we live together."

She reached for the detachable shower head to rinse the soap. "Did you tell him I'm just your roommate?"

He shook his head, holding her gaze.

"Why not?"

Nico opted to go with the truth. "He was jealous, Stevie."

She frowned, looking away as she placed the sprayer back in the clip and stepped underneath to rinse the conditioner from her hair. "Jealous of what?"

He figured he didn't need to answer that. For one, he wasn't sure what the answer was. But he did know he'd seen a flash of something in Stone's eyes. And it reminded Nico of the night the three of them had been together.

"Maybe it was heartburn," she said, trying to make a joke out of it. "You know Stone. He doesn't get jealous. If he did, he wouldn't've shared me with you."

That wasn't the first time she'd said that, and Nico got the feeling she truly believed that. He knew better. Yes, jealousy played a role for many people, and they wouldn't dream of sharing their partner with anyone. For others, it was a turn-on to be able to give twice as much pleasure as they could give on their own. No, Nico didn't know Stone's reasoning, but that was the impression he'd gotten that night.

"Not that I care," she said, reaching for the green toy. "I've got all I need right here." Stevie looked his way. "Now, if you'll excuse me, I've got a date."

Nico was disappointed that she didn't want to talk about it. They needed to. Stone wasn't someone they could shove into the dark recesses of their minds and pretend he didn't exist. It had been impossible to do when he wasn't there. Now that he was back, it would only get worse.

Stevie winked at him. "Unless *you* want to take care of me."

If he stayed, he knew exactly where this would lead, and though he ached for this woman, Nico didn't want to encourage her. Stone was back, and no matter how she tried to play that off, it bothered her that he was. Until they figured out a way to coexist in the same small town, she wasn't going to move past it. The sad part was that they would never have a meaningful, real relationship until they could get beyond what happened all those years ago. Not with each other or anyone else.

"I'll order a pizza," he said, turning to leave.

"Chickenshit," she muttered. The word was followed by the hum of the vibrator.

Nico stopped, turned. He looked at her and then did something he'd never done before. At least not without both of them having a few drinks in them. He walked right into the shower with her, clothes and all.

Stevie's eyes opened, and she gasped, her mouth falling open as he loomed over her, crowding her against the tiled wall. He was soaked from head to toe within seconds, but he didn't care.

Nico held out his hand. "Give me the toy."

Her eyes narrowed, lips parted in a silent "O." She relinquished the vibrator.

"Put your hands above your head."

Her throat worked on a slow swallow. She did as instructed.

Nico captured both her wrists in one hand and held them high above her head, resting his forearm on the tile so he could crowd her against the wall.

"Spread your legs."

She did.

He dragged the buzzing toy over her bottom lip, watching her as he did. "You think this thing can replace a man?"

Stevie nodded, but he saw the truth in her eyes.

"We'll see about that."

He dragged the toy down her chin, her neck, her chest. He kept going, down, down, down to the juncture between her thighs. He maintained eye contact as he positioned the tip directly on her clit. He saw the moment the pleasure registered because her face went slack, her eyes rolling back, those pouty lips parting with a sigh.

The woman was exquisite. He could've watched her all day.

"Nico…"

"I'm not a chickenshit," he told her.

She rocked her hips. "I know."

"We agreed this wouldn't happen again."

"I know." She whimpered, her eyes closing.

"So why can't I keep my hands off you?"

"I don't know."

"Yes, you do," he said, taking the vibrator away. "Tell me why."

Her eyes snapped open. "Please, Nico."

"Tell me," he repeated, pressing it on her clit again.

"Because … oh, yes," she hissed. "Because I *want* your hands on me."

Nico swallowed hard, applying a little more pressure, bringing her closer and closer to orgasm but not letting her go over.

The first time she told him that, he thought she'd been playing a role. They'd gotten good at that. They always turned their sexual encounters into a game. A way to keep their distance, to pretend they were merely using each other for a common goal. Although he still played along, that had stopped working on him a long time ago.

Nico hadn't been with anyone but Stevie since he broke up with Melanie thirteen months ago. For the five months of their engagement, Nico had ridiculed himself for bowing to the pressure. He had dated Melanie for nearly two years without ever wanting more than that. When she gave him an ultimatum—marry her or she walked—he panicked. He'd felt boxed in, forced to live a life he had never wanted. He'd bought this enormous house because it had been her compromise when he refused to leave Coyote Ridge. The only reason he'd agreed was because it sat on five acres and backed to Curtis Walker's ranch. At the very least, he figured they wouldn't be swallowed up by some cookie-cutter subdivision if and when the city council gave in and let the demanding home builders come in.

But the house wasn't the only thing he'd done that was completely out of character for him. He'd stopped going out with his friends, spending what little spare time he had with Melanie's friends, whom he couldn't stand because they were as uppity and pretentious as she was.

The only solution he could see was to marry her and endure. He couldn't have what he wanted, anyway. It was the lesser of two evils, so he proposed and regretted every second that followed. It had taken five months, but he woke up one morning determined to stop the insanity before it brought real heartache. No matter how he tried to convince himself otherwise, Melanie would never be able to give him what he needed. No woman could. Not *everything* he needed. And Melanie wasn't the sort of woman who would understand.

So, in order to save her some pain in the future, he'd ended things.

Three short weeks after that, Niyah and Adam got engaged, and Nico took the opportunity to move on with his life. Inviting Stevie to live here solved three problems. It helped fill some of the space, gave him some help with the mortgage, and ensured he wouldn't settle for less than what he wanted. Stevie was the only person who knew him, who truly understood him. Who accepted that he wanted something most people didn't even understand.

Nico waited until Stevie opened her eyes. "Is that all you want? My hands on you?"

She shook her head. "I want you inside me."

He released one of her wrists. "Take the toy."

She lowered her arm, keeping the vibrator firmly on her clit when he gave it to her. He shifted his hand between her legs, pressing two fingers against her entrance.

"Yes," she whimpered, her voice a harsh whisper. She lifted her foot, resting it on the teak bench she kept in there. "Fuck me with your fingers."

He pushed them deep inside her.

When he invited Stevie to live with him, Nico hadn't expected this would happen. He probably should've known since his craving for this woman had only intensified over the years, even though he'd only had her that one night.

Until eleven months ago. Valentine's Day last year. Both of them dateless and wallowing in their self-pity, they'd gotten shitfaced and ended up in bed together. The next day, they pretended it didn't happen. They went right on pretending until the next time. After a certain point, it became a routine, both of them pretending they weren't using booze as an excuse to find the closest thing to satisfaction that either of them had ever felt since *that night*.

Stevie groaned, her pussy contracting around his fingers as she trembled.

Her brown eyes darkened as the pleasure coursed through her. She continued to look at him, holding his stare as he fingered her. Nico knew what she was waiting for. The woman didn't hide her desires and never pretended she was anything but a hot-blooded woman who loved sex.

"You want it so fucking bad," he rasped, moving his mouth close to hers. "You want to come. It's right there, Stevie. So close."

She cried out as he thrust his fingers in deep, the smooth, slick walls of her cunt stroking him.

He spoke directly into her ear. "You wish it were my fat cock, don't you? Stretchin' this sweet cunt."

Her knees buckled. "Yehhh ... oh, fuck ... Yes! I want your cock!"

"You want me to pound the orgasm out of you. Don't you?"

"Yes."

"You want me to bend you over and plow your pussy until you're screamin' my name."

"Yes ... oh, oh ... yes!" She bit her lower lips. "Please ... give me your cock."

"I will, darlin'. You know that. But it's gonna be in your mouth."

Her pussy spasmed, squeezing his fingers. He pumped his hand, thrusting faster, fucking her deeper. Stevie loved rough and dirty sex. She had told him as much during one of their inebriated conversations. Because of the night he'd spent with her and Stone, Nico knew she was being honest.

The problem was Nico wasn't capable of being rough with her. He couldn't bring himself to do it for fear of hurting her. If that happened, he would never forgive himself. Stone was the rough one. That night, he'd manhandled them both in a way that had felt beyond good. No pain, only pleasure. But Stone was skilled in that arena, whereas Nico was not. Stone knew precisely how far he could take things without causing pain or injury. Nico didn't.

However, Nico had a knack for dirty talk. With Stevie, he'd learned that the more vulgar he was, the more desperate she became. He loved watching her come apart. She was so fucking beautiful.

"You're gonna come on my fingers, then you're gonna pull out my dick and suck me. I'm gonna fuck that sweet mouth of yours. Gonna drive my cock down your throat. Take what you owe me."

Stevie licked her lips. "Yes." She groaned, her pussy spasming. "Please. Oh, fuck, Nico. Please."

He released her other wrist so he could take the vibrator from her hand. He pressed it firmly on her clit and finger-fucked her until she was gasping and writhing, every muscle in her delectable little body tightening as the release built.

"Come, darlin'," he commanded harshly, ramming his fingers inside her. "Come so you can suck my cock."

She screamed, her body tensing, her inner muscles clamping down tight on his fingers.

God, he fucking loved when she came apart.

Stevie didn't hesitate, didn't take the time to come down before she was ripping at the button on his jeans, urging him back so she could go to her knees. She wrenched the wet denim down his hips, and then his cock was in her perfect little mouth.

He dropped the vibrator.

"Oh, fuck. Goddamn, Stevie. Your mouth's so fuckin' hot," he groaned, slapping one palm on the wall and grabbing her hair in his fist, holding her head so he could fuck her face. "Suck me deeper. Yes. Just like that."

Nico didn't waste time. He didn't hold back. He fucked her face and came down her throat within seconds. She did that to him. He was almost convinced he could come simply by watching her get off.

As he dragged gulps of air into his lungs, he helped Stevie to her feet. She was grinning as he pulled her close, her cheek resting on his chest. Her arms came around him, and they stood like that, the water barely tepid at this point.

"We have to stop doin' this," he told her, pressing a kiss to the top of her head.

But rather than agree with him, Stevie tilted her head back and met his gaze. "Do we?"

Nico studied her face, looking for signs she was still caught up in the ecstasy. Before he could ask her if she was serious, the shower door banged against the metal trim. They separated, their attention going to the puppy, who was insistent on getting in.

Stevie laughed as she turned the water off.

"He probably wants dinner," she said, opening the door to reach for a towel.

"He already ate."

The puppy trotted in, licking the water off the floor and pouncing in the little puddles.

Nico sighed as Stevie strolled out of the bathroom, putting another incredible encounter behind her. Just like she always did. Pretending it wasn't getting increasingly difficult not to give in to the idea that this could be more.

"Your timin' could be better," he whispered to the dog. "Five minutes sooner, and I wouldn't've fallen a little more in love with her."

It was a lie, but one he continued to tell himself because sometimes it was the only way he could make it through the day.

TEN

Sunday, January 14, 2024

"SHE'S DOIN' FINE," DEBORAH EXPLAINED AS THEY all sat around the dinner table. "Her doctor did tell her he'd prefer she not travel until after the baby's born."

Since Chelsea and Paul weren't there to share an update, Stone's mother was doing it for them.

Even without his sister and her husband, the dinner table was crowded. Like Stone, Donovan hadn't passed up a free meal. Nor had Brady. Since Reilly and Tate usually had dinner with Deborah and Owen on either Friday or Saturday, they'd pushed it out a day when Mom informed them they would be back early.

From the moment he sat down, Stone felt a sense of nostalgia. He'd missed these weekly meals. Catching up with his family, listening to their stories. Unfortunately, CJ hadn't been able to make it, so there was one chair empty. Sundays were CJ's overnights at the fire station. Because his brother mentioned trying to catch up soon, Stone agreed to meet him at the diner in the morning for breakfast.

Reilly lifted a forkful of their mother's famous tuna noodle dump—the worst name in the history of names for anything you put in your mouth—and paused before taking a bite. "Does that mean you'll be goin' up there every weekend?"

"Not every weekend, no," Mom said with a smile, clearly hearing the hint of jealousy in Reilly's tone.

All grown up and independent as hell, Stone knew that Reilly still enjoyed being the favorite.

"I've got plenty of time to help plan the wedding," she assured Reilly.

"I'm gonna need all the help I can get." She glanced at Brady. "Unless you wanna elope in Vegas. Because that's option number two. And I'm not takin' it off the list yet."

All eyes shifted to Brady.

"Not a chance."

Stone's dad nudged Brady with his elbow. "Smart choice."

"I don't know why," Reilly told Owen. "It would save y'all a ton of money."

"A ton?" Owen asked, glancing between Reilly and Deborah.

"Of course." Reilly fluttered her lashes. "If I'm forced to wear some big white gown, I've got to have all the accessories."

"I'm not payin' for diamond jewelry," Owen told her, then nodded at Brady. "That's *his* job."

With a mouthful, Reilly shook her head. "I'm not talkin' about diamonds." She grabbed her iced tea to wash it down. "I'm talkin' white doves. Lots of them."

"Doves?" Owen looked at Deborah. "*Why* do we need doves?"

"It's romantic," Reilly said as though it was obvious.

Stone was watching their mother, too, so he saw the slight shake of her head. After all this time, Stone found it amusing that Reilly still had the ability to pull one over on their father.

"Right up until they shit on the guests," Donovan said, pushing his empty plate away.

Reilly laughed. "Fine. Then I'll take white tigers to walk me down the aisle. Three of 'em."

"They'll eat the guests," Donovan mentioned as though this was a serious conversation.

"White German shepherds, then. I'll need four of those, though. That way, they can walk in pairs in front of me. Lead the way like cute little flower girls." Reilly looked at her mother. "Who *is* gonna be the flower girl?"

"You could always ask Ethan and Beau if Kiera'd be willin'," Deborah said, referring to their cousin's daughter.

"You could have Kate do it," Owen chimed in. "She's nine. Might be able to control her better."

"She's a Walker," Donovan noted. "Ain't no controllin' that bunch."

That earned a round of laughs from everyone.

Reilly took a bite, contemplating all the information. She lifted her fork as she swallowed. "I still think the doves are the right way to go."

"How about doves *and* tigers?" Stone suggested.

Reilly's eyes glittered with mirth. "That would be interesting, right?"

Donovan looked at Brady. "You sure you still wanna go through with this? It's not too late to back out."

Tate punched Donovan in the arm and earned himself a glower that spoke of the sort of retribution Stone didn't want to think about.

Clearly ready to be off the subject of over-the-top wedding ideas, Deborah looked at Stone.

"Donovan said you met with the landscaper."

"Nico Daugherty came by?" Owen asked.

Tate chuckled. "Wasn't that the guy you punched in the face for makin' Chelsea cry?"

Stone purposely didn't look at Brady. He was the only person at the table—at least that Stone was aware of—who knew about what happened that night in the hay loft. Brady didn't have specifics, but he'd been pulling into the driveway the next morning and had seen Stevie and Nico leaving. Considering Stone had been shirtless and barefoot, the guy didn't need a map for his suspicions to find a home.

Because of that ill-timed exit, Stone had ended up on the wrong end of Brady's good intentions two days later when Brady blasted him for being a dumbass. He could still hear Brady's disappointed voice all these years later.

"Chelsea's fuckin' boyfriend, Stone? You couldn't find someone ... fuck, anyone else to screw around with? You realize he's Stevie's best friend's brother, right? You could've lit a match up in that loft and not caused as much damage as you've done to more than one relationship. For what? And don't tell me it's because you're serious about either of 'em."

That conversation with Brady, which was more of a one-sided shouting match, had sent Stone into a tailspin. Up until that point, he'd spent two whole days walking around in a hazy fog of satisfaction. But as soon as Brady called him to the carpet, he'd been riddled with regret. While he hadn't appreciated Brady going postal on him, he couldn't deny the man was right.

"I thought you wanted to make somethin' of yourself, Stone. D told me you're lookin' at workin' on a ranch. Why the fuck are you stringin' along a coupla high school kids? You should be out there, figurin' out what the fuck you wanna do with your life."

Brady had single-handedly planted the seed of doubt, watered it, and made it grow from there. The more Stone had thought about it, the more he'd realized that he had no business thinking about a future with anyone. Definitely not Stevie. She had her whole life ahead of her, and the last thing he wanted was for her to end up hating him. She would've because if he stuck around Coyote Ridge, there was no way he wasn't going to insist on a repeat of that night. He figured it wouldn't take long for her to end up feeling used, and he would've ended up wallowing in a shit-ton of regret.

So he'd decided that chasing a dream was the best option. For everyone.

"Remember Chelsea walked around for a week feelin' sorry for the guy?" Reilly asked.

"But not sorry enough to take him back," Owen noted.

"She did take him back," Brady said, his gaze sliding past Stone. "For a minute."

"It was routine for her at that point," Deborah said with a wistful smile. "But she had her sights set on bigger things."

"You think they might move down here one day?" Reilly asked.

Stone wasn't paying attention, so he didn't hear his mother's response.

His only thought was that he needed to seek out Stevie. At the very least, she deserved an apology.

Whether he could tell her the truth—that he'd been in love with her, but that night had changed him—was still undetermined. Deep down, he knew he'd made the right decision by leaving because what he'd wanted was not something she had signed up for.

To this day, he couldn't see himself settling down with one person. Fifteen years ago, that had seemed like a ludicrous idea. Then again, being out and proud had been reserved for only the most determined. Luckily, that wasn't the case anymore. For a lot of people, anyway.

But it wasn't until Stone learned about his cousin Travis coming out and admitting that he was in love with Kylie and Gage that he realized it wasn't as crazy as he'd thought. Difficult, yeah. Because it wasn't as easy as it looked. Finding a soulmate when you were looking at a one-to-one ratio was hard enough. Finding someone who understood and wanted the same thing didn't happen easily, so finding two was next to impossible. Yet somehow, Travis had found a way to make it work.

With that said, Stone wasn't going to give up. Now that he'd had a taste of the best life had to offer, he would settle for nothing less than genuine happiness. Even if it meant he would be single for the remainder of his days.

"SO WHAT WAS THAT LOOK YOU GAVE Stone earlier?" Reilly asked Brady on the drive back to their house.

They were sitting in the backseat of Donovan's truck since they'd all ridden together to her parents' house for dinner. They had the illusion of privacy, but she knew her brother and Tate were listening to every word.

Brady continued to gaze out the window. "I didn't give him a look."

"Yes, you did." Reilly tapped the back of Tate's seat. "You saw it, right?

He didn't respond.

"I think you're seein' things," Brady told her.

She huffed. "They don't call me the all-seeing, all-knowing one for nothin'."

"No one calls you that," Donovan and Brady said in unison.

"Yes, they do," she countered.

"Name one person," Brady insisted.

"Tate."

Tate barked a laugh. "I do *not* call you that."

"Well, you should," she told him before turning her attention back to Brady. "That one." She pointed at his face. "That's the look. The *non-look* look."

He glanced at her. "What?"

"Stall tactic one-oh-one. Ask a question to buy time so you can come up with a lie."

Brady's smile started slow and ended with a wide grin and a shake of his head. "I'm not gonna lie to you."

"But you're not gonna tell me the truth, either. I saw it. As soon as Tate mentioned that Nico was the guy Stone punched for makin' Chelsea cry, Stone instantly avoided lookin' at you. Tate saw it. Right?"

"I saw nothin'," he said.

"Liar."

He chuckled.

"You know somethin'," Reilly accused Brady. "About what happened back then."

"Nothin' happened."

Reilly looked at Donovan and noticed him glancing back at them in the rearview mirror.

"Do *you* know?" she asked her brother.

"No."

"Really?"

He met her gaze in the mirror. "Really."

Darn it. She believed him.

Reilly glanced at Brady and lowered her voice. "This isn't over."

He laughed as he took her hand and linked their fingers. And just like that, she knew what she had to do.

Fifteen minutes later, after Donovan dropped them off at their house, Reilly filled a glass with water and faked a yawn. "I think I'm gonna turn in. See you in the mornin'."

Brady looked up from where he was, glancing at the pile of mail he'd dropped on the counter yesterday. "You don't wanna watch a movie?"

Oh, she definitely did. Especially because they'd made it their Sunday night tradition—that is, if a handful of Sundays could be considered a tradition. Because she closed the General Store early on Sundays, it gave them time to spend together. Alone. And for the past few weeks, they'd opted to camp out on the couch and watch a movie. Reilly preferred it because it always led to some spicy extracurricular activities.

"Nah. I think I'm gonna hit the hay."

"Everything okay, Rye?"

Reilly stopped at the base of the stairs and turned toward him. She pretended to yawn again, stretching her arms over her head. The move lifted her sweater, instantly drawing Brady's attention to her bare belly. The heat in his gaze was instant, just as she knew it would be.

"I could probably be persuaded," she told him, lowering her arms.

He huffed a laugh as he walked into the living room. "Could you now?"

"Yep."

"What exactly do I need to do to persuade you?"

"Never mind." She spun on her heel and started up the stairs. "You won't like it, so never mind."

Before she reached the top, she heard his booted feet on the stairs.

Reilly squealed when she realized he was chasing after her. She made a beeline for the bed and ran around to the other side. Her first mistake was thinking a king-size mattress was going to stop him.

Without hesitating, Brady scaled the mattress in two steps, then hopped down on the floor, trapping her between the wall and his big, beautiful body.

"I was doin' some thinkin'," Brady said with a smirk.

Reilly laughed as she peered up at him. "Yeah? In the ten seconds it took you to get up here?"

He nodded. "I think you're the one who needs to persuade *me*."

"Oh, really?"

Brady lifted his sweater and pulled it over his head, tossing it onto the bed.

Reilly was instantly distracted by the sheer perfection of his body. The man was freaking hot. It didn't matter that his sexy body had become her own personal playground these past few weeks, she found when he took off his shirt, she was unable to speak.

Brady took her hands and placed them on his abs. She took over from there, grazing the smooth, warm skin.

While she did that, he unbuttoned his jeans.

Her mouth watered. Really, it did.

"Dessert?" she asked hopefully.

Brady laughed as he sat down on the bed. "Take off my boots."

She helped him get them off, dropping them on the floor because she didn't want to miss a thing. When Brady McCord stripped, it was like unwrapping Christmas, Valentine's, and birthday gifts all at once.

He stood back up so he could push his jeans and underwear down before he sat down again.

When he laid back on the bed, she took over, admiring his hard cock as she tugged his jeans down his legs.

She licked her lips and met his gaze. "I can be very persuasive."

His brown eyes gleamed with desire. "I know you can."

Reilly reached for him, circling her fingers around his satin-smooth length, stroking from root to tip. She watched his face, loving the way his eyes rolled back whenever she touched him.

She teased him for a minute before stopping abruptly. His eyes opened, radiating heat as they tracked her every move. Reilly stripped quickly before joining him on the bed, straddling his thighs. She resumed her massage, using both hands, one to caress his cock, the other to gently play with his balls.

Brady moaned softly.

Reilly stopped.

His eyebrows lifted in question.

"First, you have to admit there was a look."

He grinned, reaching down to stroke himself.

Reilly stopped him by covering his cock with her hands. "This is mine. You can't touch it."

He barked a laugh.

"Only I get to touch it tonight. But I'm only gonna do it if you tell me."

Brady reached again, and she swatted his hand away.

Laughing, he said, "Yes. There was a look, okay?"

She nodded and resumed playing with his dick.

She paused to lift her butt off his legs. "Move back."

He shifted underneath her until he was stretched across the bed. She moved with him, continuing to stroke when he was where she wanted him.

"And what was the look for?"

"That's gonna require more persuasion," he told her.

"Oh, really?"

Brady nodded. "You should try usin' your mouth."

Reilly licked her lips, peering down at his long, thick length, which was still tunneling in and out of her fist. She wasn't sure he even realized he was doing it, but Brady was pumping his hips.

She scooted down his legs, pressing her breasts to his thighs while still holding his cock in her hand. She licked the tip, staring up the length of his torso to watch his face. Brady never stopped looking at her. That was what he always did when she put her mouth on him. As though he was as turned on by the sight as much as the sensation.

She kissed the tip, then circled her tongue around the crest.

He moaned.

"What was the look for?"

Brady lifted his head. "I'll tell you what. You suck me, then I'll lick you. After that, you can ride me. Then, if you make me come, I might consider talkin' about your brother. But as long as your mouth's close to my dick, I have no desire to talk about him."

Reilly chuckled. That made sense. She wasn't all that eager to talk at the moment, either.

"Fine. But if you don't tell me after…" She let the warning linger in the air around them as she set out to show him exactly how good she was at persuasion.

ELEVEN

"DO YOU KNOW HOW FUCKIN' HARD IT is to keep my hands off you?" Donovan asked Tate when they walked into the house shortly after dropping Reilly and Brady off.

"How hard?" Tate asked, opening the refrigerator.

Since an answer was impossible to put into words, Donovan changed the subject, coming to stand behind Tate, sliding his arms around him. "I know you can't possibly be hungry."

Tate leaned into him. "I'm a growin' boy, don't you know?"

Donovan leaned down and pressed his nose to the crook of Tate's neck. "Which part of you is growin' right this second?"

"Wouldn't you like to know?"

Oh, yeah. This was where he wanted to be. Home, with Tate in his arms, feeling the warmth of his body against him. The only thing better would've been if they were both naked. Based on the banter, he knew it wouldn't be long before that became a reality.

Tate tilted his head back, looking at Donovan. "Do you know how much I *hate* tuna casserole?"

Donovan laughed, releasing him and stepping back. "Seriously?"

Tate's eyes rounded as though he couldn't believe he'd admitted it.

"She's made it at least once a week for—Shit. Since *I* was a kid. And you're just speakin' up now?"

Tate nodded, and the look on his face was priceless. "Don't tell your mom. Oh, please, Donovan. Don't tell her."

He wouldn't dream of it, but he figured Tate didn't need to know that. "You don't want her to know?"

He shook his head. "It's not her cookin'. She's a fabulous cook. Amazing, actually."

"Layin' it on a bit thick, don't you think?"

"I love almost everything she makes, but warm tuna is nasty."

Donovan grinned, looking at Tate as though seeing him for the first time. He'd done that many times over the past few weeks as he learned the little things. Like how Tate preferred to wear socks to bed because his feet got cold. Or how he brushed his teeth twice in the mornings—once when he woke up and again after he ate. Or how on Saturday afternoons, when he finally woke up after working all night, he would eat cereal and watch cartoons because that was something he'd always done with Reilly.

The man was fucking adorable, and Donovan found he couldn't get enough of him.

"You want me to make you somethin'?" Donovan offered, giving him space to peruse the refrigerator.

Tate sighed and closed the door. "No. I had enough cornbread to tide me over for a month." He turned around. "But dessert would be nice."

There wasn't a hint of suggestion in Tate's tone, but that was somehow all Donovan heard.

He waited until Tate rounded the kitchen island. "I can think of somethin' *I* want for dessert."

Tate's expression was still intent when he looked up at Donovan. "Do we have any—" His eyes widened. "Oh."

Donovan closed the gap between them, then lifted Tate onto the counter.

"It shouldn't be that easy for you to do that," Tate said with a huff.

"What's that? Make you stop thinkin' about food?"

"No. Liftin' me up like I'm a kid."

Donovan stepped between his legs. "Trust me when I say there's nothin' kid-like about you."

Tate hummed softly when Donovan kissed him.

Donovan slipped his hands beneath Tate's shirt, gripping his sides as he worked his way up his torso, lifting the shirt as he went. He loved touching this man, feeling his muscles flex and shift beneath his fingers. When he wasn't touching him, he was thinking about it. Enough that it disrupted his train of thought more often than not. He thought for sure that would've only lasted for a brief time, but they'd been living together for several weeks now, and with every passing minute, Tate plagued his thoughts even more. He figured one day he would be able to focus again, but for now, he was enjoying the distraction.

He managed to strip Tate's shirt off him, tossing it to the floor.

Tate shivered.

"Cold?"

"A little."

"Hmm. If there were only a way to fix that," he said as he leaned down and sucked one of Tate's nipples.

Tate gasped, planting his palms flat on the counter and leaning back, making it easier for Donovan to nibble and suck on the little brown disc.

He slid his hands up Tate's back and curled them over his shoulders, supplying him with a little body heat while he drew several ragged groans out of him. Donovan lifted his head, pulling Tate to the edge of the counter so he could seal his lips over Tate's. When Tate's fingers teased through his hair, he felt tingles dancing down his spine.

"I want to lick you from head to toe," he told Tate. "And then I want to start over and do it again."

"What's stoppin' you?"

"Someone said they were cold."

"And if I'm not mistaken, your body heat is more than enough to warm me up."

Tate talked a good game, but he shivered again, and Donovan was almost positive his teeth were chattering. Yeah, he kept it relatively cool in the house, but it wasn't *that* cold. Or maybe he was more worked up than Tate. He reached between Tate's legs, dragging his knuckles over the hard outline of his dick. No, that didn't seem to be the problem.

When Tate shivered again, Donovan stood up. He grabbed Tate's hand and urged him down from the counter, dragging him through the house to the sauna room. They'd used this room more in the past few weeks than Donovan had the entire time he'd lived in the house.

He'd had it custom-built at the back of the house so that it was accessible from inside as well as outside. The smallest part of the room was meant as a changing area for when he had guests who wanted to enjoy the pool. There was a vanity with a sink and mirror and a large closet on one wall where he kept towels and various pool items. Because he wasn't a small man, Donovan had designed the sauna large—a ten by twelve enclosed space—giving him plenty of room to lay down for those times when he wanted to relax fully.

Of course, relaxing wasn't really an option around Tate. Donovan was primed and ready damn near every minute of every day. He'd spent his entire life—all thirty-nine years so far—enjoying sex, but never to the point he craved it. With Tate, he couldn't think of much else.

"Get undressed," Donovan told Tate after opening the door to the sauna.

While Tate did that, Donovan went to the control panel to turn on the heater, letting it warm up. It wouldn't take long, and since they would be generating their own heat soon enough, it wouldn't matter.

After grabbing a couple of towels and stripping down to his birthday suit, Donovan joined Tate, pulling the door closed to seal in the warmth. The first few times they'd come in here, Donovan had kept his hands to himself, not wanting to overwhelm Tate. That had lasted about a week before Tate confronted him, revealing his equally desperate need to be with him. They were still playing catch-up and probably would for at least the next ... oh, say, ten years or so. That might do it.

Tonight, Donovan offered no pretense that this was anything more than a seduction technique.

He joined Tate on the wooden bench that formed an oversized U, running the length of three walls. It was deep enough to lay down on comfortably, so he moved to sit behind Tate, leaning back and urging Tate to do the same.

Neither of them spoke as the space began to heat; they just sat there in silence, enjoying simply being. He progressed to massaging Tate's shoulders and back, turned on by the sight of his hands moving over Tate's skin.

When sweat began to form on his brow, Donovan tightened his arms around Tate. "Warming up?"

Tate nodded, relaxing against him.

Donovan kissed Tate's shoulder, then let his lips glide up the side of his neck. It only took a second before Tate was fully relaxed, his head tilted, allowing Donovan to lick and suck on his neck. Tate was so sensitive, so responsive. His soft moans grew heavier as the air warmed. Tate's hands began to slide over Donovan's legs, slowly at first but becoming more frantic as Donovan continued to heat him up.

"So what else do you pretend to like but secretly don't?"

Tate groaned. "Please don't tell your mom I—"

He reached around Tate's shoulder, pressing against his jaw to turn Tate's head toward him. "I won't," he said as he pressed a kiss to his lips, smiling as he did. "I just want to know your secrets."

"Mmm," Tate mumbled against his mouth before turning around completely and straddling Donovan's legs. "I can tell you, I definitely like the sauna."

"Yeah?" He slid his hands along Tate's thighs, moving to his hips. He dipped his thumbs into the crease at his torso, teasing him lightly as he pulled him closer.

"Mm-hmm." Tate sighed, resting his elbows on Donovan's shoulders and leaning forward, pressing his forehead to Donovan's.

Unable to keep his hands still, Donovan explored, letting his fingers glide gently along the contours of Tate's back and shoulders. The guy was small in stature, but he was built like a brick shithouse. More than once, Donovan had outlined those hard planes and rigid angles with his tongue.

"Besides tuna casserole, what else do you pretend to like?"

"Asparagus," Tate said, his fingertips brushing the head of Donovan's dick.

"Doesn't count. Everyone pretends to like that shit. What else?"

Tate chuckled. "Those war documentaries your dad likes."

Donovan grinned. He happened to find them interesting but to each his own.

"And…?" Donovan figured there had to be more.

"The scent of those laundry beads that Reilly likes. On her clothes, it smells fine. On mine, it smells like cheap perfume."

Donovan gritted his teeth as Tate continued to tease his cock, using his thumbs to massage the head.

"What else?" he grunted.

Tate lifted his head, meeting Donovan's gaze in the dimly lit room. "I promise, I don't make a habit of pretending to like things."

"No?" Donovan slid his hands up Tate's back, hooking his fingers over his shoulders, pulling him even closer.

Tate shook his head.

"Then tell me why you won't marry me."

Tate swallowed hard. Donovan felt his muscles tense, but he didn't let him go. They'd had this conversation only a couple of times since Donavan first asked. He accepted that it had been fast, but he didn't regret asking. He wanted to marry Tate. Hell, he would do it tomorrow if the guy was willing to go to the Justice of the Peace. Since the man had yet to give him an answer—positive or negative— he suspected there was a deeper issue.

"I'm not—"

"Don't lie."

Tate frowned.

"Answer me this. Do you want to get married one day?"

"Yes."

"To me?"

"Yes."

"That was easy."

"You're not the problem," Tate said with a sigh.

Donovan hugged him tighter, wanting Tate to know he wasn't pressuring him. He was genuinely trying to understand. "Is the problem somethin' I can fix?"

Tate held his stare for what felt like an eternity. When he finally spoke, his words dripped with despondency. "I don't want a wedding."

Donovan frowned. "Okay. Who said you had to have one?"

He shrugged. "Your family's all excited that Reilly's gettin' married. They're pickin' out dresses and napkins and shit."

"And you don't want dresses and napkins and shit?"

Tate laughed, just as Donovan hoped he would.

"I don't want to stand up in front of a bunch of people."

"Then we won't."

"But what about you?" Tate's eyes were warm. "Don't you want that?"

Donovan pulled back enough that he could look Tate in the eye. "I want you. Forever. However, I can get you."

"You say it like it's been months, not weeks."

"Do you need me to set a timer? I will. How long should I set it for? A month? Two? Ten? At what point will you know you want to spend the rest of your life with me?" He tilted his head. "Because I'm already there, Tate. If I could tell you how it happened, I would. I just know that bein' with you … it makes me happy in ways I've never felt before."

"When you say shit like that, it seems so simple."

"I love you," Donovan whispered. "If you need me to wait six months or a year, I will. If you wanna wait five years, we'll keep doin' what we're doin'. But marriage is important to me. For the sole fact that I want the world to know who you belong to."

Tate's eyes were misty, and Donovan's chest clenched.

"I want that, too."

"We don't have to have a big wedding. We can go to the Justice of the Peace, find someone to stand in as a witness. Or we can take Reilly and Brady with us. Or hell, we can go to Vegas." Donovan laughed. "Reilly'll be pissed, but I'm sure she'll get over it."

"Can we take Reilly and Brady with us to Vegas?"

Donovan could tell he was teasing but answered with a heartfelt "Yes."

Tate laughed. "She really would be pissed."

"Knowin' Reilly, she'll finagle a double wedding so the two of you can share the same anniversary," Donovan told him.

"She would."

Donovan cupped his face, still holding his gaze. "I don't need a wedding, either. But there is one thing I want."

Tate's eyebrows lifted. "Anything."

"I want you to take my name."

Donovan gave Tate a moment for that to sink in before he explained. No, it wasn't common for same-sex couples to take one name or the other. Some hyphenated, others merely kept their own. But Donovan didn't care what other people did. He wanted what he wanted, and this was important to him.

"You've been an honorary member of our family for as long as either of us can remember. Let's make it official."

This time, tears formed, and he worried he'd overstepped. But then Tate lurched forward, crushing his mouth to Donovan's.

"Yes," Tate whispered against his lips.

"Yes, what?"

"Yes, I'll marry you."

Donovan's entire chest expanded, and suddenly, the room seemed brighter and the air fresher.

"Really?"

Tate nodded. "I love you."

"Jesus," he rasped and pulled Tate into him, holding him tight as he kissed him hard and deep. They were both panting hard by the time they pulled apart, and the temperature was soaring, not entirely because of the steam.

"Anything else you only pretend to like?"

Tate shook his head.

"So you *do* like havin' my cock inside you?"

Tate's lips parted in a silent sigh, his eyes glassy. "Definitely."

Thank God for that because Donovan couldn't spend another minute without being buried balls deep inside this man.

"Fuckin' you deep and slow?"

Tate nodded.

"Prove it." Donovan grabbed the bottle of lube he'd brought with him. He placed it in Tate's hand. There was a desperation to his movements, although he was attempting to rein himself in. He wanted to be inside this man. He wanted to be joined as one so Tate could feel everything Donovan was feeling.

Tate continued to hold his stare as he opened the bottle and poured the liquid into his hand. He used both hands to slick Donovan's cock, going slow, his eyes still glistening. The moment certainly hadn't passed, but Donovan wanted to be one with him. And he couldn't wait another second.

"Do you prefer bein' on me or under me?" Donovan asked, simply because he liked knowing Tate's preferences.

"Both."

Donovan smiled. "Good answer."

"Which position do you like the least?"

Tate smiled, leaning forward. "The one when you're not inside me."

Donovan laughed, the sound echoing around the enclosure.

"Come here, then," he said, holding onto Tate as he turned to stretch his legs out on the bench. He released Tate so he could extend his arms out behind him, putting his palms flat on the bench.

Tate shifted one leg out from under him, stretching it out forward.

"Put me inside you, Tate," Donovan growled. "Now."

Propping himself on his knee, Tate guided Donovan's cock between his legs, pressing the head firmly against his anus. He lowered himself slowly, Donovan's cock sliding in slowly, filling Tate inch by inch. As he sank down on him, Tate pulled his other leg out from under him and stretched it out until they were in a see-saw position, facing one another.

Donovan's stomach muscles clenched as the pleasure tore through him. It wasn't simply being inside Tate that did it for him. It was looking at him, seeing the way his eyes glazed and his lips parted as the pleasure consumed him, too.

Tate planted his hands behind him on Donovan's knees for leverage and began to rock forward and back, fucking himself on Donovan's cock.

"God, Tate," Donovan hissed. "I love watchin' you fuck me."

So he did, admiring the flex and shift of Tate's muscles as he took his pleasure from him. The way his cock bobbed proudly, untouched by either of them. He took his time, never rushing, as the ecstasy simmered and glowed hot.

Thankfully, the timer ran out on the heater, and it clicked off. The room was a thousand degrees, and they were only creating more heat as Tate fucked him.

"Stop," Donovan said, sitting up straight and grabbing Tate's hips.

When Tate's arms went around his neck, Donovan grabbed his ass and turned, putting his feet on the floor. He stood, still lodged deep inside Tate. As soon as they stepped outside the sauna, they were blasted with cooler air. Donovan didn't make it farther than the vanity counter. He propped Tate on it, grabbing under his knees, pushing his legs back to change the angle. He began pumping his hips, fucking in deep and slow.

When the pleasure became too much, he stopped again, this time carrying Tate into their bedroom. His cock dislodged when he set Tate on the bed. He didn't waste time joining him. He paused briefly to kiss him, to taste the man's sweet surrender.

"Please," Tate groaned against his mouth. "I need you inside me."

Donovan rolled to his back and reached for the pump bottle on the nightstand, needing more lube for what he had in store for Tate next. He tucked a pillow under his head, then drizzled more lube over his cock, hissing at the chill.

"Ride my cock," he growled roughly as he tossed the bottle aside.

When Tate started to straddle him again, Donovan shook his head. "Turn around."

Tate's eyebrows popped, and a smile contorted his mouth. He liked this position, and Donovan knew it.

Tate faced away from him, straddling his hips and sitting on his dick. Donovan grabbed Tate's ass, spreading his cheeks wide, easing him down, watching as his cock slowly sank into the heated bliss of Tate's body.

"Oh, fuck yes," he hissed. "Take all of me, Tate."

Donovan guided Tate up and down, unable to look away from the erotic sight of his cock disappearing inside Tate. When the lightning storm erupted in his spine, he drove himself deep inside Tate and pulled him down, his chest to Tate's back. In this position, Donovan's lips were near Tate's ear. He curled his arms around him, flattening his palms on Tate's chest and slowly running them down, over his stomach, his hips.

"You're so tight," he whispered, holding Tate's hips and thrusting up into him. "So fuckin' hot."

They'd stopped using condoms, and Donovan found the sensation damn near addictive.

Tate gripped Donovan's forearms to keep from rocking off of him.

"I can't get enough of you," Donovan told him.

"I love you," Tate hissed, trying to impale himself on Donovan's cock.

"Say it again. Tell me you'll marry me."

"I'll marry ... oh ... fuck ... yes, I'll marry you."

It wasn't enough.

Donovan wrapped one arm around his waist and rolled until Tate was face down on the mattress. He covered the smaller man, planting his hands on the bed to hold himself up. He fucked into him, deeper than before. He tried to go slow, but it felt too good. He fucked him into the mattress, reveling in the sensations that wracked his entire body.

"Donovan ... oh, fuck. I'm gonna come."

He took that as his cue, driving into him faster, harder, deeper. He drove himself right to that mind-bending precipice.

Donovan leaned down and pressed his lips to Tate's ear. His words came out in a rough growl. "Come for me, little boy. Come so I can fill this tight little ass."

"Oh, fuck ... yes!" Tate cried out, his ass milking Donovan's dick as he surged headlong into ecstasy.

Tate cried out his name as Donovan exploded inside him, Tate's ass clenching as he bucked and trembled beneath him.

COMPLETELY SATED AND GASPING FOR AIR, TATE fought to catch his breath.

"It's your turn to wash the comforter," he told Donovan, his words slurred from exhaustion.

Donovan laughed. "Why bother? I'm just gonna make you come again in a little while."

Did it make him a sex addict because he was hoping that was true? Tate would swear that each encounter was hotter than the last.

As happened almost every time, Donovan threw an arm over him and pulled Tate close so they were touching from knee to chest, with Donovan spooning behind him.

"Were you serious about Vegas?" Tate asked when he could string more than a couple of words together.

"Do you wanna get married in Vegas?"

Did he? "Yes," he said confidently. "But can I talk to Reilly and get back to you?"

Although he was pretty sure Reilly had been teasing about eloping in Vegas, he needed to make sure that was the case before Tate went and made plans to do it. Plus, she would be upset if he didn't tell her he'd finally agreed to marry Donovan. She knew the reason, but she promised not to mention anything to Donovan. She'd kept her word, but that was Reilly for you.

"Sure." Donovan kissed him on the cheek before pulling away. "But keep in mind, if she decides she wants a double wedding in Vegas, my parents will insist on bein' there."

Tate rolled to his back, watching as Donovan walked toward the bathroom. The man was sin on a freaking stick. Literally, he was the hottest thing on two legs. It still shocked him to know that Donovan Jameson wanted him. No, he didn't just *want* him, he loved him. Although Tate was having issues reconciling the timeline, he believed Donovan when he said the words. He would have to be crazy not to want to marry the guy.

"Shower with me," Donovan called from the bathroom. "Then you can call Reilly while I make you a cherry turnover."

His favorite.

Tate squeezed his eyes shut and smiled so wide it was a wonder his face didn't split.

He wouldn't be merely crazy not to marry the guy, he would be a flipping idiot.

TWELVE

Monday, January 15, 2024

"YOU LOOK LIKE SHIT."

Stone glared at his brother. Only ten minutes into their meal and CJ was readily passing out insults. Just like old times.

"You know what y'all can do with your opinions?"

CJ chuckled. "Who's *y'all?*"

"You. Reilly. Donovan."

"So the consensus is you look like shit?"

Stone picked up his coffee mug, arranging his fingers to discreetly flip his brother off.

"Back atcha." CJ sat back in his seat. "We just tell it like it is, bro, and you, my friend, need a haircut and some…" CJ made a circle with his hand toward Stone's face. "I don't know what *that* needs, but, *man.*"

A laugh bubbled out of him. He couldn't help it. CJ had always been like that. Maybe because he was the middle child, the youngest of the boys. Or maybe because he was only a couple of years younger than Stone, so he was old enough that Stone had given him crap growing up. Whatever the reason, CJ hadn't changed much in the time Stone had been gone. Aside from growing up and making something of himself. He'd done things right somewhere down the line. Too bad all those life lessons hadn't given him an attitude adjustment.

Stone wished his brother would lay off *just* a little. He usually appreciated that his brothers and sisters didn't pull their punches. But considering he'd been back for three days and the consensus seemed to be his appearance was lacking, Stone wasn't all that fond of this morning's ribbing.

"Rough night or what? Not gettin' much sleep, huh?"

The last thing Stone wanted to think about was rough nights. It was all he *could* think about these days. And yeah, he was getting plenty of sleep. The problem had nothing to do with his ability to close his eyes and drift off. It was what happened when he did. Nico and Stevie plagued his damn dreams, and it didn't matter how many hours he clocked horizontally, he continued to wake up hard and unsatisfied.

"Shouldn't you be winin' and dinin' that girlfriend of yours?" Stone asked, trying to change the subject.

As was the case whenever someone mentioned Jamie Collier, the girl CJ'd been mooning over for years, his expression blanked. "She's not my girlfriend."

"She could be."

CJ shook his head and grabbed the bottle of Tabasco, applying a generous amount to his eggs.

"It's been what? Two years? Why haven't you sealed the deal yet?"

CJ's eyes narrowed.

Stone recognized the look. "Fine. I'll back off."

"Thank you."

"Just as soon as you tell me what the hold up is," Stone added, grinning when his brother rolled his eyes.

"That's the question of the hour," CJ replied. "So what *is* the holdup?"

145

Stone frowned. "With what?"

"You've been back three days. Mama said you've been holed up in the barn. I thought you'd be makin' rounds, lookin' to see who's willin' to sell you some land."

That had been the plan. Right up until he pulled into town. Now that he was back, Stone wasn't sure his dream of owning a cattle ranch was in the stars anymore. The worst part was, if he wasn't dreaming of a ranch of his own, he had nothing. It was the only thing he'd wanted for as long as he could remember. Now that he was questioning it, he felt … empty.

CJ tilted his head as though that might help him figure Stone out. "You thinkin' about ridin' again?"

Stone chuckled. "Hell no." That much he knew for a fact.

Bull riding had been a means to an end. A way for him to make money that he could put directly into savings. He'd made a name for himself working on the Double J and spending time on the rodeo circuit. With a few championship buckles under his belt, Stone could probably write his own ticket. But sitting astride a fifteen-hundred-pound beast and riding for eight no longer thrilled him. And not only because the last time he'd ridden—almost seven years ago—resulted in several compound fractures in his back. Those had healed nicely, but he wasn't getting any younger. Bull riding was a young man's game. Or a fool's errand. Take your pick. And Stone was neither young nor a fool.

Between the championship purses he'd won and working at the Double J, he had more money than he needed to buy up a decent parcel of land, a few heifers, and the semen from champion bloodline bulls. It was all he needed to build the legacy he'd always dreamed of building. But would it make him happy? He wasn't so sure anymore.

"You could always buy the Lassiter farm. They've got some chickens and goats. I think a couple of alpacas."

Stone flipped his brother off again as he sipped his coffee.

"What? I think you'd do fine out there feedin' oats to goats. Get yourself a rockin' chair and some Metamucil. Right fine life, if you ask me."

"No one asked you."

CJ forked eggs in his mouth and immediately reached for his orange juice.

The bells over the diner's door chimed, drawing Stone's attention as it had the last dozen times it opened. This time, he felt something kick hard in his chest when he saw Stevie walk in.

Stone put his hand on his chest as it suddenly tightened. It felt like someone had sucked all the air from his lungs. He couldn't even gasp for breath because he was incapable of moving, his eyes tracking the only woman he'd ever loved as she walked up to the hostess.

Holy Jesus. She looked the same as she had back then: long blonde hair pulled back in a ponytail, big brown eyes, and those perfect, *perfect* lips. Her face was more contoured, her cheekbones more prominent—the result of age—but she still looked as young and as sweet as the girl he'd given his heart to. And yes, she was still the most beautiful girl he'd ever laid eyes on.

"Earth to Stone," CJ said, waving a hand in front of his face.

His gaze slid to his brother. "What?"

CJ glanced over his shoulder. When he turned back, he was grinning but not making eye contact.

Stone forced his gaze to remain on his brother. "What's that look for?"

"Nothin'."

Stone kicked him under the table.

"Ow. Fuck," CJ hissed, his voice low. Even as he glowered, he didn't stop laughing.

Stone leaned forward. "What the hell is wrong with you?"

"I was just thinkin' about somethin'."

"About what?"

"Somethin' that happened a long time ago." CJ's idiot grin got bigger. "Long, *long* time ago."

Stone frowned.

"I saw y'all," CJ said, his voice lowered to a whisper. "Right before you three went into the barn. And didn't come out until the *next day*."

Stone sat back, wide-eyed.

"Don't worry. It wasn't my business then, and it ain't my business now."

Stone pushed his coffee away, his eyes sliding to Stevie. He couldn't help himself. The second he saw her, something raw and untethered churned inside him. A hunger that hadn't been sated in years. Like then, he was starved for her, and it only took one look.

Only then did he realize Nico was standing behind her, that little dog in his arms.

Were they wearing *matching coats*? What the *fuck*?

He forced himself to look at the table, the floor, his brother. Anywhere but at the two people waiting to be seated.

CJ glanced back.

"Stop lookin'," Stone hissed.

"If it's any consolation, they're watchin' you the same way you're watchin' them."

Of course, Stone had to look, and CJ wasn't wrong.

This time, when CJ turned, he motioned for them to come over.

"Jesus Christ. What the hell are you doin'?" Stone whispered harshly.

"Figured you needed some company." CJ tossed his napkin on his plate. "I've gotta get home and get some sleep. Thanks for breakfast."

Stone snarled. "I wasn't buyin'."

CJ's grin grew too wide for his face. "You are now."

"Don't ever call me again," Stone muttered as Stevie approached, Nico right behind her.

"Hey, Stevie," CJ greeted. "How you been, sweetheart?"

"Good." Stevie smiled up at CJ, but her attention quickly shifted to Stone.

Their eyes met and held. He got lost in the dark brown depths the same way he had back then. He didn't want to, but manners had him getting to his feet. He stepped toward her, closing the distance without realizing he was.

She tilted her head back, her eyes locked with his, an expression of surprise on her face.

Heaven help him. Stone was pretty sure this was what an out-of-body experience felt like. As though he was hovering elsewhere in the room, watching this interaction because the emotions that churned within him were too much for his tired brain to process.

"Hey, girl," he said in a rough whisper.

She swallowed hard. "Hey."

The soft rasp of her voice caused a chill to shoot down his spine. Because it was awkward not to, Stone pulled her in for a hug, his arms going around her. He swore he heard her gasp softly as she put her arms around him, hugging him back.

And just like that, everything he felt came rushing back, flooding his limbic system. For one brief moment, it was as though he'd never left, like the past fifteen years hadn't happened, because this—right here with Stevie in his arms—was the only place he'd ever wanted to be.

She smelled incredible. Some spicy, fruity blend—definitely strawberries—that went right to his head. One touch and every feeling he'd thought was lost forever returned, overwhelming him— mind, body, and soul.

Fuck, he had missed her, but he hadn't realized how much until this moment.

"Good to see you, man," CJ said to Nico. "Talk atcha later."

Stone forced himself to release Stevie, meeting her gaze one more time before returning to the booth. His movements were awkward, but he wasn't sure what to do or say, so he motioned for them to join him. He didn't sit down—not at first. But then he became self-conscious, so he slid into the booth.

Stevie took the puppy from Nico and set him on the floor. It took only a second before the little fluff ball had his front paws propped up on the booth beside Stone.

"What's up?" Stone asked the dog, unable to resist the urge to scratch between his ears.

"Sit," Nico told the dog, gently urging his hind end down to the ground.

The dog sat.

"Impressive."

"Not really," Nico said, although he was smiling. At the dog, of course.

"You two sit," Stone told them, pointing toward the side of the booth that CJ just vacated.

Stevie looked up at Nico as though ... what? Was she seeking permission? Or sending him a silent plea for help?

"Didn't sound like a question," Nico countered, his gaze bouncing between him and Stevie.

Using his own words against him. Clever.

Stone gestured toward the seat and said, "It wasn't."

Something flashed in Nico's dark blue eyes. He looked at Stevie one more time, and she gave a slight nod. A second later, she shrugged off her coat and scooted into the booth, leaving room for Nico to sit beside her.

"Sit," Nico told the puppy again.

"He got a name yet?"

"No."

"Why not?" Stone grinned down at the puppy trying to sit but unable to keep his hind end from wagging uncontrollably.

"His name's Jäger," Stevie answered, elbowing Nico in the arm.

"Jäger? As in…?"

"Jägermeister," she said. This time, there was a taunting gleam in her pretty eyes.

"We haven't agreed on that yet," Nico noted. "I thought about callin' him Trouble. Suits him."

Stone's gaze shot to Stevie. *We?* He was proud of himself for holding that one in, but he couldn't resist glancing at their hands, expecting to find wedding bands. When he saw there weren't any, his relief nearly sent him to the floor.

"I remember someone else who used to be trouble," Stone said, his full attention on Stevie.

"Still is," Nico added.

Stevie elbowed him.

Nico grunted, then looked at Stone. "Seems I'm attracted to it."

She giggled, her eyes lowering even as her smile widened. "Yeah?"

The waitress came over, earning a puppy lick on her ankle while she refilled Stone's coffee.

"What can I get ya?" she asked Nico and Stevie.

"The usual."

Her gaze shifted to Stevie. "You, too, hon?"

"Yeah."

"Comin' right up." She looked at Stone. "You good?"

"Yep."

He looked at Nico and Stevie when she walked away. *Real good, in fact.*

STEVIE WASN'T SURE WHY SHE BOTHERED TO order food. There wasn't a chance in hell she would be able to eat it. Her belly was flip-flopping like a fish out of water and had been from the moment she saw Stone from across the room.

The man she hadn't seen in fifteen years looked almost the same as he had back then. Same dark hair, same hard body. Only this version of Stone was more rugged, more refined. Definitely older. Bigger. Sexier. He had laugh lines around his eyes, and he'd lost the youthfulness in his face. It was replaced by a harder jawline and a slightly crooked nose.

But his eyes were the same. Not only the green-gold color but the heat and mischief that glittered in them.

"How've you been?" Stone asked her.

"Good." The word came out too quickly and without an ounce of inflection.

"Yeah?"

She nodded, feeling like an idiot. For the past few days, she'd been practicing what she wanted to say to this man when she saw him again after all this time. And she knew she would, despite the over-the-top avoidance plans she'd been trying to come up with.

And since it was inevitable—Coyote Ridge just wasn't that big— she'd come up with a variety of possible greetings.

Heard you were back. When are you leaving?

Stone who? Can't say I remember you.

Sorry, don't have time to talk. I've spent fifteen years pining for you, need to figure out how to move on with my life.

In all the different scenarios, not one time had she even considered hugging him. Punching him in the nose had crossed her mind a time or ten. Kicking him in the balls had been at the top of the list, too.

Sitting at a booth with him and Nico had not been part of the plan.

Yet here she was.

Stevie glanced at Nico, trying to figure out how he could be so calm. He didn't appear wracked by nerves or even the slightest bit put off. He was watching Stone as though he wanted to have *him* for breakfast instead of pancakes and sausage links, which were the *usual* he'd asked for.

Stone sat up straight, resting his forearms on the table, his eyes zeroed in on her.

"What?" she prompted.

"You look good, Stevie."

She didn't thank him for the compliment. Hell, her tongue was so twisted, she couldn't.

"So what're you two up to this mornin'?" Stone asked, this time directing his question at Nico.

"Headin' to work."

Stone gestured toward the logos on their shirts. "D and S Landscape Solutions."

When he looked at her, Stevie raised her eyebrows, encouraging him to read between the lines. It didn't take him long.

"Daugherty and Shepherd," he said. "Very nice. How long've you been in business?"

"Eight years," Nico answered.

Stevie chewed on her bottom lip, spinning the silverware wrapped in a paper napkin. She didn't bother opening it because they wouldn't be staying. Their *usual* included a to-go bag. Thank God.

She could feel Stone's eyes on her, and it took every ounce of self-control to keep from squirming. She inhaled deeply, wishing someone would turn down the heat.

She saw Stone's hand move, gesturing between them. "Are you two a couple?"

"No," they both said at the same time.

"But you live together."

"Yeah," they answered in unison again.

"Roommates?"

"Yep," they both chimed.

That wasn't creepy. Not at all.

A slow smile curved the corner of Stone's mouth, and Stevie felt the tension in her core. Her pussy actually clenched. That damn smirk was what had attracted her to him in the first place. Looked as though she wasn't immune to it now, either.

"Interesting."

"Why's that?" she asked, wishing she had the nerve to say something else. Something with substance. Something that didn't make her look like she was stunned (and maybe a little happy) to see him.

Which she was, of course.

But *he* didn't need to know that.

NICO WASN'T SURE WHY HIS ASS WAS planted in this seat.

He'd told himself last night after he'd jerked off in the shower to the memory of Stone that he would steer clear of the man. As soon as he'd seen his truck parked in the diner's lot, he should've pulled back onto the road. Ventured elsewhere.

Instead, he'd asked Stevie if she was hungry and pulled right in, not bothering to tell her that was Stone's truck they'd parked next to.

Yeah, it was safe to say he was attracted to trouble.

"Reilly tells me you're a landscape architect," Stone said, looking at him once more.

Nico nodded, wondering whether or not he'd solicited that information from his sister or if she merely offered it. Or why *that* might possibly matter. Who cared if he asked around about him? So what? That weird swelling in his chest was probably nothing more than pre-indigestion. If it wasn't a thing, well, it should be.

"I am," Nico confirmed. "Stevie runs everything."

Once again, Stone looked at Stevie, but Nico couldn't read his expression. He looked somewhat forlorn. As though he'd spent all these years pining for the woman he'd left behind. Nico wouldn't blame him if he had. Stevie was one of those people who was impossible not to think about. Very much like Stone.

At least for Nico, anyway.

The waitress delivered two cups of coffee in paper cups with lids, a small bowl with sugar packets, and another with little cups of cream before darting off.

Stone was still looking at Stevie. "You go that route, too? Landscape architect."

When Stevie didn't answer, Nico did for her. "She's a botanist."

"The study of … plant biology, right?"

Stevie nodded, continuing to spin the napkin-wrapped silverware on the table.

"But we both get our hands dirty," Nico said. "We're not above workin' hard."

Stone's shoulders relaxed, and he leaned back, his fingers sliding on the side of his coffee cup. "Why should you be?"

Leave it to Stone to make him look like a defensive asshole. He wasn't sure how to respond to that. He swore the other day he'd seen a hint of distaste in Stone's gaze when he thought he was a landscaper. Which he was. Technically, he wore many hats when it came to business. As did Stevie.

"What about you?" Nico doctored his coffee, adding sugar. "You workin'?"

"Not at the moment."

"Plans?"

Stone's gaze shifted to the table, and he fidgeted with his coffee mug. "Thought I had some. Up in the air right now."

"You gonna hit the road?"

Stone tilted his head. "That's the second time you asked me that. You tryin' to get me outta here?"

"No."

Aaand he might've said *that* a little too quickly.

"You want me to stay?" Stone grinned, glancing between the two of them, and Nico felt that damn smirk on the head of his fucking dick. Damn, the man was potent.

"I didn't say that."

Stone's shoulders tensed. "Is there somethin' you'd *like* to say?"

Nico lifted his coffee cup to his lips and locked eyes with Stone. There were a lot of things he'd like to say to this man. Most of which he hadn't even thought about until the other day when he saw Stone for the first time after a decade and a half. Okay, fine. Maybe he'd reflected back on them a few times in the last fifteen years. But only briefly. Definitely not often.

Dammit. *What the fuck am I doin' here?*

"Here you go," the waitress said, depositing the to-go bag in front of Nico.

Perfect timing. "Thanks."

"Y'all get your usual to go, huh?" Stone asked, leaning back in that casual way that made him look even hotter.

"Things to see, people to do," he said.

Stevie chuckled, and Stone barked a laugh.

It was then Nico realized what he said. "You know what I mean."

"I certainly do," Stevie said, patting his arm.

Stone leaned forward, his voice low and intensely seductive. "If y'all have an openin'"—his gaze shifted between them—"I'd like to get on your calendar. For the latter."

If Nico had ever had a reason to call in sick—which he'd never done before—that would be it. For fifteen years, he'd wondered if he would ever hear that guttural baritone again, ever have a chance to be with a man who could single-handedly tilt his world on its axis. Stone still had the ability to ruffle his feathers and make his dick stand up and take notice at the same time. No one else could do that to him. Not even Stevie.

However, letting this man seduce him was a terrible idea. Worse than agreeing to marry a woman he hadn't been in love with after she hounded him endlessly. In the end, he'd broken her heart. In this case, should he give in to Stone, Nico had no doubt he would be the one with the pain in his chest. He hadn't fallen for the guy fifteen years ago, and he was grateful for that. No sense tempting fate again. No, thank you.

With that said, Nico wasn't above pushing the envelope.

He drank half of his now lukewarm coffee and reached for the to-go bag. As he shifted to get up, he met Stone's sexy stare.

"We're both partial to ribeyes and baked potatoes. I'm not usually much for wine, but Stevie prefers an expensive red with dinner. A restaurant isn't a requirement, but if you don't know how to cook, I suggest you get reservations."

Stone's eyebrows shot to his hairline. "And for dessert?"

"Surprise us." Nico got to his feet, glancing down at the puppy as he waited for Stevie to get out of the booth. "Come on, boy. You ready?"

"My place," Stone called out as they were walking away.

"Don't know where that is," Nico grumbled.

"The barn behind my parents' house," Stone supplied, sounding undeterred. "Both of you. Friday. Seven o'clock."

Stevie didn't look back when she called out, "If you're lucky."

He heard Stone's sexy laugh as he walked out the door with Stevie and the little dog leading the way.

THIRTEEN

"I CANNOT *BELIEVE* YOU DID THAT," STEVIE snapped when Nico got into the truck. She punched him in the arm for good measure. "What were you thinkin'?"

"The same thing you were," he said, avoiding eye contact as he started the truck and put it in gear.

"I'm not goin'," she told him, yanking on the seat belt, trying to clip it as he pulled out of the parking lot.

"Yes, you are."

"No, I'm not," she insisted, even though she didn't believe it either.

She wanted to. God, she wanted to. But there wasn't a rational bone in her body that thought it was a good idea.

Seeing Stone for those few minutes had brought everything flooding back. So many emotions she'd locked up broke free, filling her with sensations she'd thought she would never feel again. It was almost like he'd never left, and she was back to being that carefree eighteen-year-old who had fallen in love with the sexy bad boy with the devilish smirk.

Only she wasn't that girl anymore. She was a grown woman. She had a business and bills and … and she had Nico.

Not that she was in a relationship with Nico. She wasn't. They both agreed on that. However, she cared for him.

No, she *loved* him.

It was true.

She was in love with Nico, but she didn't want him to know that. She didn't want to screw things up because what they had was a good thing. They were friends, and they enjoyed one another's company. Not to mention, they were explosive together even though they pretended their sexual encounters were entirely accidental. Stevie didn't want to lose that.

She'd been a spectator during his relationship with Melanie. No way did she want that to happen to them. Stevie knew Nico had loved Melanie. Maybe not the forever kind of love because there were things he never told her. Things about himself that Stevie knew because not only had she been part of it, but also because Nico trusted her.

Deep down, Stevie wanted the sort of happily ever after that was found in romance books, but Nico could never be that man. He needed something she was incapable of giving him. Something that Stone Jameson had introduced him to, and he'd been forever altered by. Stevie understood that because the same thing had happened to her.

That didn't mean Stone's reappearance was a sign they could pick up where they left off. She'd changed. She was no longer the love-struck girl who would follow Stone around like a puppy, craving whatever he was willing to give her. And no, maybe he hadn't treated her like she was a toy he could pull out and play with whenever the thrill struck, but she'd convinced herself he had. It had been her way of coping with the loss.

Sure, the idea of being with Stone made her blood pump faster than it had in years, but she wanted more than that. Maybe there was a chance she could find herself sandwiched between Nico and Stone one more time, but where would that get her? It certainly wouldn't lead to a promise of more. Until she found someone capable of making that promise, she wasn't willing to sacrifice her heart.

Not even for the two men who would forever hold pieces of it.

Four hours later, Stevie was in her office, her full attention on handling the month's receivables, when there was a knock on the door.

"Come in," she said without looking up.

"I'm gonna run to lunch. Want me to get you anything?" Tara Chadwell, the best receptionist on the face of the planet, said.

"No. Thanks, though."

"I turned on the answering service so you won't be interrupted."

This time, Stevie did look up. She smiled. "What in the world would I do without you?"

"Hopefully, you'll never have to find out."

No truer words had ever been spoken.

"Have a good lunch."

Tara flashed a smile and pulled the door closed.

Stevie turned her attention back to her computer. She pulled up her notes app and jotted down a reminder to check on payroll options for the new year. Tara deserved a raise and it wasn't because Stevie was currently strapped in tight on an emotional roller coaster that had started at the diner. No, Tara deserved a raise because that woman was sometimes Stevie's saving grace.

Tara had worked for them for nearly two years, shortly after she received her associate degree from Austin Community College. Tara had answered their ad on Indeed, one of at least a dozen applicants interested in the receptionist role. Nothing about her résumé had stood out necessarily, but the moment Stevie met her, she knew she was the one. It was as though the woman had a light shining from within. Even on the darkest days, she had a way of putting a smile on Stevie's face without even trying.

Tara had proven her worth, taking on more and more responsibilities over the years, and now they all relied on her. The woman never asked for anything, which was why Stevie tried to do whatever she could to show her she was valued.

After jotting down her thoughts, Stevie closed the notes app and got back to work.

Several minutes later, another knock sounded.

So much for not being interrupted.

"Come in."

The door opened, and Nico appeared.

"Hey." She sat up straight, turning her chair to face him. "What's up?"

Jäger—yes, that was the name she was officially giving him—trotted in and made a beeline for the small fluffy bed Stevie had gotten him. She'd placed it in the corner so he could sleep in peace, but it was the little toys she'd tossed in it that he was concerned with now.

Nico closed the door behind him, and she knew something was wrong. He never did that.

"The other day in the shower…"

As soon as the words were out of his mouth, an image of him standing over her, his cock tunneling in and out of her mouth, flashed in her head. For the past two nights, she'd tossed and turned in her bed, squeezing her thighs together to stave off the need. She fought the urge to slip into his room and join him in that big bed of his. She told herself it was only because he was capable of delivering mind-altering orgasms, but she knew better. She wanted those, yes. But she also wanted what came after. For him to hold her in his arms, keeping her warm and making her feel safe.

"Yes?" Her voice cracked on the word.

"You said somethin'."

Stevie frowned. She did? Just now? "What?"

"In the shower," Nico clarified.

Oh. Right. The other day. She grinned. "So did you. A lot of things." Filthy, raunchy, *beautiful* things. God, she loved his dirty mouth.

His blue eyes, usually the color of the deepest ocean waters, glittered brightly. Rather than respond, he moved toward her, taking each step as though it were measured, trying to decide what would happen when he reached her.

Maintaining eye contact, Stevie tilted her head back until he was practically standing over her.

"I told you we had to stop doin' … *that*."

Yes, he had. And she said… "I think I said somethin' along the lines of, are you sure?"

"'Do we?' That's what you said."

"Okay." Where was he going with this?

She watched as he leaned down, placing his hands on the arms of her chair. She had to lift her feet when he pushed her back, putting space between her and the desk.

"Were you serious?"

Stevie wasn't sure whether there was a right or wrong answer. She definitely didn't want to say the wrong one.

"Maybe. Why?"

He nudged her knees apart so he could make room between them, then he slowly lowered until he was kneeling before her.

"Because I don't want to stop."

She watched his face, studying his handsome features. "Why are you tellin' me this now?"

"I don't want to give you up."

She frowned. "I didn't realize I was yours to give at all."

"Stevie."

"Nico," she drawled, mimicking his warning tone.

She'd never seen him like this. Well, maybe once. Back when—

"This is about Stone," she accused.

His eyes heated even more, and she knew she was right. Stone's presence had triggered memories for him the same way it had for her. They might as well be back in the hayloft, the two of them alone while Stone went to the house to shower. Stone had been gone for half an hour or so and during that time, Stevie and Nico had shared a moment. She was the one who'd instigated it by admitting she hadn't been asleep when they'd been screwing around like they thought. Well, she had, but the moment she woke up, she'd been transfixed on the two men beside her.

She had to shake off the memory because it was too hot to think about. She would need a cold shower afterward, which wasn't an option.

"I want to have dinner with him," Nico said, his voice ragged.

"You should," she told him. "I definitely won't get in the way of that."

She would likely be devastated, but hey, that wasn't his concern. The last thing she could tell him was that she would be extremely jealous if they were to get together, and she was left on the outside looking in.

Nico's hands slid along her legs, moving higher until his fingers curled around her butt. He pulled her toward him until she was pressed intimately against him.

This was new. Usually, Stevie was the one who touched him first. Or, at the very least, she said something to trigger a response.

"Us," he said firmly. "Not me."

Stevie swallowed, not sure what he expected from her. She wanted the same thing. Of course she did, but she knew it wouldn't be good for her. Certainly not until she at least understood why Stone was back and what his intentions were now that he was.

"I don't think I can," she admitted, sliding her hand along his jaw.

She rarely touched him like this. When they were *together,* it was very much like the day in the shower. Both caught up in the heat of the moment, unable to deny the chemistry they had. But kissing was rarely even on the menu because it brought a certain level of intimacy that they both tried to leave at the door.

"But you should have dinner with him," she urged. "I know you need what Stone can give you, Nico. Don't be ashamed to go after it."

"I'm not ashamed."

A small smile pulled at her lips. "Good. Then it's settled?"

He shook his head, still holding her tightly against him. "Not without you."

Stevie instantly shook her head. "I can't."

"Then we won't go."

Frowning, she pushed on his shoulders, and he instantly released her. That was Nico. He was always so careful with her even though he was well aware of the fact she liked it rough. And she trusted him more than she'd ever trusted any man. With the exception of Stone. But she'd understood Stone in a way that hadn't made much sense to her at the time. They'd connected so completely that it had blown her mind when he had simply walked away from it.

And that was another reason she wasn't interested in getting mixed up with Stone again. She had no desire to nurse another broken heart. Hell, she wasn't done nursing the one he'd given her fifteen years ago. If she were, his appearance would have no effect on her. Instead, when she looked at him, she felt everything she had back then. All the love, the lust … it came flooding back as though not a minute had passed. Stevie didn't trust that feeling. She wasn't that naive girl anymore.

Nico got to his feet and thrust his hand through his hair, ducking his head as he walked toward the door. He stopped without reaching for the doorknob.

"Did you mean it?" he asked without looking back.

She could've pretended not to know what he was talking about, but she figured she owed him the truth. She wasn't completely on board with pretending their encounters were accidental anymore, so she didn't feel the need to lead him on about it.

"Yes," she said simply. "I meant it."

When he turned, she expected to see disappointment on his face. She was asking more of him than he'd ever offered, which wasn't fair. They had a good thing going. She was a fool for—

"I do, too, Stevie."

She scrunched her face and turned slightly, pursing her lips as she tried to tie that response back to what they were discussing. She couldn't.

"*Do, too,* what?"

Nico started toward her again. The look in his eyes told her he wasn't going to answer with words. He was going to show her exactly what he meant.

"I WANT…" NICO WASN'T SURE HOW TO put it into words.

Hell, he wasn't even sure what he wanted. Ever since he saw Stone on Friday, the man had been a constant in his head, stirring up memories. Making him remember how he'd felt that night and the days that followed. Nico had felt whole for the first time when he'd been with Stevie and Stone. They'd somehow reconciled all the confusion and gave him hope that he could have everything he wanted.

Then Stone disappeared, and that hope deflated as surely as if someone had taken a pin and poked a hole in it.

His reappearance was making it flicker to life, and though Nico knew there was a good chance he was delusional, he couldn't help but think there was still a chance. Based on the way Stone looked at Stevie that morning ... how could there not be?

"Nico? What's happening?"

He realized he'd closed the distance between them, but this time, Stevie was standing up, staring at him as though he'd lost his mind.

He had. At least temporarily, because the only thing he could think about was claiming this woman to ensure no one took her away from him.

He cupped her face and peered down at her.

"You are the most beautiful woman I've ever laid eyes on."

Her eyebrows dipped low, her forehead creasing. "Have you been drinkin'?"

"No." He leaned down, his mouth hovering close to hers. "When I'm with you ... nothin' else matters."

"Why are you tellin' me this?"

"Because you need to know."

"Why?"

Nico kissed her. He couldn't help himself. He pressed his lips to hers, forcing himself to be gentle when the only thing he wanted to do was yank her leggings down and bury himself inside her. He was overwhelmed with this primal urge to claim her. He had no right; he knew that much. She wasn't his. Never had been. Not even *that night*.

Stevie hesitated, but only for the briefest of moments. Then she was kissing him back, her mouth hungry, urgent.

Was she feeling the same thing? A need to mark her territory before the big bad wolf came knocking. And he would. Nico had no doubt that Stone was going to pursue this. He'd invited them to dinner, and the Stone he'd known didn't do something like that without an agenda.

Although he wanted to pretend he wouldn't succumb to the attraction that still pulsed in the air when he was near Stone, Nico knew he wasn't that strong. He'd spent the past fifteen years wanting more of what they'd had that night. Not just Stone, but Stevie, too. Together, they were the answer to everything he'd ever wanted.

Stevie's arms wreathed his neck. He slid his around her waist, pulling her close as he kissed her hard and deep. He was starving for her. As though every other time he'd had her had merely been an appetizer. He was craving the meal. Five courses—no, make that seven. Hors d'oeuvres through dessert. But that still wouldn't be enough. Every encounter with her made him want more. He was a junkie at this point.

Stevie stumbled, and Nico realized he was pushing her toward the wall, toward a stable surface that would allow him to do what he needed to do.

"If you want me to stop, tell me," he whispered, breaking his lips free so he could bend over and take off her boots.

She lifted one foot at a time, and he took that as a good sign.

Nico met her gaze as he slipped his fingers into the waistband of her leggings. He held her stare as he dragged them down. He tried to go slow, but the instruction wasn't quite reaching that part of his brain. He managed to get one of her feet free before she grabbed him, pulling him against her, sealing their lips together once more.

Nico groaned low in his throat when Stevie began ripping at the button on his jeans. She had his cock free within seconds, yanking his jeans down his hips. He took over, sliding his hands under her ass and lifting her, forcing her to put her arms and legs around him. He pressed her back to the wall and crushed his mouth to hers.

Using the wall as leverage, he reached down and guided his cock between her legs.

He stopped, realizing they'd forgotten a step.

"No condom," he said on a ragged groan.

Stevie's eyes blazed with heat. "Do we stop?"

"I don't know. Do we?"

He knew she was on birth control. And neither of them had been with anyone else in a year. He trusted her implicitly and provided she trusted him, he saw no reason they had to. But Nico wasn't about to make that decision for her.

Stevie pressed her heel into his ass. "Fuck me, Nico."

He pressed the head of his cock against her tight entrance.

"Oh, fuck," he growled, her slick heat coating the head of his dick sent shockwaves through him.

He gripped her ass once again and held her in place as he drove in as deep as the position allowed. He pulled out, pushed in again. This time, Stevie tilted her hips, allowing him to bury himself to the hilt.

"You have to fuck me," Stevie whispered, her head resting on the wall. Eyes closed. "I need you to fuck me, Nico."

Watching her face, he began driving into her, fucking her with long, deep strokes. His pace had a natural progression as the minutes ticked by until he was slamming into her, fucking her as hard as he could.

They were both gasping and grunting, doing their best to be silent because there wasn't a lock on that door, and there was no telling who might be on the other side. The office had been empty when he came in here, but that could change at any time.

He pounded into her, taking every ounce of pleasure from her body as he could, all while his heart constricted in his chest. It had never been solely sex for him. Not even *that night*. He'd learned long ago that he wasn't wired that way. He didn't enjoy casual sex, and she was the reason.

That night with Stevie and Stone had opened his eyes. He'd felt something. A connection. One casual sex never gave him. He wanted that again. And yes, he wanted it with Stevie and Stone, even if they weren't at that point yet. Maybe they never would be, and he would be forced to decide. But right here, right now, there was only one person he knew he couldn't live without.

Her.

He pressed his mouth close to her ear. "Do you want this, Stevie?"

"Yes," she gasped. "Yes, Nico. God, yes."

"Do you want *me*, Stevie?"

"I've *always* wanted you," she said with a husky moan.

"Then we owe it to ourselves to see where it goes." He impaled her again and again, willing her to feel the connection between them. It was stronger than mere friendship, deeper than mere lust.

"I love you, Stevie. Always have."

Stevie's arms wreathed his head tightly as she pressed her face against his neck and cried out, the sound muffled. Her pussy clenched around him as she came. He came from the intensity of it, his cock lodged deep inside her.

Several minutes later, after they'd cleaned up and he'd returned to his office, Nico realized she hadn't said the words back to him. In fact, she hadn't said *anything*.

FOURTEEN

Wednesday, January 17, 2024

STEVIE'S PHONE CHIMED WITH ANOTHER ALERT. THEY were coming more frequently now. Evidently, the winter storm that the weather service was predicting was increasing in intensity and would be swinging into their area by the end of the week at the latest.

Shit. She had no more time to procrastinate.

Hopping up from her desk, Stevie grabbed her coat from the hook behind the door. She shoved her arms into it and felt for the key to ensure it was still in her pocket. It was.

"Hey, Tara!" she called to the receptionist as she grabbed her phone from her desk and started toward the door. "If Nico comes in, tell him I ran to the nursery."

Tara gave her a thumbs-up because she was on the phone.

"Oops." Stevie smiled sheepishly, then mouthed, "Sorry."

Holding her coat closed, she headed out into the frigid temperatures. They had no precipitation, so no sleet or snow meant no ice. Yet. Since the roads were clear, she could make the twenty-minute drive to the nearest nursery without incident. If she lived in a perfect world, they would have a plant nursery in Coyote Ridge. For as long as she could remember, that had been her plan. To open one. Only when she'd had the opportunity—thanks to her inheritance—she'd gotten cold feet. Instead, she'd gone a broader route, choosing the landscaping business because she knew it was the more resilient of the two options.

She didn't regret a single second. With Nico as a business partner, they'd made a name for themselves. And word of mouth was spreading. Just yesterday, they'd gotten a call from a real estate developer in south Austin looking for a unique perspective and wanted them to design the landscaping for their model homes. Nico hadn't been thrilled with the idea, but Stevie had talked him into entertaining it. After all, the goal was to eventually give Nico the ability to work solely on the design and not have to worry about the rest of it. They needed to have a steady client base for that to happen.

But right now, Stevie wasn't worried about Nico or potential clients. She was worried about the plants in the greenhouse. The upcoming freezing temperatures were going to wreak havoc if she didn't do something. She'd learned her lesson last year, but it had been too late because, by the time she realized the germination mats wouldn't cut it, she'd lost most of her vegetables and the few flowers she could grow in the colder season.

This year, she was determined to do things differently. Or at least that had been the goal. Unfortunately, like last year, she'd been banking on a relatively mild winter, so this cold snap caught her unawares.

So off to the nursery she went, hoping Byron Cartwright would have what she needed.

Forty-five minutes later, she was standing in the nursery, debating the benefits of various ways to heat a greenhouse, when she heard a familiar voice.

"Holy shit, dude," Byron said, his handsome face lighting up.

Stevie stepped to the side to see Stone approaching. His gaze briefly shifted to her before he grinned at Byron.

"Stone fuckin' Jameson. When'd you get back?"

Stevie watched as Byron and Stone exchanged one of those back-slapping hugs that men engaged in. Only theirs wasn't quite as platonic as she was expecting it to be. When Byron cupped the back of Stone's neck and pulled back only enough to meet his gaze, she thought for a second they were going to kiss.

Only they didn't.

She shook her head and looked away, giving them a moment to catch up. What was *wrong* with her? Just because Stone liked guys and Byron liked guys did not mean they'd ever liked each other. For one, Byron was *her* age.

Oh, wait. *She* was also her age and that hadn't stopped Stone from being with her. Or Nico, who was only a year older.

"Do you know Stevie Shepherd?" Byron said from behind her.

"I do, yes." Stone's voice was warm and friendly. "Was hopin' to run into you again."

"How do you two know each other?" she asked, realizing as soon as the words were out that it didn't sound casual.

Byron's grin was wide. "We had a thing back in high school."

Stevie's eyebrows lifted. "A thing?"

For fuck's sake, stop talking. But for some stupid reason, she couldn't help herself.

"You know I don't kiss and tell," Stone said in that seductive baritone.

Damn him for being so freaking sexy.

"Anyway." Byron laughed. "You in town for a while?"

"Back for good," Stone told him.

"Maybe we can grab a beer and catch up."

"I'd like that."

She cleared her throat, waiting for Byron to acknowledge her. "I'm gonna go with the radiant heat for now. If and when I ever build the greenhouse I want, I'll go with solar."

Byron nodded. "I'll grab the heaters and bring 'em to the front."

"Thanks." When Byron walked away, she glared at Stone. "Are you *stalkin'* me?"

"Oh, hey," Byron called out, turning around. "I pulled what your mom's lookin' for. It's ready when you are."

That wicked smirk slowly pulled at the side of Stone's mouth. "Thanks, man."

When Stone pivoted back around to face her, Stevie realized it was too late to make a quick escape. Her face was hot, her embarrassment impossible to ignore. She'd accused him of *stalking* her. Ego, much? Geez.

"Buyin' stuff for work?" Stone asked, nodding toward Byron's retreating back.

Taking a deep breath, she blew it out slowly and resigned herself to this conversation.

"A little of both. Personal and work," she admitted. "I grow a variety of flowers and plants that we use in Nico's designs. Plus, I've been growin' some root vegetables and leafy greens. They're all temperamental, so this weather's not helpin' matters. I lost everything last year."

Realizing she was rambling, she stopped and forced another smile.

"Is that what you enjoy doin'? Growin' thing?"

She met his gaze. "I enjoy doin' lots of things."

Stone held up his hands in front of him. "Didn't mean to offend."

And she hadn't meant to be defensive, but he brought that out in her.

"Sorry," she mumbled, meeting his gaze. "Stressful day."

"Understood."

His hazel eyes were warm and far too sexy for her to stare into for long. Whenever she did, she felt that familiar stirring deep inside. Despite the anger she still harbored, her body still ached for his. Stevie had never been able to deny her attraction to him. She remembered the first time she talked to him, back before their first milkshake date. Every cell in her body had come to life, and she'd floated on a cloud for days afterward. It was like the guy had a magic touch, and he knew exactly where to aim it without having to make physical contact.

"Damn, it's good to see you," Stone whispered.

Stevie swallowed hard and found herself nodding. She didn't want to agree with him, but it was good to see him. Really good. *Too* good.

Time to go. "I should go pay for my stuff," she told him, forcing her eyes toward the front of the building.

"I hope to see you around."

"Yeah. Maybe." Stevie walked away, wondering whether he'd forgotten he had invited her and Nico over for dinner. She had no intention of going, but it would really chap her ass if he'd already forgotten.

Then again, maybe it was for the best.

THIS WAS A SETUP. HAD TO BE.

After picking up the stuff his mother ordered from the nursery, Stone had driven around for a while. At first, he hadn't had a destination in mind, simply driving the backroads of the country town he'd grown up in. At some point, he started looking for land that was for sale, finding only a couple of tracts. Neither were large enough for what he needed, but he'd kept going.

About two hours in, he found himself on the highway heading to Embers Ridge. He wasn't sure what prompted him to think about Dead Heat Ranch, but as soon as he did, he wanted to take a look at the place, see if it was still up and running.

It was, so he'd stopped in to talk to Jerry Lambert. He figured the guy was old enough now he might be willing to sell. It had taken about three minutes to learn that Jerry no longer ran the ranch. His five daughters did. Stone didn't even need to ask to know that selling wasn't an option. Jerry had gotten a phone call and told Stone to look around. He'd wandered for a few minutes, and the next thing he knew, he was back in his truck, heading home.

The brief detour had given him absolutely no clarity on his life. The only thing he realized was that, at least right this minute, he didn't miss the chaos that came with ranch life. What that said about him and his future, he wasn't sure because if he didn't have ranch life, what did he have?

When he pulled up to the house to drop off the stuff he'd picked up for his mother at the nursery, he was grateful to see her standing outside. He wanted to talk to her. About what, he didn't know, but of all the people in his life, his mother was always the one who would give him straight answers when he asked difficult questions.

They never got around to the difficult questions, though.

When he pulled into the driveway, Deborah was standing in the yard, an iPad in her gloved hand. She looked like an Eskimo, complete with her Ugg boots, her sherpa-lined coat, and matching beanie, all bundled up like it was negative twenty, not a relatively comfortable forty-one degrees Fahrenheit. He was pretty sure she had on her robe underneath her coat.

"Are you warm enough?" he asked as he approached.

"I hate cold weather," she said, smiling brightly. "But I do like my cold weather gear."

Obviously.

Deborah glanced at the iPad screen, then to the yard, back to the screen. "Since you're here, I need a favor."

He held up the bag he'd gotten from the nursery. "Another one?"

"When you get a job, I won't ask you to run errands. Until that day happens…"

Touché.

She let the sentence hang, and since he had no recourse, Stone waited for her to relay what she needed him to do.

"Can you drop this off for me?" She dug in her coat pocket and pulled out an envelope.

"What is it?"

"A check?"

He took it when she passed it over. "Where?"

Her smile made him regret stopping to talk to her.

Now, as he drove out to D & S Landscape Solutions to drop off the check, he wondered why his mother couldn't simply pay with a credit or debit card online. He'd asked, of course, but her answer had been a shrug and another mischievous smile. Hence the reason he thought this was a setup.

Especially now as he stood inside what looked to be a nicely renovated double-wide trailer. Based on the layout, he was pretty sure it had once been someone's house. Some of the walls had been removed, replaced by structural support posts that surprisingly didn't look awkward. What was probably once the living room was now a reception area, complete with a desk but no receptionist.

On the other side, the space that likely had been reserved for the kitchen and dining area was now some sort of design spot. There were three small round tables, each with three chairs. On the tables, catalogs were set out. Probably a way to pass the time while waiting. The same went with the flat-screen television mounted on the wall. It was currently playing the mid-day news and the news cycle was all about the winter storm that was coming. He'd gotten his fill of warnings for the day, so he continued to scope the place. At one end of the house, some sort of refreshment station was set up. Two counters were separated down the middle by a small hallway that led to a bathroom, complete with a sign on the door.

Stone waited several minutes, expecting someone to appear, but no one did. He figured someone was here because there was one of the Dodge Rams with the company logo and one of those sporty new Ford Broncos parked in the small lot reserved for customers. Since he'd seen the same Bronco in the parking lot of the nursery, he figured it belonged to Stevie.

Was she here? Or had she gone out on a job? Was she with Nico? Did they have a receptionist or something?

Of course, whoever worked here could very well be out in the metal building adjacent to the house. There were several trucks with the same logo parked in front of it.

Figuring he would walk over to the building to see if he could find someone, Stone started for the door.

That was when he heard voices coming from the other end of the house. It looked like there were two rooms, one at the far end and one on the right, and a short hallway creating a path along the exterior wall.

He walked that way, hoping he could interrupt and pass over the check and be on his merry way. The last thing he wanted to do was run into Nico or Stevie and leave them with the impression he was stalking them. His run-in with Stevie had been awkward enough. More so because she clearly *expected* him to be stalking her.

Both rooms' doors were closed, but he could hear muffled voices behind one. He raised his hand to knock but paused when he heard his name.

That was definitely Nico and Stevie.

"Yeah? Where'd you see him?"

"At the nursery."

"And?"

"And nothin'. Did you know he used to have a thing with Byron Cartwright?"

"I didn't." There was a hint of amusement in Nico's voice.

"That doesn't bother you?"

"Should it?"

"I don't know." Stevie groaned. "I really wish…"

Stone held his breath, waiting for her to finish that sentence. *What? You really wish what, Stevie?*

Nico changed the subject. "Did y'all get a chance to talk?"

"No."

"You reconsidering havin' dinner with him?"

"No," she said adamantly.

Nico laughed.

How was that funny?

"You said no but nodded. So which is it?"

"I absolutely *hate* that he's so damn…" She growled.

"So damn what?" Nico asked. "Handsome? Sexy? Infuriating?"

Stone grinned. Good to know he could be both sexy *and* infuriating.

"Yes," she said. "All of the above."

"I think we should have dinner with him. Fifteen years is a long time."

"It is. It's a long freaking time for him to have never called."

Ouch. He deserved that.

"Maybe he had a good reason." Looked like Nico still saw the good in people.

"How is it so easy for you to forgive him for what he did?" she blasted.

Nico's voice rang with sympathy when he said, "Because he didn't do anything to me, Stevie. We had one night together. You were the one datin' him. He didn't owe me anything."

"He didn't owe me anything either," Stevie countered.

Yes, I did, Stone thought. *I owed you the truth. You deserved at least that much.*

"I think *you* should have dinner with him," Stevie said. "Maybe y'all can find some common ground. Maybe even find what you had with him back then."

Was Nico interested in what they had back then? As in one night, no holds barred? Or would he be open to something more?

"Stevie, it's dinner," Nico huffed. "Nothin' more."

"You don't know that."

Yeah. You don't know that.

"I do. But if you're not goin', I'm not goin'."

Well, hell.

Stone heard the faint sound of movement, and instinct told him he needed to hustle out of the way because someone was coming. But he didn't back away from the door. He wanted to hear more. He wanted to hear them change their minds. He didn't know why he cared so damn much, but he did. Seeing them again ... Stone wanted a chance to catch up. He wasn't expecting anything other than dinner and some conversation. Maybe some laughs tossed in.

Liar.

Fine. He was *hoping* for more, but he had no expectations. After all, it had been fifteen years since he'd seen them. All three of them had changed over the course of that time. Stone wasn't sure he would have anything in common with them anymore.

"Let me know when you're ready to go," Nico said. "If the weather gets bad, I'll drive."

Stone stepped back because Nico's voice came from just on the other side of the door.

And then it opened, and there he was.

Stone instantly held up the check. "Here."

"Hey," Nico greeted, taking a step back, his forehead creased with his surprise.

Stone peered around him to see Stevie sitting at a desk, her eyes wide.

"It's a check," he explained. "My mother asked me to drop it off."

"She could've paid online," Stevie stated.

Of course she could. Not only had she set him up, but now he looked like a fucking moron.

"You could've given it to Tara," Nico told him.

Stone glanced at the empty reception desk, assuming that was where Tara belonged. Nico peeked out of the office.

"Ah." He looked at Stevie. "You know where she went?"

"No idea."

"Here," Stone said, shoving the envelope in Nico's hand. "I should go."

As he made his way to the door, he could still hear bits and pieces of their conversation.

I think you *should have dinner with him.*

If you're not goin', I'm not goin'.

Stone paused with his hand on the doorknob. He glanced down the hall to see Nico staring back at him.

"About dinner tomorrow…" He swallowed the lump in his throat. "I'm gonna have to get a raincheck. A lot of stuff goin' on."

Nico nodded, but he didn't argue, didn't suggest a better day.

Not that Stone had expected him to.

Feeling like an idiot, he walked out the same way he'd come, not bothering to look back. Even as he got in his truck, he swore he could feel Nico's eyes on him.

FIFTEEN

AFTER OVERHEARING THE CONVERSATION BETWEEN STEVIE AND Nico, Stone spent a solid week sulking.

And then he spent another week hating himself for it.

As punishment, he forced himself out of the house. He spent time in town, interacting with people he hadn't seen in years. He went to the diner for meals, got full on good food and interesting rumors. He went to Moonshiners for drinks, got a pleasant reminder of the energy that this town had. He went to the General Store when he was bored, spending time with his sister because, as had always been the case, he found being around Reilly the easiest thing in the world to do.

In between, he dealt with the occasional encounter with Stevie and Nico. Although they were rare, Stone found himself looking forward to even the slightest glimpse. It was slow going, but they were exchanging pleasantries, and Stevie was no longer glaring at him. He considered that progress, but he knew he would have to take action if he wanted them to move forward.

Which he did. More than anything.

Only there was one problem. He'd been back for three weeks, and he'd made absolutely zero progress in getting his life on track. His career path was still up in the air, and though he was rekindling friendships, that wasn't exactly where he'd envisioned himself at this point.

It didn't help that he still had boxes that needed to be unpacked. Seeing them sitting there made him wonder whether that was his subconscious's way of telling him this might not be where he belonged.

Now, as he stared at those boxes, he sipped his coffee and reminded himself that this was where he was supposed to be. From the moment he got back to town, he'd felt the sense of belonging he'd left behind years ago. It had come flooding back. And then seeing Stevie and Nico…

"This *is* where you belong," he said aloud, setting his coffee cup on the counter before wandering over to grab one of the boxes.

The least he could do was finish unpacking.

So that was what he did. Unpacking more of his boxes, using the empty ones to pack up a few of Reilly's things that she'd left behind. There wasn't much. Not enough to fill one small box, but he set it aside so he could drop it off at the store later. At the very least, it would give him something to do.

Unfortunately, they'd had some sleet overnight, and more was expected in the afternoon, so it didn't make sense for him to drive around. Wasting gas and risking running his truck into a ditch was not high on his list of things to do.

At noon, he made himself a sandwich, but before he could take a single bite, his cell phone rang.

He glanced at the screen, concern filling him. "Hey, Uncle Curtis. How're you doin'? Everything okay?"

"Just soakin' up some peace and quiet before the weekend."

Stone didn't know why, but the gruff sound of his uncle's voice had always had a calming effect. Growing up, he'd been close to his aunts, uncles, and most of his cousins. Enough that he found himself awash with nostalgia each time he heard Curtis's familiar voice.

"All those grandkids keep you on your toes, huh?" Stone teased.

"On my toes *and* my ass," he huffed. "You think maybe you could make time to stop by today or tomorrow?"

The request surprised him. "Stop by? Your place?"

"Yep."

Of course his uncle wasn't going to elaborate. Where was the fun in that? Instead, Curtis let the silence hang until Stone had no choice but to fill it with a response.

Stone glanced at the clock. "Sure. I could get by there today. Give me an hour?"

"We'll be here. I'll make sure there's a pot of coffee on."

"See you then."

Stone disconnected the call and stared at his phone, wondering what Uncle Curtis might want.

He couldn't remember the last time any of his aunts or uncles had called him. He saw them at holiday get-togethers. Some of them, anyway. Stone's dad, like Reilly, was the youngest, but he had eight older siblings, five of whom were still alive. His sisters, Celeste and Katherine, had died when Owen was four, and his sister, Adele, had died almost twenty years ago. That left Lorrie, Mitch, Bruce, Rose, and Linda. One of the benefits of living in a small town was that they saw each other often. Stone knew from experience that being away from family wasn't easy. It was another reason he was bound and determined to put down roots here.

After he finished his sandwich, he cleaned up the kitchen, trying his best not to leave too early. He didn't want Uncle Curtis to think he was just sitting on his thumbs, waiting for someone to call and invite him over.

When he ran out of ways to be productive, he pulled on his coat and hat and headed out.

Getting to Curtis and Lorrie's took twenty minutes because the roads were getting bad. The weather service was telling people to stay home if they could. Their warning wasn't too far-fetched, considering Stone nearly drove off the road twice due to some black ice on the less traveled back roads.

Thankfully, he reached his aunt and uncle's place without incident. Aunt Lorrie welcomed him at the back door, urging him inside and taking his coat.

"It's gettin' colder," she said as she walked over to the coffee pot. "I'm not a fan. These old bones prefer warmth."

Stone grinned. Lorrie was seventy-five years young and looked as youthful as she always had. There was a seventeen-year age difference between Lorrie and Stone's dad, so she was more like a mother to Owen than his own mother had been. Then again, Phillip and Dorothy Jameson hadn't been the best parents in the world. Some even said Stone's grandfather was the spawn of Satan. Not that Stone would know. The man died before he was born.

"You take it with milk and sugar, right?"

"Yes, ma'am."

While she prepared his coffee, Stone looked around the kitchen, then glanced into the living room. The house was just the same as he remembered growing up. He'd spent a lot of time over here despite Curtis and Lorrie's boys being older than him. All except Zane, who was a couple of years younger. As kids, they'd run around together at family gatherings, but as they got older, they never really became friends.

Of course, he'd lost touch after he left, only seeing most of them on rare occasions. It was his own fault, he knew, and he was hoping he could reconnect with some of them now that he was back.

"There you are, boy," Curtis said as he strolled into the room. He was wearing his usual Wranglers and boots, along with a long-sleeve shirt covered by a thick flannel shirt, which was unbuttoned, the cuffs rolled up.

"Hey," Stone said, walking over to shake Curtis's hand.

As always, Curtis took his hand like he was going to be formal, then jerked him in for a hug.

Lorrie chuckled, delivering two mugs of coffee and going back for a third.

"Have a seat," Curtis said when he released him. "Your daddy tells me you're back for good. That right?"

Stone knew that his parents were close to Curtis and Lorrie. Always had been. They got together frequently, and not only to celebrate birthdays or holidays. It wasn't until Stone went out into the world that he realized that sort of closeness wasn't the norm. It was one of the things he'd missed most while he was gone.

"Yes, sir," he said, pulling out a chair and planting his butt in it.

"What made you decide to do that? You've been gone, what? Fifteen years?"

"Give or take a week," he joked. "I wish I could say I got the itch to come back, but it was circumstance."

"You got caught with the boss's daughter."

"Curtis," Lorrie admonished.

Curtis laughed. "What? It's true, ain't it?"

"Yes, sir, it is," Stone admitted, taking a sip of his coffee.

"I know your mama and daddy are glad you're back," Lorrie told him.

"Yeah. Mom's got me runnin' errands for her right now."

Curtis's eyebrow lifted. "'Cause you ain't got a job."

Stone laughed but felt his cheeks heat from embarrassment. Curtis never did pull his punches. It was amazing how the man could pin that blue-gray stare on him and make him feel like he was sixteen, not thirty-six.

"You got any money saved up?"

"Yes, sir." He had enough to keep him afloat for a good long time at the pace he was going. If he wanted to live in his parents' barn for the foreseeable future, that is. Which he didn't.

"Jerry Lambert called me up yesterday," Curtis said, leaning back in his chair. "Mentioned you stopped by there."

"I did. Thought I'd see how they were managin'."

"You still wantin' to be a rancher?"

Stone glanced between his aunt and uncle, wondering how much he should tell them. Just being there made him want to open up and reveal everything because his family didn't judge. Could he use them as a sounding board?

"It's been my plan for a long time," he admitted, wrapping his hands around his coffee mug and staring into it. "Not sure I'm still lookin' to take the same path, but I'd like somethin' along those lines. Farming's an option I've considered, too."

Curtis gestured toward the back door. "You think you could do anything with what we've got here?"

Stone frowned. He was confused. Curtis owned a large portion of land because, at one time, the Walkers had owned every inch of the town. Back before Curtis renamed it Coyote Ridge in Lorrie's honor, it had been Granite Creek, named for the tributary of the San Gabriel River that ran through the town. From the stories he'd heard, Curtis's father had rented out some of the land to others, and when Curtis inherited it, he'd dissolved those debts, gifting the land to the renters and, ultimately, giving the town a chance to thrive.

"It ain't gettin' much use anymore," Curtis said when Stone didn't respond. "Ethan and Braydon are the only ones still livin' on it. They've got no interest in any more than what they've got. We've rented out a couple of the boys' houses, but we ain't gettin' any younger. Plus, we've still got a few thousand acres left that we haven't figured out what to do with. We'll be leavin' that to the boys when the time comes."

Stone glanced at Lorrie, curious if she might clue him in on what Curtis was getting at. She was looking at her husband with the same love he'd always seen in her eyes whenever she looked at anyone in her family.

Curtis sat forward, resting his forearms on the table. "I guess what I'm tryin' to say is, are you interested?"

"In your land?"

"Yep." He waved a hand. "Not all of it, mind you. But a good portion."

Stone wasn't sure what constituted a *good portion.*

Curtis continued. "Out here, I'd say you're good with about one cow per three acres. Four acres for a mature bull. We've got about four hundred acres we're willin' to part with. Part of it's on this side of the road. The rest is on the other side. We've rented out three acres to that landscapin' company. They've got a fifty-year lease, so you won't be able to touch it. You'd own it, though. Collect rent or whatnot."

Holy shit.

Stone glanced between the two of them.

"Provided you've got a plan," Lorrie noted. "You'd need a business proposal, of course."

"Of course." He'd actually been working on one for some time. Back when he thought he'd take over the Double J, Stone had wanted to prove to Doug that he was serious and capable.

"The boys agreed they'd be willin' to let it go as long as it stays in the family," Lorrie added.

"And provided it'll be used for somethin' worthwhile," Curtis tacked on. "There are stipulations: no retail shit, no big master-planned housin' communities. The soil's fertile. Perfect for farmin' or grazin'."

Stone wasn't sure what to say.

"It's contingent on a couple of things," Lorrie explained. "First, you've got to stay here. In Coyote Ridge."

"I'm doin' that," he told them. "No matter what path I take."

Curtis nodded, looking at his wife to continue.

"You'll have to agree not to sell it for one hundred years. That goes for your children, too. And when the time comes that it is sold, the Walkers and Jamesons'll have first option to buy at market value."

"Makes sense." Stone wasn't sure who he was supposed to look at, so he directed his question at both of them. "How much're we talkin', though?"

Lorrie looked at Curtis.

"I paid nothin' for it," he said. "It's been in my family for generations. I want it to stay there. One thing people forget is that it's not about the money."

That was generally what people with money said, but Stone didn't mention it.

"It'll be a gift."

Stone choked down his surprise.

Curtis pinned him with that blue-gray stare. "Just keep in mind, gifts like that don't come free. You incur responsibility for others when you get handed a gift like that. It's your job to help those who need help."

Stone swallowed. Was that why Curtis was the way he was? Because he saw good fortune as a reason to help others? It explained a lot. Stone had always admired his aunt and uncle for the things they did for this town. He'd never met anyone as generous as them.

But he still had one question. "Why me?"

"Why *not* you?" Curtis countered instantly.

"You've got a couple dozen nieces and nephews. Why not one of them?"

Not to mention seven sons and all those grandkids.

"Fifty-seven," Lorrie said with pride. "We've got fifty-seven nieces and nephews."

It was a big number, but not so big when you considered Curtis and Lorrie each had seven siblings. Big families produced big families. At least that was what his mother always said.

"Out of those fifty-seven," Curtis said, meeting Stone's stare. "One of 'em has been chasin' a dream and gettin' in his own way at every turn. "

"Yeah." Stone looked down at the table. "I've gotten good at that."

"You have," Curtis agreed. "But sometimes, it's that one who's capable of holdin' everything together. Even if he doesn't know it yet."

Lorrie reached over and touched his hand. "I think if you look close enough, you might see that everything you've ever wanted has been here all along."

Stone wouldn't dispute that. He'd thought the same thing when he saw Stevie again. He'd felt an echo of what he'd felt for her as though not a single day had passed. He had his work cut out for him, that was for sure.

"Are you interested, boy?" Curtis asked, his eyes warm.

"Yes, sir."

He smiled. "I guess you'll have to figure out if you're interested in countin' bushels and bales or heads and tails."

In other words, farm versus ranch.

"We'll expect a business proposal in fourteen days," Lorrie stated. "Plus, you'll need to talk to the boys."

"In person," Curtis tacked on. "Don't do that whole textin' or emailin' nonsense. Face to face. Tell 'em your plans. Get their buy-in. You'll need it."

"Yes, sir. I can do that."

His uncle smiled. "Good. I'm lookin' forward to the next time we meet."

Stone was, too.

Fifteen minutes later, after saying his goodbyes and promising to get them the information they requested, Stone left Curtis and Lorrie's.

His head was swimming, and he wasn't sure what he was feeling—surprise, anxiety, hope, or maybe a mixture of all of it. He felt as though he was outside his body, watching himself. It was surreal.

And there was only one thing he wanted to do.

As he was heading back toward town, he passed D & S Landscape Solutions. As soon as he did, he hit the brakes. A second passed before he found himself backing up and taking a turn down the narrow drive that led to their office. He wanted to talk to Stevie, so he figured it was a good place to start. His conversation with his aunt and uncle had given him an idea.

As he pulled up to the D & S office, it started to rain harder—a mixture of rain and sleet, to be more specific.

Figuring it wasn't going to get any better, he hopped out of his truck and bounded up the steps. He thought for sure the door was going to be locked, so he stumbled forward when it opened.

He took off his hat when he walked in, once again encountering no one at the reception desk.

"Anyone here?" he called out. The last thing he wanted to do was overhear a conversation like the last one. He'd spent the better part of two weeks being pissed off at himself for making Stevie hate him so much she wasn't willing to have dinner with him.

Not that he didn't deserve it. He'd done her wrong, promising he would come back and that he would call her. He never did because he hadn't meant the words he'd told her. When he left, he did so with the sole intention of moving on and letting her do the same.

Now, here he was years later, regretting that he'd been so stupid.

He looked toward the offices. "Nico? Stevie?"

Stone heard mumbling, but he didn't move from his spot.

A second later, Nico appeared, holding his cell phone to his ear and motioning for Stone to come to his office.

Nico continued his conversation, gesturing toward the empty guest chair. "Yeah. I hear ya. We're dealin' with the same."

Stone took a seat and peered around the space. It was much nicer than he'd expected it to be. On the wall were several framed certificates. On a shelf nearby were some small glass statues. They looked like awards of some sort.

The desk was free of clutter. It held a laptop and a small lamp. A black leather cup holder held several pens and more than a dozen pencils.

He wondered whether Nico was as neat and tidy all the time. Was his house the same? Or was this an exception because he didn't want his customers to think he was a slob? He had at least two dozen more similar questions because the truth was, Stone didn't know Nico all that well, and most of it was hearsay. Back in the day, Nico had been dating Chelsea, so Stone only knew what she'd shared with the rest of the family. Which, like most teenagers, revolved around how good-looking he was.

"Sorry about that," Nico said, drawing Stone out of his thoughts. "Did you need somethin'?"

"I came by to see if Stevie was here."

Nico's forehead creased, and Stone could tell he wasn't exactly pleased by that revelation, but he didn't ask why Stone wanted to see her. However, the question lingered in his eyes, so Stone opted to enlighten him.

"It's business-related," he explained. "I saw her at the nursery a coupla weeks ago. She was talkin' to Byron."

Nico still didn't prompt him to continue, but Stone didn't want him to think he was there trying to poach the woman.

"I just came from my aunt and uncle's—Lorrie and Curtis. I'm workin' on a business plan. For some of his land. I was wonderin' if she could answer a few questions for me. Regardin' greenhouses."

It wasn't exactly the full truth, but it was close enough.

Nico nodded, steepling his fingers, his wrists resting on his flat stomach as he leaned back in his chair. "I sent her home. The weather's supposed to get worse. I didn't want her drivin' in it."

Stone nodded and got to his feet. "Then I guess I'll stop by another time."

"You could go by the house," Nico said, also standing.

Stone was surprised by the suggestion. "I'm not sure she'll be thrilled with me showin' up on your doorstep."

Nico sighed. "You hurt her, Stone. When you left. What do you expect?"

"I know." Stone looked down at his boots. "I'd like the chance to apologize, but I know it'll never be enough."

"Stevie doesn't hold a grudge forever. I mean, she forgave me." A smile tugged at his mouth. "Eventually."

Stone frowned, peering up. "For what?"

"After you left, she blamed me for it."

"It had nothin' to do with you."

"I know that," he said earnestly. "But she was heartbroken. It was easier for her to blame me than the guy she was in love with."

Shit.

Stone met Nico's stare. "If it's any consolation, walkin' away from her is my biggest regret. I'd do it all over again, though." He gestured toward the space. "I would've held her back, and it looks to me like she's happy."

"She's successful," Nico clarified. "That doesn't mean she's happy. She pretends she is. But she's livin' *my* dream, not hers."

Stone wanted to ask him to explain that, but he refrained. Instead, he started walking toward the door. "Could you tell her I came by?"

"No."

He turned and looked at Nico, surprised by his adamant tone.

"Go by the house," Nico said. "Talk to her. You'll know where you stand if she sends you on your way. The least you can do is make an effort."

Stone stood taller. "I'd like to think I've been makin' an effort."

"By backin' out of dinner?"

"It saved y'all from havin' to cancel on me," he shot back.

Nico's eyes widened. "You heard that."

"Yeah."

Nico rolled his eyes. "It doesn't matter. One canceled dinner or not, you've been back less than a month, Stone. You haven't had *enough time* to make an effort."

"I invited her to dinner," he said hotly, not enjoying where this conversation was going.

Nico moved toward him. "Yeah. That was a half-ass request, and you know it. And you didn't invite *her*. You invited both of us."

Stone held his ground. "My mistake. I thought y'all were a matched set at this point."

"Don't start with bullshit excuses. That's beneath you. If you're lookin' to make amends with Stevie, you—"

Stone stepped toward him until they were practically toe to toe. "She's not the only one I walked away from."

Nico's mouth opened, then closed quickly.

Considering Stevie was doing her best to keep her distance, Stone figured this was his best chance to lay it all on the line. It might not make a damn bit of difference, but he knew he had to try.

"I was in love with her, Nico, so yeah, I owe her an apology. She deserves that much. But that night changed me. *You* changed me. I didn't just leave because of her. I left because I was feelin' somethin' I didn't fully understand."

Stone thought for sure that would spur some response, but Nico didn't say a word.

"I'll be honest with you. Walkin' away again is not in my plan. I asked you both to dinner because I wanted to know if there's even a chance of findin' a way back into your lives. Both of you."

Nico swallowed.

"As friends," he clarified but held Nico's stare. "Unless there's an option for more."

Again, Nico remained mute.

NICO HAD NO IDEA WHAT HE WAS supposed to say to that. It was exactly what he'd hoped to hear from Stone, but he damn sure hadn't expected it.

Stone lowered his voice. "Is that an option, Nico?"

Was it? "Maybe."

It was apparent his answer wasn't what Stone expected. "That's all I needed to hear."

As soon as Stone turned to leave, Nico reacted. He grabbed his arm, gripping but not hurting, wanting to halt his progress but unsure what else he wanted.

Stone decided for him, grabbing the front of his shirt and jerking him forward. Nico nearly plowed him over, but Stone was prepared, cupping his jaw to steady him as their mouths crashed together.

He was shocked, but not enough to pull back. He kissed Stone like the starving man he was, his tongue sliding into Stone's mouth, battling for dominance. Stone let him take the reins for a brief moment, but as was the case all those years ago, Stone's dominance won out. The grip on Nico's jaw tightened as Stone grabbed his belt loop with the other. In one swift move, Stone pivoted, and Nico found himself against the wall, Stone's big body pinning him in place.

Stone wasn't kissing him, but he wasn't moving away. They stood there, lips hovering for several heartbeats before Stone finally spoke.

"The desire's never gone away. For her or you. I've wanted her since the day I met her. That hasn't changed. But *I* did. That night. I had a taste of somethin' I didn't think even existed."

Nico was trying to process the words, but he wasn't sure if Stone even had a point.

"I've wanted *you* since that night. The same as I want her. That's what scared the shit out of me. I didn't want to go back to what it was before. I wanted *both of you*. Together. Stevie didn't sign on for that. Neither did you."

But Nico would have if Stone had simply stuck around long enough to find out.

And suddenly, it made more sense. Although Nico wanted the same thing back then, Stevie hadn't signed up for that. She'd been Stone's girlfriend at the time. The two of them in a monogamous relationship. *That night* had been an anomaly, a one-time thing. Or it should have been. If Stone wanted more, it made sense that he'd distanced himself.

Not that Stevie would understand since she was the one Stone left. Nico got it, though. He understood because he'd felt the same way.

Stone's eyes implored him. "Does somethin' like that even work?"

"A threesome?"

"No. I know that works. But does it work when two turns into three?"

"Yes," Nico said, his hand fisting in Stone's shirt.

Stone pulled back, meeting his gaze. "You think so?"

"With Stevie? Yes." Nico truly believed that. "But you should know I love her. I'll do everything in my power to protect her. Even if it's from you."

"Is that a threat?"

There was no vehemence in Stone's tone, but Nico answered seriously. "It's a promise."

To his dismay, Stone released him and took a step back. "I'm sorry. That was…" He exhaled heavily. "I keep forgettin' you and Stevie are together."

"We're not," Nico said, but he didn't reach for him. He remained against the wall, fearing his legs wouldn't hold him up. "We're friends."

"With benefits?"

Nico nodded.

"And you love her?"

"Yeah."

"Does she know that?"

He'd told her as much, but since Stevie hadn't brought it up at all, he wasn't sure she'd heard him. That, or she didn't reciprocate and didn't want to hurt him by saying as much.

Nico went with the simple answer, shaking his head. "And I'd like to keep it that way."

"Maybe she should."

"If I thought we could find what we're lookin' for, maybe I'd tell her."

"I don't know what that means."

"You weren't the only one who was changed by the events of that night, Stone. You left a hole when you left. In both of us. It became a spot that needed to be filled, but neither of us knew how to do that."

Stone's eyes glittered with something Nico couldn't identify. Hope? Disbelief? He wasn't sure.

Nico's gaze shifted to Stone's mouth. He wanted to kiss him again, to feel that rush he'd felt a few moments ago.

Stone took a step closer, but he didn't kiss him. His fingertips brushed over Nico's bottom lip. "I get it. I do," he said, his voice barely audible. "No one's ever made me feel that … spark. Only you and Stevie." Stone's gaze lifted. "But I need to talk to Stevie first. She already said she has no desire to get mixed up with me again. The last damn thing I want is to make her hate me even more."

Nico took that as his cue, pushing off the wall and walking back to his desk to pick up his phone. "Go to the house. Give me your number, and I'll text you the address."

Stone rattled off the number, then added, "You might wanna warn her I'm stoppin' by."

Nico shook his head. "If I do that, she won't answer the door. Y'all have to talk. Sooner rather than later."

Stone glanced down at the phone when the text came through. "I hope you know what you're doin'."

Nico did, too. "I've got to meet with a client. Today's the only day they can do it. I'll be home after that. If you're still there, maybe we can have dinner tonight."

"Dinner would be good."

With that, Stone walked out the door.

SIXTEEN

"JÄGER, NO! WAIT! COME HERE!" STEVIE SHOUTED, chasing the puppy around the kitchen island.

He thought it was a game because she was chasing him with a towel in the hopes of drying him off. What she'd thought would be a quick potty break had turned into fifteen minutes of him playing in the yard. Normally, it wouldn't be a problem, except it was sleeting. He would stand there, wait until the little ice pellets clung to his fur, and then give a whole body shake before doing it again. At first, it was cute. Now she was worried he was going to catch a cold.

"Maybe Nico was right," she said when she managed to get her arms around him, lifting him in the towel. "Trouble is a good name for you."

The doorbell rang.

Jäger stopped wiggling, his attention lasering in on the front door. He let out a little yap.

"Who could that possibly be?" She set him on the floor. "Did Nico forget his key again? I told him to keep his truck key with his other keys and not in his pocket, but he won't listen. Serves him right, huh? It's crazy to be out in this weather."

With a smile, Stevie went to the door and pulled it open, keeping an eye on Jäger so she didn't accidentally hit him with it. She was giggling at the puppy when she looked up and found Stone standing on the front porch.

Instantly, the smile was gone, and she pretended that she wasn't staring at the most gorgeous cowboy in existence. And the man was downright gorgeous. He was wearing a black felt Stetson on his head and a bulky, black Carhartt coat, his hands tucked into his pockets. It wasn't zipped, and she could see a glimpse of maroon beneath. His long legs were clad in Wranglers that were worn in all the places that hugged his impressive lower body. The boots on his feet looked like they'd seen quite a bit of action over the years.

"What're you doin' here?" She frowned, forcing herself to meet his gaze. "How'd you even know where I live?"

"Nico gave me the address. I went by the office to talk to you. He said I should come by here."

Blasted man. She was going to make him pay for that.

A gust of wind battered Stone as he stood there. He managed to grab his hat before it was blown off his head.

Stevie knew from the deepest recesses of her soul that she was so going to regret this. "Come in."

While he opened the screen, she picked up Jäger. He was doing a full-body wiggle, excited about a visitor. At least one of them was.

Stone walked in, his gaze shifting over the space. She was grateful she'd taken the time to clean up. It hadn't been on her list of things to do (because it never was), but with Jäger, she was finding either she kept her stuff off the floor, or he ended up with it in his mouth. They hadn't had him a full month yet, and she'd already had to toss three socks (none of them matching), a pair of flip-flops, one slipper (she still hadn't found the other one), and what had been a perfectly good hairbrush before Jäger chewed the handle off.

"Beautiful place."

"Thanks. You can hang your coat on the rack."

He turned to look in the direction she was pointing as he shrugged out of his coat.

"It's Nico's. The house, I mean. He bought it when he was with Melanie. His ex. She wanted somethin' big and fancy. All about perception, that one. And Nico … well, he was tryin' to convince himself he could be happy with her." Stevie spread her arms wide. "He ended up with this."

"Does it make him happy?" Stone asked as he hung his hat beside his coat and removed his boots, leaving them near the door.

"I think it's growin' on him. I love it. It's huge. Almost four thousand square feet. Open floor plan." She was rambling, but she couldn't help it. He made her nervous. "There's a huge game room upstairs. We turned it into an office. Plus, it sits on five acres with no one behind us. What's not to love?"

Now that his hat was off, she could tell he'd gotten a haircut since the last time she saw him. With the sides and back shaved short and the top stylishly messy, he looked much more like the boy she'd fallen in love with all those years ago.

Damn him.

"Can I get you somethin' to drink? I was gonna make hot chocolate. But I can make some coffee."

"I wouldn't say no to coffee."

Funny, that was the same thing Nico always said when she tried to get him to have hot chocolate. Was she the only one in the world who loved hot chocolate?

"What's up, little guy?" Stone crouched down to pet Jäger. "I think you've grown since I last saw you."

"He eats like a horse," she said as she opened the cabinet to pull out the coffee. "I *hate* that he's eatin' processed food, but the fresh stuff is so expensive. I told Nico I wanted to create my own recipe and make it for him. I know I can come up with somethin' that's healthy and a helluva lot cheaper. But I wanna talk to the vet first. I've never had a dog before. Wouldn't wanna give him somethin' that's not good for him. Or, you know, toxic."

Realizing she had verbal diarrhea, Stevie pinched her lips shut and dumped the coffee grounds into the filter before flipping on the switch.

"You can have a seat anywhere," she said when she turned around to find him standing in the kitchen, Jäger in his arms.

"Is he allowed on the couch?"

"He now owns the place," she told him, grabbing the milk from the refrigerator and a glass measuring cup from the cabinet. "Nico just pays the mortgage."

Stone laughed.

Stevie put the measuring cup, now filled with milk, into the microwave and grabbed the bucket of powdered cocoa. It was one of her guilty pleasures. She even kept some on hand all year round.

"Plus, he sleeps in Nico's bed," she continued. "I snuck him in mine one night, but when I woke up, he was gone. Since he won't jump down on his own yet, I know Nico stole him. Freaked me out at first. I thought I squished him. We got him a kennel"—she pointed to the medium-sized cage with the padded mattress—"but it's takin' some time to get him used to it. I read somewhere that they feel safer in there, so that's what we're tryin' to do. Get him to sleep in it."

And she was doing it again.

Taking a deep breath, she reminded herself she hated this man.

Although hate was a pretty strong word. She'd definitely hated him fifteen years ago, back when he shattered her heart into tiny fragments that had rattled around in her chest for years. Now, she wasn't exactly sure how she felt about him. It really sucked that he'd gotten better looking with age. He was still big. Muscular and ridiculously tall. He made Nico look small in comparison, although he wasn't.

She scooped a generous amount of cocoa into her cup and stole glances at Stone. It irked her that he was sitting on the floor playing with Jäger. Only good guys played with dogs like that. In her mind, she'd built Stone up to be this total asshole. The kind who snapped at old ladies and snatched the last gallon of milk when a single mom and her scraggly little kid were about to reach for it. It'd been the easiest way to deal with the residual heartache she felt. But she should've known Stone would still be the same, fun-loving, nice guy he'd always been.

"How do you take your coffee?"

Stone looked up. The moment his eyes met hers, she felt a blast of heat. He still looked at her the same way he had back then. Like someone just rang the dinner bell, and she was on the menu.

"Little sugar, splash of milk."

She had to put effort into remembering to breathe as she tore her gaze from his and grabbed what she needed. When the coffee pot was half full, she pulled it from the warmer and poured him a cup.

By the time she joined him, Stone was sitting on the couch with Jäger curled up beside him, fast asleep.

"You have a secret for that?" she asked, nodding toward the puppy as she passed him the coffee mug. "When I'm with him, he won't stop movin'."

"He doesn't realize you're in charge."

But you are. And he always had been. Without even trying, Stone could dominate an entire room. She'd been in awe of it. And yes, turned on by it back in the day.

"So, what brings you by?" she asked, forcing herself not to think about the past. Or him laying her out on the couch and having his wicked way with her right now. Or her curling up on his other side and falling fast asleep like Jäger.

Yeah. She was ridiculous. So what?

"My aunt and uncle called me this mornin'," Stone explained. "Asked me to come by. They know I've been lookin' for some land to buy."

"To build a fancy bull breedin' ranch, right?"

As soon as the words were out of her mouth, Stevie realized he'd never told her that. She'd picked up bits and pieces over the years, usually from running into Reilly or Donovan at the General Store. From time to time, Stevie would ask how he was doing. It usually got her the low-down.

Based on the sparkle in Stone's eyes, he realized he'd never told her that, either.

"Yeah," he said. "That was my original plan."

She sipped hot chocolate and pretended this was just a casual conversation between casually acquainted people. "But not anymore?"

"I don't know." His expression shifted from smoldering to contemplative. "At one point in my life, that's all I wanted. Now … especially if this opportunity comes through, I think I wanna go a different route."

Figuring he would relay what that was, Stevie waited.

"Then I talked to Nico at the office, and he said somethin' that made me want to do somethin' … else."

"Sounds like you don't know what you want."

His eyes took on that smoldering look again. "Baby, I've always known what I wanted. That wasn't the problem."

Baby. For fifteen years, she'd despised that word as a term of endearment. But when Stone said it, she was shot right back in time to when it made her feel like the most precious thing in his world.

Her insides clenched, and she found she couldn't look away from him. He was talking about her. She knew he was. This was her opportunity to tell him he'd missed his chance, but she couldn't get the words out. Her throat was constricted by a knot of emotion.

So she waited, praying he had more to say.

STONE DIDN'T MEAN TO SAY THAT.

It was the truth, yeah, but he'd come here in a professional capacity. His last encounter with Stevie hadn't gone quite the way he'd hoped, and he didn't want to risk a repeat. Not this soon, anyway.

It wasn't that he was ready to give up on talking to Stevie. Quite the opposite. But he was willing to give her space. With some time, he hoped she would come around, be willing to have him in her life again. He understood why she was hesitant to talk to him about what happened when he left. It had been a cowardly move on his part, and he owed her more than an apology. He owed her an explanation.

"I'm sorry," he told her. "I didn't mean—"

"What *was* the problem then?"

That was new. The Stevie from fifteen years ago never would've questioned him. It wasn't that she'd been amenable to everything he said or did; it was that they'd never gotten onto subjects that required her to voice a different opinion. Back then, they'd gone from getting to know one another on a friendly, casual level to a sexual exploration that had taken over everything.

"Me," he said truthfully.

"So it wasn't that you were freaked out because the three of us had sex?"

"Freaked out? No."

Stevie snorted.

"I wasn't freaked," he assured her. "Obsessed, maybe."

And he hadn't meant to say *that* either.

Her eyes narrowed. "Obsessed?"

Stone nodded, considering his words carefully. This was a touchy subject. Not the threesome part, but the fact he'd left town. He wanted to give her an explanation that made sense.

Unfortunately, he didn't have one.

"It was all I could think about for two days after," he admitted.

Her eyes shifted over his face, but he couldn't read what she was thinking. "What made it different than all the other times you'd done it?"

He couldn't blame her for thinking that. He'd had a reputation for screwing pretty much anyone back in the day.

"That's the only time I'd ever done somethin' like that."

"Really?" She snorted again. "The town playboy never shared his girlfriend with another guy?"

He pretended not to hear the utter disgust that dripped from every word.

"You're the only girlfriend I've ever had."

Her eyes widened. She obviously noticed that he wasn't referring to past tense. It was true. He'd never had a girlfriend before or after her. Yeah, he'd had some ongoing sexual relationships with women, but nothing serious. He'd never made any promises or claimed he would be monogamous. Only with Stevie.

"What about boyfriends?"

"Never had one of those either."

"But you've been with other men? Since you left, I mean."

"Yes." He wasn't going to lie to her.

"Have you had any more threesomes?"

"No."

"Why?"

Stone chuckled.

Stevie looked frustrated. "What?"

"I didn't prepare myself to have this conversation with you today."

"That's a good thing. Now I know you'll tell me the truth."

"I've always told you the truth."

Her eyebrows shot skyward. "I distinctly remember you tellin' me you'd call and you'd see me the next time you came into town."

"You're right. I did say that."

"So you lied."

Stone could've told her he'd intended to call her, but that would've been a lie. He'd cut all ties when he left town. It was his only option. Otherwise, he would've come running back, and it wasn't the best thing for her back then.

"Yes." It pained him to admit it. "I left with no intention of contactin' you."

Her shoulders remained square, and there was sadness in her eyes, but it was the twinge in her voice that hurt the most. "Why?"

"Because you were too young to get mixed up with me."

"Too young? But I wasn't too young for you to share with another man."

Every memory of *that night* included both Stevie and Nico as willing participants. Hell, he'd even left and come back to find Stevie with Nico's face between her legs. Had he missed something? Had he pushed her into something she didn't want to do?

"I thought we were all on board," he said hesitantly. "Was I wrong?"

God, he hoped not. It would kill him to know that Stevie had felt pressured that night. Stone didn't regret a single second, but he would if she said she hadn't wanted to do it.

Her eyes skidded away, landing on the puppy, where they remained for what felt like an eternity.

"No," she finally said. "You weren't wrong."

Thank Christ.

"What about you?" he asked, needing a minute to breathe. "Did you ever have another threesome?"

"Oh, yeah. All the time. Every Friday nigh—No, *Jesus*. That was the only time."

He remembered what Nico had said.

You weren't the only one who was changed by the events of that night, Stone. You left a hole when you left. In both of us. It became a spot that needed to be filled, but neither of us knew how to do that.

"Did Nico?"

Her expression softened. "Not that I know of. Melanie certainly wasn't the type of girl who'd let some other guy touch her while Nico got off on it."

He didn't miss the vehemence in her words. It seemed she was overcome by emotion whenever she spoke about that night, but he couldn't quite pinpoint what she was feeling.

Stone leaned forward and put the coffee mug on the table. "Tell me somethin'." He looked at her. "Do you regret that night?"

"No."

Considering the speed at which she responded, he believed her.

He rested his elbows on his knees and dropped his head in his hands, staring at the floor. "Stevie, that night made me want somethin' I didn't think I was ready for. Let alone you." He forced himself to sit up and look at her. "I wanted to explore more of that. With you and Nico."

"Why didn't you?"

"You were too damn young. Shit, you were still in high school." He put his hand up before she could argue. "And Nico was Chelsea's fuckin' boyfriend."

"Ex."

"By a minute."

She opened her mouth but then closed it. A few seconds later, she said, "That's fair."

"Think about it, Stevie. I never hid the fact that I was bisexual or that I liked to play the field. And everyone knew Donovan was gay. Back then, it wasn't acceptable. Not as the norm. People looked at us like we were lepers sometimes. There wasn't a chance in hell that we could've had somethin' real. Not the way I wanted it to be. We would've had a spotlight on us. And the rumors ... *Jesus.* You would've been the topic of conversation for months."

"Me?"

"Yes, you. The *woman* who was screwing two guys." He huffed. "No matter how far the world claims it's come, women are still viewed differently than men. I would've received high fives if I had two women in my bed every night. The same doesn't apply to you. And certainly not back then."

At least some of the fury faded from her expression. "So you thought leavin' for fifteen years was the answer?"

"I didn't even know where I was goin' when I left," he exclaimed, emotion beginning to choke him. "I just knew I needed to protect you from that. If word got out that we did … what we did…"

Stevie took a deep breath. "You're right. I'm not contesting that part. But you shouldn't have lied."

"I shouldn't have," he conceded. "You deserved a helluva lot more from me. I'm sorry. Sincerely sorry."

Her gaze shifted to the mug in her hand. "I don't know if I can forgive you."

"I won't blame you if you don't." He waited until she looked up. "It might not mean anything, but I've never loved anyone but you, Stevie. I've never even tried because I knew it wouldn't matter. You were it for me, and I left. I punished myself by rememberin' everything I loved about you. And I compared every woman I met to you. No one could ever come close." Her eyes glittered with unshed tears, but he forged ahead. "I'd already found the one, but I was stupid enough to let that go. I deserved to be alone."

Stevie jumped up from her seat and raced to the kitchen. The coffee mug clanged in the stainless-steel sink, and a second later, he heard her crying.

Hating himself for upsetting her, Stone followed her into the kitchen.

He reached for her but stopped at the last second, choosing to stand directly behind her instead. "Oh, girl. Please don't cry."

She shook her head.

"I'm so sorry, Stevie."

She shook her head again.

Stone couldn't resist. He put his hands on her shoulders, and a flood of sensation filled him. Touching her brought back so much, and he wasn't referring to a sexual response, although that was impossible to deny. But touching her, being with her … back then, it was all he cared about. It didn't matter where they were or what they were doing. As long as he was with Stevie, he could breathe.

Stone leaned down, keeping his voice low. "Baby, I'm so fuckin' sorry."

She continued to cry, her body jerking from her sobs, so he urged her to turn around. When she finally did, he wrapped his arms around her, propping his chin on her head and holding on tight. It felt like someone kicked him in the chest, knocking the air right out of him. And it was still the best feeling. Maybe the only thing he'd actually felt in the past fifteen years. With the exception of kissing Nico a short time ago.

"Please don't cry," he whispered, running his hand over her silky hair. "I'll spend the rest of my life makin' it up to you as long as you'll let me into your life. As friends," he tacked on, so she didn't think he was expecting anything else.

He wanted more. Damn straight, he did. Even with a decade and a half separating them, Stone knew without a doubt that Stevie was still the only woman he would ever love. She was just as vibrant now as she had been then. Maybe even more so. And when he looked at her, it was like coming out of a gloomy gray fog that had shrouded him all that time.

When she finally tilted her head back, Stone used his thumbs to brush the tears away. Her dark brown eyes were the color of rich coffee, brighter because of her pain. He hated that he was the one responsible.

He didn't lean in, didn't attempt to kiss her. Instead, he whispered, "God, I've missed you, Stevie."

"I've missed you, too. Even though I still hate you."

Those words would've felt like a gut punch, but she smiled softly.

"Think maybe we can try to move past that?"

"Maybe. But you're gonna have to work for it."

"I'll do whatever it takes." And he would. Stone intended to prove to her that he was worthy of her. And yes, he would settle for friendship if that was all she was willing to give him.

He was still cupping her face, and she still had her arms around him. Neither of them moved. Remaining just like that until a thump sounded from the front of the house.

Stevie laughed.

"What was that?"

"Your boot. Jäger's got a thing for boots."

Reluctantly, Stone released her and headed toward the door. Sure enough, Jäger had his boot's pull strap in his mouth and was attempting to drag it across the floor, but he couldn't get traction on the hardwood.

"You know that's not yours," Stone told him, snatching up one of the many toys on the floor. He traded his boot for a toy.

Jäger wasn't fooled. He lunged at the boot and yipped.

"You're gonna have to grow into that bark. It sounds a little weak. Like your mama was a bird. Try somethin' deeper."

Jäger yipped again.

"Nope. Sounds the same."

He was attempting to pique his interest with the toy when the front door opened. They both looked over.

"Hey," Nico said, taking off his coat and hanging it on the rack beside Stone's. "It's a mess out there."

Jäger forgot all about the boot and bounded over to Nico, who bent down to give his head a rub. "What's up, Trouble?"

Stone stood tall. "I guess I should probably get goin'."

Nico stood. "Might be too late for that. They've closed the Granite Creek bridge. I'm just lucky the office is on this side of it."

Fuck. There wasn't another way to get around unless he wanted to drive about five miles out of his way. If the roads were bad enough for them to close the bridge, a ten-mile trek would likely take him a couple of hours. His truck wouldn't have too much trouble, but anyone else on the road would cause a delay.

"You can stay here," Stevie said from behind him.

Stone turned. She had wiped the tears away, but her eyes were red-rimmed.

"You okay?" Nico asked Stevie, although his glare was directed at Stone.

She laughed it off. "Yeah. Stone was just bein' Stone. Tellin' it like it is."

Nico rounded on him.

Stone held up both hands. "I didn't set out to make her cry."

"He didn't," Stevie said, curling her hand around Nico's muscular forearm.

It was clear Nico wasn't ready to believe that, his expression skeptical as he looked down at her. "You want me to hit him for you? It'll make us even."

Stone grinned at the thought. He still remembered that day. That punch had led to the most incredible night of his life.

"Nah." Stevie huffed a laugh. "I think we're good. For now. But maybe you could start a fire?"

Nico nodded, continuing to glance between them as though, in doing so, he might be able to see what happened while he wasn't there.

"You hungry?" Nico asked Stevie.

"Yeah. I've got a pot roast in the oven. It'll be"—she looked at her watch—"thirty minutes or so before it's done. I made the cornbread already. I'll warm it up in a little while." She looked at Stone. "You good with pot roast?"

He was good with whatever she wanted him to have. But he kept that to himself. "Yeah. If you've got enough."

"More than," she noted, motioning toward the couch. "Might as well get comfortable."

That was exactly what he did.

SEVENTEEN

NICO FIGURED HE SHOULD PROBABLY BE CAREFUL what he wished for.

Of course, getting Stone to the house had been half the battle. The other half had been hoping Stevie wouldn't saw his nuts off when they were alone together. He was pretty sure Stone's family jewels were safely intact. In fact, he would go so far as to say she was … happy. At least based on the conversation and laughter that'd been coming from the living room for the past hour. It was a far cry from the tears he'd witnessed when he first got home.

"What about you?" Stone asked.

Nico realized he was talking to him. Only problem was, he hadn't heard the question. "What was that?"

Stevie and Stone shared a look.

Stone's expression was … unreadable. "We were wonderin' if you wanted to play truth or dare."

Nico frowned. "With the two of you? That would be a solid *hell no*."

Stevie laughed, and the sound was so damn beautiful. He loved to hear her musical laughter. It was the highlight of so many of his days. More so after he'd done something questionable—sending Stone to the house ranked at the top of that list—because it meant she wasn't mad at him.

After he texted Stone the address, he'd worried that Stevie might never speak to him again. Then he'd worried that he'd pushed them together and he was going to be the one on the outside looking in. *Then* he'd worried he would come home to find them screaming at each other. Then—yes, there were more—he wondered if he would find them fucking like bunnies in his bed. No one said his thoughts were rational.

He'd fretted over all the possibilities the entire hour he spent on the phone with a client. He would have to make that call again on Monday because he didn't remember a damn thing they'd discussed.

"We weren't gonna play truth or dare," Stevie admitted. "But maybe we should so I can ask you where you were at just then."

"What?"

Stevie looked at Stone. "That's what he does when he needs time to formulate an answer. Usually, it comes after I've spent fifteen minutes telling him something that happened to me durin' the day. He stalls with a"—she lowered her voice, presumably to mock his voice—"*what?* Then I'll watch while he tries to replay whatever bits and pieces he might've heard so he can respond correctly."

Stone glanced between them. "Does it work?"

"About seventy percent of the time," Stevie said at the same time Nico said, "About eighty percent of the time."

"Hey, you want somethin' to drink? A *real* drink, I mean," Stevie offered, hopping up from the couch and carrying her empty plate to the kitchen.

If Nico didn't know better, he would think she was running away.

"I'll clean," Nico offered, following behind her. "You cooked."

"I don't mind," she told him. "See what Stone wants to drink. It'll only take me a minute."

Nico looked across the room to see Stone was watching them intently. The guy had been doing that quite a bit this evening. Like he was consuming every part of their lives that he could in case they threw him out of the house. The vulnerability Nico sensed in Stone was new. Back in the day, Stone had been one of the most confident people Nico knew. He'd idolized that.

This particular version of the man was ... well, he was more human. And though Nico was still putting him on a pedestal, it wasn't quite so high anymore.

"Hey," Nico called to him. "You wanna beer?"

"I'll take Sprite and vodka," Stevie told him. "Be generous with the vodka or stingy with the Sprite; I don't care which one."

Stone's eyebrow quirked. "I'll have what she's havin'."

Nico grabbed the Sprite from the fridge and the vodka out of the freezer. He pulled three glass tumblers down from the cabinet.

"You're wanderin'. And you're sniffin'," Stone said, obviously talking to the puppy. "You need to go out?"

"I can take him," Nico offered, setting the two-liter down.

"I don't mind." Stone grabbed his boots from the barstool where someone had set them earlier.

Nico tried not to watch as he pulled them on in a hurry, clearly understanding puppies don't wait for anyone, and grabbed his coat before herding Jäger out the back door.

When he was alone with Stevie, Nico turned to her. "You good?"

She nodded, but she didn't look away from the sink.

"Are you sure?"

She nodded again.

Nico moved to stand behind her. He leaned down and kept his voice low. "Would you tell me if you weren't?"

Her hands paused. Her chin tilted toward him. Her voice was whisper soft. "I don't trust myself with the two of you."

He stepped to the side, wanting to look her in the eyes. He didn't understand. "What do you mean?"

Her eyebrows lifted slowly, and she gave him that look that said *I'm giving you a few seconds to let it sink in.*

"You don't trust yourself with—oh."

Her smile was back, and this time, it made her eyes glitter. Yep, that was his dick twitching behind his zipper. Since he could also tell she wasn't thrilled with that admission, it probably wasn't the correct response.

"I won't let you do anything you'll regret in the mornin'."

A boisterous laugh bubbled out of her. "Regret? I wouldn't regret it. I just don't want to do that to myself again."

Nico understood. When it came to Stone, he didn't trust himself either. Because of the intensity of *that night*, Nico had convinced himself he had been dangerously close to being in love with Stone back then. It was the only rational explanation for the emotional upheaval that had followed the man's departure. For years, Nico had thought about him, about what might've been if he'd stayed. It was complete fiction, but it had become real in his mind.

"Let's just see where it goes," Stevie said as she went back to handwashing dishes. "But ... if it does..." She looked back at him again. "Would you run out of the house screamin'?"

He didn't even have to think about it. "No."

Nico still thought about that night. For the longest time, he'd tried to analyze it to death. To figure out why that particular formula—Stone plus Stevie—had done it for him in ways nothing else ever had. He could never figure it out since he only had one night to draw from. But that didn't stop him from trying. A repeat would probably bring as much clarity as confusion, though. Still, he wouldn't pass it up.

Stevie huffed. "Who's to say Stone would even be interested?"

Everyone, Nico thought. Everyone who knew the man would say that Stone was interested.

Nico had seen the way the guy was looking at Stevie. There was the same worship flickering in his gaze now as he'd seen back then. Fifteen years might've passed, but it was safe to say that Stone Jameson was still in love with the girl. That much hadn't changed. However, Nico's feelings for Stevie certainly had. He pretended they were friends, but Nico loved her. And there was no questioning it. What he felt was definitely love because it choked him up when he least expected it.

But he knew Stevie. You didn't rush her into things. You took it slow and let her come up with the idea herself. Otherwise, she would need time to think about it. And Stevie Shepherd could think things to death if you let her.

The back door opened.

"Good job, Jäger," Stone praised as they came inside. "You got a treat for him?"

"In the jar over there," Stevie said, pointing toward the cabinet near the door.

Stone opened the glass jar with "Treats" etched into the side and pulled out one of the small training treats Stevie was using to work with the puppy.

"Good job," Stone repeated and gave the dog his treat.

Nico finished pouring the drinks. He wasn't quite as generous with the vodka as Stevie would've preferred. She would thank him for that in the morning.

When he went to hand Stone one of the drinks, Stone didn't reach for it. "I was thinkin' I should go." He looked toward the back door. "The sleet's let up some. I've got four-wheel drive, so I'm sure I can get home."

Stevie turned off the water and grabbed a towel, turning to face him. "Stay. Please."

Stone stared at her for the longest time. Long enough Nico was certain they were having a silent conversation, speaking only with their eyes. To Nico's surprise, Stone looked at him, seeking his response.

Nico attempted to pass him the drink again, nodding. "Stay. I think a conversation is long overdue."

Stone's gaze snapped between them once more. "I don't think that's a good idea."

Stevie came around the island. "Why?"

Stone swallowed hard, his Adam's apple bobbing slowly in his throat as he peered at her. "Because I don't trust myself around the two of you."

Nico snorted a laugh.

When Stone's eyes darted to him, he nudged his chin in Stevie's direction. "She said the same thing."

Nico stood there, captivated by the gleam in Stone's eyes when he looked at Stevie again. Neither of them bothered to hide what they were feeling. It was damn potent, too, warming the house better than the fire that was crackling in the fireplace.

"This isn't why I came here," Stone said, his voice dropping an octave when Stevie stepped toward him.

"I know," she said, closing the distance between them.

Nico couldn't look away. The same way he hadn't been able to that night. These two… Separately, they were attractive. Together, they were unforgettable. The contrast between them was staggering. Stone, at six feet, three inches, towered over Stevie's petite form. He outweighed her by at least a hundred pounds. Of solid muscle. The guy had always been big—a trait that ran in his family—but years of hard work had honed him into something spectacular.

Stone inhaled sharply when Stevie curled her fingers into the waistband of his jeans. Nico's muscles clenched as though she was touching him and not Stone. As though Stone was the conduit, and simply being in the same room allowed Nico to feel what he was feeling.

Stevie's eyes closed when Stone cupped the side of her face. His hand was bigger than her head; his long, wide fingers looked as though they could easily break her. Yet he was so gentle.

"God, baby," Stone whispered, now completely enraptured by her.

Nico understood what that felt like. He'd endured it for months on end, looking at this woman and seeing only the best that life has to offer.

"I want you to stay," she replied, her voice equally as soft.

"I don't think it's a good idea," Stone said, but he didn't sound like he believed it any more than Nico did.

"Why?"

Nico felt the full impact of Stone's gaze when it shifted to him. He wasn't sure what the guy was thinking, but he held his stare, waiting.

Then Stone looked back at Stevie. "I kissed him earlier."

Well, hell. Nico hadn't expected him to say *that*.

Stevie's gaze darted between them, coming to rest on Stone. "And?"

"And I didn't think about what I was doin' when I did," he admitted, holding Stevie's gaze.

Stevie frowned. "What's there to think about?"

"For one, the two of you … it seems you're buildin' somethin' between you. I didn't even consider that I could be comin' between that. It was selfish."

Stevie looked at Nico. He saw her understanding and the mischief that lived inside her. She was up to something.

"I kiss him from time to time, too," she said, a smile pulling at her pretty mouth. "He doesn't complain."

Nico choked on a laugh. What the hell was going on here? And how had *he* become the topic of their conversation?

Stevie's gaze returned to Stone. "In fact, I'll kiss him now if it'll make you feel better."

"It would," Stone said, his tone serious although the smile on his face was devastatingly roguish.

Nico knew when they both turned to look at him that there was a better-than-good chance he was not going to survive this night with his heart intact.

STEVIE NEVER MEANT TO TURN THIS INTO a dare.

Her brain was aware she was making a grave mistake by letting her hormones dictate her actions. Stone had shattered her heart once; there was nothing to say he wouldn't do it again. And as much as she pretended she only cared about sex, it was a front. A way to protect herself. If she were to wake up tomorrow without Nico, she would be as devastated—if not more so—than she'd been when Stone left. What she had with Nico was significantly deeper because it was built on not only friendship and a mutual attraction but also years of spending time together, getting to know one another, and simply being there.

Releasing Stone's waistband, Stevie stepped around him and walked toward Nico. If he didn't want this to happen, he would tell her. She trusted him to be honest with her. About everything.

She stepped up to him, holding his gaze as his head tilted down.

"You know what you're doin'?" he asked, and there was so much passion in the words.

"When it comes to kissin' you? I know *exactly* what I'm doin'."

"And the rest?"

"Not a clue," she answered truthfully, but she wasn't going to let it stop her.

For the first time in a really long time, Stevie had the opportunity to be the carefree girl she'd once been. And yeah, she had these two men to thank for that. It was like falling back on the familiar, knowing what to expect. She could even predict the aftermath, although she wasn't interested in analyzing it right now.

Stevie went up on her toes so she could reach Nico's lips. She aimed for chaste in an effort to goad him, but he was onto her. Without warning, he grabbed her hips and lifted her, dropping her butt on the counter. His mouth was on hers instantly, hot and needy. She groaned, her arms sliding around him, palms flattening on his back so she could keep him there.

Nico kissed her like a starving man. His tongue dueled with hers, battling for dominance. He would win. She had no doubt because surrendering to him was so much fun.

No, Nico wasn't rough with her. The very most he would do was grab her hair from time to time, but even that was gentler than she would've preferred. She missed the intensity of her encounters with Stone. No one had ever taken her the way he had. They were either not into it or worried they would hurt her. Nico fell into the second category.

Was Stone still as dominant and aggressive? Would he toss her like a rag doll and make her feel that same sweet ache in her core as he had back then? She wanted that. Hell, she *needed* that. It had been too long since she'd been with a man who looked like he was trying to keep it together when really he wanted to fall apart because he couldn't resist her.

A hand moved along her thigh. She knew it belonged to Stone because Nico's were on her face as he plundered her mouth.

She reached for him, keeping one arm around Nico, her other hand sliding over Stone's. His knuckles were rough, a sign he worked with his hands. It turned her on to think about what those sexy hands could do to her body.

Nico grabbed her hair and tipped her head back, their lips separating. She gasped for breath, her chest heaving from both exertion and a hunger so powerful that it was a good thing she was sitting down.

Without moving her head, she looked at Stone. "Are we even yet?"

Stone was looking at Nico. "I don't know."

Before she could suggest anything, Stone moved, stepping closer to Nico, taking his arm. Nico released her hair and turned, following Stone's movements until Nico's back was to her, his hips between her thighs. When Nico leaned against the counter, it allowed her to see over his shoulder as Stone moved in.

As though they'd done it a thousand times before, Stone cupped the back of Nico's head, holding it firmly as he leaned into him.

Stevie was mesmerized, completely unhinged by the sight of these two men kissing. The two sexiest men on the planet were different in so many ways, yet when they came together, it was like they belonged that way.

Nico rested his forearms on her thighs, his hands cupping her knees as Stone devoured him. Stevie couldn't resist sliding her hand beneath his shirt, seeking warm skin. His torso was a wonderland of ridges and valleys. All those delectable muscles were a playground for her fingertips.

A soft hum escaped him as she let her hands wander. Higher at first, then back down. She dipped her fingertips into his waistband, sighing as she grazed that mouthwatering V that led down, down, down.

When Stone and Nico continued to kiss, Stevie gripped the hem of Nico's shirt and lifted it. Stone must've sensed what she was doing because he stepped back, releasing Nico's mouth so he could watch as she revealed Nico's rock-hard body.

Nico would've been the perfect choice for one of those art classes where people painted or sketched the human form. Every single muscle in his body was perfectly defined. From the steely contours of his shoulders to the perfect muscles in his calves and every inch in between, the man was built as though someone had created him from a mold labeled *Perfection*.

She got Nico's shirt off, and Stone whistled a definite sound of approval that matched the appreciation in his eyes.

Jäger yipped, causing all three of them to look at him where he sat near the table.

"We're good," Stone assured him. "You can go back to your nap."

As though he understood every word, Jäger flopped back down with a sigh.

"Your turn," Nico told Stone.

Stone looked confused. "My turn?"

"To take your shirt off."

Stone's eyes darted to Stevie.

"He's right." She smiled. "It's only fair."

Something flashed in Stone's eyes, but she couldn't make out what it was. Nico must've thought he was taking too long because he did the honor of removing it for him.

Nico still blocked much of her view, but not all of it. Stevie gasped when she saw that Stone had her name tattooed on his body. It arced along the curve of his shoulder muscle; the calligraphy letters, probably originally done in a rich black ink, had faded some. Enough that she was prompted to ask, "When did you do that?"

Stone glanced down at his shoulder. "About two years after I left."

Two years? He'd still been thinking about her after that long? And yes, that lent credence to his confession that she was the only woman he'd ever loved, but still, it didn't make sense. He was the one who left. He'd walked right out of her life. Why? If he'd loved her enough to tattoo her name on his body, why hadn't he ever come back? Or just called?

Nico didn't say anything, and she briefly wondered if it bothered him. But then he stepped to the side, and she saw the reason he was speechless. On Stone's other arm, covering his entire arm from his shoulder down to his elbow, was a finely detailed Mayan design made up of circles and blocks. As she looked closer, she saw what was inside those blocks. Nico's name wasn't as obvious as hers was, but it was there nonetheless.

Stone was looking at Nico. "I told you it changed me."

"What?" Stevie asked, realizing she hadn't been privy to whatever conversation he was referring to.

"That night." He looked like he was ashamed to admit that.

"Tattoos are permanent," she mused, staring at her name again.

"So are my feelings."

What was he trying to do? Make her blubber like a moron? She didn't remember Stone being quite so honest about his feelings.

Stevie wasn't sure what to say or do, but Nico didn't seem to have that problem. He grabbed Stone by the back of the neck and slammed his mouth over his. They stumbled back, but Stone kept his feet under him. Stevie watched as the passion ignited all over again, only it was like someone had added jet fuel to a grease fire. It burned hotter than before.

Except it didn't last as long. Nico released Stone and turned to her. He closed the gap between them, approaching slowly. But when he reached her, his kiss was as intense as the one he'd planted on Stone, only with less momentum. But then he was gone, and Stone was there, drowning her in ecstasy as he kissed her hard and deep.

A switch had been flipped. All reservations had disappeared. Her fingers curled along the indention of his waist, shifting higher, her fingertips tracing the sexy hard slabs of muscle that created a masterpiece. She kept going, purposely clipping his nipples with her fingernails before gliding her thumbs between his pecs. Higher still, to the long, strong column of his neck. Wanting more, Stevie wrapped her arms around Stone's neck, tasting his hunger and the same driving need she'd felt all those years ago.

Stone gripped her hips, lifting her off the counter with ease. She wrapped her legs around him and held on as he relocated to the living room.

"Where's Jäger?" she asked when he leaned down, depositing her on the couch as he hovered over her.

Nico was the one who answered. "Under the kitchen table. Sound asleep."

Hopefully, he would stay that way. At least long enough for her to sate the ache that was building with each passing second.

Stone attempted to stand up, but Stevie made it impossible, holding onto him, pulling him down with her. He settled his knee between her legs, balancing over her with one hand planted on the couch.

"You sure about this?"

"I think we all are." Stevie looked up at Nico to confirm. "Right?"

He responded with a nod, followed by, "But I think we need to move this to a bedroom."

"What about Jäger?"

"I'll move him," Nico said.

She met Stone's gaze and nodded. She was ready.

EIGHTEEN

WITH HER ARMS WREATHING HIS NECK AND her legs wrapped around his waist, Stone picked Stevie up again. This time, he followed her directions, making his way down a short hallway.

"Ignore the mess," she whispered.

Stone laughed. "What mess?" He was unable to see anything beyond her. Not because she blocked his view but because he was so focused on what he'd ached for all this time that he didn't see anything else.

He dropped her on the bed but didn't move with her this time. He wanted to look at her—*really* look at her—so he could gauge whether she was ready for this or if this was a momentary lapse in judgment. He did not want to wake up tomorrow and find that Stevie hated him all over again.

They were moving fast. The red flags in his brain warned him that this could backfire quickly. At the same time, he didn't care because, for the first time in years, he could breathe again. Walking away from it was no longer an option, which meant he had to shift gears to adjust for the speed at which they were moving.

She reached for the button on her jeans, but before she could free it, Stone smacked her hand away.

Her eyes glazed over, her lips parting on a soft moan. And that smile. Fuck, he'd missed that knowing smile.

"You still like it rough?"

"God, yes." She squirmed, rubbing her thighs together. "You still like to *be* rough?"

"Yeah."

She smiled. "Good. Because it's been a long, *long* time."

He wanted to ask how long, but he honestly didn't want to know the answer. Stone preferred to go on pretending that Stevie hadn't been with anyone for the past fifteen years. It wasn't true, but the thought of her with anyone else made him crazy.

"Take off the shirt first," he commanded, reaching for her foot so he could pull off the thick socks covering her feet.

Stevie stripped the cotton off slowly, clearly realizing that the pre-show was as powerful as the act. Stone looked his fill, admiring the soft body beneath. She wasn't as soft as she'd been at eighteen. Her muscles were more defined, proof that her job required physical labor. It was sexy as hell to watch her body flex and shift as she moved.

"Now, the jeans."

Her eyes remained locked with his as she unbuttoned them. She chewed on her lower lip as she slid the zipper down. His gaze followed her hands as she pushed the denim down her hips, then her legs. He didn't help, wanting her to do the work, giving her time to ensure this was what she wanted.

When she was left wearing only a pair of silky red panties, he thought he might need to sit down. She was the most beautiful thing he'd seen. And he wasn't merely talking about other women. Compared to the most glorious sunset or the highest peaks of the snow-tipped mountains, this woman's beauty made it all look like a cheap painting. She was God's greatest creation, of that he was certain.

Looking at her made him feel like he was twenty-one again and noticing her for the first time. He felt that same rush of adrenaline as he had back then. His skin tingled, and there was a fuzzy sound in his ears. The entire world faded away, leaving nothing but the two of them.

He was so distracted he didn't notice her move until she was on her knees, reaching for him.

She flattened her palms on his chest, and he grabbed her wrists. "Did I say you could touch?"

Another gasp, and her eyes dilated. She definitely wasn't afraid. She was turned on. It fueled the raging beast that wanted to dominate her.

He peeled her hands from his skin and shoved her back.

Her giggle was exquisite as she fell back and bounced on the mattress. He followed her down, coming over her, pinning her beneath his weight.

Stone hissed when her cool fingers glided up his back, her fingertips teasing a path along his skin.

"God, I missed you, Stevie," he whispered. "Missed you so goddamn much."

He crushed his mouth to hers, angling his head so he could deepen the kiss. She kissed him back with a passion that mirrored his own. It took tremendous effort to maintain control, to not give in to the driving hunger that urged him to slide into her heat and claim her the way he had so many times back then.

Stone broke the kiss, trailing his lips along the smooth line of her jaw. He wrangled her arms down, pinning them to the bed as he licked a path down her chest. He licked her nipple lightly, then sucked her into his mouth. He wasn't gentle, causing her to cry out as she arched her back.

"God, yes!" The rest of her words were a strangled mixture of vowels and consonants as he continued to worship her tits.

He couldn't stop, fueled by a primal need to feast for fear of spending the rest of his life hunting and never finding something as succulent as her.

Stone was aware of Nico coming into the room. His hunger intensified, multiplying tenfold. He'd only had the man once, but that had been all he'd needed to create a devastating addiction. The high he'd experienced that night was one he'd never been able to duplicate, and God knows he'd tried. Maybe not as hard as he could have since he'd never attempted to replicate the situation. Never with two people. Deep down, he'd known it would be futile. What the three of them had shared that night was impossible to replicate. Not with other people, anyway.

Forcing himself to slow down, Stone lifted his head and looked at Stevie's pleasure-ravaged face. Her eyes were bright, her lips pink and glossy, her smooth skin reddened by the stubble on his face. She was panting and humming.

And so goddamn beautiful, she stole his breath.

Stone shifted over, stretching out beside her, his legs hanging off the side of the bed.

He looked up at Nico. "Join us."

It wasn't quite a command, but not a request, either. Stevie all but broadcast her need for his dominance, but Stone hadn't detected the same in Nico yet. He didn't want to put an end to this before it started.

Stevie tilted her head, peering at Nico, where he stood in the doorway. He was shirtless and so goddamn gorgeous. The guy Stone remembered hadn't been as ripped as he was now. There was no telling what Stone would've done to him that night if he had been.

Nico moved to the end of the bed, his eyes blazing when Stone cupped Stevie's perky breast, teasing the nipple with his finger and thumb. Nico put one knee on the mattress, staring as though seeing a mostly naked woman for the first time. Based on the way Stevie had kissed Nico in the kitchen, Stone knew it wasn't their first time.

"When was the last time you two fucked?" Stone asked, being blunt and gauging their reactions.

Stevie gasped. "It's been a while. A couple of weeks ago. In my office."

Oh, hell.

"Before that, he fingered me in the shower," Stevie said, gasping when Stone pinched her nipple.

"She was taunting me." Nico smirked.

"Which time?"

His blue eyes blazed. "Probably both. That greedy pussy always needs attention."

That was new. And unexpected. And hotter than fuck. Nico's dirty mouth was going to add to the heat.

"What did she give in return after you fingered her?" Stone asked when Nico stretched out along Stevie's other side.

"Her wicked mouth. Around my dick."

"I would've loved to've seen that," Stone admitted, putting his fingers on Stevie's lower lip. "You suckin' his big cock between these pretty lips." He pushed his fingers into her mouth. "Suck."

She did, her tongue adding to the wet heat as she licked and laved his fingertips. It felt like she had her mouth wrapped around the head of his dick. Goddamn.

Stone pulled his fingers from her mouth and reached over. "Suck."

Nico's eyes flashed hot, and he opened his mouth, taking Stone's fingers inside. Just like in his memories, Nico stared at him, eager for another command.

Stone glanced at Stevie briefly. "Does he like it rough, too?"

"He wants to be dominated, yeah," she said, her eyes locked on Nico as he sucked Stone's fingers.

Stone met Nico's gaze. "By me?"

He pulled his fingers from Nico's mouth so he could answer. He received a nod.

"Tell me," Stone commanded, ensuring he kept his tone hard. It was obvious nothing less than forceful would suffice.

"Yes."

"Yes, what? You want me to dominate you?"

Nico's blue eyes flashed. "I want you to *annihilate* me."

Jesus fuck.

Stone growled, unable to contain the hunger. He moved with lightning speed, straddling Stevie's thighs and leaning over her so he could kiss Nico.

"Don't think I won't," he whispered.

"Do your worst," Nico hissed.

A memory from that night flashed in his head.

"You've never had a dick in your mouth."

Nico shook his head.

"Mine's gonna be the first."

It wasn't a question, but Stone was seeking permission to a degree. He would only give Nico what he was willing to take.

Nico held his stare and dared to provoke the beast. "Do your worst."

They were the same words Nico had taunted him with that night. They'd been unexpected but the perfect opening for what had transpired after.

Stone thrust his tongue into Nico's mouth, mimicking what he intended to do to him later. He wanted nothing more than to dominate a lover who could take anything he could dish out. With Stevie, he had to be careful. Back then, he'd pushed his own boundaries with her because he sensed she wanted it. And the more aggressive he was, the hotter she got. But there was always that niggling in his brain. A warning that he needed to be careful. He wanted to make it good for her, but he didn't want to hurt her.

With Nico ... he didn't think that was going to be an issue.

Stevie's fingers teased the hair at Stone's nape, and he felt her watching them.

He reluctantly pulled back from Nico. "What do you say we make it about her tonight?"

Nico's eyes shifted to her. "That's a great idea."

Stone sat up, straddling Stevie's thighs. He cupped her tits, kneading the firm mounds with both hands, rubbing her nipples between his index fingers and thumbs. Her back arched, so he increased pressure until she whimpered.

"Too much?"

"No," she gasped.

He pinched a little harder.

She whimpered again, her lips parting. He tugged for a few more seconds and then released them, letting the blood flow return.

Stevie gasped, eyes wide.

Holding her stare, Stone tugged her panties down enough that he could slide his thumb between her smooth, bare lips.

"You're wet, baby."

She nodded.

"Does this pussy need some attention now?"

She nodded again.

"Good. Because my tongue needs a workout."

Stone shifted back until he could get off the bed, dragging her panties down her legs as he went. When he had them off, he tossed them onto the nightstand.

"Spread your legs."

She did, but not the way he meant, and based on the sparkle in her eyes, she knew that.

"You want that pussy spanked, don't you, baby?"

She gasped.

"Pull your knees back and wide. Let me see that pretty cunt."

Nico assisted, sliding his hand under her knee and pulling it back, spreading her open.

"Fuck me," he hummed. "Damn, baby. That's pretty."

Stone gripped her hips and pulled her to the edge of the bed as he dropped to his knees. He inhaled her, eager to feast. Before he leaned in, he met Nico's gaze.

"You ready?"

He smirked. "I've been ready for fifteen years."

Stone grinned. "Me, too."

IT WAS LIKE THAT MADONNA SONG.

Like a virgin.

Touched for the very first time.

Only she wasn't a virgin. And this wasn't the first time she'd been touched. Not even the first time they both had their hands on her. Yet, Stevie felt like she was experiencing arousal in its unfettered form. Raw and powerful, her entire body was one giant nerve center.

Lightning struck as soon as Stone's tongue glided over her clit.

She screamed. The explosion came from the inside, blowing out all the windows and walls of her existence. It was unexpected and brutally beautiful in its intensity.

"Jesus Christ." Nico's breath rasped against her lips. "Did you come, sweet girl?"

She whimpered, trying to shift her hips because Stone wasn't finished, but she was too sensitive. She tried to close her legs, but Nico's hand rested heavily on one knee, and Stone's hand was pressed firmly to the inside of her thigh, her pussy vulnerable to his sensual assault. As though Stone knew, his tongue went soft, wet heat dragging along her slit, pressing gently at her entrance before wandering back to caress her clit. Velvet-soft strokes gave her back some of her sanity, but she was still on edge, her body vibrating with the need for more.

Stevie curled her arm around Nico's neck and kissed him. He mirrored Stone's ministrations, his tongue lapping gently at her tongue, his lips so soft against hers.

"That's only the first of many," he promised.

She believed him. At the pace at which Stone was renewing the tension, his magic tongue stroking nerve endings she didn't know she had, Stevie figured the next would come very soon.

"Yes," she moaned softly, pulling her lips from Nico's so she could savor the exquisite thrust of Stone's finger as he slowly penetrated her. "More. I need you inside me."

Suddenly, Stone was on the bed again, lying beside her, his finger still filling her, pumping gently.

She reached for him, finding his mouth with hers, tasting herself on his lips. She didn't linger, reaching for Nico and urging him closer until they were hovering over her, swapping air, their tongues sparring. Watching as Nico tasted her on Stone's mouth … it sent a wave of heat crashing through her. They were beautiful like that. She'd never seen anything as hot as them kissing.

But her attention rocketed elsewhere when Nico's hand grazed along her thigh. Higher. A moment later, she felt him push his finger inside her, gliding against Stone's as they fingered her at the same time.

"That's a good girl," Stone crooned, taking a break from kissing Nico to peer down at her.

When he claimed Nico's mouth again, Stevie growled, arching her back, trying to stave off another release because it was too soon. She wanted this to last all night. At this rate, she would be obliterated before they fucked her. And she wanted that. It was a heady sensation to feel them inside her at the same time. She wanted them to fill her with their cocks.

At the same time.

Oh, God. And now that was all she could think about.

Stevie managed to wrangle herself under control by sheer force of will, but then they stopped kissing, and their mouths descended on her breasts. They latched onto her at the same time, their fingers still fucking her.

She came.

A whoosh of air escaped as her body tensed violently, her pussy clamping down on their fingers. That didn't stop them. They fought against the resistance, their mouths sucking harder, prolonging the orgasm until she thought she would shatter into dust particles and float off in the air.

"So sensitive," Stone said when he released her breast and kissed her chest. "So goddamn beautiful."

"Fuck me," she growled, not caring that she sounded desperate. "Both of you. Fuck me."

That got their attention.

"Have you ever had your ass fucked?" Stone asked, clearly as direct and curious as back then.

"No," she admitted. "But I want it."

Stone's smirk was devious. "One of these days. But not today, baby."

Nico and Stone shared a look before Nico said the most promising words. "But we can give you what you need."

Then, they both disappeared from the bed. She was still gasping for air as she watched them undress. Those yummy V's appeared as pants were discarded and more muscles were revealed. She vowed she would take a trip through that beautiful wonderland at some point. Maybe not tonight, but she would insist on having free rein to roam those delectable ridges and valleys.

Nico procured condoms while Stone returned to the bed.

"Put it on me," Stone ordered Nico. "But suck me first."

Not wanting to miss *that*, Stevie rolled toward Stone, propping her head on her hand so she could stare down his body as Nico leaned over him. His hands flattened on Stone's thighs and worked upward slowly.

"I watched y'all that night," Stevie mentioned.

Stone glanced at her. He started to speak but swallowed whatever he would've said with a soft rumble in his chest.

Nico had taken him to the root and was easing off slowly.

Stevie continued with her story. "I woke up while you were fingering his ass."

"Keep talkin'," Stone urged, his arm banding around her, his hand warm on her hip. "Tell me."

"Then I watched as you fucked him. Face to face."

Stone reached for Nico's hair, holding on while Nico bobbed up and down. "Fuck, you're good at that."

"I couldn't look away. Like now." Stevie gasped when Stone bucked his hips and buried his cock in Nico's throat. "It's so hot."

She remembered that encounter more than she remembered anything else. Watching Stone as he fucked Nico … it hadn't been solely physical. There'd been something else there. Something more. And after Stone left, she'd been pissed at him for Nico's sake, too, even while she'd existed on her hatred for both of them. Her heartache had disillusioned her, made her blame Nico for something he hadn't been responsible for.

"Don't make me come," Stone snapped, jerking Nico's head up. "Not yet."

There was a hint of satisfaction in Nico's expression as he rolled a condom on Stone and then himself. Before Stevie knew what was about to happen, she found herself trapped between them, Nico spooning behind her.

Stone fixed that by turning toward her. Nico pulled her with him so she was lying on top of him, her back to his chest. Then Stone was shifting and moving, attempting to get situated. Stevie planted her feet on the mattress, knees pointed outward, making room for Stone. There were too many knees to account for, but somehow, he made it work.

"Fuck," Nico hissed. "Oh, fuck yes."

Stone was stroking Nico's cock, his knuckles grazing her pussy as he did. He was watching his ministrations, his face contorted by pleasure. Beneath her, Nico's chest vibrated as he rumbled his pleasure.

Stevie felt the blunt head of Nico's cock against her entrance as Stone looked up. She held his gaze, relaxing as he guided Nico inside her.

Nico's fingers curled under her knees as he pulled her legs back, spreading her wide, trapping her arms in the process. She was pinned to him, her knees pulled back, his enormous cock tunneling in and out of her pussy.

God, he was big. He filled her exquisitely, her body stretching to accommodate his girth.

He shifted, pulling her, changing the angle, allowing him to fuck her deeper. Stevie was wracked by pleasure as she stared at Stone, willing him to join in. She wanted to feel both of them inside her.

Stone inched forward on his knees, stroking his cock before guiding it between her legs. Stevie held her breath when she felt him tease the head of his cock along her slit.

"You sure you can take both of us?"

Stevie wasn't sure of anything, but she didn't care. She *needed* this. "Yes. Fuck me."

His gaze swept over her, lingering between her legs as Nico continued to fuck her slowly. Finally, Stone pressed against her entrance, stretching her impossibly as he pushed inside, his cock sliding alongside Nico's.

"Oh, shit," Nico hissed at the same time Stevie said, "Oh, fuck!"

Stone's eyebrow rose, but he didn't stop. "Hurt?"

"A little," she admitted, even as her pussy gushed with excitement. It wasn't so much pain as a sense of being stretched beyond capacity. Her body gave way to the intrusion, accepting them both.

But it wasn't enough. "Fuck me. Please, Stone, just fuck me."

What she was asking for felt impossible. Especially as her body stretched to accommodate the girth of not one cock but two. Relief came instantly when Nico retreated, and Stone pushed in. They alternated, ramming their incredible cocks inside her, lighting her up from the inside. They kept that up for long minutes, keeping her filled, then they were both inside her at the same time again, stretching her more than she thought possible.

"Stay still," Stone finally said, the command barked at Nico.

Buried balls deep inside her, Nico stopped moving. Stone leaned forward, pushing in alongside him. He propped himself up on one hand beside Nico's head. His free hand began rubbing her clit as he pumped his hips, fucking into her, stroking Nico in the process.

"Oh, fuck," Nico growled, his voice guttural. "I'm gonna come."

That admission had Stevie skyrocketing toward release. Stone stroked her clit with his thumb and rocked into her. She watched his face, waiting for the moment of no return. When she saw it, she let go, succumbing to the sensation that ripped through her.

Stone grunted. Nico growled.

And together, they came as one.

NINETEEN

NICO WOKE IN A DARK ROOM, A soft body against him. He moved slowly, not wanting to wake Stevie. He didn't know what time it was, but based on his internal clock, Jäger was going to need to go out soon. He'd put him in his crate, keeping him safe before he'd joined Stevie and Stone, but no doubt he would get restless because that was what puppies did. And his puppy was no exception.

He eased out from under the blanket, grabbed his jeans from the floor, and slipped out, heading for the living room. As he pulled on his jeans, a sense of panic washed over him when he noticed the crate door was open. Flipping on a light, he looked around, expecting to find Jäger on the floor with something he shouldn't have chewed to little bits around him.

There was nothing on the floor. Not even Jäger.

And then he heard it.

The soft rumble of Stone's voice came from the back of the house. A second later, the screen door squeaked.

"Good job, little guy," Stone told him. "Let's get you a treat."

Nico moved closer, smiling when Jäger saw him. The puppy started hopping in his direction like he was his favorite thing in the world. Of course, Jäger did a quick U-turn when he heard the lid on the treat jar. He snatched his treat and bounded over to Nico again.

"Did he wake you?" Nico asked as he picked up the puppy and scratched his little head.

"No. I couldn't sleep."

"Strange place?" Nico asked.

Stone glanced down, not meeting his gaze. "No, I ... uh ... didn't want to close my eyes. I didn't want to wake up to find it was all a dream."

Nico hadn't expected Stone to reveal so much. He also hadn't expected Stone to be the sort to talk about what he was feeling. He'd hardly known the man back then, aside from things that all the high school kids knew about the guy they wanted to be like. Whenever they'd talked, it had been mostly in passing, a couple of times over the Jamesons' dinner table on the off chance one of Chelsea's siblings—besides Reilly—came around for a meal.

"It wasn't a dream," he told Stone, carrying Jäger into the living room. He urged him back into the crate, digging one of his chew toys out from under the small bed, hoping it would keep him busy until he fell asleep. Since he slept a good majority of the time—something that was normal, according to Stevie—he figured it wouldn't take long.

"It still feels surreal," Stone noted, taking off his coat and laying it over one of the bar stools. He wasn't wearing a shirt, only his jeans and boots. "Mind if I get some water."

While Stone toed off his boots, Nico returned to the kitchen to grab a glass from the cabinet. He handed it to Stone and nodded toward the refrigerator. "Water pitcher's in there."

While Stone poured himself water, Nico leaned against the counter, crossing his arms over his chest. He couldn't help but stare at the tattoo on Stone's right arm. He would admit he'd been shocked as shit to see his name etched inside those blocks. It was almost undetectable unless it was your name and you were used to seeing it. The N and the I were sitting on top of the C and the O, so it probably didn't look like anything more than random letters to most people.

Stone set down his now empty glass, his gaze shifting to his arm. He obviously saw Nico looking.

"What made you do that?" Nico asked.

Stone exhaled heavily. "I wanted to remember what I walked away from." He paused for a beat but then continued. "For a long time after I left, I was unhappy. But I was determined to make somethin' of myself. And to resist the urge to come back."

He glanced at Stevie's name on his other shoulder. "I told myself it was for the best. That Stevie was too young to know what she'd be signin' up for if I had stayed. I wanted more for her."

"She mourned you like you'd died," Nico told him. "She went through the five stages. It started with denial, which lasted for about a month. She insisted you would be back. The anger stage lasted the longest." Nico met Stone's gaze. "Two years, I think. She hated me as much as she hated you."

There was surprise mixed with guilt in Stone's hazel eyes. "Why'd she think it was your fault?"

"She needed someone to blame. She accused me of interfering. Said if I hadn't been there, that night wouldn't've happened, and you wouldn't've left."

"That's not true."

"I know that," Nico admitted.

He didn't bother telling Stone he'd had his own stages of grief. He'd been pissed at himself for thinking he even had the right to grieve the loss of something he'd never had in the first place.

"I felt somethin' that night," Stone said, holding his stare. "Somethin' I'd only ever felt for Stevie. Lookin' back on it, I don't understand how I could. I hardly knew you. It didn't make sense."

No, it didn't. But Nico understood what he meant because he'd felt something, too.

"I'd never done that before," Stone continued, now leaning on the counter, mirroring Stone's posture. "Been with two people like that. I haven't done it since." He nodded toward the bedroom. "Not until tonight."

"And?" Nico hated himself for asking, but he needed to know if this was just Stone's way of reminiscing.

"I felt everything I felt back then." Stone looked away. "Even if I don't have the right to."

"She's not as tough as she pretends to be, Stone. She doesn't love easily. It's still there, though. She'll pretend it's not if you take it away, but it's gonna hurt."

Stone stood tall, his arms falling to his sides. "I wouldn't be here if I only wanted one night."

Nico's heartbeat picked up speed as Stone approached.

"What about you?" He moved closer. "What is it that you want, Nico?"

He didn't know how to answer that because his feelings for this man had never made sense. That one night had altered him mentally and emotionally, and the result was devastating. Even after fifteen years, Nico still hadn't found what he was looking for. He hadn't been sure it even existed. Until last night. Until he was with Stevie and Stone again. Everything felt right. Like all the puzzle pieces were present, accounted for, and securely locked into place.

Feeling a little too raw and exposed, Nico pushed off the counter and took two steps forward, placing his palms on the island. It prevented Stone from meeting him face to face. He didn't want the man to see that much of him yet. He didn't want Stone to know that he'd felt whole twice in his life, and Stone had been there both times.

Nico was aware of Stone standing behind him, his warmth blanketing him even before Stone pressed his chest to his back.

"I can't explain it," Stone whispered, his breath fanning Nico's shoulder. "It doesn't make sense, but at the same time, it's the only thing that does."

"I know," he admitted, then closed his eyes when Stone's lips grazed his shoulder.

Stone's hands joined the fray, sliding around his waist, then up over his chest as his lips got bolder. Nico found himself leaning into him, tilting his head as the sensations tore through him.

"You love her," Stone whispered, his lips trailing along Nico's neck.

It took a second to process what he meant.

"I do," he admitted. "I have for a long time."

"It's more than obvious."

"Not to her."

"She deserves to know."

"I told her," he admitted.

"What did she say?"

"Nothing. Not then or since."

"When was this?"

"A couple of weeks ago."

Nico had considered bringing it up again, but he was scared to because he didn't want to ruin the good thing they had. If she wanted to talk about it, she would confront him. Until then, he didn't want to rock the boat. He wouldn't only be risking their business relationship if she didn't reciprocate his feelings. He could also lose her friendship, and that meant more to him than anything else.

Stone sucked on his neck, and Nico gasped, reaching back to grab his thigh. He held on, succumbing to the sensual assault, unable to resist. He'd been with a few men since his night with Stone, but none of those encounters had ever felt right.

This...

This felt right.

Being with Stone felt right.

Like he was exactly where he belonged.

With both Stevie and Stone, Nico felt that sense of completeness that had evaded him for so long. He wanted more, but he was scared to admit that. Scared he was going to push them in a direction that would have catastrophic repercussions if it didn't work out.

Stone's hand slid over Nico's throat. He applied pressure, pulling Nico's head back. The sensation was unlike anything he'd ever felt. Not since *that night*. The dominance in his touch rekindled that longing that had been simmering inside him.

"Take me to your room, Nico." Stone bit that sensitive spot where his shoulder met his neck. "Take me to your bed."

Unable to resist, that was exactly what Nico did.

STONE EXPECTED NICO TO RESIST. AT THE very least, come up with an excuse.

He didn't.

Nico led the way through the dark house, past the living room, past the door to Stevie's room. He continued down a long, narrow hallway that ended at the door to his bedroom.

Testing the waters, Stone instructed Nico to get on the bed.

"Face down," he demanded when Nico didn't hesitate. "Don't move."

He found a switch for the lamp on the nightstand. It provided enough light to see by, so he perused the room, taking it in, wanting to get a feel for Nico's personal space.

The room was enormous and felt even bigger because there wasn't much furniture. A king-sized bed, two nightstands, and a large armoire were all that it held, aside from the large shag rug on the floor and the curtains hanging over a sliding door on the back wall. The curtain was pulled back so that half of the door was uncovered. Beyond, it was pitch black, making the glass act as a mirror, allowing Stone to see Nico's form on the bed.

"Condoms?"

"Nightstand."

Stone assumed he meant the one he was standing beside, so he opened it. Sure enough, there was a box of condoms already open. He retrieved one. He found a bottle of water-based lubricant tucked inside. He grabbed that, too.

Setting both on the nightstand, Stone moved to the side of the bed. He stripped off his jeans, then helped to rid Nico of his pants, leaving both on the floor. He joined Nico on the bed, forcing his legs wide so he could kneel between them. Starting at Nico's calves, Stone gently kneaded his muscles, working his way higher. He lingered momentarily at Nico's ass, his thumbs dipping low, grazing Nico's heavy ball sac.

Nico's body quivered, but he didn't move.

To show his approval, Stone pressed his lips at the base of Nico's spine, then trailed his mouth over the hot, firm skin of his back. The guy was ripped, every muscle perfectly contoured, as though he'd been molded by an artist.

Stone worked his way higher until he reached his neck.

"Turn over."

Nico rolled beneath him, flipping to his back. Stone stared down into his face, admiring the smooth lines of his cheekbones, the high arch of his brow. His face had matured with age, making him not merely attractive but downright gorgeous.

"You know what I liked most about that night?"

Nico's eyes flashed with curiosity. "What?"

"Your vulnerability. Your willingness to do whatever I wanted. I could've done anything to you that night."

"You still can."

That admission made Stone's chest tighten. He still wasn't sure this wasn't a dream, but he prayed if it were that he never woke up. He wanted to live this out for the rest of his life. One night hadn't been enough back then, and it certainly wouldn't be enough now. But he didn't know where this was headed. And if he had to choose between spending one night with them or none at all, he would certainly choose this.

He lowered his hips, rubbing his cock along Nico's. He watched as the pleasure caused Nico's expression to change, his jaw relaxing as his eyes drifted closed. Stone rocked gently, the friction causing his skin to tingle.

"When was the last time you were with a man?"

Nico's eyes slowly opened. "It's been a while."

"How long's a while?"

"Five years."

That shouldn't have pleased him the way it did. "I'll try to be gentle, but I won't make any promises."

"I don't want gentle."

"No?"

Nico shook his head.

"You want rough?"

Nico's eyes flashed with heat. "Rough and dirty. That's your promise, right?"

Stone wanted to tell him he'd give him anything he wanted, but he kept that to himself. Unlike earlier with Stevie, he sensed Nico's vulnerability. It seemed that when it was just the two of them, he was nervous. Why? Because he couldn't hide what he was feeling? Because he couldn't distract himself? Couldn't hide from it?

Or was Stone merely seeing something that wasn't there? Was he fooling himself into believing that tonight could turn into more?

Propping himself on one arm, Stone reached between them, fisting both their cocks. He held firm, rolling his hips, using the momentum to guide his hand as he stroked them both, their cocks rubbing together.

Nico gasped, his head tipping back, his neck stretching. It was a beautiful sight.

"I want inside you, Nico." Stone continued to watch him. "I want to feel you wrapped around me."

Nico was breathing harder, his chest rising and falling faster.

"You want me inside you?"

"Yes, goddammit. Fuck yes."

"Put your hand on your cock," he instructed.

Nico reached down, his fingers grazing Stone's dick as he wrapped his fingers around himself.

"Stroke it."

When he started jerking himself hard and fast, Stone put his hand over his and squeezed.

Nico groaned, his hand stilling.

"Slow. I want you to come when I'm inside you. Not before."

A slight nod was Nico's only response.

Stone released his hand, watched as he resumed the up-and-down motion, slower this time.

Content he was following instructions, Stone reached for the condom and lube. He quickly sheathed himself and then generously applied the lube. He coated his fingers for good measure, then tossed the bottle aside.

"Pull your knees back. Show me where you want me."

Nico's eyes were heavy-lidded, his lips parted as he stopped stroking to do Stone's bidding. He pulled his knees toward his chest.

"Farther."

Nico gripped behind his knees and pulled them closer to his ears.

The sight was erotic as hell, and Stone knew tonight wasn't going to be rough and dirty. He would reserve that for tomorrow. Or the next day. Or every day after. Right now, he wanted to fill this man, to lodge himself deep inside and luxuriate in the heat of Nico's body as it enveloped him.

Sitting on his heels, Stone pushed one finger inside Nico's hole. He watched as it stretched around him. He was tight. Almost too tight. He fingered him for long minutes, waiting for Nico to relax, his cock hard as steel and growing harder by the second. Figuring there was no harm in pushing him, Stone worked two fingers in deep and curled them just the right way to find—

"Fuck!" Nico jerked and twitched.

Stone massaged his prostate, tormenting him with pleasure as Nico writhed and panted. It was obvious no one had ever done that to him before, and Stone loved that he was the first.

"I could make you come like this. Hell, I could make the orgasm last forever if I wanted to."

Nico gritted his teeth. "Fuck ... it feels ... *god* ... *damn*."

"Good?"

"Too good." Nico groaned. "You're gonna make me come."

Stone stopped, slowly withdrawing his fingers and replacing them with his cock. He leaned forward, gripping Nico's ankles to keep himself upright and to force Nico's hips to tilt as he sank inside him slowly. He watched as Nico's hole stretched around him, accepting him.

"Take all of me, Nico," he hissed as the pleasure robbed him of breath. "All. Of. Me."

When he was met with too much resistance, Stone slowly pulled back, pushed in again until he was fucking Nico with long, jolting thrusts.

"Oh, yeah." Stone heaved a breath when he was balls deep inside him. "Tell me what you need."

Nico was watching him. "Fuck me."

Stone began to move, rolling his hips. Slow, deep strokes. Nico's ass caressed every inch of him. He maintained a steady rhythm, which came to a jarring halt when he looked up at the sliding glass door and saw Stevie's reflection behind him.

"Come here, baby," he said, not looking at her.

Nico's teeth clamped shut, a hint of fear in his eyes.

Stevie joined them on the bed, lying beside Nico, her eyes glued to where their bodies were joined.

"You're a dirty voyeur, baby."

She smiled. "Can't help myself."

"You like watchin' me fuck him?"

She nodded, her eyes still fixed on Stone's cock moving in and out of Nico.

"Kiss him," Stone grunted, enduring the pleasure of being deep inside Nico's ass.

Nico turned his head, his gaze sliding over Stevie's face. She was the one who leaned in, initiating the kiss.

Stone wondered if she could feel Nico's tension. Her presence was increasing his anxiety, but Stone wasn't sure why. Then she brushed her fingers along Nico's jaw, and Stone felt him relax. She had the same effect on him.

Stone continued to move, rocking into Nico, retreating slowly. The friction was exquisite, the slow drag of that tight ring of muscle along Stone's dick.

Stevie pulled back, releasing Nico's mouth when Nico gasped. Her gaze returned to the point where Stone was buried to the hilt.

"Stroke his cock while I fuck him."

Her small fingers curled around Nico's cock, and Stone's dick swelled even more. He started moving again, slamming his hips forward, sinking in as deep as Nico's body would allow. As Stevie began stroking faster, Stone matched her rhythm until he was plowing into Nico.

"Oh, fuck! Stevie … Stone … holy fuck, that feels good." Nico cried out. "I'm gonna come. Oh, shit, I'm gonna come."

Stone couldn't hold back. As soon as Nico's cock erupted in Stevie's hand, he drove into him one last time and gave himself over to his release.

STEVIE CRAWLED UNDER THE BLANKETS WITH NICO when Stone disappeared to the bathroom to clean up after he'd grabbed a hand towel and cleaned Nico's chest. She had stared in awe, surprised by the sweetness of the gesture. For whatever reason, she hadn't expected it.

She wasn't sure what had compelled her to come in here. She hadn't intended to be caught watching, but she would admit it was a relief that Stone had invited her to join them. Not because she'd been jealous—although maybe a little—but because she'd wanted to be closer to them. She'd woken alone in her bed and almost instantly felt the cold chill of their absence.

Nico slid his arm under her head, pressing his naked body close to hers.

"You okay?" he whispered in her ear.

"Yeah. You?"

"Never again," he mumbled.

Before she could ask what that meant, Stone returned. He watched them for a moment, his eyes filled with something she hadn't seen in a long time. Something she thought she would never see again. Back then, she hadn't doubted Stone's love for her because she'd seen it in his expression. Either he couldn't hide it, or he didn't want to. It was there now, glittering in his eyes as he stared at them.

Stevie pulled the blanket back and patted the mattress, urging him to join them.

He hesitated for a moment but then clicked off the lamp. His enormous body dented the mattress as he lay down beside her. She waited until he moved closer, then draped her arm over his stomach. It caused him to move even closer until she was sandwiched between them.

Several minutes passed, and Stevie felt herself drifting. Just as she relaxed completely, she heard Stone's soft words whispered into the darkness.

"Thank you for lettin' me stay."

She wanted to tell him to promise he would never leave, but she held back the words. She wasn't a naive teenager anymore. There was no telling what tomorrow would bring, and she wasn't interested in promises he couldn't keep.

For now, she was content to have him there.

And though she wouldn't anticipate forever, she would continue to be content every day that he was.

TWENTY

Friday, February 2, 2024

STONE WOKE UP TO A WARM BODY curled up against his side, a soft arm draped over his stomach.

His first instinct was to shove out of bed, but he remained still, waiting until the events of the night flooded his brain. Something told him this wasn't going to be one of those instances when he snuck out to put distance between himself and whoever was next to him.

A familiar hint of strawberries and cream stirred his body.

No, there would be no running away from this.

He pressed a kiss to Stevie's forehead and let his fingers roam the warm skin of her back.

"We've never done this before."

Her soft words floated into his sleepy brain.

"No, we haven't." Fifteen years ago, they'd had sex numerous times, but never had they woken up together. He had lived with his parents, and she'd lived with hers, so the opportunity hadn't presented itself. The few times they'd gone to the barn, Stone hadn't wanted her to wake up like that. It was one thing to fool around, but he'd loved her enough to want more for her. Like a bed and a real room. And hell, air conditioning.

No, this was a dream come true. Waking up with her soft and warm against him, the day underway.

Stevie's hand wandered the way his did; only hers moved across his ribs, his stomach, inching lower.

Shifting his arm, Stone reached for Nico, but he wasn't there.

"He's makin' breakfast," Stevie said, her voice still whisper-soft.

"Does he need help?"

She pressed a kiss to his shoulder. "I offered. He said no."

"So, should we go back to sleep until it's ready?"

Stevie chuckled as she draped her leg over his. "Probably not."

"Did you have somethin' else in mind?"

"Mmm-hmm." Her lips trailed toward his nipple.

Helping her along, Stone shifted her so she was lying on top of him, straddling his hips. He brushed her hair back from her face and looked at her in the dim light filtering in through the partly open curtain.

Her dark eyes glittered as she met his gaze. Stone swore he saw a wealth of emotion in those mocha-colored irises.

"Good mornin'," he said with a smile.

"It's definitely about to be."

A second later, Stone grunted when Stevie rubbed her pussy along the length of his cock. He grabbed her thighs and guided her, letting her rub herself against him. She was hot and wet, and he longed to be inside her, but he was awake enough to realize they didn't have protection. Considering who she was, Stone didn't really care. He would've gladly slid home regardless of that, but he'd trained himself to pay attention. With the exception of Stevie, he'd never screwed a woman he intended to have a future with, so protection was crucial. For both of them.

With Stevie, he would leave the choice to her.

"Stone…"

"Want me to get a condom, baby?" he asked, keeping his voice low. "Or do you want to slide that slick pussy down my cock."

She lifted her head.

He could see the questions in her eyes, so he answered them. "I'm clean. You're the only person I've ever been bareback with."

Her eyes widened.

"I get tested regularly," he assured her.

She whimpered, continuing to rub herself along his dick, which was now a steel rod between them.

"How do you know I'm on birth control?"

Stone held her gaze. "I don't."

Evidently, it was the wrong thing to say because Stevie jerked. Before she could scramble off of him, Stone banded his arms around her and held on tight.

"You can't be serious," she hissed. "You don't know me anymore, Stone."

She was right. He didn't. But he knew enough to be certain that what he felt for her all those years ago was still just as potent as ever.

"Don't run," he said firmly. "Stay with me, Stevie."

He held her stare and rocked his hips, grinding his cock along the seam of her pussy. She gasped, her eyes closing, but she fought to open them again. Her ire was etched in the lines on her face, but even that looked good on her.

"If you want a condom, get one," he told her, keeping the hint of command in his tone because he knew she loved that.

Her jaw muscle bunched. "How do you know I don't have a disease?"

"Do you?"

"No," she huffed. "But you don't know that."

"You're right. I don't." Stone lifted his head so he could kiss her lips. "But I trust you, Stevie."

And he did. He trusted her with his whole heart. He probably shouldn't, considering how callous he'd been with hers all those years ago. There was a good chance she wanted to hurt him the same way he'd hurt her. However, he knew Stevie well enough to know she would launch an emotional attack, not a physical one if she wanted to get back at him.

"What if I wasn't on the pill and I got pregnant? You'd be screwed."

No, he would be right where he wanted to be. Stone didn't tell her that because he knew the question had been rhetorical. She was working through her emotional pain. He had hurt her, and she wanted him to know it. He knew. He did. And he would spend the rest of his life making it up to her. Even if the most he ever got from her was a few fleeting moments of intense pleasure.

Stevie whimpered as she continued to grind against him. "You should ... oh, God..." She inhaled deeply and started over. "You should know I don't love you anymore."

He ignored the vise that gripped his chest at her admission. "I know."

She gasped and groaned, her pussy growing wetter by the second. Stone held himself together by sheer will.

"And I don't plan to," she whimpered.

"I know."

Her eyes opened. "I'm serious."

Stone ensured she saw his sincerity when he whispered, "It's the least I deserve, Stevie. But that doesn't change the fact that I still love you." He brushed a strand of hair back from her face. "Let me love you, Stevie."

Tears filled her eyes, but she didn't let them drop. He gripped her hips even as she sat up. Her gaze snagged his as she wrapped her fingers around his cock and guided him where they both wanted him.

Stone's eyes rolled back as the heat of her body enveloped him. She was slick and hot, and ... God, she felt so damn good. Nothing had ever felt like this. Not in fifteen years.

He threaded his fingers with hers and let her use him as leverage as she rode him. She never looked away. Neither did he. The pleasure consumed every inch of his being. Heart, body, and mind.

Some would call him crazy, but Stone was still head over heels for this woman, and nothing would ever change that. He'd suspected it would all come flooding back if and when he ever saw her again. That was part of the reason he'd steered clear on his brief visits over the years. Now that he was here, now that she was with him, he knew it would be impossible for him not to spend the rest of his life loving her.

Even if she didn't want him to.

STEVIE COULDN'T BELIEVE SHE WAS DOING THIS.

She couldn't believe she was throwing caution to the wind, yet here she was, letting Stone weave his way around her heart once again. He was good at that. Sneaking in when she least expected it.

As much as she wanted to harden her heart against him, it was impossible. As though she'd been designed to love this man even if she didn't want to. And she didn't. She didn't want to love him because she knew he was capable of hurting her. He'd already wrecked her once. There was nothing to say he wouldn't do it again.

"You're so fuckin' beautiful."

If he was feigning the awe in his voice, he was a master manipulator.

She was panting heavily—with both exertion and the overwhelming heat that consumed her. This man made her feel things no one else ever had. The only person who'd come close was Nico, but they'd purposely kept this sort of intimacy at bay.

"Stevie … baby…" His eyes closed, head tipped back. "Oh, yeah. Fuck me, baby."

God, she hated that he was so damn sexy, especially when he was encouraging her to take what she wanted from him. And this was what she wanted. Nothing more. She would be content to have his body and only that for the rest of her life.

Liar.

And if she kept telling herself that, one day, it would be true.

Maybe.

"Stone…"

"Tell me, baby. Tell me what you need."

"You," she insisted. "Fuck me."

"You're doin' a mighty fine job of fuckin' me right now."

Stevie stopped moving.

Stone laughed.

She hated that he did because it made her feel lighter. Freer. She'd always felt that way with him. As though the world couldn't hurt her if he were around.

"How do you want me?" he asked, his voice gruffer than before.

She considered that for a moment.

"You want me to bend you over and fuck you from behind?"

Stevie nodded.

He chuckled again. "Or you want me to bend you in half and plow my dick into this sweet cunt?"

He prefaced those words by rubbing his thumb on her clit.

She nodded again.

Stone rolled his hips, lifting her, his cock buried so deep inside her, she wasn't sure where he ended and she began.

"Which is it gonna be, Stevie? Tell me."

"You decide," she told him, hissing through clenched teeth as his cock rubbed so perfectly inside her.

"You sure?"

She nodded.

Stone moved faster than a man his size should move. Stevie found herself on her side with Stone straddling one of her legs, the other he was holding up, her foot pointed at the ceiling. He rammed his cock deep inside her, the angle causing her to cry out as exquisite pleasure ripped through her entire being.

He didn't stop. His hips pistoned so fast it was impossible to keep up with the delicious sensations battering her body.

"Yes ... oh ... fuck ... yes! Stone!" She screamed his name again and again as she came in a violent rush that was so powerful it knocked the air from her lungs.

"You want me to come inside you?" he growled, continuing to fuck her like a man possessed.

She met his stare. "Yes."

"Fuck." He clamped his teeth together, his eyes lowering to the point where their bodies were connected.

Stevie watched him as he watched himself fuck her. It sent her spiraling again, another orgasm pummeling her as intensely as the first.

"That's it, baby," he grunted and groaned. "God, yes, Stevie. Oh, fuck..." Stone slammed into her one final time, holding himself there.

Stevie watched his face as he came deep inside her. It triggered another mini eruption that had her pussy locking down on him. His expression contorted into something that resembled pain.

When they were both wrung dry, he fell forward, catching himself before he crushed her. Giving herself over to the moment, Stevie wrapped her arms around his neck and kissed him.

As she did, she prayed that this man wouldn't stomp on her heart again. It was bad enough that the damn thing was already belly up, begging him to love her the way she'd always wanted him to.

Nico was pouring coffee into a mug when Stevie appeared.

"Mornin'," he greeted.

"Mornin'," she rumbled, her response not quite as cheerful. In fact, he'd go so far as to say it was hesitant.

"You should be hungry after that," he said, keeping his tone nonchalant.

"Oh, God." She covered her face with her hands.

Nico figured he could approach this a few different ways. One, he could act like he had no idea Stevie and Stone just fucked in his bed. Of course, he would have to be deaf to think that since Stevie's cries had echoed through the entire house. Or two, he could acknowledge that he was aware of her early morning extracurricular activities and pretend it was an everyday occurrence. Or three, he could greet her the way he'd wanted to greet her for the past couple of months and hope that it didn't make things weird between them.

Nico set the coffee mug on the counter and walked over to Stevie.

Option three was the only one that made sense to him.

Tilting her chin up with one finger, he pulled her hands away from her face. Her eyes were wide, glittering with what looked like concern or maybe embarrassment. It was difficult to tell.

Leaning down, Nico tilted his head and pressed his lips to hers. He waited until her mouth softened before he kissed her, licking his way inside and taking what he'd wanted for so long.

She kissed him back. Hesitantly at first, then with the same vigor he'd grown accustomed to.

Yeah, he was in love with this woman and had been for a long time. It hadn't happened *that night*, but a strong affection had, and it'd been building ever since. At this point, Nico wasn't sure he would make it through a day without her in it.

Her cool fingers caressed his cheek as she kissed him back, a soft hum coming from deep inside her. Her touch soothed him. It effectively erased all his worries because she kissed him with both passion and affection.

"Are you mad?" she whispered when he pulled back.

Staring down at her, Nico grinned. "How could I possibly be mad?"

As though trying to speak with her eyes, Stevie's head jerked, and her eyes popped open wide. "Because I had sex with Stone in your bed." She practically ground the words out through clenched teeth.

"What a coincidence. So did I."

Her smile was slow and rife with disbelief. It grew wider until she was shaking her head and laughing.

"Tell me there's coffee."

"There's coffee."

To his surprise, Stevie went up on her toes and kissed him on the lips. Softly this time. "Last night was incredible."

He processed the words as she hurried over to the coffee pot. She was correct; last night had been incredible. All of it. What threw him was the fact she mentioned it. Their encounters in the past were never discussed. Afterward, Stevie always walked away as though it had never happened. Even after he told her he loved her, he hadn't garnered so much as an acknowledgment. This time was different.

And fine, it was different any way you sliced it. For one, Stone was there.

Speaking of…

Stone walked into the room wearing the clothes he'd been wearing yesterday. His hair was wet, so Nico assumed he'd taken a shower. His expression was wary as he glanced at Nico, then Stevie, and back again.

Leave it to Jäger to liven things up. As soon as he saw Stone, he came running toward him, tripping over his own little paws but rebounding quickly.

"Hey, little guy," Stone greeted, going down on one knee to greet the puppy. "Have a good night?"

Jäger yipped and rolled onto his back, a silent request for a belly rub.

"Mornin'," Stone said when he looked up at Nico again.

"Mornin'. There's coffee."

"I should probably head out," he said hesitantly as he stood tall.

"That might not be possible," Nico informed him. "The roads are worse now than they were last night. Good news is, the temperature's supposed to get in the forties today, so it'll melt."

"Are you really tryin' to run out?" Stevie asked.

Nico heard the disappointment in her voice.

"I'd prefer to stay," Stone said, his gaze locked on her. "I just don't wanna overstay my welcome."

"You won't," Nico assured him.

Stone's expression was one of doubt, but he didn't say anything more.

"Grab some coffee. I haven't started cookin', but there's bacon and eggs in the fridge," Nico urged. "I'm gonna take a quick shower."

Not only did he need one, he also needed a few minutes to process what was transpiring. There was a weirdness in the air. One that he didn't recall after *that night*. He wasn't sure what it meant— if anything—and since he was known to overthink things on occasion, he figured there was no better time than the present to do just that.

TWENTY-ONE

WHILE NICO SHOWERED, STONE STOOD AT THE stove, finishing up the scrambled eggs while the bacon crisped in the oven.

"I did not know you could cook," Stevie said from behind him. "Your mom always teased that it wasn't safe to eat food you made."

"Yeah. But she's the one who taught me." He glanced back at her. "And I might've picked up a few things while I was workin' on a ranch or two. Nothin' fancy, mind you. But I can scramble some eggs, and I make a mean steak. What about you?"

"I like to cook, but I usually do less fryin'. That's Nico's specialty."

"How long've you two lived together?" Stone tried to play it off as a casual question, but he wasn't sure it came across that way.

"About a year now. I moved in when Niyah and Adam got engaged. They wanted to live together, and I would've been a third wheel. Nico offered to let me rent one of the rooms after Melanie moved out."

"Tell me about her," he said, curious about a woman who'd managed to get Nico to propose to her.

"She … uh…" Stevie sighed. "Melanie was nice enough. I think she loved Nico in her own way."

"Meaning? What? She loved his money?"

"No." Stevie set her mug down. "I think it was more than that, but she was very possessive. Once she came in and took over his life, she did her best to push everyone else out. Includin' Niyah. And if you know his sister, you know she doesn't stand for that. They butted heads a little."

That was interesting. More so, that Nico would've allowed someone to do that. From what he recalled, he'd been close to his sister.

"And the company? What prompted you to start your own company?"

Stevie answered more easily. "My grandpa left me some money when he died. Since I didn't want to work for anyone else, it was my only option, really." She took a sip of coffee. "Nico already had his degree by then. I knew if he could venture out on his own, he could make some real money. He worked for this other company after he graduated college. They were holdin' him back, so it seemed like the right thing to do."

Stone glanced back at her over his shoulder. "So it was his idea?"

She shook her head, smiling. "No. God, no. He argued with me for weeks about it. But I won in the end."

"And you love it?"

"I do," she said, and there wasn't an ounce of insincerity on her face. "I'm my own boss, plus, I get to work with plants. It's all I ever really cared to do."

Admittedly, Stone hadn't known what Stevie's plans were back in the day. She'd been close to graduating high school, but they never discussed what she would do afterward. And then he left.

He plated the eggs and placed them on the island before grabbing the oven mitts to get the bacon out.

Nico strolled in, his hair damp from his shower, just as Stone dumped the bacon onto one plate and set it in front of Stevie. He glanced between them and then headed for the coffee pot.

"If you leave her alone with that, she'll eat every piece," Nico teased, gesturing toward Stevie with his elbow.

"Only because I have to fight you for it," she said, smiling up at him.

Not for the first time, Stone saw the pure adoration on Stevie's face when she looked at Nico. They played it off as though they were merely roommates, but Stone could tell it was more than that. Nico had told him as much, and Stone was almost positive Stevie reciprocated his feelings. They were certainly more than merely friends with benefits.

"Tell me this," Stone prompted. "What would you be doin' right now if you hadn't inherited that money?"

Stevie's left eye squinted—which was fucking adorable—and he could tell she was giving it serious thought as she bit off the end of the bacon strip.

"She'd have a farm full of fruits and vegetables," Nico answered for her, returning to take the stool beside Stevie.

Stone leaned against the counter with his plate, eating while he watched the interaction between them.

"That's not true. I would've ended up doin' exactly what I'm doin' now."

Nico looked at Stone. "Don't let her lie to you. She hates sittin' in the office all day."

"I do *not* sit in the office all day," she countered with a laugh, and it was clear this was an argument they'd had before. "I get outside as much as you do."

"Maybe." Nico conceded. "But don't deny you'd rather be out there more."

Her eyebrow quirked as she looked at Stone. She shrugged. "I don't know. I love what I do, so does it matter?"

Stone figured there was no better time than the present to discuss the opportunity he was looking at.

"I talked to my aunt and uncle yesterday," he explained. "Lorrie and Curtis."

"I haven't seen them in a while," Stevie said as she continued to eat. "How're they doin'?"

"They're good. I saw 'em back in December when I came back for Christmas."

He realized his error as soon as the words were out of his mouth. Stevie's interest shifted to her food, and she avoided looking at him.

Figuring it was pointless to apologize profusely for something he couldn't change, he forged ahead. "Anyway. Curtis and Lorrie are willin' to give me about four hundred acres to do what I want with."

"Four hundred?" Nico whistled. "That's a lot of land."

A rapid thump sounded, drawing their attention to the floor. Jäger was sitting, his little tail thumping on the hardwood as he stared up at Nico. Stone didn't think it was the whistle that got his attention, but rather the smell of food.

"You're cute," Nico said casually. "I know. You want the bacon, but you don't *need* the bacon."

Jäger made a cute little whimper sound.

"Give him a bite," Stevie said, nudging Nico with her elbow.

"He doesn't need people food," Nico countered.

"It's *bacon*. It's *everyone* food."

Stone smiled, watching the interaction. He grinned even more when Nico caved, dropping Jäger a small piece of bacon.

"Four hundred's a lot of acres, is it not?" Nico asked him when Jäger was content.

"Dependin' on what you wanna do with it. If you're lookin' to raise cattle, you can get about one head per three acres. If you wanna work the land, it's enough to do pretty much anything."

Stevie waved her fork, not bothering to look up. "He wants to put some bulls out there."

Stone saw the concern in Nico's gaze. It was obvious he was worried about the shift in Stevie's demeanor.

"Actually," Stone said. "I was thinkin' about doin' somethin' else with it."

He set his plate aside and reached for his coffee.

"That's where you come in," he told her, waiting for her to look at him.

Stevie's eyes slowly lifted. "Me?"

"You're right," he continued. "Raisin' champion bulls was my goal at one time. Not necessarily my dream because I never quite nailed down what I wanted to do, but it felt like somethin' I'd be good at."

Stevie's eyebrows dipped low. "Not anymore?"

"I was thinkin' I'd rather farm it."

Her eyebrows popped toward her hairline. "As in what? Corn?"

"We could do that," he agreed. "Right now, we'd probably yield about a hundred bushels per acre."

Stevie looked at Nico, then back to him. "We?"

Stone swallowed hard and met her gaze. "The three of us."

Nico frowned, but he didn't speak.

Stone kept his focus on Stevie. "I heard you talkin' to Byron the other day. You were talkin' about greenhouses."

She waved her hand, but before she could interrupt, he continued.

"I was wonderin' if maybe the three of us could work together to come up with a plan for how to use the land. I'm thinkin' it'll give you enough room to build the greenhouses you want so you can produce whatever you want. Then maybe we could use some of it to open a farmers' market. We make it large enough to allow other vendors to sell their produce."

Her eyebrows were practically at her hairline. "Farmers' market?"

He nodded. "For the town. I hear they're all the rage."

She huffed a laugh, and the noose on his chest relaxed a little.

"I don't know if I'd go that far." She glanced between him and Nico. "But we could do a lot with it. Four hundred acres would be plenty to work with. But if you want to grow corn, we'd have to use quite a bit for that."

The fact that she used the word *we* gave him hope.

She rambled on, throwing out several ideas. Stone made a mental note of all of them, figuring he could easily work it into a business plan. It wouldn't take much to research the area and develop a market analysis and financial projections.

"You know that'll cost a lot of money," Nico added when Stevie exhaled with a sigh.

"I've got money," Stone noted. "More than I need to get this underway. What I don't have is the know-how. That's where you come in," he told Stevie.

"But I've already got a full-time job."

To Stone's surprise, Nico said, "But we both know this is more along the lines of what you'd rather be doin'."

"That's not true." She was offended. "I happen to love what I do." Her forehead creased as she glared at Stone. "And I don't appreciate you comin' in and tellin' me I don't."

He held up his hands. "That is not at all what I'm doin'. Swear it."

She shoved off the stool. "Coulda fooled me."

"Stevie, wait," he said, setting his coffee mug on the counter.

"No." She planted her hands on her hips and spun to face him. "What gives you the right to come in here thinkin' you know what I want? You don't know me, Stone. You don't know the first thing about me."

"You're right," he admitted, moving closer. "I don't. And I'm not pretendin' to."

When she didn't move back, he took that as a good sign, reaching for her hands.

Lowering his voice, he tried to defuse the situation. "I don't have an agenda, Stevie. Honest to God. This is merely an opportunity, and as soon as my uncle presented it, the only person I could think about was you."

"Too little too late, Stone," she said, tears filling her eyes. "You had your chance. And I've already told you, I—"

Before she could rip his heart out of his chest with her words, Stone pulled her closer, forcing her to look up at him.

"Don't say it."

"But it's true."

"Maybe so," he whispered. "But I've told you already, I'll do whatever it takes to make it up to you." Stone looked over at Nico. "And to you, too. Last night…" He looked back at Stevie. "Last night wasn't just sex."

"Maybe not for you, but it was for me," Stevie huffed and tried to pull away, but Stone held on, not letting her get away.

"It wasn't," he said, his tone harder than before. "You can lie and say it was, but we all know better."

"That doesn't mean I want anything from you," she countered hotly.

"I know." And he did. This wasn't going to be easy, but he was willing to put in the work.

Hell, at this point, he was willing to do whatever it took to show them both that the three of them were meant to be together. He felt it in his soul, and he just needed some time so they could feel it, too.

NICO WASN'T SURE WHAT TO SAY, BUT he couldn't ignore the sincerity he saw on Stone's face.

He also couldn't ignore the pain that glittered brightly in Stevie's eyes. He knew her well enough to recognize when she was shutting herself off. Stevie wasn't willing to open herself up to the heartache she believed Stone capable of. Who could blame her? The guy had left fifteen years ago and hadn't looked back. They'd both obviously been hurt by that decision, and Stone was looking to make up for it now. Nico respected that.

At the same time, it'd been *fifteen years*. Stone had been back for less than a month and while Nico didn't think there was a time requirement on relationships, it felt like they were moving fast. One night together … and yeah, Stone was right, it wasn't just sex. But that didn't mean they needed to jump into something as permanent as a business proposal. But he also didn't want to let Stevie pass up an opportunity he knew she would've jumped at if Nico had been the one to suggest it.

"Give me a chance, Stevie." Stone's voice quivered. "That's all I'm askin' for. From both of you. A chance to show you what we had … it was real. It's *still* real."

Nico was honestly surprised he was being included. Considering what they'd shared all those years ago had been nothing more than one night of intense pleasure, he didn't expect more than that now.

Did he want it? Yeah. More than he was willing to admit.

Last night … with Stone … Nico had felt everything he'd felt back then, only now it was multiplied by a million because he'd honestly thought he'd conjured it all up. That the past decade and a half had been filled with memories he honestly believed he'd simply exaggerated. But he hadn't. It felt right to him. Being with Stone. Being with Stevie. And being with both of them… After years of not finding anything that even remotely came close … that was what made him realize this wasn't something that happened every day.

And fine, maybe they were moving at warp speed. Stone could very well disappear tomorrow. But Nico didn't think that would happen.

He exhaled a hard breath when he realized he'd just mentally run himself in one big fucking circle.

"It was sex," Stevie snapped. "If you think it's more, that's on you. But I—"

Stone silenced her by crushing his mouth to hers.

Nico stared, watching as Stevie instantly surrendered. He wasn't sure she even realized she was doing it, but she stopped fighting him.

"It's not just sex," Stone snarled, his mouth hovering over hers. "Not for me. I've never felt anything like what I feel for you and Nico."

It stunned him that Stone was still including him in this conversation. He wanted to pretend he didn't care, but the truth was, it validated the emotions that had been churning inside him since he realized Stone was back for good.

"Tell me you feel nothin' for me," Stone insisted, his hand sliding to her neck, his thumb pressed under her chin, his big fingers curling around.

Goddamn, the two of them were hot together. Nico was surprised by how much it turned him on to see them like that. Stevie surrendering to Stone. It awakened parts that he'd thought were long dead.

"Hatred," she hissed. "That's what I feel for you."

It was a lie. Nico knew it as soon as the words were out of her mouth. But that was Stevie. She was erecting those walls, trying to keep her heart from getting pummeled. He couldn't blame her, but Nico wanted Stone to knock down those fucking walls. God knows Nico hadn't been able to. And yeah, maybe Stone was right when he said he should tell Stevie how he felt. Until he did, Nico couldn't fault Stevie for pretending there was nothing between them but intense heat.

"You can hate me," Stone told her. "But that won't stop me from lovin' you. And it won't stop me from provin' that deep down, behind all that hatred, you love me, too."

Stevie's mouth opened and closed.

"I don't expect either of you to trust me right now," Stone said. "I just want a chance to prove it. Can you give me that chance, Stevie?"

"I don't know." Her gaze shifted sideways. "Can *you?*"

Nico realized she was asking him.

His first instinct was to side with her because he knew that was what Stevie wanted. She wasn't asking him to be honest. She was seeking validation for her pain. But Nico knew her better than anyone else. He knew she would latch onto that and use it to shield herself for as long as she could. Nico wasn't willing to let her shut herself off from him anymore. They'd been doing this dance for a year, and he knew they could keep right on going at this pace for another and another. But they didn't have to. This was a chance for them to get it all out in the open, to admit what they were pretending didn't exist.

"Yes," he said, getting to his feet. "I'm willin' to let this play out. See where it goes."

Her eyes widened as he neared.

He moved to stand behind her, leaning down so he could speak directly in her ear. "And I think you are, too."

"No."

"Are you sure about that?"

There was a brief pause before she said, "What part of no don't you get?"

"The part that's a lie," Nico told her, feeling her resolve weaken as he stood there.

"Then the joke's on you," she hissed, attempting to pull away from Stone.

Nico stepped closer, pinning her between them. "We can make you admit it, Stevie. Is that what you want?"

She shivered, and it was followed by a huff that didn't have as much conviction as before.

"Make me, then," she snapped.

"You asked for it. Remember that." Nico slipped his hands underneath her sweatshirt, sliding higher so he could cup her breasts.

"I didn't ask for shit."

He breathed against her ear. "Your mouth says one thing, but your body's sayin' somethin' else."

Stevie whimpered, leaning into him. Nico knew without a doubt that this was what Stevie needed. She wanted them to fight her. She wanted them to prove her wrong.

And for the first time in his life, he was willing to do exactly that. Fight for what he wanted. And Stevie and Stone were the only two things he'd ever truly wanted. Now that he had a chance to have them, he wasn't about to pass that up. Not without a fight.

STEVIE DIDN'T KNOW HOW THEY'D GOTTEN HERE.

One minute, they were having breakfast; the next, she was crushed between Nico and Stone.

Although she didn't want to admit it, she'd never felt more alive than right now. Here, with both of them. And yes, she was filled with too many emotions to count. Hate. Lust. Love. The last one was what she had a problem with because if she allowed herself to love Stone again, she was going to end up getting hurt.

But if Nico was willing, would she be hurting him by fighting this? His presence made it bearable. He had the ability to settle the chaos. She trusted him implicitly.

Worst case, if Stone disappeared again, she would have Nico, right? He'd told her he loved her. Yes, it had been in the heat of the moment, and he hadn't mentioned it since, but surely there'd been a fraction of truth to it. Then again, Stone had tossed out the sentiment more than once since he showed up on their doorstep last night, so she wasn't convinced it meant the same to them as it did to her.

And yet, she was entertaining his proposal.

Stone's thumb brushed along her jaw, his hand still firmly around her neck. He wasn't applying pressure, merely holding her, but it was so erotic. No one had touched her like that but him.

Nico jerked the cups of her bra down, freeing her breasts, surprising her by the roughness of his touch. It sent sparks skating across her skin.

"Oh, God." She moaned, leaning into him as he plucked her nipples.

When she opened her eyes, she saw Stone watching, his gaze boring into her. Pure lust radiated from every pore, and she found herself desperate to soak it up. It pissed her off that he still had that much power over her. At the same time, it made her feel alive.

Before she realized what was happening, Nico pulled her sweatshirt over her head, but her arms were still in the sleeves. He grabbed the fabric, twisting it so that her arms were pinned behind her. She had nowhere to go. Stone was in front, Nico behind.

She tried to pull away, but they held her tighter.

Stevie gasped when Stone dropped to his knees and took her breast in his mouth. The heated suction dragged a moan from her. Her body betrayed her as she thrust her chest forward, silently urging Stone for more.

Nico bent down, his mouth near her ear. "This is what you want, Stevie. It's what you've always wanted."

"No," she argued, watching as Stone licked and sucked her nipple.

She gasped again when Nico cupped the back of Stone's head while he feasted on her breast. That simple touch ignited a firestorm in her veins.

It was true. The three of them were combustible together. She'd known it since *that night*. She'd fantasized about it for so long. Even after she gave up hope that Stone would come back, she'd imagined what it would be like if the three of them were together again. She'd tried to replace Stone with other men, but she'd always come back to this very scenario because, while she hated to admit it, Stone was irreplaceable. So was Nico.

"I've waited years to see him do that," Nico whispered in her ear. "To watch him feast on you."

She inhaled sharply when Stone bit her nipple before moving to the other one.

"You want our hands on you," Nico continued.

"Yes," she said, although she didn't mean for the word to come out.

"Only us."

"Yes." Even as she admitted it, she tried to fight them. It was part of the game, and she knew they understood that.

Nico pinned her arms tighter, his mouth sliding along her jaw, lower. He sucked on her neck while Stone bit her nipple.

She fought some more, loving the way they held her more firmly. It was their dominance that she craved. It made her burn hot.

Stone's mouth released her, and she tried to squirm away again. She thought for a second he was going to relent because he shifted away. But he was only reaching for the stool, dragging it closer. He shoved it toward Nico.

Then Stone was roughly jerking her leggings down, her panties with them. When she was naked from the waist down, he reached for the front clasp of her bra, unhooking it and letting it flap open.

She wasn't sure what they were doing, but then Nico pulled her backward onto the stool. He still had her arms shackled behind her, but he kept her from falling by using his body.

"Oh, shit!" she cried when Stone's big hands pushed under her knees, lifting her legs, spreading them wide. He buried his face between her legs, licking her from entrance to clit again and again.

She was going to come. Not only from the sheer ecstasy of Stone's wicked tongue but the way Nico was keeping her pinned in place. They had complete control of her body. The only thing she could do was endure.

"Fuck, that's pretty," Nico rasped, his chest against her upper back. "His mouth on your cunt."

God, she loved when Nico talked dirty.

"You're gonna come on his face, aren't you, Stevie?"

She whimpered, trying to hold back the release that was barreling down on her. She didn't want to give them the satisfaction. But refraining was futile. She wanted this more than she'd wanted anything in a long damn time.

"That's it, girl," Nico urged. "Come for us."

Us.

She loved that word. She loved the vivid images it painted in her mind. The two of them with her always.

"Oh, God!" Stevie screamed when Stone wrapped his lips around her clit and flicked it ruthlessly with his tongue. She came in a heated rush, her body vibrating. If it hadn't been for Nico behind her, she would've crashed to the floor. But he was there, holding her.

She gasped for air, panting like she'd run a mile, her limbs like noodles.

"My turn," Nico stated.

"Wait," she mumbled, but they ignored her as they traded places, working together to keep her where she was, sitting on the stool, her legs spread wide, arms shackled.

Then Nico was between her legs, his mouth working her until she was nearly in tears from the overwhelming pleasure. She was too sensitive, but he knew just what to do to keep the pain at bay.

Stevie writhed and moaned, leaning into Stone, grateful he was there to hold her up while Nico fucked her with his tongue.

Nico lifted his head, meeting her gaze. He pinched her clit between his forefinger and thumb, gently applying pressure. Enough that she saw stars.

He teased her entrance with one thick finger.

"Will you agree to give this a chance?" Stone asked, his voice rasping from behind her.

"I don't know," she admitted, crying out when Nico applied a little more pressure on her clit.

"Agree, and Nico'll make you come again."

Stevie held Nico's stare. "Please."

"Agree," Nico insisted.

"I can't."

He pushed one finger inside her. Slowly. Delicately.

"Fuck me," she demanded, grinding her teeth together.

"Agree," he repeated.

"I can't."

"Yes, you can," Stone insisted, his hand sliding over her chest, his other hand still banding her hands behind her back. He pinched her nipple. "Just agree, Stevie. And we'll give you everything you need."

Nico gently fucked her with his finger. It wasn't enough. She needed more. She was so close.

"Nico..."

"Agree, darlin'," he said, his eyes hot.

She didn't want to. Yes, she wanted it more than anything, but she was terrified this was going to backfire in her face. If she gave in...

Stone's beard scraped along her cheek as he leaned down. "Give us this, baby. Give *us* a chance."

She knew he was referring to the three of them as the *us* in that statement, and it caused her heart to pinch.

"Okay." She nodded. "I will."

"You will what?" Nico asked, pushing his finger in deep, curling it just right.

"Oh, God." She clamped her teeth closed as the pleasure intensified. "I'll ... oh, fuck ... I'll give us a chance."

They'd clearly been waiting for that because Nico began fucking her with two fingers as he leaned down and sucked her clit. Stone stood tall, crushing her arms between them so he could use his hands to pinch and pluck her nipples.

It took mere seconds before Stevie detonated. She came with a violent scream, her body shattering into a million pieces.

TWENTY-TWO

"I'M TELLIN' YOU. SHE'S DONE THIS BEFORE. I'd go so far as to say she's a pro."

Stone glanced over at Nico, fully expecting to see ... well, to be honest, his mind had gone in a vastly different direction because what he expected to see was Stevie on her knees in front of Nico, giving him the blowjob of a lifetime. She wasn't on her knees. In fact, she was a few feet away from Nico, both of them on the couch in the living room.

"Hey. You still over there?"

Nico was now waving his hand, attempting to get Stone's attention.

"Yeah. Sorry."

"She can help you. All you've gotta do is ask. Who do you think did the business proposal for D and S?"

Stevie pointed at herself with both thumbs, then mouthed, "That was me."

Damn, she was cute.

"Or, you know, you could come cuddle up on the couch, and we can work on"—her arm shot straight up in the air, hand tilted, finger pointing as though she was aiming over his head—"*that* later."

She was sitting with her back to the corner of the couch, a blanket covering her from the neck down, while Jäger slept in her lap. Stone wasn't one to lay around the house and do nothing, but she made it look inviting.

She patted the cushion beside her. "I don't bite."

Stone sat up straight, planting both hands on his head so he could stretch. "But I do."

Even from where he sat on the stool in the kitchen, he could see her eyes glitter.

It had been two hours since their rendezvous in this kitchen—on this very stool, actually. The three of them had retreated to their separate corners, finishing their breakfast and keeping the conversation off the topic of their relationship. As far as Stone was concerned, there was no need to hash it out anymore. Stevie had promised to give them a chance, and he was going to hold her to it.

After breakfast, Stevie disappeared to take a shower, and Stone asked Nico if he could borrow the iPad that had been sitting on the counter. As soon as Nico gave him the go-ahead, Stone started researching business plans pertaining to farming and he hadn't left this stool since he started.

"Lorrie told me fourteen days," he said, forcing himself to his feet. "And I've got to talk to their boys to get their blessing."

"You think they'll give it to you?" Nico asked as Stone approached.

"Curtis said they have no desire to do anything with it. Plus, he's got more set aside to pass on to them when…" He waved his hand, not wanting to think about the day his uncle was no longer of this earth.

Stone flopped down on the couch between Nico and Stevie, stretching his legs out in front of him. He looked at the television but wasn't paying attention to what was on the screen. He had too much on his mind.

"When's the last time you talked to your cousins?" Nico asked.

"It's been a minute," he admitted. His trips to town generally didn't involve visiting anyone but his parents. And his brothers and sisters if they were around. He would see everyone else on holidays, mainly those who popped by his parents' house for something.

"Your family's close, though," Stevie acknowledged. "I'm sure they'll be happy to catch up."

Stone nodded, peering over at her. "How're your folks?"

Her expression shuttered. "They ... uh ... divorced. My mom's in New York with her new rich husband. My dad's taken up internet dating."

"Oh, shit." He twisted to face her more fully. "I'm sorry. I didn't know."

Her eyebrow quirked, and to his surprise, she didn't blast him with a remark meant to make him feel like shit. He would've deserved it, obviously.

Stevie waved a hand. "It's no big. I'm sure my dad won't get swept up in some catfishing scam where he gives what little money he has to some burly dude pretending to be Sally McBigBoobs."

Stone glanced at Nico to see what his reaction was. His response was a shrug.

Knowing he was only digging a deeper hole, Stone directed his next question at Nico. "And your mom?"

"Dead," he said without an ounce of emotion.

Way to go, Jameson. Sure know how to ruin the mood.

Fuck.

Stone sat up, planting his elbows on his knees. "I—"

Before he could make an excuse to go home, Stevie slipped out from under the blanket, carefully crawling over Jäger, who was far too comfortable to notice Stone was mastering the art of putting his foot in his mouth.

"I'm sorry," she said, urging him back so she could straddle his legs.

Stone relaxed, staring up at her as she planted her hands on his shoulders.

"I said I'd give this a chance, and I meant it. But I should warn you. Parents—mainly mine—are a sore topic in this house. But now you know."

His body warmed as she settled on his lap, her fingers trailing along the neck of his shirt.

Stone couldn't explain the sense of calm that settled over him when he was around Stevie. It had always been the case. She had a way about her that made people comfortable. Even when she was ratcheting up the temperature on his internal thermometer.

Her eyes trailed the path of her fingers. "Let me see if I can get you caught up."

He smiled. This was the Stevie he remembered. She'd always been quick to defuse a situation.

"After you left, we all graduated high school. Me, Nico. Your sister."—she lifted her hands, balling them into fists, and cheered—"Class of 2009. Yay!"

Stone laughed, content to listen and watch.

"Then, Nico went off to college." She flashed a grin. "Landscape architect, which, if I recall correctly, was an idea he came up with after he learned that Donovan and Brady had gone the traditional architect route."

Stone glanced at Nico. He laughed when Nico both shrugged and rolled his eyes.

"Don't deny it," Stevie told him. "I started community college and lived at home. I worked in the diner for about a week. Hated it. Luckily, my dad told me I should focus all my efforts on school and not try to do more than I could handle. I didn't argue, filling my class schedule. I got my associate degree in business management. My dad was proud of me, so he urged me to apply to a big university because he knew business was not where I wanted to focus my life. Since Niyah was going to UT, I figured it was worth a shot. I got in. Plant biology is my jam. It was awesome. Meanwhile, Nico was still learning to rake dirt and make it look pretty."

Nico snorted.

Stone huffed a laugh. The tension had faded completely, and it was all due to Stevie's efforts. But he wanted to know more.

"Keep goin'," he urged.

"Okay." She sat back on his thighs, forehead creased in thought. "I finished my bachelor's degree, but unlike the overachievers I associate with, I stopped there. Niyah and Nico, not so much. They like to shine. Nico got his master's degree. Niyah, the *real* overachiever, went for her doctorate. That's how she met Adam. He's cool. A nerd like her. They make a good pair."

She took a breath. "Niyah and I rented a house here in town, and that's where we were when Nico finally came home. I think he slept on our couch for about a week. Maybe a month."

Nico was shaking his head. "I did not."

"But you could have." She flashed another grin. "Shortly after that, my grandpa died."

Her gaze shifted back to Stone, and he could see the echo of sadness still there.

"Long battle with cancer. I spent a lot of time with him after I graduated high school because my parents were always fighting. We were close. Me and Grandpa. I figure that's why he left me money. He wanted me to be independent of my parents. I used it to bribe Nico into startin' a business."

Nico laughed. "Bribe? Is that what you're callin' it?"

"Works." Her grin grew wider. "We started the business. It was slow at first. Real slow. But we were both determined. That's how he met Melanie. Her parents are clients of ours. *Were*, I guess, is the better word. They don't like him much anymore since he broke up with her."

"They like me just fine."

Stevie giggled. "I know. Which is weird. He broke their little girl's heart, but they still like him." She shrugged. "Anyway. *Before* he broke her heart, he planned to live happily ever after with her in this great big house. They were gonna have a horde of kids and at least three house servants." Stevie canted her head. "After all, Glamour-life Barbie didn't intend to pay for anything or, God forbid, get her hands dirty with kid slobber. She preferred to spend her days at the hair salon getting ready to have tea with her bitchy ass friends."

Nico snorted. "She's not too far off on that."

"I take it you didn't like her?" Stone asked Stevie.

"I liked her just fine—right up until she decided she'd fill Nico's schedule so he didn't have time to spend with his sister. That lasted a while. And then, as a shock to everyone who knew them, Nico proposed." She gasped dramatically, pressing her hand to her chest. "With wedding bells as the soundtrack to her new future, Glam Barbie morphed into Psycho Barbie and became downright mean."

Stone looked at Nico again, trying to gauge whether there was any truth to this story. He was surprised when Nico nodded, his gaze shifting to his lap.

"But thankfully, he came to his senses and realized good ol' Mel couldn't give him what he needed."

"Which was?"

"Penis," Stevie answered, her expression serious.

Stone barked a laugh.

"What? It's true. Don't believe me?"

He planted his hands on her thighs. "I believe you."

She sighed. "Anyway, last year, Niyah and Adam got engaged, and they borrowed the wedding bell soundtrack for themselves, so I knew it was only a matter of time before I would be lookin' for a new place to live, and I mentioned as much to Tara. She's the receptionist at the office. Nico, who likes to eavesdrop, overheard us, and the next thing I know, he's offerin' to let me rent a room in this great big mansion."

"I didn't eavesdrop," Nico told her. "Niyah told me."

Stevie rolled her eyes, smiling at Stone. "So he says. And somewhere in there, my mom decided that Texas was much too small to contain all her big dreams, so she got on the internet and started searchin' for the Barbie life that Mel had tried to design for herself—I think they drank from the same well or somethin'. Anyway, my mom found some rich dude who would give her not just the Barbie dream house, but the Barbie sports car, the Barbie swimmin' pool, the—" She waved a hand and exhaled heavily. "You get the picture."

"You have somethin' against Barbie?"

She laughed and rubbed his chest. "A little bit, yeah."

He'd missed this woman so damn much.

Stone tapped her thigh to get her attention. "While Nico was shackin' up with Glamour Barbie and Niyah was datin' her future husband, who was keepin' you company?"

Stevie snorted. "Oscar. And no, it was never serious. He entertained me—in bed and out—but he was not boyfriend material. The guy still sleeps on his mom's couch from time to time. I ended it a few months before I moved in here."

Good to know.

Still watching her, Stone asked, "At what point in this story did you and Nico start doin' the nasty?"

She laughed, the sound so beautiful, he couldn't resist reaching for her.

"That wasn't planned," she said cautiously, glancing at Nico.

Stone looked, too, and saw Nico nod as though giving her permission to reveal their secret.

"We ... uh ... we found ourselves alone last Valentine's Day. We might've sucked down a little too much rum and Coke and ended up horizontal."

"I'm pretty sure we were vertical that first time," Nico supplied. Her eyes lit with amusement. "Maybe."

"And since then?" Stone probed, wanting desperately for these two to finally admit that what was happening between them was far more than mere sex.

"SINCE THEN, WHAT?" STEVIE ASKED, PLAYING DUMB.

She knew exactly what Stone was getting at, but she wasn't ready to go there yet. It was one thing to agree to this orgasm-producing triangle thing they had going on, but something else entirely to start putting names to the feelings that came with it.

"How often do you sleep in your own beds?"

"Every night." That much was true.

Although they'd had sex a few times over the past year, Stevie made a point to walk away after. She knew what would happen if she stuck around, and she refused to make things awkward for Nico.

"What about you?" she asked Stone. "Give us the CliffsNotes of your life in the past fifteen years."

His eyes glittered. He obviously knew a redirect when he heard one. Question was, would he fall for it?

Finally, Stone nodded his head slowly, his hands once again moving leisurely over her thighs. His gaze lowered as though he was interested in where his fingers were, but Stevie got the feeling he couldn't look her in the eye when he shared his story. Regardless of whether they were moving forward, there was still a lot of residual pain there.

"I hopped around from a few ranches after I left here. Worked as a temporary hand where I was needed. About a year in, I landed a more permanent gig. Stuck around for a while, worked my way up to foreman." His gaze lifted slowly. "Got fired, moved on."

Stevie probably didn't want to know, but she asked anyway. "Why'd you get fired?"

"I was ... uh ... fuckin' the owner's wife."

She did her best not to react, but since she was sitting on his lap, she knew he felt the tension that took up residence in her muscles.

"It was stupid," he said, his hands resting more firmly on her thighs as though he feared she would move. "But I was reckless back then. I didn't give a shit about anything but makin' a name for myself. I did what I needed to do to numb myself."

"And sex with a married woman was your drug of choice?"

"I didn't want strings," he said, his gaze lifting. "And I knew she'd married him for the money—something I didn't have—so I wasn't worried she'd get attached."

"That's one way to do it," Nico said flippantly.

"Yeah." Stone cleared his throat. "After that, I went to work at another ranch. Started from the bottom again. Worked my way up as far as the owner was willin' to let me go. Ended up gettin' a job offer from the owner of the Double J. Didn't have to work my way up that time. That's where I was before I came back here."

"Why?"

Stone met her gaze. "Why what?"

"Why'd you leave to come back here?"

He held her stare for what felt like years before he finally said, "Boss found out I was screwin' his daughter."

If it weren't for the shame she saw on his face, Stevie would've hurried off of him. Instead, she forced herself to remain still, wanting him to elaborate.

"Was it serious?" Nico asked.

"Not at all." Stone's eyes swam with regret. "Not on my part, at least. I didn't even like her. She was a grade-A bitch, and she wanted everyone to know it. I looked past that, and we became friends."

"With benefits," Stevie noted.

Stone shrugged. "I didn't realize she wanted more. Or that her dad would *expect* more. He gave me an ultimatum: marry her or move on. I opted for the latter."

Stevie hated herself for asking, but… "So you didn't love her?"

Stone was still looking at her, his hazel eyes intent. "No. I've never loved anyone else." His voice dropped an octave. "Only you."

Stone wasn't proud of what he'd done; that was clear. It was then she realized she wasn't the only one who'd been hurt by his actions. Walking away hadn't been easy for him, either. Whether she should or not, Stevie believed him.

Not that it solved all her issues, but it helped. She still harbored a lot of hurt from him leaving her with promises he never intended to keep.

"Are you stickin' around this time?" She needed to hear him say the words. She needed to see the truth in his eyes.

"Yes." His hands stilled on her legs. "That's about the only thing I'm certain of right now. I'm not leavin' again."

"Okay."

As soon as the word was out of her mouth, Stone exhaled heavily. Had he been worried she'd think he was lying? She'd never seen this vulnerable side of him before. Back when they'd been together, he'd been the larger-than-life, cocky man who knew what he wanted and didn't take no for an answer.

"I'm startin' over," Stone said, glancing between them. "And I'm hopin' to do it with y'all in my life."

Stevie looked at Nico. He was watching her, not Stone. She wasn't sure what he was thinking because he had a way of masking his expression, making him impossible to read.

Jäger stirred on the couch and a second later, he was crawling into Stone's lap, his tail wagging as he sniffed and snorted.

"I should take him out," Nico said, getting to his feet.

Stone shifted back when Nico reached for Jäger, picking him up and carrying him toward the back door.

When it was just the two of them, Stone looked at her. "I should probably head home. The roads should be fine now."

She knew he was right. The sun was out, and the temperature was above freezing. The remnants of yesterday's mild storm would be gone completely by nightfall. It was one of the benefits of living this far south.

Stevie nodded. "Maybe we can meet up to go over your business plan. You know, once you put it together."

Stone's hands slid over her hips, cupping her butt as he pulled her closer. "How about dinner? Tomorrow night. My place."

"Maybe."

He flashed a grin, urging her closer with his hands on her back. Stevie leaned in, unable to resist him despite knowing this was moving too fast. She already wished he wouldn't leave, but she knew it was the best for all of them. They needed some space, some time to process what happened last night.

"You think one day you might forgive me?" Stone whispered, his breath fanning her lips.

"There's a good possibility."

"That's all I need to hear." He cupped her face, his thumb brushing along her cheek. "The one thing I've learned over the years is to never take anything for granted. I did it once, and I've been unhappy ever since. I don't intend to do it again."

Warmth curled like smoke ribbons in her chest. She wanted to believe him. Right now, she actually did. And that scared her because she was nothing if not pragmatic. She tried to see the best in people, but she was quick to dismiss them when they hurt her. Stevie had convinced herself that life was too short to dwell on the hurt and anger. Sure, it'd taken years for her to believe that, and this man was the reason.

"I won't let you break my heart again," she whispered.

Stone's eyes turned glassy. "I'll do my damnedest not to."

"And I'll never forgive you if you break Nico's."

His gaze bounced over her face. "I don't intend to."

"Good."

Stevie started to get up, but Stone pulled her in, pressing his mouth to hers. She surrendered to the kiss, leaning into him, teasing his silky hair as their tongues did a slow waltz.

When they finally separated a few minutes later, Stevie knew he'd successfully burrowed right back into her heart. Almost as though he'd never left.

TWENTY-THREE

STONE WOULD'VE PREFERRED TO SPEND THE ENTIRE day holed up in Nico and Stevie's house with them, but he had things to do, so after checking with Nico to ensure he wasn't upset about what Stone had revealed, he'd made his exit.

The first thing he did when he got home was pull out his laptop so he could work on the proposal for Curtis and Lorrie. It had been on his mind since yesterday, and though he didn't get a firm agreement from Stevie about it, he'd come up with a better idea. Rather than go off half-cocked, he decided to put together a proposal for her as well.

Last night, when he'd been unable to sleep, Stone had run through a dozen ideas in his head, but one in particular had lingered. It had surprised him that he'd gone from wanting to raise championship bulls to tending the land to looking forward to designing a farmers' market that the entire town could utilize. But the more he thought about it, the more he liked the idea. Plus, it incorporated Stevie's dream, which felt right to him.

No, he couldn't make up for leaving town fifteen years ago and leaving her behind, but he could prove to her that he wasn't the same selfish guy he'd been back then. Plus, it was something that would benefit his hometown, which not only appealed to him greatly but would likely appease Curtis and Lorrie, too.

Granted, he still had to broach the subject with Curtis and Lorrie's sons. There was no telling how that would go. At one point, he'd been relatively close to his cousins, but all those years away hadn't benefited him in that regard. He no longer had the same bond he'd had back then. These days, he knew only what the annual Christmas cards told him.

Shifting his attention to his laptop, Stone cleared his head of the clutter. He could overcome all those obstacles if he simply put it all down in a manner that made sense.

He got to work.

Three hours later, Stone had just finished whipping tuna fish in a bowl when a knock sounded on the door. He looked over to see Donovan standing on the porch. Before he could wave him in, his big brother opened the door and strolled inside like he owned the place.

"Come on in, I don't mind."

Donovan glanced around. "I didn't think you did. I figured you'd be hard at work."

"Doin' what?"

"I don't know. Gettin' settled, maybe." Donovan was looking directly at the stack of boxes Stone had shoved into the corner of the living room.

"Haven't gotten around to it yet."

Donovan chewed on his bottom lip as he leaned against the kitchen island. "Not enough time? Or you're not sure you're stayin'?"

"Why's everyone keep askin' me that?"

"Maybe 'cause you're actin' like it's a vacation."

Stone frowned as he scooped tuna fish onto a slice of bread. "How so?"

"For starters, you're livin' in the barn."

"And that bothers you?" Stone didn't understand why Donovan thought it was a problem. Where the hell else was Stone going to go? "Shouldn't you be at home givin' your man shit instead of me?"

"He's workin'."

It was impossible to miss the disappointment in Donovan's tone.

Stone chuckled. "Can't convince him to quit and become your personal servant?"

"Don't think I haven't tried."

Stone looked up at his brother.

"Kiddin'. It took everything I've got to get him to accept my marriage proposal."

"Well, that's—wait." Stone stared at his brother. "He accepted?"

Donovan's expression morphed into one that radiated happiness. "He did, yeah. Finally."

"Y'all been together what? Two weeks?"

"A little longer than that," Donovan said with a smirk. "Timin's everything, ain't it?"

Leaving the bowl of tuna on the counter, Stone walked over to Donovan. "Congratulations, man." He hugged his brother. "That's fantastic. It's only *a little* weird that you found the guy on the playground. But hey, to each his own, right?"

Donovan hugged him back, slapping his back harder than was necessary. "I knew you'd give me grief."

Stone returned to his tuna fish. "Just make sure you've got life insurance. He's gonna be around a *long* time after you're pushin' up daisies."

Donovan barked a laugh. "Fuck off. Fifteen years ain't that much—" He cut himself off and rolled his eyes. "Yeah. I hear it. I'm shuttin' up now."

Stone chuckled. "Think of it this way. If nothin' else, he'll keep you on your toes. Plus, he's young enough to care for you when you're wearin' diapers and sittin' in your recliner all day."

"Fuck off."

Stone chuckled. "Seriously, man, I'm happy for you. This is a good thing. Tate's a good guy."

Truth was, he wasn't interested in giving his brother shit about his newfound love. He really was happy for Donovan and Tate. Hell, he was happy for anyone who found love.

"Why're you here? I know you didn't come by just to announce your weddin' plans." He slapped another piece of bread down. "You want some tuna fish?"

"I'll pass. But thanks." Donovan took a seat on one of the bar stools. "Actually, I came by because I ran into Trey Walker in town yesterday."

Stone didn't know Trey all that well, but he'd gone to school with Trey's brother, Cal.

"What'd he have to say for himself?" Stone asked, sensing his brother had a reason for bringing him up.

"He owns Camp K-9 with his husband and wife."

Stone canted his head and grinned. "You know, there are more people in this town who've got two spouses than there are probably anywhere else in the world."

"Coyote Ridge is a diverse town."

"Not to mention inclusive," Stone noted. He liked that about his hometown.

"The whole triad thing's not as uncommon as you think," Donovan said before continuing his original topic. "When Trey and them bought the land to move their trainin' facilities to, they also purchased some adjacent land. Trey's lettin' the high school use it."

His brother paused as though *anything* about that sentence made sense.

"And this means somethin' to me because…?"

"Relax and eat your sandwich," Donovan said with a snort. "I'm gettin' to the point. Give me a second."

Stone laughed.

"Anyway. Trey mentioned the high school's lookin' to hire someone to manage their FFA program."

"I'm not a farmer, D." *Not yet, anyway.* Since he wasn't ready to reveal his land proposal to anyone yet, he left it at that.

"It's about agriculture, you dumbass."

"Semantics."

"No," Donovan stated firmly. "You've got significant experience in both leadership and in—"

Stone set down his sandwich. "Look, D, I know you mean well, but trust me when I tell you, you don't want me teachin' anyone's kids."

It did foster a few more ideas for his proposal, which he made a mental note of for later.

Donovan held both hands up. "Fair enough. Thought I'd pass it along." He lowered his hands. "What is it you wanna do?"

276

If ever there were a more difficult question…

"Right now, I wanna take a minute to eat my damn sandwich."

Donovan chuckled as he got to his feet. "Got it."

"You don't have to go," he said when Donovan started toward the door. "You mean well, I know that. I'm just…"

"Confused?"

"Tired," he admitted. "Tired of not knowin' what I wanna do."

Donovan stared at him from where he stood by the door. "But you wanna stay here? In Coyote Ridge, I mean."

"Yeah," he said, and meant it. "It's about the only thing I do know right now."

"Good. Believe it or not, I'm glad you're back."

"Thanks." He glanced at his sandwich, then back to his brother. "You're welcome to stay if you think you can shut up for five minutes so I can scarf this down."

Donovan laughed and waved a hand. "I'm headin' home. I was avoidin' it because Tate's at work. He's only lived there for a few weeks, but it's a little lonely when he's not there."

"You're serious about this, huh?"

"More than I've been about anything in my life."

Stone watched as Donovan waved and walked out the door. He stared at the space his brother had vacated while he ate his sandwich. As he did, his thoughts drifted to that night so long ago. The night that shifted something inside him, even though he hadn't been willing to look too closely at it at the time.

"You awake?" Stone whispered, talking to Nico.

"Yeah."

For the past hour, Stone had been drifting with Stevie in his arms. He was exhausted, but the adrenaline was still steadily flowing in his veins, making it impossible for him to relax completely.

Carefully, he eased out from under Stevie, tucking a pillow under her head and pulling the blanket over her. She didn't budge, making him smile. He kneeled beside her for a moment, admiring her. His girl slept like the dead after sex. He loved that about her. He loved everything about her.

Convinced she wasn't going to wake up, Stone crawled over to Nico, aware the man was watching him intently as he got closer.

"I told you I wasn't done with you." Stone urged Nico to his back, straddling his thighs, rubbing along the length of him as he got comfortable. *"You have a problem with that?"*

"No."

"Then touch me."

There was hesitance in Nico's touch, but his hands flattened on Stone's thighs, inching higher. They were both naked, so there was nothing to hinder him from exploring, but he didn't.

"I'm not gonna hurt you," he whispered. He flashed a grin and added, *"Much."*

As he stared down into Nico's eyes, Stone looked at him. Really *looked* at him. The guy had been dating his sister for years, but Stone had never paid too much attention to him. Superficial, sure. He'd noted that Nico was a good-looking guy with a body worthy of an exploration. Not that he'd ever thought about it. Not until today.

At the moment, it was all he could think about. He wanted to lick this man from head to toe. He wanted to taste every inch of him, to learn what made him moan.

"You've really never been with a guy before?"

Nico shook his head.

"But you've wanted to?"

Nico shrugged.

Stone grinned. *"I'll take that as a yes."*

He wasn't here to force Nico to acknowledge his desire for the same sex. It wasn't a question. They'd proven that theory already. What he wanted was to show this man how good it could be. And he wanted to be Nico's first. Not because of some alpha desire to dominate and claim but because he had this overwhelming desire to make it good for Nico.

"I'm gonna touch you now," he warned, shifting so that he was straddling only one of Nico's legs.

Stone leaned down, resting on his elbow as he pressed his forearm across Nico's throat. He didn't cut off his airway because his goal wasn't to hurt him. It was to force him to surrender. He got the feeling that was what Nico needed. Someone to show him what he was missing.

"Kiss me," he ordered.

Nico had to lift his head in order to reach Stone's mouth. It increased the pressure on his throat, but he did it, so Stone met him halfway, licking at his lips. Teasing at first. He intended to keep it light and fun, but his plans disintegrated when Nico's arms came around him, and he moaned softly against Stone's mouth.

He found himself swept away by this strange connection he seemed to have to the man. Stone used his free hand to explore, caressing Nico's smooth chest, his rippled abs. He worked his way down, grazing his cock. Stroking softly. He was hard as steel. But Stone didn't linger there. He kept going, trailing his fingertips over Nico's balls, teasing lightly, continuing south.

"Spread your legs."

Nico did, moving his left leg over and angling his knee out to the side.

Pausing briefly, Stone brought his fingers to his mouth, sucking two fingers, lubing them with spit before sliding them between Nico's legs again. The entire time, he maintained eye contact with Nico, gauging his response based on his expression.

"No one's ever fucked you here?" he asked as he slowly, gently pushed one finger inside Nico's ass.

Nico shook his head.

"I like that I'm gonna be your first," Stone admitted, gently prodding Nico's hole, fingering him. As he did, he kissed Nico again, distracting him as he worked the tight passage.

"That's only one finger. You want two?"

Nico nodded.

Stone's dick throbbed with anticipation as he pushed two fingers inside him, pumping them faster, wanting him to relax so he could eventually take Stone's cock inside him.

As though he knew what Stone's intention was, Nico pulled his leg toward his chest, opening himself to Stone's intruding fingers.

"Relax," Stone told him, shifting his arm off Nico's neck so he could hold himself up. "Let me stretch you."

"Lube," Nico whispered.

Stone pulled his fingers free and reached for the bottle of lubricant that he'd retrieved from his bedroom earlier when he'd been getting them food. He'd known it would be needed if and when Nico did give in to him.

He squeezed a generous amount between Nico's legs, then used those same two fingers to work it inside Nico's hole.

"Better?"

Nico nodded, and for the first time, he started to relax, his ass stretching under Stone's ministrations.

Stone tossed the bottle away, leaning forward and resting on his arm so he could kiss Nico again. It helped, too. Nico relaxed even more, his muscles loosening. The distraction was helping, so Stone decided to keep his attention elsewhere.

"Did you enjoy fuckin' Stevie?"

Nico's eyebrows angled down, confusion contorting his handsome face.

"Tell me you haven't thought about it before? Your sister's smokin' hot best friend."

"Yeah," Nico whispered. "I've fantasized about it."

"Of course you have. She's amazing." He briefly stilled his hand, then said, "Three fingers," and added another, fucking him deeper.

Nico grunted, pulling his leg back again. "Fuck me."

"Not yet."

"I want your dick inside me."

"You have to earn it first."

Stone rammed his fingers inside Nico, fucking him, showing him what he would get when Stone finally gave him what he wanted. Nico grunted and groaned, his hand clutching Stone's arm, holding onto him as he panted and moaned.

"You ready to earn it?" Stone asked, scissoring his fingers, working him open that much more.

"Yeah."

Unable to hold back any longer, Stone pulled his fingers out and grabbed a towel from the floor to clean himself off. He opened the cabinet beneath the television to retrieve a condom. He didn't waste time, sheathing himself quickly before stretching out beside Nico, kissing him, keeping him in the moment. When Nico's shoulders relaxed again, Stone took the time to lube his cock before rolling to his back, grabbing Nico's hip so he could bring Nico with him.

"Straddle me," Stone told him, tucking a pillow under his head.

Nico shifted, his knees bracketing Stone's hips.

"Now take my cock and put it inside you. I want you to sit on me. Take me as deep as you can. Go slow. We're not in a hurry." Stone grinned. "Not yet, anyway."

He could see the gleam in Nico's dark eyes, but he couldn't tell if it was fear or anticipation making them glitter. Whatever it was, Nico didn't hesitate. He gripped Stone's cock and guided it between his legs, rubbing the head against his hole before he lowered himself onto him.

Oh, fuck.

Stone gritted his teeth as the pleasure tore through him. Nico grunted, but he took more. Or tried to. Inch by inch, he eased down, but not all the way.

Because Nico seemed at a loss for what to do, Stone pressed one hand in the center of Nico's chest, holding him up while he fisted Nico's cock with the other. He set the pace, stroking him as Nico began rocking forward and back.

"Relax. You can take more of me if you relax."

Nico's head tipped, and his chest expanded as he drew in a deep breath. He exhaled slowly, his hips lowering. He was now sitting on Stone's cock.

"Let it feel good, Nico. Fuck me. Right now, it's all you. Take it."

Nico grunted, lifting and lowering. Up, down. Up, down. He was so fucking tight, and Stone could tell the discomfort far outweighed the pleasure. At least for Nico.

"Lean forward."

He wanted Nico to change the angle to relieve some of the discomfort. Stone pulled his arm back, his hand still pressed to Nico's chest, guiding him to where he wanted him to be.

He stopped when Nico's expression went slack, and his eyes rolled back. "Oh, fuck."

"Better?"

Nico nodded as he began moving again, impaling himself. Long, deep strokes along Stone's cock caused goosebumps to form as Nico took what he needed.

He encouraged him with soft words, loving every second. And when Nico's movements became jerky, he knew it was time to take control.

"You're ready for me to ride you, huh?"

"Yeah."

"You want me to split that ass open with my cock."

Nico groaned.

Stone moved, bucking his hips, forcing Nico backward. The move surprised him, but Nico knew what to do, drawing his legs back as Stone moved into position. He planted his hands on the back of Nico's thighs, folding him in half before guiding himself home.

Stone fucked him. Hard. Fast. He didn't relent, staring down at Nico the entire time, watching the way his eyes glazed as the pleasure intensified. It was everything he'd imagined it would be. Actually, no. It was more. So much more. He couldn't explain it, but he felt a connection to this man.

"Fuck ... oh, fuck ... Stone!"

"Jerk yourself off," Stone commanded.

Nico grabbed his cock, yanking on it as Stone pumped his hips, chasing the inevitable release.

"So tight." Stone gasped for breath. "So hot." He rammed in harder. "God, you're fuckin' perfect."

"Fuckin' perfect," Stone said now, drifting out of the memory, but not before every fiber of his being went rock fucking hard.

He knew exactly what he needed to do next, so he grabbed his cell phone off the counter and pulled up his text message app. He added Nico and Stevie to the thread and typed up a message.

DINNER AT MY HOUSE TONIGHT. BOTH OF YOU. PLEASE.

Stone didn't waste any time waiting for a response. If they declined, he would adjust his plan, but for now, he was going on the hope that they would agree. He grabbed his key and started for the door. Before he reached it, he did a U-turn and headed for the bathroom to brush his teeth.

It usually wouldn't've mattered that he had tuna breath because his goal was to go to the grocery store. Only he had one stop to make first.

STEVIE WAS STANDING ON THE BACK PORCH waiting for Jäger to do his business when her cell phone chimed.

DINNER AT MY HOUSE TONIGHT. BOTH OF YOU. PLEASE.

She pretended she wasn't overcome with relief by seeing the text from Stone.

Ever since he left, she'd been overanalyzing everything that happened last night. And again this morning. Wondering whether she would find out Stone had skipped town the way he did the first time they'd found themselves in this situation. It was easy to believe he would stay as long as he was there, but the moment he walked out, her doubts had returned.

Stevie wanted to believe he was committed, but it was difficult to think he was when she still wasn't sure how she felt about it all. On one hand, she got giddy at the idea of seeing him, talking to him, kissing him. She'd never felt anything like what she felt for Stone. Not even with Nico. With him, her love had grown slowly, organically. With Stone, it had been instantaneous, and she found it difficult to believe that she was still in love with him after all this time. But it felt the same.

"Doesn't mean it's love," she admonished.

The screen door opened behind her, putting an end to her self-recrimination.

Nico cleared his throat. "Hey, did you see the text from Stone?"

She took a deep breath and looked down at Jäger, who was swatting at a strand of dead grass. "Yeah."

"Thoughts?"

Turning to face him, she cocked an eyebrow and aimed for casual. "I think I can handle dinner. What about you?"

Nico moved closer, coming to stand directly in front of her. Funny the difference a day could make. If he'd done that yesterday, she would've come up with a joke to make him laugh so she could pretend his proximity didn't set her aflame. Today, she didn't feel the need to hide it. Plus, she liked the way he was looking at her. The look was the same, but it felt different. More intense.

"I'm willin' to give it a shot if you are."

"Okay." It was all she could think to say. She had a million questions, most pertaining to what the future held—*if anything*—for the three of them. She was terrified to voice those questions, though, worried she wouldn't like the answers.

"You sure?"

She nodded.

His eyes implored her. It was obvious he wanted her to elaborate, but Stevie didn't know what to say. She didn't want to think this to death for fear it might screw it up. She figured her best option was to ride it out for as long as she could.

Nico reached up and cupped her neck, his hands warm against her skin. "You wanna talk about anything that happened last night?"

"Like what?"

He shrugged.

"I'm good," she assured him. "With all of it."

His eyes heated, and she saw the moment he intended to kiss her. She tilted her head back, welcoming his mouth on hers.

She'd been attracted to this man for so long that it felt surreal for him to be kissing her. After all, the only kisses they'd shared before today had been the passionate kind that usually preceded them getting naked.

Something pressed on her foot, causing Stevie to pull back. She looked down to find Jäger staring up at them. He barked once, clearly expecting their attention to shift to him.

"Why don't you respond to Stone, and I'll get him a treat," Nico suggested.

Although she was disappointed that their brief make-out session had come to an end, Stevie smiled and pulled out her phone. She shot back a message that they would be there, then followed it with a question as she was walking into the house.

Still looking at her phone, she didn't realize Nico was standing there until she ran directly into him, her face bumping his incredibly impressive chest.

She looked up. "Sorry."

The way he was looking at her gave her a moment of pause. Like usual, she couldn't read his expression, couldn't tell what he was thinking.

He solved the problem when he cupped her face, his fingers sliding under her hair, his thumb brushing along her cheekbone.

"What's wrong?"

"Nothing," he said, peering into her eyes, the look so intense, she swore he could see into her soul.

"You sure?"

"For the first time in a damn long time."

Stevie smiled, some of the anxiety dissipating. Her phone chimed, and a second later, Nico's did, so she knew it was Stone. She glanced at it quickly.

"Seven o'clock," she read aloud before looking up at Nico again. "That gives us a little time."

"For?"

Rather than answer, Nico took her phone, set it on the counter, then took her hand and led her through the kitchen, the living room, where Jäger was curled up in his crate—which she took to mean this was premeditated. When they reached the hallway, he took a left, heading toward his bedroom.

"Nico? What's goin' on?"

As soon as he stepped into the room, he pulled her into him. Stevie wasn't expecting it, so she crashed into him, but he seemed ready for that because his arm came around her as he crushed his mouth to hers.

Instantly, her blood went from simmer to boil. She kissed him back, grabbing for him because it seemed the right thing to do.

"We have to clear the air," he mumbled against her mouth.

That sounded ominous. "Meaning?"

She wasn't even aware they were moving until Nico was lowering her onto the bed, moving over her. He never broke the kiss, never stopped touching her. Not even when he began tugging on her clothes.

Although she was eager for answers, she got with the program, helping to remove them until there was nothing between his hard body and her much softer one.

Nico lifted his head, holding himself over her as he met her gaze again. "I told an untruth earlier."

Stevie frowned. "About?"

"You asked if I was mad that you fucked Stone in my bed."

A cold chill swept over her. He'd told her he wasn't mad. "You lied?"

Nico shook his head. "I wasn't mad. I'm *not* mad. I'm…" He hesitated, his eyes glittering. "I was jealous."

Stevie continued to look at him, holding his gaze, waiting for more.

It finally came, but not in words the way she'd expected. His response was made with his body as he shifted her legs apart and settled himself between them. She pulled one knee up and back, urging him where she wanted him.

Stevie whimpered when the broad head of his cock pressed against her entrance. She dug her fingertips into his sides, urging him deeper, wanting him more than she ever had. It reminded her of the day in her office. The day he'd fucked her against the wall. So much emotion had churned between them that day, so many things left unsaid.

"I was jealous that he had you all to himself," Nico whispered as he pushed in deeper. "That he got to wake up to you, that he got to feel the heat of you first thing. I've wanted it for so long."

"You have?" She hadn't known. Until that day in her office, she had honestly thought her feelings were one-sided. Yeah, she knew he enjoyed the sex—it was incredible—but she hadn't realized he was looking for anything more than that. But then he had told her he loved her. Her heart had swelled that day, but it deflated quickly when he never mentioned it again.

Nico held himself still when he was fully seated inside her. Stevie wanted him to move. She wanted to feel him, wanted him to bring her the unbridled pleasure her body expected from him.

"Do you remember that day in your office?"

She nodded, wondering if he could read her thoughts.

"I told you I love you."

She swallowed hard, nodding again.

"You didn't say anything," he whispered, his eyes locked with hers.

"Neither did you. I thought…" She cupped the back of his head, teasing his hair with her fingers. "I thought it was just the heat of the moment."

"No." He shook his head for emphasis. "I'm not holdin' back anymore, Stevie." His words were gruffly rasped, a slow, sexy scrape over her senses. "When it comes to you, I'm all in."

She cried out when he slid out of her and pushed himself back in deep. His eyes implored her as their bodies remained one.

Nico began to move, pumping his hips, filling her, stretching her. She wrapped her legs around him, dug her ankles into the small of his back, and urged him deeper.

"Tell me you want me," he groaned.

"Yes." She knew he wasn't referring to her physical desires. "I've always wanted you, Nico."

He fucked her harder, deeper. It seemed her words sparked something inside him.

"I want that, too," she continued. "To wake up in your bed ... oh, God ... Nico ... yes..."

He shifted, his hands fisted beside her head as he began driving down into her. She felt every thrust, not only with her body. She felt something more than corporeal pleasure, more than sensual gratification. She felt a bone-jarring intensity that reached the depths of her soul.

"Tell me it's more than sex," he ground out.

"It is," she assured him even as their bodies moved together in the very act they were discussing.

"Tell me you trust me, Stevie."

"Yes." She held onto him, his thrusts more punishing, driving her closer to orgasm. "More than I trust anyone."

He groaned, his gaze sliding down her body and locking on where they were joined. He pulled out and pushed in. Out and in, watching as he fucked her. Stevie continued to watch him, loving how expressive he was when they were like this. He was usually so guarded, but not when they were together like this.

She was still watching him when he looked up, meeting her gaze. "Tell me you love me."

Stevie exploded. Her world detonated in an outward burst so intense she could practically feel her molecules separating as the orgasm ripped through her.

She didn't realize Nico had stopped moving until she came back to herself. He was still watching her, buried deep. When she took a breath, he began moving again. Slower this time. He built her right back up within minutes.

"Tell me," he whispered.

She wanted to, but she was scared to. The only time she'd ever told a man she loved him, he'd ended up walking away.

"You tell me," she retorted, her eyes rolling back as his hips lowered, his pelvis pressing perfectly against her clit.

Nico leaned down, his arms and shoulders flexing as his weight shifted. His mouth came closer to hers, but he didn't kiss her.

"I love you, Stevie. I have for a long time."

She grabbed him, wrapping her arms around him, pulling him until he was on top of her. Nico slid his arms under her, holding his weight on his forearms as he began to move again. His lips covered hers, his tongue lazily teasing into her mouth as he continued to fuck her. Slow and deep, she felt every inch of him as he filled her and retreated. It was too much. She was overwhelmed. Heart and body.

"I love you, too," she whispered between kisses. "I always have."

Nico growled, and his hips bucked. He slammed into her as he lifted his head, looking at her again.

"God, Stevie." He squeezed his eyes closed. "Fuck."

She grabbed his ass, pulling him into her. They rocked together as he held on, refraining longer than she needed, but she wasn't about to stop him. She let the sensations tear through her again, rode the wave of ecstasy until it crashed, and she raced headlong into another orgasm, this one more intense than the first.

"Oh, yeah," he groaned, lifting up. "That's it. Come for me, Stevie."

She dug her nails into his ass, holding him inside her when he finally succumbed to his release.

When he fell on top of her, she held onto him, burying her face in his neck and sending up a silent prayer that he didn't break her heart.

Because Stevie knew that if she broke this time, she would never be the same again.

TWENTY-FOUR

NICO WAS WALKING ON A CLOUD.

At least, that was what it felt like. He could've rationalized that it was the result of what had to've been one of the top three most incredible sexual experiences of his life. It should've only been on the better-than-great list because of the missionary position and the lack of dirty talk, but no. He was relegating it to the top of the incredible pile, and he knew it had everything to do with Stevie telling him she loved him.

He honestly hadn't expected her to say the words. And he damn sure hadn't intended to coax them out of her, but he wasn't lying when he told her he'd been jealous that morning. He hadn't realized it until much later, but something about it had niggled at him for most of the day. Nico finally figured out that it wasn't so much that Stevie and Stone fucked in his bed, but rather they'd woken up together and had the opportunity.

Nico wanted to wake up with Stevie in his bed. Every day. For the rest of his life.

And yeah, taking her into his room, fucking her in his bed, urging her to admit her feelings ... he'd been selfish on every angle because Nico wanted—no, he *needed* Stevie to acknowledge what they had before things progressed even more with Stone. And he knew they were going to. Despite the rocky past they shared, the connection was still there. It was as strong as if Stone had never left.

"You think he knows how to cook?" Stevie asked from the passenger seat of his truck as they pulled into the Jamesons' driveway.

"He made breakfast this mornin'," he reminded her.

"True. But anyone can make eggs and bacon. Even me."

"Eh. Mostly." He chuckled. "You can *mostly* make eggs and bacon?"

Her eyes were wide when she looked at him. "Meaning?"

"Meaning... if you let *me* cook eggs and bacon, then you're capable of making them."

Stevie laughed, smacking him on the arm. "Shut. Up."

She grew quiet as they neared the barn behind the house. Nico parked next to Stone's truck and admired the place. He'd seen glimpses of it since the renovation, but he'd never stopped long enough to really see what they'd done. No, it didn't look like it had back in the day. Nor did it look like much of a barn anymore, aside from the actual shape of the structure. It certainly wasn't what he'd expected.

However, it did bring back a flood of memories from *that night*.

Fortunately, Jäger kept his mind from wandering. The puppy realized they'd reached their destination and hopped up from his bed in the back seat, peeking over the console, panting softly.

"Yep, we're here, boy," he told the dog as he turned off the truck.

Jäger let out an excited yip and tried to put his front paws on the console. He was still getting his legs under him, but it wouldn't be long before he was getting where he wanted to go without help from anyone.

"You good?" Nico asked, reaching for Stevie's hand.

"Yeah. You?"

He nodded.

"You jealous?"

"No." He huffed a laugh, releasing her hand so he could open the door. "I intend to have you in my bed from here on out." He got out of the truck. "What's there to be jealous about?"

Nico walked to the front of the truck to wait for her to get Jäger out, his rumbling stomach reminding him of the reason they were there. It had been an incredibly long day. Probably because yesterday had bled right into it, and they were still going after an eventful night.

"I hope you're—" Nico cut himself off when he realized Stevie was no longer smiling.

"Did you mean it?"

He figured now wasn't the time to play dumb, so he turned to face her, putting his hands on her hips and pulling her against him. This was Stevie, so he knew what she was referring to. It was obvious she'd been thinking about it ever since he said the words a short time ago.

"When I said I love you?"

"Or was that your way of—"

He cut her off. "I meant it, Stevie. Both times I said it. I love you. It wasn't about me bein' jealous."

"You sure?"

"Definitely." He tipped her chin up as he leaned in. "Did *you* mean it?"

"Yeah." Her smile was shy. "But don't let it freak you out, okay?"

"Why would it freak me out?"

"You're a guy. Shit like that sometimes freaks you out."

"Shit like that?"

"You know, emotional crap."

"You say the sweetest things," he teased, using the phrase she used on him so often.

"I try."

Nico pressed his lips to hers. "You said you trusted me."

"I do."

"Then know I'll never lie, and I'll never run."

As soon as the words left his mouth, he wished he could take them back. He didn't mean to paint a target on Stone, and he knew that was the fastest way to get Stevie to question what they were doing with him. It wouldn't take much for her to reconsider or, worse, let her fears get the best of her. Nico wanted this, and so far, Stone hadn't given them any reason to doubt his intentions.

Granted, Stone had been back for a whopping three weeks, so Nico wasn't sure he could make that determination. What he did know was that he wasn't interested in fighting this. For the first time in as long as he could remember, he was happy.

"Come on," he urged, pulling her by the hand. "Let's see if he knows how to cook."

"If he doesn't, I'm gonna feed mine to Jäger when he's not lookin'."

Jäger yipped, clearly on board with that plan.

As they were walking up onto the porch, the door opened, and Stone was there, looking good enough to eat. He was wearing Wranglers, boots, and a black button-down shirt with the sleeves rolled up to reveal his muscular forearms. He'd shaved at some point, the stubble gone completely. It was a good look for him.

"I was startin' to think y'all were gonna make out on the porch all night."

"We thought about it," Stevie teased. "But we figured we might as well invite you to join."

Stone's eyes heated.

"Of course, it depends on whether you can cook."

He laughed. "And if I can't?"

Stevie shrugged one shoulder. "I guess you could always watch."

Oh, boy. She was sassy tonight. They might have their work cut out for them.

CURTIS WALKER CARRIED TWO GLASSES OF ICED tea into the living room so he could join his wife on the couch. Lorrie was curled up with her blanket, her reading glasses on, and a book in her hand.

It was their Friday night ritual. She would read, and he would flip through channels, pretending he gave a shit about what was on the television. Truth was, he didn't care. He would gladly stare at a blank screen just for the opportunity to sit in the same room with the woman he loved more than life.

He set one of the glasses on the end table near her. The movement had her looking up at him, a beautiful smile on her face.

"Did you talk to Travis today?" she asked, setting her book aside.

Curtis put his tea glass on the other end table and took a seat close to her. "I did. Why?"

Lorrie turned so that she could stretch her legs out on his lap. "Did you mention our conversation with Stone?"

"I might've brought it up."

"What did he say?"

"He's got other things on his mind."

She smiled sweetly. "Understandable. But that's not an answer."

Curtis chuckled. "He said we should do whatever we want with it. He's got no interest in the land."

He didn't bother to tell Lorrie that Travis mentioned he would have interest in other sections down the line, so he'd insisted that they not divvy up every acre and pawn it off on someone without coming to him first. Curtis had assured him that wasn't the plan.

"He did ask why we chose Stone," Curtis relayed, adjusting her feet on his legs so he could slide his hands beneath the blanket and touch her.

He loved touching his wife. Even if it was just to hold her hand or warm her ankles, as was the case now. Curtis had always felt calmer when she was near. He'd fallen in love with her long ago, back when she was just a girl and he an unruly boy who didn't know what he wanted out of life. They'd been blessed. With sixty years of marriage, seven sons, and twenty-three grandchildren, they'd built a good life together, one full of love, laughter, and a tremendous amount of good fortune.

"It feels right to me," Lorrie said, her arm stretched out along the back cushion, her fingers brushing over his shoulder.

"It does," he agreed. "I know Deb and Owen'll be happy if he sticks around. He can finally stop runnin'."

"I don't think he ran so much as he went in search of something."

Because they lived in such a small town, he'd heard plenty of rumors over the years. Many of them about members of his family. He took each with a grain of salt and *always* considered the source. There was plenty of speculation over why Stone had up and left fifteen years ago. One minute, he was there; the next, he was off trying to build a life elsewhere.

"He didn't find it." At least Curtis assumed he hadn't. The boy was different than Curtis remembered. Not quite as cocky. A little more reserved.

"I think he did," Lorrie corrected. "But he found it before he ever left."

Curtis looked at his wife. "Little Stevie Shepherd?"

Lorrie laughed. "She's not so little anymore."

"She's pocket-sized," Curtis teased.

She flapped her hand at him. "Be nice."

He slid his hand up her smooth calf. "I'm always nice, darlin'."

Her eyes heated just as he knew they would.

"Deb told me he spent the night over there last night."

"Where?" he asked, not sure what they were talking about.

"Did you forget already?"

He shook his head, continuing to caress her leg. "Nope. Just found somethin' more interestin' to focus on."

She giggled. "Be serious."

"I *am* serious. I'm always serious when it comes to touchin' you."

Her laughter filled the room and warmed his heart. "We're talkin' about Stone and Stevie."

"No, *you're* talkin' about Stone and Stevie. I'm…" He let the sentence trail as he massaged her foot.

"You think he'll get the proposal done?"

That wasn't the first time she'd asked him that. Ever since their conversation with Stone, Lorrie had questioned whether Curtis thought the boy was serious.

"Yeah. I think it's what he needs."

"Stability?"

"Home," Curtis corrected. "The boy needs a place to call home."

And that was the real reason Curtis had brought it up in the first place. As soon as he heard Stone was back, he knew it was for good. A rambling man continued to ramble. Stone wasn't a rambling man, although he'd pretended to be for far too long.

Curtis had paid attention over the years. He knew Stone was looking for a place to settle, but for whatever reason, the boy hadn't thought that place was here. Now that he was back, Curtis got the feeling nothing could pull him away.

"It'll be good for him," he told his wife. "I think it'll take him a bit to figure out how he fits with the land, but he'll do right by it. And it'll give him the purpose he's been seekin' all this time. We've just gotta be patient with him." He met Lorrie's gaze. "That goes for Deb, too. Tell her to give him a chance. He'll make the right decision this time."

"Well, the boy ain't gettin' any younger, Curtis."

He grinned. No, he wasn't.

None of them were.

TWENTY-FIVE

STONE WOKE UP EARLY ON SUNDAY, FEELING inspired for the first time in a long time.

He'd spent all day Saturday working on his proposal, ignoring the urge to slack off. He would've preferred to spend the day with Stevie and Nico, but he resisted the urge, reminding himself that his future was riding on this, and he wanted to get it right. There would be plenty of time to spend with them once he got his life back on track.

And that was the real goal here. To find a track and stay on it. Stone wanted to stop looking toward the future, outlining his existence with words like *eventually* and *in the long run*. He was finally living in the now, measuring success on what he did today rather than what he would do one day.

Not only was he out to prove to Nico and Stevie, as well as his family, that he was someone they could rely on, but he also wanted to prove to himself that he had it in him to make the hard decisions.

At the moment, nothing was more difficult than spending time away from them, but he was making it work. He'd kicked off the tough decision-making on Friday night when Stevie and Nico had come over for dinner. He'd been a gentleman the entire night. They ate, they talked, they laughed. He played with Jäger for a little while, and then he'd graciously escorted them out to their truck and sent them on their way.

He knew he'd surprised Stevie when he didn't make a move. The boy she used to know would've coerced them both into staying the night, then let the tide take them where it may. But Stone wasn't that boy anymore, and though he ached for them in a way that he'd never experienced before, he was trying to be good. He wanted to slow down this train to ensure it didn't derail before they reached the end of the line. They had their entire lives ahead of them.

He laughed, shutting off the water and grabbing a towel. Like he was some sort of saint who would've turned Stevie or Nico down if either of them had put the moves on him. He couldn't resist them if he tried.

Thankfully, they hadn't put his resolve to the test that night.

And fine. He hadn't been quite so good yesterday, but he had remained focused for the entire day. The only reason that was possible was because he'd holed up in the barn, communicating with them via text message. He'd nearly caved when Stevie got sassy and started taunting him. Apparently, after a busy day—which she said they'd had—she preferred some extracurricular activities to reduce stress. Since Stone could think of a few dozen things he'd like to do to help her out, he'd wanted to rush right over to deliver. Hell, he'd gone so far as to put on his boots and grab his keys. But he'd glimpsed the laptop on his way to the door and knew he had to put work before play. At least for a little while.

But today was a new day, which was why he was getting ready to go see Stevie and Nico. His business proposal was complete. To the best of his ability, anyway. Now it was time for Stevie to review it. He'd put a lot of effort into mapping out a plan for them, and he was hoping it would be enough to convince her to take a chance on him.

Stone finished getting ready, then stopped in the kitchen to down the rest of his coffee before rinsing the cup and putting it in the dishwasher. He grabbed his iPad and pulled up his proposal, wanting to make sure he was prepared. With one final deep breath, he resigned himself to tackling the hardest part: getting Stevie on board with the plan.

Ten minutes later, Stone parked in the lot in front of the D & S Landscaping office. He hesitated because he didn't see any of the company trucks parked anywhere. Not in front of the office or near the other buildings on the property. Stevie's little Bronco was there, but that didn't necessarily mean she was.

He got out and looked around, getting a feel for how large their lot was. It was part of the tract of land he was looking to get from his uncle. In his proposal, Stone had left it exactly as it was—the fifty-year lease in place—but he'd added an option for expanding if the company needed additional space.

Although he hadn't notated it anywhere, he'd also considered relocating them to a spot closer to the central part of town to increase walk-in traffic. He didn't intend to bring it up because the last thing he wanted was for Stevie to think he intended to take over what they'd already built for themselves. He didn't, but he was willing to help them in whatever way he could.

His only hope now was that Stevie saw this as a positive opportunity and not as Stone attempting to steamroll over all that she'd built for herself.

The humidity had increased, warming the morning significantly. According to the weather channel, another cold front was moving in sometime in the next few days, but the potential for precipitation was low. He had nothing against cold weather. It was the rain and shit that he wanted no part of.

"Good morning. Welcome to D and S Landscaping," the woman at the desk said before looking up.

"Mornin'," he greeted, looking at her for the first time.

"Stone Jameson." Her dark brown eyes flashed with what looked to be recognition, but he knew he'd never met her before.

He moved toward her. "That's me."

She stood up quickly and thrust her hand in his direction. "Tara. Tara Chadwell."

"Nice to meet you." He shook her hand, wondering why she seemed nervous. "I'm sorry. Have we met?"

Tara shook her head, causing her long, reddish-brown curls to bounce on her shoulders. "I'm a … uh … a friend of CJ's."

Ah. Well, that explained it.

"He's told me all about you," she added. "Not that we talk about you all that much. He just…"

Stone chuckled. "No need to explain. My brother likes to talk. Whatever he told you, I'm sure it was a lie."

She giggled, looking more at ease. "Only good stuff. I promise."

"Then we're not talkin' about the same CJ." He glanced toward the offices at the end of the building. "Is Stevie in?"

"She is." Tara sat back down, reaching for the phone receiver.

Stone stepped back from her desk to wait as Tara pressed a button on the phone. A second later, she was talking—presumably to Stevie—explaining someone was there to speak to her.

"It's Stone Jameson," Tara whispered, ducking her head as though that would make it impossible to hear.

He smiled, looking around the room, taking it all in once again.

"She said you can go on in," Tara said, hanging up the phone.

"Thanks."

He could feel her watching him as he walked away, but Stone didn't look back. He would have to ask CJ how he knew Tara. She didn't seem like his type. Tara was on the voluptuous side. Big boned, he believed, was how Chelsea had always described women of her stature. Whatever you wanted to call it, it wasn't an issue for most men, Stone included, but CJ had always leaned toward the women with little meat on their bones. The kind who sucked back health shakes and picked through a salad when they weren't spending time at the gym or climbing rocks or strolling through nature. Not that Tara wasn't one of those women. Just because she was bigger didn't mean she wasn't in shape.

But her size wasn't the only thing that differed from CJ's usual type. Despite Tara's initial shyness, she was far more outgoing than the women CJ had dated. Like she had nothing to hide. The few women his brother had introduced him to had been the exact opposite: quiet, shy, and, yes, rail-thin.

Thankfully, he wasn't here to figure out whether or not CJ had expanded his tastes to include smiling redheads. He was here to see Stevie.

Taking a deep breath, Stone rapped his knuckles on her office door before opening it. The first thing he noticed was Stevie's fingers flying over the keyboard, her full attention on her computer monitor. The second was the little fluffs of white on the carpet near the dog bed. Jäger's head popped up, his little eyes wide with curiosity. There was a puff of white dangling from his mouth and he looked guilty, but not sure what to do about it now.

"You've got to at least hide the evidence, little guy," he told the dog as he walked over.

Stevie stopped typing. "Oh, man. Jäger. Dude. Come on." She huffed. "That's the second toy he's chewed up since yesterday mornin'."

"He's actin' out," Stone told her. "We're gonna need to find him a job. Somethin' he can focus on. That way, he'll want to chill in his downtime."

Stevie's forehead creased. "Why does that sound like a good idea?"

"Because it's a good idea," he said with a laugh. "Dogs, especially his breed, need somethin' to focus on. That's why they're often used as service animals. They're smart. They enjoy havin' tasks to complete."

Her wide-eyed stare remained on him.

"That or he simply missed me, and he wants you to hang out with me more," he said, glancing back at Jäger. "Right, buddy?" Stone rubbed his head. "At least that's the story we should go with."

Stevie brought over the small wastebasket so he could dump the toy's innards in it.

"The question is, did *you* miss me?" he asked, peering up at her.

She was watching him as though she hadn't seen him in a month rather than two days. Stevie pursed her lips and shook her head. "I didn't really notice you weren't there."

He rubbed the puppy's head before standing tall and turning toward her.

"Liar," he whispered, tipping her chin up. He lingered there for a moment, ensuring she knew he was going to kiss her. When she didn't pull back, he closed the distance and brushed his mouth over hers.

It took tremendous effort not to fall into the kiss and make up for lost time, but he managed.

"Well, I missed you." He caressed her cheek with his thumb before dropping his hand. Touching her was far too much temptation for him.

"I might've missed you," she said softly. "A little."

Stone took a step back. "Is Nico around?"

Stevie walked back to her desk. "No. He went to talk to a client in south Austin. Won't be back until lunchtime. Why? You miss him, too?"

"As a matter of fact, yes," he admitted as he took a seat in one of her guest chairs.

Jäger joined him, planting his front paws on Stone's knee. His little tail wagged as he watched him, hope glittering in his eyes.

Stone set the iPad on the other chair and picked up the dog.

"Seriously though," he said, looking at Stevie. "I came here to talk to you."

"About?"

"The future."

IT SHOULD BE ILLEGAL FOR A MAN Stone's size to cuddle a little puppy the way he was right now. The action was extremely heartwarming, filling her with a weird, fuzzy feeling.

"What ... umm ... *about* the future?" Stevie asked, doing her best to hold his gaze and not watch as his big, work-rough hands gently petted Jäger's head.

She was kinda jealous. No, make that a lot jealous. Since Friday night, she'd been jonesing to feel this man's hands on her. She'd gone so far as to declare that the next time she was in the same room with him, she was going to ensure he had the opportunity.

Of course, she hadn't intended to see him in her office. But, hey, no one ever said this place was off-limits.

"I finished the business proposal." He reached for something beside him, then held out his iPad.

She took it from him and placed it on the desk, surprised by the disappointment that filled her. He'd honestly come here to talk business, and she was already undressing him with her eyes.

"I was hopin' you'd look it over. Change what you think needs to be changed. Maybe give me some advice."

She shoved down the disappointment and resigned herself to being an adult for a little while. "This is the one for Curtis and Lorrie?"

"Yeah."

Stevie tapped the screen, and it brought up the keypad for his password. She held it out to him.

He looked up. "I've got nothin' to hide. The password's the date of the night the three of us were in the barn."

Her eyebrows snapped up. "Seriously?"

He smirked. "Is that you stallin' because you don't remember the date?"

"No," she blurted. "It was May fifteenth."

"Two digits of the year," he added when she started to type the password.

She keyed in the number, including *09* for the year, and found the presentation was already pulled up. It surprised her. She'd expected to see a half-finished Word document outlining a few things he intended to accomplish if he got the land.

That wasn't what she found.

Stone had put tremendous effort into compiling this information. His business acumen was far more developed than she would've given him credit for.

"It could probably be more in-depth," Stone noted. "But I was considering my audience. I didn't want to overwhelm my aunt and uncle at the beginning. I figure my best option is to give them enough information to make a decision, but then I'll keep them in the loop as I move forward."

"No," Stevie said, still staring at the screen as she flipped from one slide to the next. "This is actually… wow. It's really good." She looked up. "And these numbers are accurate?"

"Based on my calculations, yeah. Start-up will be slow, obviously. Crops take time, but I thought we could offset the lack of revenue by building the farmers' market and allowing people to rent space. It won't supplement all the potential revenue, but it's something."

Stevie wasn't sure what to say. She wasn't even sure why he wanted her to review it. The man had created something far more in-depth than anything she'd done before.

She flipped to another slide, and a gasp escaped her.

"Did you draw this?"

Stone stood up, leaning forward to look at the screen. "Yeah. There are several pages. It was just my initial idea of what it could look like when we're done."

Forget building a farmers' market; the guy needed to do something with his drawing skills. He'd created a 3D mockup of the farmers' market and the surrounding land. He'd even incorporated D & S in the drawing since they occupied a portion of the land he would acquire.

She squinted before remembering she could zoom in on the image, which she did. This allowed her to see a smaller section adjacent to the property she and Nico were leasing from Curtis Walker.

"Are these…?"

"Greenhouses," Stone supplied, once again sitting with Jäger in his lap. "I thought that would be the best location for them. Depending on what you wanted to grow, you'd also have access to them for the landscaping company."

Her head snapped up, her eyes wide. "You're serious about this? About me partnering with you."

His expression sobered. "I am. And Nico, if he wants to be part of it."

"Why?"

He looked surprised by her question, but Stone took it in stride. "Because I want to build a life with you, Stevie. And I want you by my side."

She frowned. "You don't need my help." She lifted the iPad. "You've got an eye for business. You could do this by yourself."

"Maybe. But I'd prefer to have your help."

Stevie wasn't sure what to say. Hell, she wasn't sure what to think. She felt as though the tornado sirens were blaring, and she was being forced to decide which shelter to take. On the one hand, there was the safety and security of what she knew—the business she'd built with Nico—or the other option, which involved venturing into the unknown with a man who'd broken her heart once already.

The logical side of her brain said she needed to politely decline because there was too much risk. Not financial because, based on this outline, Stone wasn't seeking any capital from her. No, the risk was to her emotional well-being. If this didn't work, if they hit a snag that directly conflicted with this well-thought-out plan, what would happen? Would he up and leave again? Would she be left stitching herself back together again?

"You don't have to give me an answer right now," Stone said. "I can send you the proposal. I'd like Nico to look it over, too. He might see somethin' I didn't. Y'all have seen the ups and downs of the small-town economy over the past eight years. You'll have insight that I don't."

He was being so logical about it all. It didn't suit the memory of the man that was still rooted deep in her brain. Stone had been impulsive and reckless back in the day—traits she'd found incredibly sexy because she'd been young and naive. This man ... he was putting tremendous thought and effort into what came next.

Strangely, that was ridiculously sexy to the older, grown-up version of herself.

Stevie set the iPad down. "What you've got is impressive. I won't lie. And it's tempting. But I do need to mull it over a bit. And yeah. I want to talk to Nico."

His smile lit up his entire face. "That's all I was hopin' for."

Stone rubbed his knuckles on Jäger's head one more time before setting him on the ground and standing tall.

"I'll let you get back to it." He stared down at her. "I'm gonna move forward and talk to my cousins. See if I can't get their approval. You'll let me know?"

She nodded.

Stone came around the desk. He waited until she turned in her chair before he leaned down and pressed another quick kiss to her lips. She wished he would linger because she missed the warmth of his body. The other night, she'd been anticipating staying the night with him. That hadn't happened, and while she didn't want to admit it, her patience was running thin. He'd generated a welcome heat inside her, and it continued to churn—more so with his proximity—so it wasn't easy to do the adult thing and let him walk away without exploring that a little more.

But she did because that was the correct response. She wasn't that impulsive young girl who would follow this man anywhere, and it was important that he knew that.

"I'll call you later," he said as he started toward the door. "Maybe we can have dinner again."

She nodded. Not so much because she agreed but because she knew it was necessary. Especially if she was supposed to keep it together. What it was about this man, she didn't know, but he had the uncanny ability to make all common sense flee.

Stevie figured the best bet was to sate those urges before they turned into a wildfire that burned out of control.

"HOW ABOUT DINNER TONIGHT? OUR HOUSE. WE'LL invite Stone?"

Nico grinned because it was unusual for Stevie to answer the phone with questions rather than some sort of pleasantry. He'd called her to check in and to let her know he was heading back after the morning from hell. But he didn't get the chance to because she was focused on other things.

"You miss him, huh?" he asked.

"I just saw him," she said, her tone a bit higher than usual. "Why would I miss him?"

"He was there?"

"Yep. Dropped by unannounced and then dumped this brilliant business proposal on my desk."

"Brilliant business proposal," he echoed. "That sounds like a positive."

"It's not," she drawled. "Here he is, mappin' out a future, and the only thing I can think about is gettin' him naked."

Nico laughed. She sounded forlorn and a bit testy. He was used to Stevie pretending she wasn't going up in flames. However, he'd known the woman long enough to see every side of her. Even those she tried to keep under wraps. Stevie Shepherd was a hot-blooded woman with a libido that burned out of control all the time. He knew because she didn't have a problem sharing those little nuggets of information. At one point, he'd been as much her sounding board as his sister had. So much so that Nico worried she was relegating him to the friend zone.

"I'm more than happy to sign up for the job," Nico noted while driving into the Coyote Ridge town limits. "I'll be back in ten minutes."

"I got you naked last night," she countered.

She had. And it had been fucking incredible.

Although he'd stated his desire to have her in his bed every night, Nico had expected Stevie to pretend it never happened. To his surprise, she was the one who brought it up after they'd gotten home from Stone's on Friday night. He wouldn't pretend not to notice that her desire was ramping up whenever she spent a little time in Stone's company. That was to be expected. After all, it affected Nico in much the same way. And it was working out for both of them that they had each other to lean on.

Which they'd definitely done.

"So? Do you wanna invite him, or should I?" Stevie asked, interrupting his memory of the past two nights.

"I will. I can do it now."

"No," Stevie blurted. "Wait until you get here."

He frowned. "Why? Somethin' goin' on?"

"Nope."

"Stevie?"

"Just wait until you get here," she said, her tone holding a hint of determination. "I've got an idea."

"Why is it that I always fear there's gonna be trouble when you say that?"

She giggled. "Maybe because you know me so well. Now hurry up. Tara's goin' to lunch, so we don't have much time."

Before Nico could ask her what that meant, Stevie hung up on him. His curiosity had him pressing the pedal closer to the floor.

Ever since Stone's reappearance, and especially since the night he stayed at their place, Nico had noticed a shift in Stevie. As he said, she'd always been open about her desires, and yeah, he'd allowed her to seduce him more than once simply so he could be with her on her terms. However, Stone brought out a different side to her. The hot-blooded woman he knew now smoldered at all times. And yeah, he was as hot-blooded as she was, so he was curious what she had in mind.

As he was pulling down the driveway leading to the office, he saw Tara driving toward him. When she slowed, he did, too. She lowered her window and waved up at him. "I'm takin' Jäger with me to grab some lunch. I thought I'd walk him through the park, get him a little exercise."

"You're gonna spoil him."

"That's the plan." She waved again and pulled away.

Nico turned his attention to the building directly in front of him. There was only one vehicle out front—Stevie's—because the crews were all out taking care of clients today. Sundays were busy for them. Their non-commercial customers appreciated them working on weekends because it worked better with their schedules.

Nico parked the truck and got out, his phone in hand. He considered calling Stone to warn him that Stevie might be up to something but decided against it.

As usual, the office was empty when he walked in. Saturdays were busy with walk-in traffic, but Sundays were hit or miss. Since they weren't close to town, most people didn't venture out this way. Only those who knew they were here or those who stumbled upon them accidentally while out for a leisurely drive. Except for their word-of-mouth customers, their clients tended to be businesses— apartment complexes, new-build communities, etc.—because of it. Nico hoped to change that because he wanted nothing more than to cater to his hometown.

"Stevie?" Nico called out as he headed toward his office.

He was about to stop at her open door but didn't have to because she came racing out, grabbing him by the hand and dragging him with her into his office.

"Jäger's with Tara."

"I saw that."

She stopped long enough to close his office door. "Did you call Stone yet?"

"You told me not to."

"Good." She stopped in front of his chair, then turned, still dragging him along. "Sit."

Evidently, she was serious because she shoved him, causing him to fall back into his chair. "What is goin'—"

"Call him," she demanded. "Actually, no. Let me."

Nico stared at her wide-eyed as she took his phone, held it up to his face to unlock it—a trick she'd learned from his sister—then began tapping the screen. A second later, he heard it ring because she'd put the call on speaker.

"Hey," Stone greeted. "I just left your office. Sorry I missed you."

Nico felt a flutter in his chest. One of those weird sensations you couldn't quite name. The kind that was rife with anticipation and pleasure.

"Nico wants to ask you somethin'," Stevie said into the phone, then passed it to Nico.

Stone chuckled. "Okay."

"I have no idea what she's up to," Nico told Stone. "I just walked in and—oh, goddamn."

"What?" Stone asked.

"Fuck. Stevie. What're you doin'?"

The woman was kneeling in front of him, her hands sliding up his thighs, inching higher. She cupped him through his jeans before continuing until she reached the button.

"What's she doin'?" Stone asked.

"Tell him," Stevie insisted as she worked to free him from the confines of the denim.

"Right now she's … fuck me. She's takin' off my pants."

A soft growl sounded from the phone. "Tell me, Nico. Tell me what she's doin'."

Oh, damn. That gravel-rough baritone was something he'd heard in his dreams for so long. He'd fantasized about Stone for years after *that night*. Enough that hearing his voice now made his dick thicken even more.

"I don't know what to say," Nico said honestly. "I called her on my way back, and she asked if I wanted to invite you to dinner. Next thing I know, she's draggin' me into my office and—"

Nico stared at her as she jerked his jeans down his hips. He couldn't do much to help her because the chair had wheels, and when he tried, it moved him farther from her.

Not that Stevie seemed to notice. She was a woman on a mission, working diligently until she got his jeans and underwear around his ankles.

"Oh, shit," he groaned, dropping the phone on his desk so he didn't risk crushing it as Stevie took his cock in her mouth. He grabbed both armrests, gripping tight as pleasure annihilated him.

"Nico," Stone growled through the phone. "Tell. Me."

"She's got my cock in her mouth," he said, sliding his fingers into her hair so he could guide her. "God*damn*. She's good at this."

Stevie peered up at him, releasing him from her mouth briefly, her brown eyes glittering with intent. The little minx knew exactly what she was doing.

"It could've been you, Stone," Stevie noted, then licked her lips and set her attention on his dick once again.

"Damn, baby. Why didn't you say somethin'?" Stone asked.

"Oh, fuck me," Nico groaned when she deep-throated him again. "I think this is her way of punishin' you. Or me. Or both."

Stone chuckled. "Sounds to me like it's one helluva punishment."

"Oh, it is." Nico tightened his grip on her hair, trying to wrangle control of the situation. "She's a feisty one."

"Always has been," Stone noted.

"Yes, she has. God, Stevie. Suck me. Shit, yes. Her mouth…"

"Tell me," Stone urged.

"She's so fuckin' good at this." Nico couldn't look away as she held his stare, her mouth working him up and down with exquisite precision. "She might need a spankin' after this."

Stevie's eyes widened, and Nico saw the intrigue that lit her brown eyes.

"I think you should come over tonight and deliver it," Nico told Stone.

"I can definitely do that."

"Is that what you want?" Nico asked Stevie. "For him to come over and paddle your ass?"

To his surprise, she nodded, her hand curling around the base of his dick as she began stroking while she sucked. She knew he loved it when she did that.

"She said yes," Nico told Stone.

"What time works for y'all?" Stone asked.

Stevie paused, his cock still lodged deep in her mouth. She held up six fingers.

"She says six."

"I'll be there. Want me to bring somethin'?"

"A bottle of wine," Nico told him, grabbing Stevie's head with both hands. "And a belt."

Her eyes flashed hot.

Stone's groan echoed through the phone. "Wine and a belt. I'm game." He paused. "But I'll only deliver if she can make you come in the next minute."

It was Nico's turn to groan as the suction of Stevie's mouth intensified.

"Damn, girl. That's it," Nico urged, guiding her up and down on his cock. "Make me come, Stevie. Make me come while Stone listens."

Her eyes closed, and he could tell she was spurred by the request. This might've been her idea, but they'd taken control from her, which was all Stevie ever wanted.

"I'm gonna come, Stone," Nico warned. "I'm gonna come down her throat."

Stevie bobbed faster, her hand stroking firmly.

He was so damn close.

"Oh, fuck yes. Stevie … I'm comin'. Swallow," he grunted. "Swallow all of it."

"Fuck," Stone crooned.

Nico grunted and growled as he came, loving that Stone was on the phone to hear this.

When his dick finally stopped pulsing, Nico flopped back in the chair, completely spent.

"A bottle of wine and your belt," Stevie reminded Stone. "At six."

"I'll be there, baby."

"Promise?"

"You couldn't keep me away."

Stevie reached over and disconnected the call. As soon as she did, Nico pushed his chair back and got to his feet so he could right his clothing. He noticed a hint of caution in Stevie's eyes as she sat back on her heels and watched him.

"I got carried away," she said. "I'm sorry."

With his jeans back on, he reached for her, helping her to her feet. "I'm not. That was…" Nico leaned down and kissed her, cupping her head so he could stroke her mouth with his tongue. "I'm a big fan of spontaneity."

She smiled, peering up at him. "Me, too. I'm also a big fan of spankings," she said, her words followed by a giggle as she backed away from him.

"Noted."

Nico was still smiling as she left his office to get back to work.

In fact, the smile remained firmly affixed to his face for the rest of the day.

TWENTY-SIX

STONE BROUGHT WINE, JUST AS HE'D PROMISED to do. He also wore his belt, but that wasn't unusual. He always wore his belt, but now that he knew Stevie was so fond of them, he was going to have to remember it had multiple uses.

"Stevie showed me the proposal," Nico said as they sat together on the back porch, sharing dinner and wine while Jäger hopped and sniffed around the yard. "Quite impressive."

That was Texas for you. One minute, it's sleeting, and the roads are closed; the next, it's warm enough to sit outside and share a meal.

"Thanks." Stone was trying to pay attention but was having a hard time because this dinner—what Nico referred to as a classic quick meal—was one of the best things he'd ever tasted.

He pointed his fork toward the meat and potatoes on his plate. "What's *in* this?"

"Flank steak, potatoes, and carrots," Nico told him. "I add a garlic mustard butter sauce. It's quick and easy. Some people make it in a skillet. I roast the potatoes and carrots on a baking sheet in the oven while I fry the steak in the skillet. The key is to ensure you sear the steak, not steam it, so you've got to make it in batches."

"You need to teach my mother how to make this," he told Nico. "She can make this instead of tuna casserole."

"It's Stevie's favorite."

Stone looked at the woman who'd been quiet since he arrived at the house. He wasn't sure if she was embarrassed about what happened earlier or simply anticipating what was to come. Whatever the reason, she'd kept herself busy entertaining Jäger while Stone had kept Nico company in the kitchen.

He reached for his wine. "Somethin' on your mind?"

Her brown eyes darted to his face. "What?" She was still chewing as her gaze moved to Nico and then back.

In that moment, she looked so much like the young girl he'd first fallen in love with. Sweet, innocent. God, he'd fallen for her so fast. It was strange that a decade and a half stood between then and now, yet Stone felt as though not a minute had passed. He still felt the same ache in his chest when he looked at her. That longing to be with her at all times, to see her smile, to feel her smooth, baby-soft skin.

"You've been quiet. Just wonderin' what you're thinkin' about?"

She shook her head and speared another potato. "Nothin'."

Stone nodded, contemplating his next move as he sipped his wine. He opted for the casual route. "What happened earlier in Nico's office … does that happen all the time?"

Stevie didn't hide her reaction in time because Stone saw the flash of heat that made her eyes glitter. She sat up, wiping her mouth with her napkin before grabbing her wineglass.

"Why? Jealous?"

She was being catty, which meant she was nervous.

"A little bit, yeah," he said honestly.

Her expression fell. "That makes no sense."

"No?" Stone glanced at Nico to see if he was paying attention. He was. "You get jealous when I'm touchin' her?"

Nico's gaze shifted to Stevie, and Stone was positive they had a silent conversation before he said, "Yeah. What man wouldn't?"

"Exactly."

"But y'all know about … each other or whatever."

Stone liked that her feathers were ruffled.

"That doesn't mean we don't get jealous. I had to listen while you sucked his dick."

"You didn't *have* to," she said, and this time, he noted a hint of trepidation in her tone.

"Baby, trust me. I wasn't hangin' up that phone unless my life depended on it."

"Why?" She tipped her head and stared at him. "Why does it turn you on to … share your … uh…" She fluttered her hand. "Your girlfriends or whatever."

He could tell she was expecting a serious answer, so he gave her one.

"I've only ever shared one girlfriend. You. And that was with"—he looked at Nico—"you." His attention returned to Stevie. "I can't explain *why* I wanted it in the first place, but I can tell you, seein' you with him… It's arousing to watch his hands and mouth on you. To see him bring you pleasure the way only he can and know I've got the same opportunity. Watchin' the way your body reacts, hearin' those soft, sexy moans… it turns me on like nothin' else."

Stevie's cheeks were rosy, and he doubted it was from the cool breeze since they'd turned on an outdoor heater that was keeping it at bay.

"So it's only me you watch?" she asked. "Not him?"

Stone smiled. "Oh, I watch him, all right. The two of you together are the best aphrodisiac in the world. Trust me; I would've loved to've been in that office today. To see you on your knees, suckin' his cock between those pretty lips."

Her face flushed even more, but this time, she fanned herself.

"You wanna know what the best part is?" he prompted, realizing no one was eating anymore.

"What's that?"

"Both of us touchin' you at the same time. To see you overwhelmed with pleasure is a high no drug can offer."

Stevie looked at Nico, so Stone did, too. "Do you disagree?"

"No. He's right," Nico told Stevie. "Nothin' compares to it."

"Is it just me, or does she look like she doesn't believe us?" Stone asked.

"I think you might be right."

Stevie's eyes widened. "I didn't say that."

"You didn't have to, baby." Stone smirked. "Don't worry. We know just how to make you believe us."

Her eyebrows arched. "How's that?"

Nico was the one who answered. "We'll show you."

"And we won't stop until you're convinced."

Stone loved the way her lips parted on a soft gasp, and he was pretty sure she crossed her legs under the table, attempting to stave off the desire that was pumping through her.

Stone knew the feeling. He was hard as steel and ready for the next course.

STEVIE PROBABLY SHOULD'VE LEFT WELL ENOUGH ALONE.

That was what a smart woman would do when faced with two alpha males whose eyes sparked with lust. She should've changed the subject, talked about the weather, or the adorable puppy sitting eagerly near their feet, hoping for a yummy morsel to fall so he could snatch it up.

Unfortunately, she didn't do either of those things. Although flustered and slightly embarrassed by her earlier actions, she wanted more of what these two offered. The last thing she wanted was for them to believe otherwise.

"I'll have to take your word for it," she said off-handedly before downing the rest of her wine.

"Is that a dare?" Stone asked. "I think it's a dare."

She gave him her best cocky smile as she pushed her chair back and grabbed her plate. "I'll be in the kitchen washin' dishes."

"I'll help." Stone got to his feet before she could decline the offer.

Stevie grinned, hurrying into the house, careful not to step on Jäger as he bounced along beside her, still hoping for a snack.

She set her plate and empty glass down on the counter, then snuck him a small piece of the plain steak Nico had set aside before he added the sauce. Stevie knew she was being a helicopter mom, but she was looking up every ingredient they came across to see whether dogs could have it. Apparently, garlic was toxic to dogs, so she'd told Nico as much. She was pretty sure one bite of their food wouldn't hurt him, but she wasn't taking any chances.

"That's all you get. Don't tell on me, okay?"

Stone and Nico were right behind her, bringing in the rest of their dishes. Before she knew what was happening, Stone was elbowing her out of the way so he could take over dish duty.

Before she could pelt him with feigned outrage, Nico picked her up and set her on the counter beside the sink.

"What're you—"

She didn't get the sentence out because his mouth fused to hers, his lips warm and soft, his hands gentle as they cupped her face. Her train of thought vanished, her entire existence zeroing in on the feel of his tongue sweeping into her mouth.

Oh, yeah. She could get used to this. A hot, sexy cowboy doing the dishes while another hot, sexy man kissed her. This had to be what heaven was like.

Nico's hands shifted from her face, sliding downward. Slowly, gently. She loved the way he touched her. More so now that they'd come to this understanding. They weren't pretending anymore. They were making their desire for one another public, no longer ignoring the combustible heat that churned between them.

He tugged the hem of her sweatshirt, lifting it, urging her to raise her arms. She did, allowing him to drag it up and over her head, setting it on the counter beside her. His hands returned, curling around her ribs as his thumbs slid underneath her bra to tease her nipples.

Stevie pulled back, giving him more room to maneuver, gasping for air as her body pulsed with arousal. He was hardly teasing her, but combined with the fact Stone was there, it was too much.

"Take it off," Stone commanded from his spot at the sink. He was diligently rinsing the dishes and tucking them into the dishwasher, but he was watching both of them.

Nico flipped the front clasp of her bra, then slowly peeled it off her breasts, his eyes locked on the flesh he revealed. A chill swept over her, but it had nothing to do with the temperature in the room.

Stevie whimpered when Nico cupped both breasts, plumping them as he leaned in and licked her nipple. He teased one, then the other, until they were taut. Only then did he close his lips around one, sucking gently. Too gently.

She stared down at him, watching as his mouth did magical things to her sensitive nipples.

"Harder," she rasped, wanting to feel a bite of pain.

Nico delivered, sucking hard. Her head fell back on her shoulders as she cried out. She grabbed his head, holding him to her so he wouldn't stop.

She was aware of the water turning off, her attention shifting to Stone as he grabbed a towel to dry his hands. He was watching intently, his heated gaze locked on Nico's mouth as it did wondrous things to her.

Clearly aware that Stone was finished with his task, Nico stepped to the side, focusing on her right breast, leaving room for Stone to join in the action. He didn't hesitate, his gaze meeting hers as he stepped forward. But he didn't touch her the way she expected. Instead, he cupped the back of Nico's head, his other arm sliding around behind her, his big palm flattening on her back.

Stevie couldn't resist touching him, so she slipped her fingers into the cool softness of his hair while they watched Nico lick and lave her breast. Her breaths were ragged, sawing in and out of her lungs because it was overwhelming. Both of them here. It was what she'd dreamed about for so long. It felt almost surreal.

"Kiss me, Stevie," Stone growled softly.

She shifted her attention to Stone, although she didn't release Nico's head. She was still holding him to her, her fingers brushing Stone's as he did the same.

She moaned when he nipped her lower lip before kissing her with that alpha aggression she'd craved for so long.

Every cell in her body was sparking, her nerve endings buzzing as the pleasure radiated through her being. Their touch was intoxicating, making it hard to breathe. She was grateful she was sitting down; otherwise, she would've been a puddle on the floor.

"More," she whimpered when Stone released her mouth.

"Baby, we're not gonna stop until you've come a dozen times."

Although she wasn't sure that was even possible, she certainly hoped he would try because right now, she was strung so tight, she thought she might snap in two.

Nico nipped her one last time before he stood tall, turning toward Stone. They came together in front of her, their tongues sliding together in a slow, sexy caress. She moaned. Watching them together was a thrill she still couldn't quite understand. It made no sense that she wanted their full attention on her, yet she could probably get off on watching them like this.

Stone shifted to stand in front of her, his back to her. She trapped him between her knees, taking the opportunity to touch him even as he continued to kiss Nico. She inhaled that rich, musky scent of his skin as she kissed his neck. When he tilted his head, she sucked harder, chills rushing down her spine when he moaned his approval.

With Nico's help, they managed to rid him of his shirt. Her mouth trailed over his broad, muscled shoulders while her hands roamed freely over the hard planes of his chest. He was so big, so powerful, so warm. She could've spent hours learning every inch of him, tasting, touching, inhaling his delectable scent.

A soft huff and a flop drew her attention. Stevie looked over to see Jäger on the floor, eyes closed, clearly tired of waiting for them.

Stone chuckled. "I think maybe we should move this somewhere with a little more room to maneuver."

"Bedroom," Stevie said. "But you two go, I'll put Jäger in his crate."

She could see the surprise on their faces.

"Be naked before you get in there," Stone said, his tone gruff and raspy.

"Yes, sir," she teased, watching them as Stone put his hand on Nico's back and urged him toward the bedroom.

Not wanting to miss a thing, Stevie got to work.

NICO LED THE WAY TO HIS BEDROOM, his skin humming from the light touch of Stone's hand on his back. It was a strange feeling, but he liked it just the same. He'd never considered himself submissive in any form of the word, but when it came to Stone, he found he was capable of anything.

"You sounded surprised earlier," Stone said when they walked into the room. "When I was on the phone."

Nico turned when Stone grabbed his arm and halted him from going farther. "When Stevie...?" He smirked. "Yeah. That's not her usual MO."

"No?"

Nico shook his head. "It's you."

Stone frowned. "Is that a bad thing?"

"No." At least Nico didn't think so. "She's still got that wild streak she had when she was younger. She suppresses it most of the time, but it's still there. You bring it out in her." Nico smirked. "It's not a bad thing at all."

In fact, Nico liked that side of Stevie. She was a strong, independent woman who asked for what she wanted. And if that didn't work, she took it. He'd always admired that about her.

"And you enjoyed it."

It wasn't a question, but Nico nodded in response.

Stone tugged him forward until they were chest to chest. Nico fell into him, into another scorching kiss that had his blood pumping hotter, thicker.

Ever the multi-tasker, Stone managed to pull his shirt up to his neck before Nico even realized what he was doing. He pulled back, allowing Stone to take it off him. He started forward again, but Stone stopped him, his gaze raking over Nico's chest, lower.

"I wanna lick every inch of you," Stone rasped, wonder ringing in his voice.

Nico appreciated the approval he heard in his tone.

"But first..." Stone jerked him forward again; this time, his arms banded around him, and he crushed his mouth to Nico's.

No man had ever kissed Nico the way Stone did. With an unbridled passion that nearly swept him off his feet. The few men Nico had indulged over the years had been the submissive sort, seeking a firm hand. Nico had provided because there was nothing else to do. And each time, he knew it wasn't what he was seeking.

This was what he craved. A man who took without asking because he knew that was what Nico needed. A firm, dominant partner who knew just how to touch him to make him burn.

Stone hit the wall with a thud, Nico crashing into him as they devoured one another.

"Take off my belt," Stone commanded, holding Nico to him.

He worked the big buckle free even as Stone's tongue thrashed in his mouth. Nico's lungs were working overtime, his muscles coiling tighter as his body heated more.

Nico tugged the leather belt from the loops, then pressed it into Stone's hand.

Stone released his mouth, smiling as he did. Nico knew something was coming but didn't know what until Stone put a firm hand on his head and urged him down to his knees. He didn't resist, eager to do this man's bidding.

As he kneeled before him, Stone flipped the button on his jeans free with one hand, then lowered the zipper. All the while, Nico felt his eyes on him. Stone didn't ask for assistance as he pushed his jeans down, his thick, heavy cock bobbing proudly when it was freed.

Nico's mouth watered with the need to taste him.

"Show me how she did it," Stone instructed, gripping the base of his cock and angling it toward Nico's face. "Suck me like she sucked you."

Nico leaned forward, licking the broad head, relishing the salty taste of him. He inhaled deeply, drawing Stone into his mouth at the same time he breathed in that musky scent that was uniquely Stone.

He felt an odd sense of déjà vu as his lips dragged over Stone's thick, throbbing shaft. His cock filled his mouth as it tunneled deeper. Nico laved and sucked in tandem, letting his taste overwhelm his senses.

"Oh, fuck yes." Stone grabbed him by the hair, pulling him forward, sending a shard of pleasure/pain coursing down Nico's spine. "I forgot how fuckin' good you are at this."

Nico curled his fingers around the base of Stone's cock, gripping firmly as he sucked him as deep as he could.

He felt something cool slide along the back of his neck. He heard the jangle of metal near his ear. Opening his eyes, he noticed Stone was holding his belt in both hands, the leather curved behind Nico's head. Stone used it to pull him forward, forcing more of his cock down Nico's throat. When Stone loosened the belt, Nico pulled back, dragged air in, and they repeated the action again and again.

Footsteps sounded in the hall, but Stone's belt behind his head made it impossible for him to look over. He knew Stevie was there. He could hear her soft gasp and feel her presence as she entered the room.

"Goddamn, you're beautiful," Stone whispered, his tone rife with wonder and awe. "Come here, baby. Join him."

Stone released the belt, so Nico shifted to the side, making room for Stevie without stopping what he was doing. Stone grabbed him by the hair, not allowing him to stop. His dominance ratcheted up the pleasure swimming in his veins.

Stevie's cool fingers curled around the back of his neck as she knelt beside him, her bare breasts rubbing his arm. She moved in close, her other hand fisting around the base of Stone's cock. She stroked him while Nico bobbed and sucked.

"Fuckin' heaven," Stone crooned. "Both of you … doin' that."

Nico could feel a slight tremble in Stone's legs, knew he was having a difficult time remaining upright. Intense pleasure tended to do that. It weakened the knees.

"Stop," Stone barked.

Nico released him instantly, shifting back.

Stone's expression was hard, but his eyes glittered with promise. "I'm not ready to come yet. Baby, I want you to show me what you did to him earlier."

Nico barely had time to brace himself when Stevie turned to him, urging him back as she pounced. His back met the hardwood at the same time Stevie started yanking on his sweatpants, jerking them down his legs.

"Eager?" he teased, watching her brown eyes gleam in the dimly lit room.

She nodded, leaning forward and taking his cock as deep as she could. Stone remained standing, watching them as he removed the rest of his clothes. When he was naked, he dropped to his knees, his cock in his fist. It hovered over Nico's face, taunting him.

Nico tilted his head back, silently requesting Stone to put it in his mouth, to force him to take it. He needed Stone's dominance. Needed him to take what he wanted.

The man was nothing if not perceptive. He painted Nico's lips with precum, then dipped the swollen head between his lips.

Nico was in heaven. Stone's cock in his mouth, Stevie's mouth on his dick. He wanted to remain just like this for the rest of his life, right here with both of them.

"I think you need some attention," Stone told Stevie. "Sit on his face. Let him eat that sweet pussy while you suck me."

Stone's cock disappeared as he shifted back a few feet, giving Stevie room to move into position. A moment later, with Stevie straddling his head, Nico curled his arms around her thighs, his fingertips spreading her wide so he could feast on her. He would never get enough of this woman. He could spend hours just like this, his tongue on her pussy, her soft mewls echoing in the room.

"Ride his face," Stone urged. "Don't stop until you come."

Stevie's hips pressed down, angling so his mouth was on her clit. Nico focused his attention there, laving with the flat of his tongue before sucking it between his lips and flicking the tiny bundle of nerves.

"Nico!" Stevie sat up, staring down at him as she fucked her pussy on his face. She fisted his hair, holding tight as she trembled and whimpered.

Above him, Stone moved in close, plucking Stevie's nipples while Nico drove her to the breaking point. She rocked her hips, taking what she needed. Nico could tell she was close, but she was holding back for whatever reason. He took the choice away from her when he pushed two fingers into her pussy, curling them at the angle he knew would cause her to detonate.

Stevie screamed, her back arching as she came.

Before she could fall, Stone was lifting her up, carrying her to the bed.

"My turn, baby."

Nico got to his feet, not wanting to miss what happened next.

Earlier, Stone had said that watching her with him was an aphrodisiac. Nico knew that to be true. Trying to unravel why it worked was impossible. It was a mystery. One that Nico no longer cared to figure out. He was content to simply accept that this was where the three of them were meant to be.

TWENTY-SEVEN

STONE SMILED DOWN AT STEVIE. "TIRED?"

She shook her head.

"Want more?"

He laughed when she nodded. Damn, the woman was perfect. Sweet and sexy. Deviously mischievous. Wanton and proud of it. He loved that about her. Hell, he loved everything about her. He always had.

"Can you handle more?"

"Try me."

"I want that ass," he said, holding her stare, gauging her first reaction.

"What're you waitin' for?"

Oh, yeah. She was still a wild cat. Stone was pretty sure she had no boundaries. Not when it came to sex.

Because he knew she thought he meant he wanted to fuck her ass—which he certainly did, just not at the moment—he held up his belt, shifting the narrative.

Her eyes widened, but not from fear.

"Turn over," he commanded.

She rolled slowly onto her stomach, then shifted onto her knees, her chest flat on the mattress.

He rubbed the smooth, rounded globes of her perfect ass, then trailed his finger along the crack, his fingertip brushing lightly over the tiny, puckered hole. "You know the belt's gonna hurt, right? It's vastly different from my hand."

Her response was a shake of her ass.

"How many?" Stone asked Nico.

Nico pondered it for a moment before he said, "What's a fair number, Stevie? Three? Five?"

She turned her head toward Nico when he joined her on the bed. Stone couldn't look away, admiring the long, delectable length of Nico's impressive body. He was ripped, his muscles highly defined because of his lean stature. It was obvious his body was honed from manual labor, and Stone was more impressed by that than if Nico spent hours a day at the gym. He was a work of art.

"Can we try one, and then I'll decide?"

Stone chuckled. Apparently, she wasn't as sure of herself. Not that he blamed her. He'd never spanked anyone with a belt. He wasn't even sure how he'd feel about it, but he was willing to give it a shot. Admittedly, he'd practiced before he left the house, trying to get a good grip on the leather, figuring out the best way to swing. It was how he figured out that he had to remove the buckle to avoid a mishap. After all, he wasn't out to hurt her, merely to give her the pleasure she sought.

He cupped her pussy, teasing her with a gentle touch while he let the anticipation build. When she relaxed, he rubbed her buttocks, grinning when she flinched. He continued to play, allowing her a few minutes to catch her breath after her orgasm. He wanted to build her back up slowly. Tonight was about her, even if she didn't know it.

When she came inside the house, Stone took the opportunity to share his plan with Nico, wanting to ensure they were on the same page.

Stevie finally relaxed when Stone dragged the leather down her spine, lightly caressing. He swept it across her ass. Back and forth, again and again. When he pulled it back, he kneaded her ass.

"Right here, baby." He patted her ass softly. "I'm gonna warm you up. I'll put the belt right here. You ready?"

"Mmm-hmm."

Stone focused, pulling his arm back, angling the leather so the swing would land where he wanted it. He delivered three rapid smacks, using very little force.

She moaned softly, shaking her ass. "More, Stone. Please."

He looked at Nico. He was watching him, and his subtle nod was the encouragement Stone needed.

He spanked her with one well-placed hit, landing it on his mark. Stevie whimpered.

"Another?"

"Yes."

He spanked her again, landing the blow in a different spot.

She moaned again, louder when Nico reached between her legs to fondle her cunt.

"Darlin', you're wet."

"Mmm-hmm. More, please."

Stone remembered the first time he'd spanked her. They'd been fooling around up in the hayloft. Stevie had teased him with her mouth but stopped before she finished him off. He'd threatened to punish her for it. Her response had been to taunt him more, pushing him until he made good on his promise. He'd smacked her ass with his hand, and she had begged for more. He'd tested the waters, landing one of the smacks directly on her pussy. Stevie had orgasmed from the impact, surprising them both. It was then that Stone realized she wasn't merely playing along to please him. She craved a rougher touch.

From that point on, they'd experimented. He'd learned what she did and didn't like, and they went from there. He had trusted her to tell him when it was too much, and that was how their bond had formed.

"Two more," Stone told her. "You want me to leave a mark?"

Stevie turned her head, peering back at him. "Yes."

He wasn't sure he was capable of delivering that mark with the belt since he was still uncertain about his ability to land it without hurting her, but he would try. And if that didn't work, his handprint would look just as lovely on her sexy little ass.

Stone delivered the next one with force and precision. Stevie shot forward, crying out. Instantly, she pushed her ass back.

"One more! Now, Stone."

He could feel Nico's eyes on them as he did her bidding, spanking her again, this time as hard as he was comfortable with.

Stevie cried out, her back arching.

Stone dropped the belt and thrust two fingers inside her. Her pussy spasmed around his fingers.

"Jesus, baby. You're comin'."

She nodded and whimpered as she tried to fuck his hand.

"Get under her," he instructed Nico. "She needs to be fucked."

While Nico gladly shifted into place, Stone pulled his fingers from inside her and went to the nightstand to retrieve the lube.

He paused when he noticed something was different. The last time he'd been here, there hadn't been anything on the nightstand. Now there was a little white alarm clock, one of those colored bands Stevie used to pull her hair up, a tube of watermelon-flavored lip balm, and what looked to be a romance novel.

All of the things that had been on the nightstand in Stevie's room.

Had she moved in here? Were they now sharing a bed?

Stone swallowed hard, ignoring the hurt that took up residence in his chest. He'd been hanging onto the notion that they were still roommates, and the three of them were exploring this thing together.

Evidently, he was wrong.

He cleared his throat and opened the drawer. The box of condoms was still there. As was the pump bottle of lubricant. Stone retrieved both, intending to give Nico a condom, but when he turned back, it no longer mattered.

Stevie was sitting astride Nico, his cock lodged deep inside her.

Stone tried to hide his surprise, but he knew Nico saw it.

"She's on the pill."

"I know." And he did, but it didn't lessen the pang of disappointment that ripped through him. Stone had fucked her without a condom, and as he'd told her before, he trusted her. He knew Nico would as well. But still. Stone had mistakenly believed that this was something new for all of them. Right or wrong, he felt betrayed, and *that* ... well, it fucking hurt.

Not that he didn't deserve it.

Shrugging off the emotional turmoil, Stone pumped lubricant into his hand, coating his fingers before rubbing a generous amount on Stevie's asshole. When he did, she stopped moving.

"Just my fingers this time," he promised, his tone flat.

When she began rocking again, fucking Nico, Stone made good on that promise even as it felt like his heart was crumbling into dust.

"STONE…" STEVIE WANTED MORE BUT HE WASN'T delivering. "Please."

She wanted all of him, but she knew that wasn't his intention. She wasn't sure whether he was punishing her or himself, but no matter how much she begged, he wouldn't fuck her ass. But this was good, too. Or it would've been, except he wasn't putting much effort into it.

"Stone?"

"Lean forward," he ordered, pressing one hand on her back when he put one knee on the bed.

Stevie dropped her chest to Nico's, relaxing against him when he claimed her mouth while his cock tunneled deep inside her. It felt good, but she wanted more. She wanted to feel them both inside her at the same time.

She whimpered when Stone added another finger. He stretched her back hole, but she could tell he was holding back. She wasn't sure what had changed, but she'd felt the shift as soon as she seated herself on Nico's cock. If she hadn't been watching their reflections in the glass door, she would've been none the wiser, but she'd witnessed Stone's surprise when he turned back to find Nico buried to the hilt inside her.

He didn't say anything, but the way he'd tossed the condoms aside told her what he wasn't saying. And then Nico had clarified that she was on the pill, and she knew what his problem was.

Why? That was the question. Why was he bothered by it? He trusted her, right? He'd said he did. Did he not trust Nico? Or was this some fucked up male pride that was getting in his way?

Whatever it was, it was ruining the mood, and that pissed her off.

"Stop," she said, pushing herself up.

Nico stopped instantly, his concern etched on his face as he stared up at her.

Stone backed off, too, but rather than wait to see what she had to say, he disappeared into the bathroom.

She heard the water turn on, figured he was washing his hands.

"What's wrong?" Nico asked, his voice low.

"That's the question, isn't it?" she retorted, climbing off of him as Stone joined them. "Are you mad that we're not usin' a condom?"

"Mad? No. Surprised? Yes."

"Why?" she snapped. "You didn't have a problem fuckin' me without one. Why should Nico?"

His eyes darted to the nightstand as he started to say something, but he closed his mouth and shook his head.

"Tell me," she bit out. "I deserve that much, don't I? Or do you plan to run away again?"

His head snapped up, his eyes slamming into her. His flinty gaze narrowed as he took one step forward, then another.

"I'm not runnin'," he growled.

"Coulda fooled me." Stevie knew she should probably leave well enough alone, but she couldn't help herself. This confrontation had been a long time coming, and though the trigger wasn't what she expected, she knew it had to be done.

Nico sighed. "Stevie, we should—"

"He's pissed," she told Nico, cutting him off. "He's pissed because we're not usin' a condom."

"I'm not pissed."

"Yeah, you are. Admit it. You wanted to be special. You wanted to be the only one, didn't you?'

The muscle in his jaw bunched, but he didn't argue.

"Well, tough shit, Stone. It's *our* choice. Not yours." She snorted. "You fucked me without a condom when Nico wasn't here. How's that any different?"

"It's not."

"Damn right, it's not. I love him," she blurted. "And he loves me."

"I know." Stone swallowed. "And I know you don't love me."

Stevie's eyes widened. She hadn't expected that. To maintain this anger, she needed him to be angry, too. But he wasn't. He sounded … defeated.

Stone remained there, unmoving, which pissed her off more. So much so that she ignored the hurt that flashed in his eyes. She pretended not to see it because she didn't care. It was the least of what he deserved. After all that he'd put her through, Stone should feel some of that ache she'd grown accustomed to for so long.

She talked to Nico while she stared at Stone. "He pretends he's okay with this, but deep down, he's selfish. He wants—"

"I'm jealous, all right!" Stone bellowed. "But it has nothin' to do with—" He waved his hand toward her nightstand and took a deep breath, his tone cooler when he said, "The condom. I thought this was new for all of us. I was wrong."

Stevie was confused. What the hell was he talking about?

She glanced at the nightstand when he looked over again.

And there it was. All her stuff, probably glaring right in his face.

"I moved in here," she told him, tipping her chin up, daring him to give his opinion. She didn't care. Plus, she was still riding the wave of retribution. The need to make him feel a fraction of what he'd made her feel when he left her all those years ago was too powerful to ignore.

"I see that." He took another deep breath. "I was mistakenly under the impression this would be a conversation the three of us would have. Clearly, you two had it without me."

A second ago, she'd wanted to blast him with hurtful words. Now, she was on the verge of tears. It wasn't fair. She shouldn't care.

His voice was low, tormented. "I get it, Stevie. I do. I'm the third wheel."

"You're the one who likes to share," she managed. "This shouldn't be a problem for you."

Stone nodded. "I'm tryin' to be okay with it."

Nico sat up, and Stevie could feel his eyes on her.

Stevie gritted her teeth. This wasn't supposed to happen. They were supposed to be having fun, right? That was all she wanted. So why was Stone making this so hard?

Stone reached down to pick up his jeans. "I need—"

Stevie lost it. She bounded off the bed, racing over to him. She grabbed his jeans before he could and flung them in the opposite direction.

"You don't get to run," she hissed.

He stood tall. "I need a minute, Stevie. I wasn't goin' to leave."

"Liar!" She wasn't sure what came over her, but her anger and frustration gripped her by the throat. The next thing she knew, she was hitting his chest with her fists. He didn't stop her, and he still didn't stop her. She wished he would because she couldn't stop herself. Her anger, her hurt … it was a living, breathing thing inside her. She didn't want to love this man, but it seemed no matter how hard she tried not to, she was succumbing to it.

"Stevie," Nico barked from behind her.

"I hate you," she told Stone, realizing that tears were streaming down her face.

His tormented expression broke her heart.

She hit him one more time, then fell forward, pressing her face to his chest. His arms came around her, holding her tight.

"I don't want to love you," she sobbed, sliding her arms around him. "It's easier to hate you."

"I know," he whispered near her ear. "I've hated myself for a long time."

She believed him. And that was one of the reasons she loved him.

NICO HAD KNOWN FROM THE MOMENT HE learned that Stone was back in town that this inevitable collision was coming.

Stevie was good at pretending she didn't feel anything, that Stone's reappearance hadn't affected her, but she was only fooling herself. Nico knew better. She would end up processing it in some way that didn't involve pretending she didn't care. This was it. This was her coming to terms with the fact her life had come full circle.

He wasn't sure what to say, so he kept his mouth shut. The moment was lost, but that was okay because this was more important. Stevie needed to get it out so they had a chance of moving forward. He knew deep down she wanted this as much as he did, but as he'd told her before, he didn't harbor the same animosity toward Stone as she did. Yeah, he'd been disappointed when Stone left town, but they'd shared exactly one night together. His life had been altered, but not the way hers had.

"I'm gonna give you two a minute," he told them, grabbing his sweatpants off the floor.

Stevie pulled back. "Don't go."

"I'm gonna get some water and check on Jäger," he assured her. "I'll be right back."

Nico met Stone's eyes as he pulled on his pants. He saw more emotion in those glittering brown-green depths than he'd ever seen before. Stone was tormented by what he'd done because he'd hurt Stevie. It was evident that walking away from her was something he'd spent the past fifteen years regretting.

As Nico walked past them, Stone reached out and grabbed his arm. Nico stopped, looking down at where Stone's big fingers curled around his forearm. Stone's thumb brushed back and forth over his skin, and Nico didn't realize how much he needed that small reassurance.

"I'll be back," he promised, then slipped out of the room.

Jäger was in his crate, head lifted, eyes widely curious. Figuring he might need some attention after hearing raised voices coming from the back of the house, Nico got him out and took him out to the yard. It was cool but not cold—too much humidity to allow for that—and since he was half-dressed, he appreciated it.

While the puppy sniffed the grass around the patio, Nico sat down and waited. His chest felt oddly tight because he was on edge. Not from the argument but from the concern that Stevie and Stone might not be able to reconcile their differences the way Nico hoped.

He wished he could help them. Wished he knew how to put the past behind them. It was far easier said than done, though, which meant he had to let it play out however it was going to.

Jäger bounded over, tail wagging. He looked almost proud of himself for doing his business in the yard versus the house. It was enough to make Nico laugh as he got to his feet and led the way inside. He offered Jäger a treat, which he gleefully took, before putting the puppy back in his crate. Jäger snuggled right into the blanket, obviously appeased that all would be okay.

Nico wished he could be as sure.

Still, he headed for his bedroom, not sure what he would find.

He paused in the doorway. Stone was sitting on the bed, Stevie standing in front of him, both of them still naked. Stone's big hands rested on her hips while hers teased his hair.

Stone noticed him first, jerking his chin in the signal for him to join them.

Hesitantly, Nico made his way over.

Stevie's cheeks still had tear tracks running down them, and it broke his heart to see.

"I didn't mean what I said earlier," she said, looking at Nico.

Since she'd said a lot of things, he waited for her to elaborate.

"I do love you," she told Stone before looking at Nico again. "And I love you. It's a curse, I guess." She forced a smile, but there was a hint of amusement in her eyes to go with it. "I want to pretend all is good now, but I can't. However, Stone kindly reminded me that we've got a lot of time to make up for and there's no reason to rush anything."

Nico agreed. At the same time, he didn't want to go backward. The progress he'd made with Stevie wasn't something he was willing to give up.

"I'm gonna do my best to be more open about what I want," she told them both. "And not just with sex. Although…" She stopped playing with Stone's hair and put her hands on their chests. "I'm gonna be more vocal about that, too."

Nico glanced at Stone. "I didn't think she was havin' trouble with that. Did you?"

Stone's smile was small, but it was there. "No."

She smacked their chests lightly. "Hush it."

Stone reached for her, but she danced back out of the way.

"Are you playin' hard to get?" Nico asked, curious what her end game was.

"No. I'm takin' a step back."

"Why?"

She looked at Stone. "Remember how you said seein' me and Nico together is an aphrodisiac?"

He nodded.

"It's the same for me when I see the two of you together."

Nico continued to stare at her. He wasn't sure where she was going with this, but he got the feeling he was going to enjoy it.

"I say we get up in that bed and get comfortable, and perhaps y'all might let me watch for a little while."

"Tonight was supposed to be about you," Stone told her.

"In that case, I *definitely* want to watch you two together."

Nico frowned. "I'm lost."

"No, you're talkin' too much," she said, the teasing note returning to her voice as she moved around them and climbed onto the bed.

Nico twisted to look as she pulled the blankets back and got under them.

"Come on. Join me."

"You good?" Nico asked Stone, keeping his voice low.

Stone nodded. "As long as y'all aren't kickin' me out, then, yeah."

Nico didn't bother telling him he'd prefer he stay forever. Now didn't seem to be the time to make any significant adjustments to their future plans.

With that in mind, Nico walked around to his side of the bed and climbed in with Stevie. A moment later, Stone joined them.

This was exactly where Nico wanted to be.

Only he would've preferred there to be some spark left in Stone's eyes.

Unfortunately, it wasn't there. And Nico had no idea how to get it to shine again.

TWENTY-EIGHT

Tuesday, February 6, 2024

AFTER LEAVING STEVIE'S HOUSE YESTERDAY MORNING, STONE had put his spare time to good use. He started calling his cousins, requesting time to talk. Once he was able to nail that down, he'd put a few finishing touches on his business proposal.

While he focused on the critical task that would outline his future, he thought about Stevie and the conversation they'd had on Sunday night. Or rather, the heated words that had been exchanged. He wished more than anything that he could change the past so he didn't have to hear the venom spew from her beautiful mouth. She hated him. Deep down, he knew she did, but despite all his wishful thinking, he wasn't sure she could get past it. Maybe one day she would come around, but he got the feeling she was still pretending. Until she stopped doing that, progress may not even be an option.

Unfortunately, he didn't know how to fix it, so he did what he usually did. He focused on what he could fix.

That was why he was in his truck, heading to the diner to meet Travis, Kaleb, and Sawyer. When he talked to him yesterday, Travis told him that a discussion wasn't necessary—he had Travis's blessing already—but Stone insisted on seeing him. Travis relented after a bit of persistence—something his cousin never would've done before the events that had changed his entire life.

As he was pulling into the diner parking lot, his phone rang. His caller ID flashed on the truck's navigation screen, and he nearly ran over the parking stone.

"Hey," he greeted, hitting the brake and putting the truck in *park*.

"Hey back," Stevie said, a smile in her voice. "Whatcha doin'?"

Stone tried to play it cool, to pretend he wasn't shocked as shit that she had called him. Or that she seemed to be in a chipper mood. Up to now, he'd been the one to initiate all their phone calls and texts.

"Meetin' my cousins for dinner. What're you doin'?"

"Takin' some sage advice and callin' you."

Stone smiled. He was sure it was the first real smile since their argument the other night. He'd been in a weird place since then, unsure how to move forward but unwilling to stop trying. This felt like an olive branch, and he wasn't about to pass it up.

"I'm glad you did."

"Really?"

The vulnerability he detected in her tone made his chest ache. "Yes, really. I miss you, Stevie."

A brief pause filled the truck with silence before Stevie finally said, "I miss you, too."

Stone stared at the diner. It was busy for a Tuesday night, but through the windows that lined the front, he could see several tables open.

"I'm gonna have dinner with Nico," Stevie said after another long pause. "After, I was wonderin' if I could come over."

"I don't know when I'll be done here, but yeah. I'd like that."

Another pause, followed by, "Stone, I want to spend the night. Just the two of us."

He swallowed hard and shifted his gaze to the screen as though he would be able to see her. His chest expanded and filled with a longing so powerful he was grateful he was sitting down.

"Stone?"

"I'm here." His voice was rougher than before. "And I'd love for you to spend the night."

"You sure?"

"Positive."

The smile in her voice returned. "Okay. I'll see you in a coupla hours?"

"I'll text you when I'm leavin' here so you'll know."

"See you in a bit."

Stone disconnected the call but didn't move for several minutes. Hope now flared hot and bright in his chest. It was almost enough to make him turn around and head home, but he forced himself to turn off the truck. Seeing Stevie was the only thing he wanted to do, but this was important. After all, this was the only way he could secure his future so that he could give Stevie and Nico everything they deserved.

The longing and hope he'd been feeling morphed into confidence as he walked into the restaurant. It wavered slightly when he saw Kaleb and Sawyer but not Travis.

"Look at you, boy," Sawyer greeted with a wide grin as he got to his feet. "All grown up and shit."

Stone couldn't remember ever seeing his wild-as-fuck cousin without one of those grins. Back in the day, Sawyer had been the troublemaker every wild boy in town wanted to be like.

Sawyer pulled him in for a back-jarring hug. When he stepped back, his grin widened.

Kaleb was standing now, holding out his hand. Stone shook it but ended up in another brotherly embrace.

"And you two," Stone said as he pulled out a chair. "All domesticated and shit."

Sawyer flashed a proud grin as he ran his hand down his shirt like he was showing off his new duds. "Looks good on me, huh?"

"It does, actually." Stone looked at Kaleb. "You don't look half bad either."

Kaleb snorted a laugh. "Thanks. I've got twice as many kids as he does. I expect to look a little more worn."

"How are those rugrats, anyway?"

"Wild and untamed," Kaleb teased.

"Mason's what? Ten now?"

"About to be. In a few days. He's countin' down."

"Double digits is a big deal," Stone joked.

"That's what they tell me."

"That makes Kellan what? Eight? Barrett seven and Gabe Six?"

"You do read those Christmas cards we send."

"I keep track as best I can." Stone looked at Sawyer. "Matthew's seven and Brody's five, right?"

"I'm impressed, Jameson."

"What? That I keep track? Or that I can count to ten?"

Sawyer barked a laugh, which drew the attention of several people.

Stone looked around, expecting Travis to walk up any second.

"He's not comin'," Kaleb finally said. "He doesn't leave the house much these days."

Stone knew his cousin had a lot going on, so he decided to leave it at that.

The waitress appeared, so the three of them rattled off their orders.

"He said to tell you to do whatever you want," Sawyer informed him when she was gone. "And just to ease your mind a bit, we're right there with him."

"Well, hell. I worked on a presentation and everything. I was gonna have the waitress bring out a projection screen. Got my laser pointer."

Kaleb looked at Sawyer. "I don't think he's kiddin'."

"Only half," Stone said. "I do have a presentation, and I'm happy to send it to you. It shows my intentions with the land."

"Is it gonna benefit the community?" Sawyer asked.

"It is, yes."

"Will it help the schools?" Kaleb inquired.

"Actually, yes," Stone said, meeting his gaze. "I made some changes yesterday. Donovan came by last week and mentioned Trey's lettin' the high school use some of his land for the Ag department."

"I heard that, too," Sawyer noted.

"Since I'm anglin' for a farmers' market, I thought it might benefit them if they could let some of the kids grow and sell their own produce. I've still gotta talk to the school, but I was gonna offer to oversee it."

"That's actually kinda brilliant." Kaleb sounded pleased. "You know how Home Depot has that kids' buildin' thing on the weekend? You could do that for the younger set."

Stone had no idea what Home Depot did, but he understood what Kaleb was getting at. "I'll definitely outline a plan for it."

Sawyer grinned. "When Pop told us what they were plannin', I'll admit, I was curious why they picked you."

"You're not the only one." Stone was unable to hide his confusion. He still wasn't sure why Curtis had picked him out of the lot, but what was the old saying? Don't look a gift horse in the mouth. Yeah. Stone was adopting that as his new mantra.

"I don't question Pop's motives," Kaleb said. "And since Mom's on board, I figure they know what they're doin'."

Stone only hoped their brothers felt the same.

STEVIE WATCHED AS NICO MOVED AROUND THE kitchen.

"You sure you don't want me to do that?"

He peered at her over his shoulder. "Do what? Cook?" He grinned. "Nah. I've got it."

"I can cook," she told him.

"I know."

"Do you?"

Nico stopped and turned to face her. "If I didn't know better, I'd think you were tryin' to pick a fight."

There was a good chance he was right, but Stevie didn't want to admit that. She also didn't want to admit that she was conflicted about what she wanted. More so about what she felt she deserved.

She'd spent the past two days feeling guilty about the things she said to Stone on Sunday night. The words had come from a dark, ugly place inside her. She was embarrassed to have been so cruel. It was one thing to harbor hurt feelings, another to make a blatant attempt to inflict that sort of pain on someone else.

Rather than explain it, she shrugged.

Nico came around to stand behind her, his hands sliding over her shoulders. He didn't stop there, though. His hands flattened on her chest, urging her back until she was leaning against him. His big hand cupped her throat, his thumb grazing her jaw in a gentle caress. She took a deep breath and let it out slowly.

"I think tonight'll be good for you and Stone," he said as his hands shifted, his skilled fingers massaging her shoulders.

"I don't."

"Why?"

"Because I feel myself caving," she admitted.

"Do you want to cave?"

"Yes." Stevie hated that it came out so quickly, but it was the truth. She wanted to trust Stone because, deep down, her love for him had never died. It felt like it had been compartmentalized all these years, kept safe and secure, waiting for him to return. Now that he was here, now that she had his attention again, she wanted to take it out and give it all back to him.

At the same time, she wanted to smack herself upside the head for wanting to be so reckless. He'd broken her heart once before. What if he did it again?

"I think you need this, Stevie. I think you both do."

She spun herself around so she could face him. He didn't move back, so he stood, towering over her, his eyes warm and kind. "What about you? This feels ... weird."

When he cupped her face, she hooked her hands on his wrists.

"Like you're cheatin'?"

"No. Yes." She sighed. "I don't know."

It did feel like she was cheating, but it didn't. What she had with Nico ... it was as new and confusing as what she had with Stone. The only difference was she was sleeping in Nico's bed every night. That was nice, though. Being close to him, having him there. But it still felt like something was missing, and she knew that Stone's absence weighed heavily on them. He'd only been back in town for a few weeks, but it felt like he never left, and she wanted to spend every spare minute with both of them. To make up for all that lost time.

Nico grinned, cupping her face. "Would it help if you knew I wanted the same thing?"

"Alone time with Stone?"

"Yeah."

That did help, actually. She wasn't sure why, nor did she care to overanalyze it, but it made her feel a little better for wanting this so badly.

"We're gonna make this work, I promise."

He sounded so confident it was difficult not to believe him.

An hour and a half later, Stevie was driving to Stone's house. He'd texted a little while ago to let her know he was home. As soon as she saw the message, her heart fluttered, and her body warmed. Considering how they'd left things the other night, it was an odd reaction. After their argument, they'd agreed to set it aside for the time being and to let things happen as they were meant to happen. She'd told herself she was going to make Stone work for it, that he would have to be the one to pursue her if he wanted anything from her. Now, here she was, making the first move, asking to spend the night.

It was what the old Stevie would've done. The girl she'd been before Stone broke her heart and shattered her dreams. She'd been steadfast in her desire to go after what she wanted. Back then, she'd wanted Stone. And after *that night*, she had wanted Stone and Nico. Only she never had the chance to tell Stone that because he up and left.

When she thought about a future with Stone, she was conflicted. She was waiting for the other shoe to drop and feared that was her permanent setting. He had broken something inside her when he left, and she didn't know if it was possible to repair it.

But she wanted to be able to say that she tried. If she didn't, she would always be left wondering, and that was no way to live.

She took a deep breath as she pulled down the Jamesons' driveway. The lights in the house were on, and she was taken back to years ago when she'd spent so many hours inside that house. Stevie had not only loved Stone back then, but she'd loved his entire family. She'd envied how close they were, and when Stone left, she'd lost that, too. It didn't help that her parents had been only a few years from divorce at the time, their relationship crumbling a little more each day.

Stevie parked her Bronco beside Stone's truck and turned off the engine. She sat there for a moment, staring at the barn that was no longer a barn. It was now a home. One that lacked the memories of old. Did Stone walk around inside, thinking about what had once been? Or was it so different that his memories had faded?

"Only one way to find out."

She grabbed her backpack and got out. She shifted it onto her shoulder as she made her way up the steps to the front door. She lifted her hand to knock but stopped when she saw Stone coming toward her.

How was it possible for the man to take her breath away like that? Just looking at him brought a rush of emotion—relief, fear, anger, desire, and, yes, love. It was all there.

"Hey," he greeted when he opened the door, his hazel eyes warm.

She smiled, unable to speak.

"Come in," he urged.

When she walked inside, she paused to take her boots off while he took her backpack. When she was finished, Stone took her hand, leading her deeper into the house. He set the bag on one of the barstools.

"Can I get you somethin' to drink? I've got pretty much everything."

"What're you havin'?"

He gestured to the highball glass on the counter. "Rum and Coke."

"I'll take one of those."

"Comin' right up."

While he poured her drink, Stevie went into the living room, admiring the space the same way she had the other night when she and Nico were there. What they'd done with the place was remarkable. Never in her wildest dreams could she imagine living in a barn, but they'd somehow turned this into something warm and cozy.

"Did they use any part of the old barn to make this place?"

"More than you think. It looks new, but it's not. Brady and Donovan managed to salvage a good portion of it."

Stone appeared at her side, passing her a glass.

"Thanks." She took the glass from him. "What about the loft?"

He glanced toward the stairs at the far end of the room. "Reilly's got some stuff up there right now, but it's mostly the same. They added stairs and replaced all the rotted wood, but it's still there."

Stevie found herself staring up at the section of the space with a second floor. It felt smaller than she remembered.

"We can go up there if you'd like."

She cut her gaze to his. "I … uh … Nah. I'm good."

He gestured toward the couch.

With her drink in hand, she took a seat. She was nervous, and she didn't know how to hide it, so she did what she usually did: she addressed it.

"This feels weird."

"Bein' here?" Stone asked. "Or bein' with me?"

Stevie heard the uncertainty in his tone and stalled by taking a large gulp of her drink before admitting the truth. "Both."

"A lot's changed, Stevie."

That was an understatement. For one, they'd both grown up. She'd made something of herself, and up until a week and a half ago, she'd been content with the direction her life was going. Stone, on the other hand, seemed to be starting over, and for some insane reason, she was thinking about coming along for the ride.

Rather than fidgeting in the silence, Stevie filled it. "How'd it go with your cousins?"

His smile returned, and it reached his eyes this time. "Good. Travis, Sawyer, and Kaleb gave me their nod of approval."

"That's great. Only four more to go?"

"Yeah."

"You meetin' with them soon?"

"Not as soon as I'd like. I'm seein' Braydon and Brendon on Monday at Moonshiners—Brendon's out of town until Sunday. And I'm meetin' with Ethan and Beau next Thursday. They invited me over for dinner."

"That sounds positive."

"I'm hopin'."

"That leaves one?" she asked.

"Yeah. Zane." He chewed on his lower lip briefly. "I've reached out but haven't heard back from him."

Stevie detected a hint of worry in his tone, but she didn't push him on it.

"What happens once they all sign off?"

"I'll go over the plan with my aunt and uncle, get their input."

She nodded.

"But I can't do that until I get yours."

Stevie wanted to leave him hanging for a bit longer but couldn't bring herself to do it. She'd spent every waking moment thinking about his plan. As much as she wanted to deny it, she was excited by the prospect. More so than she ever was about the landscaping business. Not that she would admit that.

"But you'll have to look at it again," Stone said. "I ... umm..." He took a heavy inhale, and she swore he was nervous. "I added somethin' to the plan. Nothin' major. I just thought it might benefit the school if we could do somethin' to give back."

She eyed him curiously. "Like?"

"Since I'm movin' forward with the farmers' market idea, I thought it might help if we sectioned off an area and let the school use it to grow their own produce so they could sell it."

Her heart slammed into her ribs. That was very generous on his part. Not to mention wildly attractive. The fact that he was thinking about people other than himself...

Stevie took another drink, set the glass on the coffee table, and turned to face him more fully.

"I'm in."

His expression was priceless. He obviously wasn't expecting that.

"But there are some conditions," she added.

"Of course."

"If we're goin' into business together, we've got to outline it accordingly. It has to remain separate from..." She waved her hand between them. "I need to know I'll be protected if this doesn't work."

"The paperwork's all drawn up. For you and Nico."

It was her turn to be surprised.

"This isn't a rash decision on my part, Stevie. I've thought long and hard about it." He put his glass on the table and scooted closer. "But I need you to know, I'm not givin' up on us."

She swallowed hard, meeting his gaze.

"What I want from you and Nico has nothin' to do with business. I want *that* because I think we'll make a good team, and if that's all I get, I'll find a way to be happy. At least I'll have you in my life, Stevie."

She hated that he sounded so sincere. Keeping the hard shell around her heart was much easier when she doubted him. She feared she had no resistance to this man, the one whose heart was on his sleeve.

"But I want more. I want a life with you. I've missed you for so long," he whispered, brushing a strand of hair behind her ear, his fingertips gently caressing her cheek. "I never stopped thinkin' about you."

Tears formed, but she fought them back.

"And I've never stopped lovin' you."

"I'm a sure thing tonight, Stone." She swallowed the lump of emotion clogging her throat. "You don't have to seduce me."

He pulled back and met her stare. "I'm not. I'm tellin' the truth."

She detected no dishonesty, and her attempt to hold back the tears became futile.

"I want so much more than tonight, Stevie. I want the rest of our lives."

She was a goner. The tears began to fall as she threw her arms around his neck, crushing her lips to his. She let his heat consume her, his strength reassure her.

"I want that, too," she whispered, ensuring her words were too soft for him to hear.

TWENTY-NINE

STONE HELD ONTO STEVIE LIKE HIS LIFE depended on it. At times, he was sure it did. Or it felt like it, anyway.

"I'm sorry about the things I said the other night." Her words were mumbled, broken up by her sniffling.

Reluctantly, he released her when she pulled back.

"I didn't mean them." She wiped her eyes.

"You don't have to apologize. I deserve it."

Her eyes widened. "No, you don't. God, Stone. Nobody deserves to be talked to like that. I had no right, and I'm ashamed of what I said. At the time, I wanted to hurt you." She shook her head adamantly. "But what I said … it's not true."

Stone didn't want to argue with her. He'd accepted the blame long ago. He'd come to terms with the fact he'd fucked up his own life by leaving. He didn't need her to tell him that. If he had stayed, there was a good chance he would've married her, had babies. It would've been hard for them, and he had no doubt they would've struggled to get to this point, but he liked to think they would be happy even though he'd told himself for years that there was no way he could've been what Stevie needed.

Still, he wished he'd given himself a chance. Given *them* a chance.

"I loved you so much back then," Stevie whispered, her big brown eyes shining with unshed tears. "I was so lost when you left."

"I was, too." He cupped her face, shifting closer because he couldn't not touch her now that she was here.

Stevie's hand curled around his wrist, her eyes imploring him. "I went through all the stages of grief."

Nico had mentioned the very same thing to him, stating that Stevie had hated them both for a long time.

"For a while, I even pretended you were dead. I finally accepted that you weren't comin' back, so it was easier that way. I didn't want to believe you could walk away. I thought we had somethin'."

"We did," he assured her. "We absolutely did. We *do*. I fucked up. I loved you then, and I love you now, Stevie. You have to know that."

She nodded, holding his stare.

"I thought I was doin' right by you."

"You hurt me."

He swallowed, emotion churning in his gut. "I know. And I'll spend the rest of my life makin' it up to you."

Stevie shook her head. "You can't."

"But I—"

She placed her hand over his lips. "What I mean is, we have to put it behind us. If we're gonna move forward, we can't let the past define our future."

He wanted to believe that. More than that, he wanted her to mean it. A future with Stevie and Nico was the only thing he wanted. He had a lot to atone for, and he was prepared to prove to them he was in it for the long haul this time.

"I want a future with you," she whispered.

Stone pulled her into his lap, hugging her tight to his chest. He was at a loss for words, so he settled for holding her, listening to her breathe, feeling the warmth of her body beneath his hands. Her proximity stirred his body to life, but he ignored it. And he was successful, right up until she kissed his neck, her fingers teasing the hair at his nape.

"I miss the way you used to touch me," she said between nibbles on his neck.

He closed his eyes and got lost in her exquisite touch, her delectable scent teasing his nose. He couldn't count how many nights he'd laid in his bunk thinking about her. When he closed his eyes, he swore he could feel her touch, hear her soft sighs. He'd dreamed about her for nights on end, constantly waking frustrated and angry with himself for leaving.

"Stone?"

"Hmm?"

"Touch me."

He slipped his hands beneath her sweater, her smooth skin teasing his fingertips. She was so soft.

Stevie pulled away, getting to her feet. His brain began working overtime, trying to figure out what he'd done wrong when she pulled her sweatshirt over her head. She held it to her chest for a moment, then tossed it away.

Stone exhaled, flopping back on the couch as air began circulating in his lungs again. He stared at the most beautiful creature in the universe as she unhooked her bra and slipped the straps down her shoulders. Again, she held it there momentarily before baring herself to him.

"You are. So beautiful." His sentence was broken because lust slammed into him, thickening his cock, making his jeans uncomfortably tight.

She reached for the button on her jeans. "Back when we were together, I went after what I wanted without apology."

He remembered. He'd loved that about her.

"When you left, I forgot who I was. I buried that girl down deep." She flashed a smile. "I think it's time for her to reemerge."

Stone caught his breath when she shimmied her jeans down her legs.

"Do you have a problem with that?" she asked as she hooked her thumbs in the elastic of her panties.

"No, baby." He shook his head to reiterate. "No problem at all."

"Good."

And then there she was, naked and gorgeous, nibbling on her lower lip like she was unsure what to do next.

"Don't move," he whispered, soaking up the sight of her, memorizing every curve all over again.

When she shivered, Stone got to his feet. He gripped her waist and lifted her off her feet. When he started walking, her legs went around his waist, her arms circling his neck.

"Where're we goin'?" she whispered, her mouth hovering near his ear.

"Somewhere I can lay you out and have my wicked way with you."

He made his way into his bedroom and headed right for the bed. He tossed her on it, watching as she bounced and laughed. God*damn*. She was everything he'd been missing all these years.

Before she could get too comfortable, Stone grabbed her ankles and jerked her toward the edge of the bed.

Next came the internal conflict. Did he make love to her sweetly, savoring every touch and showing her how gentle he could be? Or did he take what she was freely giving him because the Stevie he loved needed that rougher touch?

Stone decided to reserve sweet and gentle for a later date. Right now, he wanted to remind her how explosive they were when they were together.

Holding her gaze, he ran his hands down her sculpted calves, stopping behind her knees. He leaned down, bending her in half while spreading her legs wide.

"Hold your legs," he ordered.

She took over, gripping behind her knees, spreading herself wide.

"I wanna look at you," he told her, admiring her as he took his shirt off and threw it to the side.

He towered over her, staring down at her beautiful body, loving how vulnerable she was right then. He trailed his finger along her inner thigh, from her knee down, down, down. He teased over her glistening flesh with the lightest flutter of his finger. She shivered again, her eyes locked on him.

"You need my mouth on you, don't you?"

Stevie nodded.

He slid his finger between her pussy lips, lightly, gently. He added a little pressure when he reached her clit.

Stevie gasped. "Stone…"

You want my tongue here?" He rubbed a circle over her clit.

"Yes." She grunted. "Please."

"What about here?" he asked, sliding his finger down to the snug entrance of her pussy. He pushed in to the first knuckle. "You want my tongue here?"

"Yes," she hissed, her eyes closing.

"Me, too." He lowered himself to his knees. "You don't know how long I've dreamed about tastin' you again. Lettin' you fuck my tongue with your sweet little cunt."

She whimpered.

"I'm hungry, baby," he warned, licking her soft pink flesh.

"Stone, please."

He slipped his hands under her ass, lifting her to his mouth. He pressed a soft kiss on her clit, smiling when she grunted her disappointment.

"That's not enough for you?"

"Lick me, Stone," she demanded.

"I think someone forgot who's in charge." He bit her labia, then licked away the sting. "Don't worry, baby. I'll remind you."

HE WAS GOING TO KILL HER SLOWLY.

Stevie should've expected it. And maybe she did. Maybe her inner bad girl was hoping he would punish her the way he used to. The man was responsible for teaching her what she liked. She'd been too young back then to know, but he'd had no problems letting her set her own path. She knew she wouldn't be the woman she was if she hadn't met him.

Stone's tongue trailed over and around, licking, nipping, teasing, but never where she wanted him. She tried to be quiet, hoping he would reward her for her patience.

Only they both knew she had none. Zero. Not when it came to him and his skilled mouth. The man ate pussy like it was both a delicacy and a dessert. Sometimes, he savored; others, he devoured. Problem was, Stevie wasn't sure which he was in the mood for.

"Look at those pretty nipples," he said, his rough words vibrating over her skin. "Pinch them for me."

She wasn't sure how she was supposed to hold her legs back *and* do what he wanted. It took a moment for her to realize she could do both, but it required her to contort her body into a less-than-comfortable position, her arms curling under her knees.

"That's better," he said as he dipped his tongue into her pussy, fucking her, tormenting her.

Did she mention the position made her even more vulnerable to his wicked tongue? It was impossible to focus while he was doing that. She pinched and tugged her nipples, the sensation warring with the delectable things he was doing between her legs.

But when he circled her clit with the tip of his tongue, she lost her grip, her inner muscles clenching as pleasure stole through her.

"Ahh. That's what you needed, huh?"

"Stone…"

He continued to play with her clit, flicking it, rubbing it with the flat of his tongue, then flicking it again.

"I can't!" she told him, her hands returning to her legs as she pulled them to her chest, desperately urging him to send her over.

Stone chuckled and the vibrations nearly did her in.

"One, Stevie. I'll let you come one time, but only to take the edge off."

"Yes." She rocked, trying to get more friction on her clit, when he licked her again. "Please, Stone. Oh, God. Make me come."

He wrapped his lips around her clit and sucked, sending shards of electricity through her, shorting out her circuits when he ruthlessly flicked the sensitive nub. She detonated, screaming as she let the waves crash over her, through her. She was drowning in pleasure, and she didn't care if it took her under, and she never emerged.

"You do know you owe me, now," he said as he got to his feet. "And I'll take my payment in increments."

She smiled, watching him pull his boots off, dropping them to the floor with a thud. He discarded the rest of his clothes without rushing. She ogled him when he was naked, her mouth watering at the sight.

"Your first installment's due now. The last in the mornin'. Then we'll discuss future terms."

This was the Stone she remembered. Sex with him had always been an adventure. There was no wham-bam-thank-you-ma'am with him. Stone had always taken his time. He was the reason she craved it. And she'd had decent sex with other men, but nothing compared to what she found with Stone and Nico. Separate or together, what they gave her was above and beyond anything she'd felt with anyone else.

"You are so sexy," he whispered as he crawled onto the bed with her.

She welcomed him into her arms as he draped himself over her so she could feel the heat of his body.

His mouth found hers, and she lost herself in the kiss. She could taste herself on his lips, which meant he could, too.

"How should you repay me?" he teased, his lips trailing down her jaw.

Stevie turned her head and whispered in his ear. "Put your cock in my throat."

He growled, a sound so animalistic, chills danced along her arms. "You say such pretty things."

She giggled as he lifted his head, smiling down at her.

But Stone didn't rush to shove his cock in her mouth. He wouldn't. The man had infinite patience, and sex had always been a give-and-take for him. Only, he usually found some way to give far more than he took. Which had always been a conundrum for her since she'd wanted nothing more than to worship him, to give him as much pleasure as he gave her. But ultimately, it was a win-win, as far as she was concerned.

He sat up, straddling her hips, his heavy cock bobbing out from his beautiful body. Her fingers itched to touch him, so she did, curling them around his thick shaft, stroking lightly while she watched him watching her.

His hands didn't remain idle. They skimmed her sides, moving higher, teasing her flesh with the gentlest brush of his skin. She gasped when he gently pinched her nipples, pulling on them until they were once again beaded. Feeling bold and brazen, Stevie angled his cock toward her mouth. She wanted to taste him, but Stone had other ideas.

Shifting, he positioned so that his cock rested between her breasts. She stopped stroking when he pressed her breasts together, pillowing his rigid shaft between them. His eyes heated as he watched his cock tunneling between her breasts.

Stevie loved watching him. His face was so expressive, so otherworldly beautiful. Although that word did nothing to describe his rugged, bad boy good looks. He had a devilish appeal about him, one she'd been drawn to instantly. She'd go so far as to say she'd fallen in love with his roguish charm.

When his lips parted with a groan, Stevie helped him along, pushing her breasts together so he could change the angle of his thrusts. It gave her what she wanted, his cock closer to her mouth. She lifted her head, sticking her tongue out so she could lap at the bead of precum on the tip when he rocked forward.

"Damn, baby. Ah, yeah. I need that sweet mouth."

She flashed a grin when he abandoned her tits and shifted his focus to her mouth. She thought he would lean over and take what he wanted, but this was Stone. She should've known he had something else in store.

In one quick move, he was on his back, and she was laid out over him. He banded his arms around her and laughed, his eyes glittering with amusement.

He was even better looking like that—carefree and happy, living in the moment. She wasn't sure she'd seen that look on his face since he returned, but she was glad it was there now.

His hands cradled her ass, kneading softly at first, but with every passing second, he became more aggressive, and the temperature of the room increased as her desire shot up a few thousand degrees.

Stone rolled his hips, his cock sliding between her thighs, rubbing sensually against her clit. He was watching her, and she knew he was following her lead, using her reactions to set the pace. There was no one better at reading her than Stone Jameson. He always knew what she needed and just when she needed it.

She cried out when he gripped her ass and shifted her so that his cock pressed against her entrance.

"You need my cock, don't you, Stevie?"

She nodded, gasping as he pushed the blunt head inside. Just the tip. Not nearly enough, but the sensation was exquisite.

"You can have it," he crooned. "But you've gotta take all of it. Think you can handle that?"

Stevie met his stare, daring him to give her everything his heated gaze promised. She felt the shift in him, his primal side coming alive. He was going to fuck her. There would be no sweet words or gentle caresses. He was going to fuck her like she needed to be fucked.

"Yes. Fuck me, Stone." She lifted her hips, giving him room. "Fuck me. Hard."

He held himself there for one heartbeat, two. His gaze held warning and promise, and she welcomed both. She knew he would wait until he was ready, so she didn't speak, only breathed. In, out. In, out. In—

Stevie screamed when he drove his cock deep inside her, filling her in one brutal thrust. He held her hips so that she couldn't move. She could only accept what he was giving her as he drilled her rough and hard, pumping into her from underneath, gravity doing its duty as she dropped down on him each time he rammed inside her.

It was just the beginning. Stevie did what she could to hold on for the ride.

"Aw, fuck. Such a tight little pussy. Squeeze my dick, Stevie."

Her inner muscles locked on tight, dragging a ragged growl from him.

"Yes. Just like that. Fuck. Feels. So. Good."

Stone never stopped fucking her. Not even when he flipped her onto her back. His hands were rough as he contorted her body, his cock tunneling deep with every stroke.

"I fuckin' love this pussy," he snarled. "So fuckin' wet for me. Did you miss this, Stevie? Miss the way I *own* this pussy?"

"Yes! God, yes!"

"I want your orgasm, baby. I want you to come all over my cock. But not yet." He slammed into her again and again. "Not until I'm done with you."

She cried out her pleasure, whispered his name, pleaded for more and more and more. He gave her everything she needed, nipping her skin, tweaking her nipples, pounding her pussy. It was wild, unhinged, and so perfect that she briefly wondered if she would even survive it.

Stone shifted forward, bending her in half, pounding down into her, hitting that spot inside her that made her see stars. He wasn't gentle, and she loved every second. She'd always loved watching the need overwhelm him as he took his pleasure from her.

"Stone!" It was a warning. She couldn't hold back. She was going to come.

"Take it, baby," he hissed, his eyes locked on her face. "Take *me*, Stevie. I wanna feel you come."

She tried to hold on, not wanting it to end, but the electricity ignited the flame, and it grew hotter and hotter until she was boiling over, every cell in her body charged and sparking.

"Let go," he demanded, his eyes hot.

Digging her nails into his arms, she did as he instructed. She let go. Falling, falling. She was overwhelmed by pleasure, drowning in ecstasy that was far more intense than anything she'd ever felt.

Or so she thought.

She learned how wrong she was when Stone slammed into her one final time.

"I love you, Stevie," he rasped, his eyes closing, teeth clamping together as he pulsed deep inside her.

Intense didn't even begin to describe the feeling that swept over her then.

STONE DIDN'T WANT TO SLEEP.

He didn't want to miss a minute with this woman.

But after he'd cleaned them both and joined her in his big bed again, the tug of exhaustion was impossible to resist as he held Stevie in the dark, her soft body warm against his. He didn't fight when sleep took him, dragging him into one of the most restful nights of his life. He woke numerous times, stirred by his body's desire for the woman he held in his arms. He ignored that need, content to simply be.

When morning finally came, Stone woke with small, determined hands moving over him. And lips. Those were definitely lips that were trailing across his chest. And a tongue.

He groaned softly when Stevie licked his nipple, teasing it to a little point.

"You're a bad girl." His voice was rough with sleep, so it came out more of a rasp.

"You have no idea," she whispered as she continued to work her way south.

Stone relaxed, letting her have her wicked way with him. Her soft mouth explored his cock, bringing him fully awake with her skilled ministrations.

"What time do you have to be at work?" he asked, staring down his torso at the woman who was making love to him with her mouth.

She paused long enough to lift her head and say, "Seven thirty."

He glanced at the clock. 6:03 a.m. glowed brilliantly red from the nightstand.

They had time.

"You're workin' my dick like you've got a goal," he said, sliding his hand over her hair.

She smiled with his cock in her mouth—which was a sight that every man should witness at least once in his lifetime because god*damn.*

"Stevie … baby…" He gripped her hair tightly, watching as her eyes sparked with pleasure/pain. "You sure you wanna do this?"

Her eyebrows rose, but she continued to take him to the root.

"I'll need recovery time before I fuck you in the shower."

Another smile, but this time she pulled off his dick. "I like the way your mind works."

He laughed. "And I like the way your *mouth* works."

She leaned down and pressed a kiss to the sensitive head of his cock, and he saw stars. Jesus. The woman was going to kill him.

"Shower then?"

He nodded, hoping his legs would work.

She didn't seem to have the same problem because she hopped out of bed like she had springs in her lower extremities. She strolled naked out of the room, her footsteps disappearing.

When Stone reached the bathroom, she was already in the shower, but rather than standing under the water, she was pressed up against the wall.

"What's wrong?"

"Cold," she said, frowning. "Don't people know that instant hot water is the only way to go?"

"I take it y'all have tankless water heaters at your place?"

"Well, duh."

He laughed as he stepped in to join her, turning his back to the barely lukewarm water and shielding her with his body.

"I'll warm you up," he promised, pulling her against him as he leaned down to claim her mouth.

The kiss started slow but increased in intensity when Stevie's hand curled around his dick, her fingers stroking as she attempted to climb his body.

"I thought for sure I wore you out last night."

"I've recharged since then."

She definitely had.

"I can't get enough of you," she said, nipping his lower lip. "Plus, you've got a lot of time to make up for."

There was no animosity in her tone, and the relief that swept through him nearly knocked him to his knees.

"It'll take the rest of my life, but I aim to make it up."

Her eyes were clear and unguarded when she stared up at him. "I'm gonna hold you to that."

She pressed a kiss to his lips but then disappeared as she stepped under the water. He took the opportunity to watch her as she tilted her head back, wetting her hair. When she went to work shampooing her hair, he grabbed the body wash and poured a generous amount in his hand, then started soaping her body, working his way from her shoulders down. He gave his full attention to every inch of her. On his way back up, as the water rinsed the soap away, he took more liberties, teasing her with his fingers.

"Stone..." She whimpered, putting her foot on the small ledge near the floor, opening herself to him. "Keep doin' that."

He fingered her. Slow and deep, surrounding her with his much bigger body as the water rained down on them, loving the soft mewls that escaped when he hit the right spot inside her.

"Stone ... I want..."

She gasped when he added a third ringer.

"Tell me."

Her eyes opened, water dripping down her face, droplets forming on her lashes. "Fuck me."

"I thought I was."

She shook her head, grabbing for his hand. His *other* hand, which was cupping her ass.

"Here," she rasped, urging his fingers between her ass cheeks.

Stone dipped his middle finger along the crack, seeking the tiny hole she was urging him toward. He pressed the tip inside her, and she attempted to spread her legs wider.

He pushed in to the second knuckle, three fingers still buried in her cunt. Water wasn't the best lubricant, but it worked in a pinch. It allowed him to sink his finger in all the way.

"You wanna be filled by both of us at the same time," he whispered. "Don't you, baby?"

"Yes."

"How does it feel?"

"Full."

"Hurt?"

"No."

He slid his finger in and out of her ass, alternating those in her pussy.

"Stone?"

"Hmm?"

Her eyes implored him. "Fuck my ass. With your cock."

"You sure?"

She nodded.

Removing his fingers from the tight warmth of her body, he stepped back. Knowing there was no way he could fuck her in the shower—their height difference made it impossible—Stone turned off the water and took her by the hand.

She giggled when he dragged her out of the bathroom and back to the bedroom. They left a trail of water in their wake, but his cock was too determined to care.

"On the bed. All fours. Ass to me."

While she did that, he grabbed the bottle of lubricant from the bedside table. Ever since he'd seen Stevie again, he'd been jacking off two or three times a day, attempting to stave off the heat. It was a temporary fix but a necessity nonetheless.

Standing behind her, he pressed his hand to the center of her back, urging her to bend over more.

"Chest flat. Knees wide."

She widened her legs, her sweet pussy and her little puckered hole beckoning him.

"You ready for me?"

"Yes."

He smacked her ass. "Liar."

"Ow." She laughed. "What was *that* for?"

"For thinkin' you could take my cock without any preparation." He chuckled, then smacked her other ass cheek.

When she giggled, he dropped to his knees and licked her from clit to asshole.

"Oh!"

"You like that?"

"Mmm-hmm."

He licked her again, tending to the sensitive nerve endings, rimming her hole.

"Oh. My. God. Stone…" She pushed her ass back. "More."

He paused to tease her hole with his finger. "You ever had someone eat your ass?"

"No."

He licked her some more, teasing her clit with his thumb. He didn't stop until she was rocking against him, whimpering and pleading. When her moans grew louder, he lubed his fingers and her back hole liberally. He started with one finger before adding another, scissoring them to stretch her. He wasn't sure she would be able to handle him this time around, but he was going to make her come regardless.

The entire time, he teased her clit.

"More, baby? Or do you want my cock in your pussy?"

She hesitated, and her lack of certainty was the only answer he needed.

Stone stood up, angling his cock and guiding it into the slick depths of her cunt.

"Fuck me," he told her.

"That's not my—"

He smacked her ass, the crack of skin on skin silencing her.

"Fuck yourself on my cock."

She began rocking forward and back, slowly at first, pulling off his dick and then sliding on again.

"Good girl."

She shivered, and he remembered how she used to swoon when he said that.

"Keep fuckin' me, Stevie. Aw, yeah. Just like that. I love this tight little pussy."

She moaned and gasped, her tempo increasing. While she brought them both pleasure, he pumped lube in his hand and coated his thumbs.

She paused when he pressed against her asshole.

"Don't stop," he growled, keeping the edge in his tone because he knew she loved that.

When her hips began rocking again, he pressed his thumb past the tight ring of muscle, fucking her ass while she fucked his cock. When her sphincter relaxed, he thrust his hips to meet her, driving his cock and thumb in deeper.

"Oh, fuck ... that feels good ... Stone ... don't stop. Please don't stop."

"Make yourself come so I can fill this little pussy."

She cried out as their bodies slammed together, his cock lodged deeper and deeper each time. When she began moaning his name over and over, he thrust his other thumb into her asshole, fucking her with both while he drove his hips forward.

"I'm ... Stone!"

She came, her pussy milking his dick, stealing his breath and his release without warning. He slammed into her, feeling the tight pulse of her asshole on his thumbs as he filled her.

"Don't move," he warned, slowly pulling out of her ass.

As soon as he did, she flopped forward with a sigh. "That was..."

"Incredible? Amazing?" He laughed. "Only the beginning?"

She peered back at him over her shoulder, her smile blinding. "I *definitely* like the way your mind works."

"Remember that when you're beggin' for mercy next time."

THIRTY

Thursday, February 8, 2024

ON THURSDAY NIGHT, STONE FOUND HIMSELF AT Donovan's, his mind still drifting back to the night he spent with Stevie. He hadn't seen her since she left for work yesterday morning, but he'd talked to her a few times via text message. Both of them. His exchanges with Nico were becoming more frequent, as though the night Stevie had stayed at Stone's was a turning point for all of them.

He would've preferred to be at their house tonight, but he had an ulterior motive for seeking out his brother. Yeah, he enjoyed the time he got to spend with Donovan, but he was looking for business advice. And since Donovan had the experience that came with creating and building a successful business, Stone knew his input would be invaluable.

So here he was, drinking a beer while Donovan skimmed the business proposal on his laptop. Stone tried not to read too much into his facial expressions, but he couldn't help it. His future was riding on his successful presentation of this to his aunt and uncle. Considering Lorrie and Curtis had a wealth of nieces and nephews who would likely jump at the opportunity to do what Stone was trying to do, he refused to half-ass it.

"This is good," Donovan finally said as he sat up and reached for his beer. "You sure you didn't take a business class or two in college?"

"I didn't go to college."

"I know. Maybe you should have. You've got a knack for it."

"For what?" Stone snorted. "For puttin' together a PowerPoint presentation?"

"This is more than that," Donovan countered, pointing at the screen. "The numbers tell a story, Stone. They outline the potential and this… I'm impressed. Really."

Stone felt a sense of pride swell in his chest, but he played it off. "That's the easy part. The hard part's gonna be gettin' this thing off the ground."

"Maybe." Donovan leaned back in his chair. "Looks to me like you've got it mapped out pretty well."

"I've had a lot of time to think about it."

"So what're you waitin' for? Why not take it to them now?"

"I've gotta get the green light from their boys."

"Ah." Donovan tipped his beer bottle to his lips. "How's that goin'?"

"Travis, Sawyer, and Kaleb are good with it. I'm meetin' with Braydon, Brendon, and Ethan next week."

"I can't imagine they'll have a problem with it."

Stone hoped not, but he wasn't assuming anything at this point. He was prepared to put in the work, and if that meant convincing them that this was the right thing, he was willing.

"That leaves Zane," Donovan noted. "What's he say about it all?"

"He hasn't called me back."

Donovan frowned. "You try again?"

"I've left him four messages." Stone sighed. "He's avoidin' me."

"Maybe he's busy."

Stone gave his brother a *get-real* look. Yeah, maybe Zane was busy but too busy to answer the damn phone and agree on a place to meet and talk? Or even just return his call or shoot him a text to say there's not a chance in hell he'll give his approval. No fucking way. Zane was definitely avoiding him. He just didn't know why.

"He *is* the baby," Donovan noted. "Maybe he thinks it's his duty to hold out."

"He's also an adult," Stone shot back. "He could own it and fuckin' call me."

"True. Did you piss him off?"

"I haven't seen him in years."

"Did you piss him off the last time you saw him?"

Stone rolled his eyes. "No."

"You sure about that?"

He wasn't sure about anything other than the fact Zane was ignoring him.

"Do you know his wife?"

Stone knew where that question was leading and didn't appreciate the accusation. "I didn't fuck Vanessa Carmichael."

"Walker," Donovan clarified.

"I know what her name is *now*. But back in the day…" Stone shook his head. "She's a few years older than me."

"Can't blame a guy." Donovan smirked as he took a pull on his beer. "You did fuck pretty much anything that walked when you were younger."

He couldn't argue that point because it was true. But Stone wasn't that guy anymore.

"What about Beau?" Donovan asked. "You have beef with Beau?"

He frowned. "What would that matter?"

"Zane and Beau have been best friends since they were kids."

"No," Stone stated. "I didn't. I knew who he was, but…" He shook his head. "No."

"Hmm. It's a mystery, I guess."

A mystery that could be solved if Zane would just fucking call him back.

"Track him down and make him talk to you," Donovan suggested.

"Oh, sure. That's a damn good way to get him to agree. Force him to face me."

"What else are you gonna do?"

Stone honestly didn't know. He would have to come up with something, though. Especially if he got the green light from Braydon, Brendon, and Ethan. If they were on board, he would have no choice but to confront Zane.

"ARE WE DONE TALKIN' ABOUT YOU?" DONOVAN asked his brother.

Stone stared at him like the question had come out of left field.

"Just checkin'. You're sensitive. I wanna make sure you get all the time you need to feel whole."

Stone's eyebrows narrowed. "Fuck you."

He laughed. "I'm gettin' married."

"I heard that rumor." Stone rolled his eyes. "You forget you already told me the good news, bro?"

"No, I mean, we're actually makin' plans. It's happenin'."

His brother's expression relaxed, and a genuine smile formed. "That's great news. You tell Mom and Dad yet?"

Donovan shook his head and downed what was left of his beer. He went to get another.

"So what's the holdup?" Stone asked when he returned, setting two more beers on the table.

"Tate wants to talk to Reilly first."

"Are they on the outs?"

"No."

"Are their phones broken?"

"No."

"Is there a reason they're avoidin' each other?"

Donovan shook his head. He knew Stone would keep going if he let him. "We've decided to get married in Vegas."

Stone's smile was slow and mischievous. "Dad's gonna be thrilled. Mom's gonna kick. Your. Ass."

Donovan feared his brother was right. Which was part of the reason he hadn't talked to his parents yet. He needed to, but he was making excuses, pretending he was waiting for Tate and Reilly to finalize their plans.

"Not just Tate and me," he admitted, watching Stone's reaction. "Reilly and Brady wanna get married in Vegas, too."

Stone's eyebrows launched skyward. "No shit? A double weddin'? In Vegas?"

Donovan nodded.

Stone barked a laugh. "Mom's gonna shit kittens."

There was a good chance he wasn't wrong about that. When Donovan mentioned a double wedding to Tate, he'd been joking. He never would've said anything if he thought Tate would run with the idea. But that was where they were at. As soon as Tate mentioned it to Reilly, his baby sister exploded with ideas. To the point that Donovan realized he and Brady didn't have a say in the matter anymore. They were simply along for the ride.

"How's that work?" Stone asked. "Isn't Brady supposed to be your best man? And vice versa?" He laughed. "And wouldn't Reilly be Tate's? And—"

"Vice versa," Donovan supplied for him. "Yeah. They're tryin' to come up with a solution."

Stone laughed, the sound echoing through the kitchen. "Man, I guess there are worse problems to have."

He wasn't wrong.

"Speakin' of problems." It was Donovan's turn to smile. "How *are* Stevie and Nico?"

Stone went still, his eyes searching. Donovan knew he was wondering how he had found out. He gave him a minute because, seriously, the answer was simple.

"Reilly."

"Bingo."

"How does *she* know?"

Donovan shrugged. "I don't think she does. Not entirely. My guess is she's fillin' in the blanks. At one time, you were with Stevie. Nico and Stevie are business partners."

"Plus, they live together," Stone noted.

"That, too."

Stone frowned. "How the fuck does that equal me and Stevie and Nico?"

"It doesn't." Donovan pointed at his brother. "But *that* does. The look on your face says it all."

Stone opened his mouth but closed it again.

"Is it serious?" Donovan wasn't sure what he expected Stone to say, but it certainly wasn't what came out of his brother's mouth next.

"I love them."

"Oh." Donovan stalled by taking a drink. "This is real."

"It's definitely real." Stone gestured toward the laptop. "Did you not notice I'm wantin' to go into business with them?"

Donovan chuckled. "I went into business with Brady. Didn't mean I wanted to spend the rest of my life with him."

"Yet here you are, havin' a double weddin' with your boy at your side."

Donovan flipped him off.

Something churned in Stone's eyes. Worry? Fear?

"It's not all rainbows and unicorns?"

"We're workin' through ... some stuff."

"That's to be expected. Doesn't explain the constipated look, though."

Stone's attention shifted to his beer bottle. "I'm worried what Chelsea might say."

"She's gonna say she's happy for you."

Stone met his stare. "The first time I fucked him was the night they broke up at the house. The night I punched him."

"Same night." Donovan took a long pull on his beer. "Wow."

"I didn't plan it."

"So where did this ... uh ... take place?" He held up a hand, halting his brother as the puzzle pieces clicked into place. "The loft. Right. CJ mentioned somethin' about you and Nico and..."

"Stevie," Stone noted. "Yeah."

Donovan did not want details. He didn't want to know what went down between the three of them, but he could tell his brother needed to get it off his chest.

"It just happened," Stone finally said, picking at the label on his beer bottle.

"Do you regret it?"

Stone's gaze snapped up. "Not a single second."

"I don't think you have to worry about Chelsea. She's happy."

"I want this," Stone said. "To be with them. I've never wanted anything this fuckin' much."

"Not even to own a ranch?"

His brother was quiet momentarily, his gaze lingering on the beer bottle. When he looked up, Donovan knew what he was about to say was the honest-to-God truth.

"I'd give up everything just to have them in my life."

Donovan understood that all too well. He felt the same about Tate. And it had hit him like a wrecking ball. Hard and fast. When he realized he was in love with Tate, nothing had been the same. His entire existence had shifted as though it was now taking place on a different plane.

And no amount of money, success, or anything else could make him want to go back.

THIRTY-ONE

Friday, February 9, 2024

💬 **WOULD Y'ALL BE UP TO LETTING ME COOK YOU DINNER TONIGHT?**

> 💬 Nico will be there, but I've got plans with my dad. Y'all have fun, though.

> 💬 I'm not a sure thing yet. Depends on what you're making me.

CHICKEN OR STEAK. YOUR CHOICE.

I'll always choose steak.

STEAK, IT IS. BAKED POTATO?

Definitely.

WINE?

Leave the drink to me.

YOU SURE YOU WON'T JOIN US, STEVIE?

I think you boys need a night alone together.

IF YOU SAY SO.

Several hours later...

STONE STOOD IN THE KITCHEN, STARING AT the closed lid of the countertop grill that had become his best friend over the years. He loved this damn thing. It had been a while since he'd had a reason to use it. While on the Double J, most of his meals had been consumed at the Johnsons' main house because Leah had insisted on it. Since it kept him from having to spend money on groceries, Stone hadn't objected.

Had the weather been better, he would've borrowed his dad's fancy Traeger grill he was so proud of, but it was sleeting, and his father would've shit monkeys at even the suggestion of that grill getting wet.

So here he was, flipping ribeyes in the kitchen. Baked potatoes were in the oven, and plates were waiting for both on the counter. The only thing he was missing was the wine or whatever drink Nico chose. Oh and Nico. He wasn't there yet.

Although Stone called Stevie an hour after that text exchange in an attempt to change her mind, she stuck to her guns, insisting she really did want to talk to her father tonight over dinner. Plus, she insisted he and Nico deserved some alone time. He hadn't argued because he was looking forward to spending time with Nico. He simply wished Stevie was coming, too.

Stone did his best not to look at the clock. It was almost seven thirty, which meant Nico was more than fashionably late. There was a good chance he wasn't coming, which was the only reason Stone had started cooking. At the very least, the food wouldn't go to waste. He could heat it up for lunch tomorrow.

As the thought flittered in his mind, headlights sliced through the darkness outside, blinding Stone momentarily as someone pulled up to the barn. He waited until the headlights turned off before looking out again. A sigh of relief escaped him when he saw it was Nico's truck.

A minute later, he was opening the door as Nico stomped his boots on the mat before coming inside carrying Jäger in his arms.

"Sorry I'm late."

"Jesus, you're soakin' wet."

Nico turned back to go outside. "Sorry about the floor."

"I'm not worried about the floor," Stone told him, grabbing his arm and urging him deeper into the house.

"I shoulda gone home to change." Nico placed Jäger on the floor. "Mrs. Jeffries called. Asked me to come by and cover her plants. Begged me, really."

Jäger took off for parts unknown.

Stone grinned. "I didn't realize you make house calls. I'll keep that in mind."

"She's eighty-seven and calls me up every year to have me add somethin' to her yard. Devoted customer. I couldn't tell her no."

"Here, let me take your coat. I'll toss it in the dryer."

Nico shrugged out of his coat. His shirt and jeans were both dark from the water.

"You wanna jump in the shower to warm up?"

Nico started pulling off one boot. "Nah. I'll be—"

"At least change into somethin' of mine," Stone told him, gesturing toward the bedroom. "I've got sweatpants and shit in the closet."

Nico swallowed, his gaze sliding toward the bedroom.

"Go," Stone said firmly. "Bring back the wet clothes. I'll toss them in the dryer, too."

He hesitated again, but only for a moment before doing as he was told.

It was impossible not to watch the man walk away, admiring his ass in those damn jeans. The guy looked good enough to eat.

Thankfully, Stone had the presence of mind not to follow him. Instead, he carried Nico's jacket to the laundry room and opened the dryer. When he turned around, he nearly stepped on Jäger, having to dance around the little guy to avoid a collision. He laughed as he leaned down and rubbed his little head.

"I'm gonna have to pay attention, huh? You're just so damn little. I don't—Oh, shit," Stone huffed, hurrying back to the kitchen island. He lifted the lid on the grill and found the steaks hadn't burned. Thank God.

He flipped them once more before closing the lid. When he looked down, he found Jäger staring up at him with those big brown eyes, his little nose twitching as he sniffed the air.

"What's up, little guy? You need somethin'?"

Realizing the puppy was wet, Stone grabbed a hand towel out of the drawer and rubbed the water off Jäger's back and head.

"Better?" Stone laughed when Jäger attempted to steal the towel.

Footsteps sounded on hardwood, so Stone stood tall. Nico approached wearing a pair of dark gray sweatpants and a dark blue long-sleeve T-shirt. His hair was mussed as though he'd just crawled out of bed. He tried to remember if that was what Nico looked like when he woke up in the morning. He honestly hadn't been paying attention when he'd stayed over. Too many other things had been going on. But now he had a raging desire to spin the man around, lead him back to the bedroom, get him into the bed, and keep him there until morning simply so he could do the comparison later.

"Dryer's in there," Stone told him, gesturing toward the laundry room at the far end of the kitchen. "I hope you're hungry."

"Starvin'. Skipped lunch when I realized the weather was turnin' bad."

Yeah, they were expecting ice on the roads tonight. That was never a good thing around these parts. Because they didn't get snow on a regular basis, there wasn't an abundance of salt or sand trucks to take care of the roads, so getting out in it was a gamble.

"How do you like your steak? Before you answer that, you should know they're well past raw, so medium or well?"

"Medium-well's fine."

"Good. Me, too. Food should be ready in—" Stone's words died when he saw more headlights coming toward the barn.

Nico's attention also shifted to the window. "Expectin' company?"

"Nope."

Hope sprung eternal. Maybe Stevie had changed her mind.

Neither of them said anything until the headlights turned off, the outdoor flood light doing its job of outlining the vehicle.

"That's Brady's SUV," Stone told Nico.

A minute later, Reilly bounded up the porch, holding a coat over her head. She rapped knuckles on one of the glass panes before opening the door and coming inside.

"Hi!" Her gaze flitted between Stone and Nico.

Stone wanted to ask why she was there, but the only sound that came out was, "Uh…"

"Hey, Reilly," Nico greeted.

She gave a small wave, then looked at Stone, cocking one eyebrow. "Don't worry. I'm not stayin'."

"Did you need somethin'?"

Her smile was so wide it was a wonder her face didn't split. "I saw Stevie at the store earlier. She said you had a date tonight."

Why did he feel like he had that one time he'd been in his parents' living room, watching a movie with … God, he couldn't even remember her name … and his parents came home. He'd had his hands down what's her name's pants beneath the blanket when his dad decided to take a seat because he "loved this movie," or so he said. Needless to say, what's her name didn't come over again after that.

This was very much like that—a perfectly good evening made awkward by family stopping in unexpectedly.

"That's what this is, right?" Reilly glanced between them. "A date?"

"Yup," he answered, doing his best not to clear his throat and give away his discomfort.

"I thought I'd come by and offer to babysit."

Stone frowned.

"The puppy," she said, clearly recognizing Stone's confusion.

As though Jäger realized he was the topic of conversation, he hopped toward her, tail wagging.

"Oh, my God! You're just so darn cute. And big. You're a growin' boy, huh?" Instantly, she was on her knees, pulling Jäger into her arms so she could cuddle him and shower him with kisses.

Reilly looked at Nico. "Would you mind?" She clasped her hands together as though praying. "I promise I'll bring him back tomorrow."

Stone looked at Nico. "I swear I had nothin' to do with this."

Nico flashed a grin. "It's fine. Just warnin' you, he's a handful. You can't take your eyes off him for a second, or he'll chew up whatever you didn't want chewed up."

"My whole night's gonna be dedicated to him." Reilly addressed Nico. "I've been beggin' Brady to let me have a puppy since you brought him to the store. This is gonna be a trial run. That way, y'all don't have to worry about him while you're … uh … *eating*."

Nice save, Rye.

"Totally up to you," Stone told Nico. "He'll be fine here."

"No, it's cool. I … um … I brought a bag with some food. It's in the truck."

Stone couldn't hide his grin, especially since the color was rising in Nico's cheeks, and he wouldn't look at him. Had he anticipated staying the night? Enough that he made the dog an overnight bag? Damn, that was cute.

"Yay!" Reilly scooped Jäger up into her arms. "You hear that? We're gonna have a slumber party!"

"Truck's unlocked," Nico told her.

"I'll text you in the mornin'. Or you can text me so I can bring him home."

"Thanks, Rye," Stone told her as he followed her to the door, opening it for her.

"Yup. Have fun. Don't do nothin' I would do."

He laughed, watching as she hurried down the steps to Nico's truck. She opened the rear door, closed it a moment later, then hurried to the SUV, getting into the backseat instead of the front. The headlights came on a second later.

"I swear I had nothin' to do with that," Stone told him again as he went to the grill.

"No, but I think Stevie did." Nico shook his head, grinning. "It's the same thing Niyah would've done if she were here."

"She wants us to be alone, huh?"

Nico chuckled, then grabbed the bag he'd brought in with him. "I picked up a bottle of wine. The guy at the store said to let it breathe. I don't have a clue what that even means."

Stone laughed. "I thought you said you liked red wine."

"Stevie's a fan. I've only had it once. I just wanted to see how far you were willin' to go."

Stone met his gaze, unable to hide the fact that the simple statement lit him up from the inside. "You might come to regret that later."

Nico's sharp inhale made him smile.

NICO WAS NERVOUS, AND HE HAD NO idea why.

It wasn't like he hadn't been on a date in a year or anything.

Oh, wait. He hadn't. He didn't count his outings with Stevie because they did everything as friends. And they hadn't had a chance for anything formal since they shifted their relationship status into the more serious range. Aside from sleeping in his bed every night and fucking like rabbits, nothing had really changed.

And it had been significantly longer since he'd been on a date with a man. He could count on one hand how many of those he'd had in his lifetime. None of them had been remarkable or worth a repeat.

"You ready to eat?" Stone asked as he pulled the steaks off the small grill.

Even if he weren't, he would've said yes because he needed something to do other than stand there like a complete fool.

"Can I help with anything?" he offered, still holding the wine bottle.

"Nope. Just take a seat."

Nico pulled out one of the bar stools since those were his only options.

"Not that one," Stone said.

Nico frowned and moved to the next one.

"Or that one."

Realizing there was amusement in Stone's voice, Nico turned to look at him.

The guy was smiling, and damn if that smile didn't amp up his sinfulness to the nth degree. Stone Jameson was by far the most attractive man Nico had ever laid eyes on—dark hair, chiseled features, and a smile that warned of devilish deeds to come. And yeah, maybe Nico was a little biased since Stone had quite literally altered the course of his life in one single night. He'd opened Nico's eyes to things he never knew about himself—and yeah, even a few things he'd suspected. In doing that, he'd allowed Nico to connect so many dots.

"You can sit anywhere you want," Stone said, his eyes glittering with mirth.

Nico took a seat in his second selection, then got up almost instantly to grab the glasses that were sitting on the counter. Before he sat, he poured wine into both.

Until *that night*, with Stone and Stevie, Nico hadn't realized he was gay. Well, technically, *bisexual* was probably a better term since he was quite fond of women, too. One in particular. However, after *that night*, he realized he had a preference. Not so much for a gender specifically, but rather a particular aspect of his encounters. His night with Stone and Stevie had opened his eyes to what it felt like to be truly dominated by someone. For years, he'd hoped to find it again, but he learned that most women, and even the few men he'd been with, expected him to play that alpha role. He could, and he did, but it only took a few times to realize he preferred to be on the opposite side. At least when he was with a man.

Stone placed one of the plates directly in front of him.

"Thanks."

When Stone was walking around the island, Nico found himself admiring how the man moved. He still had that swagger that Nico had admired when he was a teenager. The guy carried himself like he was completely comfortable in his own skin. But why wouldn't he? From what he could tell, Stone accepted who he was, faults and all. Another thing Nico had admired about him back in the day.

"Thought we'd watch a movie after," Stone said when he returned with a second plate.

"What'd you have in mind?" he asked, wanting to contribute something to the conversation.

"Depends on your mood."

Nico's gaze slid up to meet Stone's. That damn smirk was plastered on his face.

"You have any musicals?"

Stone barked a laugh. "Not on hand, but I'm sure we could find somethin'. If you're really into musicals."

"I'm not," he admitted, chuckling. "Just wanted to see your reaction."

"Baby, if you wanna watch a musical, I'm all for it."

Baby? No one had ever called him that before. His ex-fiancée had called him *honey,* but it never sounded like that. As though the words were an actual sex act.

"You mentioned your sister earlier," Stone said as he began cutting his steak. "How's she doin'? You said they moved to California. For work?"

Nico nodded. "Adam got a job at Primal Instincts."

Stone's fork paused near his mouth. "They make workout equipment, right? Those exercise bikes everyone's goin' crazy for?"

"Yeah. He's some kind of computer whiz. Coding and shit."

"So he moved to California to do it?"

Nico nodded, chewed. "Niyah's always wanted to move outta Texas. And accordin' to Adam, the amount of money they're payin' him is insane. Why wouldn't they?"

"What about you? You ever had the desire to move halfway across the country?"

"No." Nico reached for his wineglass. "I prefer the devil I know."

Stone smirked again, and Nico realized how that sounded.

Thankfully, Stone didn't call him on it.

The rest of the meal went like that: small talk that never ventured into anything too deep or meaningful. Two old friends catching up, but neither bringing up a subject that might cast a light on their history together.

It probably should've been awkward, but Nico felt comfortable with Stone. The guy was one of those people who could weed out your deepest, darkest secret before you even realized you were telling him all the sordid details. He was easy to talk to.

Probably a little *too easy*, which was how Nico found himself staring at Stone, attempting to process the question he'd just asked: *Have you ever been in a serious relationship with a man?*

"I didn't mean for it to be difficult," Stone said with a chuckle as he pushed his empty plate away and poured more wine into his glass.

"No, it's um…" Nico shook off the surprise and shook his head. "No, I haven't."

"Because that's not your preference? Or because the opportunity didn't arise?"

Nico reached for his wineglass and downed what was left, then held it out when Stone reached for the bottle.

"Didn't arise," he said, watching as Stone poured the rest of the wine into his glass.

"Prefer a safer topic?" Stone asked, sounding as though he was thoroughly enjoying Nico's discomfort.

"What about you?" Nico asked, turning the tables. "You been in a serious relationship with a man?"

"No," he answered easily. "Nor with a woman. Only Stevie."

"Never?"

"Never."

"Allergic to commitment?"

"When I was younger, maybe. Until Stevie," Stone answered as though Nico hadn't been goading him. "As I got older, the idea of one didn't make me violently ill." He laughed, rinsing the plates in the sink. "But I never found what I was lookin' for."

"Because you'd already found it. And left it behind."

Stone's discomfort was etched on his handsome face.

"Sorry. That was uncalled for."

"But true," Stone conceded.

Nico swallowed hard. "And what *are* you lookin' for, Stone? Now, I mean."

Those mischievous hazel eyes locked right on Nico when he said, "Nothin'."

Nico frowned.

A smirk pulled at Stone's wicked mouth. "I don't have to look anymore. Like you said, I've already found it."

It was a wonder Nico didn't go up in flames.

THIRTY-TWO

STONE COULD TELL HIS ADMISSION SURPRISED NICO.

Enough that the guy choked on the last gulp of wine. Since he didn't need the Heimlich maneuver performed, Stone finished rinsing the dishes and loading them into the dishwasher, giving Nico a moment to compose himself.

"Did you ever wonder if what happened *that night* … did you wonder if it was a one-time thing?"

That was a fair question. It was also something Stone had considered for years after he left. That night in the barn with Stevie and Nico had been rife with serious lust. Stone might've been compelled to think the memory had been altered over the years, and a repeat wouldn't live up to the hype.

"Are we talkin' about the three of us? Or…" He waved a hand between them. "Or what we did?"

"The second part."

Was that insecurity he detected in Nico's tone?

Drying his hand with a towel, he turned to look at Nico. "I was your first."

Nico didn't respond, but Stone wasn't asking. He was acknowledging it since he'd never really given much thought to the fact that he was Nico's first. He knew he was because he'd pushed the issue at the time, but it had felt right that night. Stone hadn't thought too long or hard about how that might've affected Nico.

"Let's just say, with you, it's different," he admitted, watching as Nico's cheeks turned pink.

"How so?"

Stone had to admire the guy because he didn't back down.

"I think it'll be easier if I just show you," Stone told him.

He didn't ask Nico whether he was interested because Stone figured he wouldn't be here if he weren't. Stone tossed the hand towel on the counter before walking around the island to join Nico on the other side.

When he approached, Nico's gaze shot up to his face.

Stone stopped directly in front of him. "What's with the insecurity, Nico?"

Another shrug. "I don't know."

"Tell me," Stone insisted because he could tell something was on Nico's mind.

"I guess I never considered what a one-on-one thing would be like."

"You mean with me?"

Nico nodded.

"Are you opposed to it?"

"No."

"Good."

Unable to resist, Stone leaned in and pressed his lips to Nico's. Just a light brush of their mouths.

"I'm interested in what you're interested in," Stone whispered, reaching for his hand. "And right now, I'm interested in watchin' a movie."

"You were serious?" Nico chuckled, and it sounded strained.

"This is a date. That's what you do on dates. You have a nice meal, watch a movie, talk." He stopped before they reached the couch, turning so he was toe to toe with Nico. He leaned in and lowered his voice. "Unless you want me to strip you right now and torture you until you beg me to fuck you."

God, Nico's shocked gasp made Stone's dick hard. Well, he figured hard*er* was a better description because the damn thing had been making his jeans uncomfortably tight ever since Nico walked in the door.

When Nico didn't say a word, Stone gripped his jaw, sliding his thumb along the smooth contour. He smelled good. Not like he had back then. Back then, Nico had smelled like sweat and man, and damn, that sensory memory still got Stone off at night. But now … now, Nico had a spicy, fresh scent that told Stone he wasn't a rambunctious teenager anymore. He was a grown man whose desires had transformed over the years.

"Have a seat," Stone told him, enjoying that he could feel Nico's pulse beating faster.

Nico nodded, responding like Stone had asked a question, but then he took a seat. Awkwardly at first, but then he seemed to snap out of it. Stone went through the house and turned off the lights, leaving only the mood lighting above the kitchen cabinets on.

Stone joined him on the couch, grabbing the remote and passing it to Nico.

"You pick."

The tension began to ease as they talked their way through the menu of movie options. A few they discussed at length while Nico continued to scroll through. By the time they landed on one, the tension had dissipated completely. That lasted until about twenty minutes into the movie when Stone grabbed the throw blanket off the back of the sofa and scooted closer to Nico so they could cover up. Reilly had warned him that the house was drafty due to the high, vaulted ceilings, and she wasn't wrong.

Stone lasted for another half hour before he couldn't resist the urge to touch Nico's leg, which was now pressing against his, their bare feet resting on the ottoman.

"Keep watchin' the movie," Stone instructed when Nico's gaze shifted to his lap.

"It's kinda hard when you're doin' … that." He gasped on the last word because Stone dipped his fingers into the waistband of Nico's sweatpants and brushed against the head of his dick.

"Are you tellin' me to stop?"

"God, no." Nico moaned, his hips lifting as Stone pushed his hand deeper, stroking the long, thick length of him.

Stone chuckled, unable to pretend he was even slightly interested in the movie. He appreciated the light that came from the television, though, because when he pulled the blanket down, he was greeted by the glistening tip of Nico's cock.

"You're fuckin' hard for me," he growled as he got to his feet, sliding the large ottoman so that it butted up against the couch. "Do you remember the rules?"

Nico's eyes were glassy as he peered up at him. "Yeah."

"What are they?"

"There are no rules," he groaned when Stone straddled his knees, shoving the blanket aside before tugging his sweatpants down his hips.

Stone grinned, memories from that night flooding back. He'd never been able to pinpoint exactly what it was about Nico that set him off that day, but the only time he'd ever experienced an adrenaline rush that compared was when he'd been atop a bucking bull coming out of the gate. He'd chased that rush over the years, trying to duplicate it in whatever way he could. He'd achieved his goal, but never with sex. Nothing had ever come close to being as intense as that one night when he had the man and the woman he'd spent the last fifteen years dreaming about.

"You're gonna beg before the night's over," he warned as he rocked his hips, grinding the hard ridge of his dick against Nico's legs.

"I fuckin' hope so."

Stone laughed. "That's the same thing you said back then."

NICO HADN'T EXPECTED THIS WAS WHERE THEY would end up.

Not because he didn't anticipate the temptation. Of course he did. This was Stone Jameson.

However, when Nico had been driving over, he'd promised himself he would leave before they ever had a chance to get this far. He'd expected Jäger to provide enough distraction for Nico to keep his distance. He'd tried to convince himself they needed to slow things down. As it was, his feelings for this man had intensified tenfold since the first night Stone stayed at his house. And every day since, he caught himself wondering what the future looked like for the three of them. Worse, he found himself daydreaming of making that a reality now. After all, they weren't getting any younger.

He was wrong about taking things slow, and he'd known it the second he walked through the door. Even before Reilly came to pick up the puppy.

Nico was unable to resist this man. And when Stone was looking at him like he wanted to have him for dessert, he knew it was futile to pretend otherwise.

"Rough and dirty," Stone said, his eyes zeroing in on Nico's cock as his hands slid up Nico's thighs.

Those two words had changed Nico's life all those years ago. He'd had no idea what Stone had in mind then, but he knew now. More than that, he knew how much he wanted him to live up to the promise.

Stone's hands slid to his hips, and the next thing he knew, the man was shifting back and jerking Nico so that his spine was curved and his ass was on the ottoman and not the couch.

Nico could feel the blood rushing in his cock, the head engorged to the point of pain. He wanted Stone's mouth on him, but he knew better than to ask. He'd done that before and endured the torment that came with thinking he was in control. That had been the first of many lessons he'd learned during the hours he'd spent with Stone in this very barn. Only back then, it hadn't been converted into a comfortable living space. They'd been up in the old hayloft with a lumpy mattress, the only padding between them and the splintered boards laid across the beams.

But that wasn't the only thing different now.

Although Stone looked like a man with a single-minded focus, Nico noticed the way he was watching him. Gauging his reactions. That hadn't been the case back then. Or maybe it had, and he'd been too far gone to notice. He couldn't deny he'd been lost in a haze of pleasure so intense, it was a wonder he'd remembered to breathe.

Stone sat astride his thighs and rubbed his cock, stroking with one hand, then both, back to one hand. His grip alternated between intensely gentle to fiercely firm. He was playing with him the same way he had then.

"You came in my mouth that day," Stone said, slowing the pace of his stroking. "Do you remember?"

Nico huffed air in and out of his lungs, nodding because he couldn't find his voice. The humiliation had consumed him that day because he'd come within minutes of Stone putting his mouth on him. He'd been overwhelmed, confused, and so turned on he couldn't control it. But Stone hadn't degraded him for it.

"You've got more self-control now," Stone said, rubbing his thumb along the sensitive spot beneath the head of his dick.

It wasn't a question, but Nico nodded. He prayed he wasn't lying.

"Don't worry if you don't. I've got plenty of ways to get you hard again. I've even learned a few more over the years."

Nico gasped, pressing his head back against the pillow as Stone stroked his cock faster. He was playing with him, seeing how much he could take.

Stone reached forward with his free hand, pushing two fingers into Nico's mouth. He closed his lips around them, meeting his gaze as he sucked.

"How many times did you suck my cock that day?"

Stone pulled his fingers out so he could answer.

"Not nearly enough."

A smirk tugged at Stone's wicked mouth. "Good answer. Mine was the first cock you ever took in your greedy throat."

It was. And that first time, Nico had been hesitant. But Stone had pushed him way past his boundaries with his rough tactics. Once Stone had confirmed Nico was willing, he'd robbed Nico of his control completely, introducing him to a side of himself he hadn't realized existed. By the second time, Nico had been begging for it. Literally.

"How many cocks have you had since then?"

"Four," he admitted.

"Did you give or receive?"

"I was the top three of the four times."

"Preference? Or circumstance?"

Nico could tell he was getting at something. "It was just how it ended up."

Stone's eyes blazed with heat. "Do you wanna top me, Nico?"

He swallowed hard. "No."

"Really?"

Nico nodded, grunting when Stone's hand tightened around his cock.

"You want me to dominate you."

It wasn't a question, but Nico nodded.

Stone smirked again. "Good."

"How many have you had?" Nico dared to ask.

"More than four." Stone's gaze shifted down again. "But none as good as this one."

Nico's chest filled with a foreign sensation. A mixture of warmth and anticipation that made his body quake.

Stone leaned down, and Nico's eyes rounded as he watched the man. The way his lips parted, his tongue snaking out to wet them before he licked the head of Nico's dick. He gasped, the sensation more powerful than he anticipated.

He watched as Stone sucked his cock. Slowly at first, teasing, tormenting. His pace increased and decreased in equal measure for long minutes while Nico's circulatory system cranked harder with every second.

Suddenly, Stone stopped, lifting his head. Nico didn't register the light that beamed across Stone's face immediately. It wasn't until Stone whispered, "Someone's here," that his breath halted in his throat.

Self-preservation had him reaching to pull up his sweatpants, although it was impossible to do with Stone straddling his thighs.

He earned a slap on his hand.

Whoever it was would see them as soon as they entered the house. The living room and kitchen ran the length of the front wall of the barn.

Stone smiled, peering down at him. "Looks like our girl couldn't hold out."

A knock sounded.

"Come in," Stone called out.

In his position, Nico couldn't see her. His neck was craned in an odd position, so he had to trust that Stone wasn't fucking with him. The surprising thing was he did trust Stone. He had no reason not to.

"Hey, baby," Stone crooned.

"Hey."

Yeah, that was definitely Stevie's sexy rasp.

"You're just in time to join us."

Nico stared into space, waiting for her to appear. When she finally did, his heart thumped hard in his chest. "You okay?"

She nodded, her gaze shifting to his exposed cock. "Better now. Don't let me interrupt."

Stone patted the cushion beside Nico. "Have a seat. Watch or join. Up to you."

Then Stone's mouth was on his cock again, bringing the damn thing back to life instantly. He thought he would drown in the pleasure, but then Stevie stripped off her sweatshirt, tossing it to the floor, and he knew without a doubt that they were just getting started.

STEVIE'S NEW FAVORITE PASTIME WAS WATCHING THESE two men together.

She'd debated whether she should go home after she left her dad's. She had intended to give them the night alone because she felt guilty since she'd had them both to herself already. Try as she might, she couldn't get her car to go in that direction, and she'd ended up here.

However, she didn't intend to intrude. Mostly. She was just stripping so that they wouldn't feel awkward, that was all. She was simply going to sit back and watch.

She could feel Nico's eyes on her as she stripped off the rest of her clothes.

"Don't mind me," she teased as she sat on the cushion beside them. "I'm just gonna sit here and enjoy the show."

Stone released Nico's cock from his lips, his fist continuing to move up and down slowly over the iron-hard length.

"Did you tell him what we did when you stayed over?"

She was surprised by Stone's question, though she wasn't sure why. The man was as vocal now as he had been back then.

"He didn't ask."

Stone looked at Nico. "You should ask. I think you might like the story."

Stevie was watching him, curious what his response would be. She knew Nico had been turned on by the fact she'd stayed with Stone because she'd felt it in his touch when he'd fucked her last night. However, he hadn't asked for details, so she'd kept them to herself.

"Tell me," Nico finally said.

Stevie opened her mouth, prepared to start the story, but Nico held up a hand.

"Wait." He inhaled sharply, his eyes rolling back as Stone continued to work his dick with his mouth. "I think a reenactment would be better." Nico gasped again, his fingers sliding into Stone's hair. "Don't you?"

Stone lifted his head, using his free hand to point at her, then toward his bedroom. "Remember what we did after the shower?"

Her eyes widened as the memory slammed into her. Stevie had thought about little else since that morning when Stone had fucked her pussy with his cock and her ass with his thumbs. She was all but counting down the seconds until a repeat.

Stone snapped his fingers. "On the bed. All fours. Ass toward the door."

She stared at him for a moment, her brain a few seconds behind. Fortunately, her body had no problem reacting to the gruff command. She could feel their eyes on her as she padded through the room and down the hallway that separated the bedrooms from the bathroom.

"Oh and get the lube from the nightstand."

A wave of heat washed over her, leaving goosebumps in its wake.

The lamp on Stone's bedside table was on. She noticed his bed was made and wondered whether he'd done that for Nico. She didn't remember it being made the other night when she was here. Then again, she didn't remember much about that night, aside from the intense orgasms Stone had delivered or the way he'd held her through the night, his big, warm body providing warmth and security as she slept.

The pump bottle was sitting on the nightstand, so she grabbed it and put it on the bed as she crawled up on it. She felt ridiculously exposed as she got into position the way he'd instructed. As the minutes ticked by, she nearly lost her nerve, but then she heard the heavy thud of footsteps approaching.

"Fuck."

More heat swept over her at the gravel-rough sound of Nico's voice.

"I think she should greet us like that more often," Stone noted.

"I had some errands to run yesterday, so I picked up somethin' I thought she might like."

They were both behind her, so she couldn't see what they were doing, but she heard the sound of plastic.

"Figured it might prepare her for the future."

"This'll work," Nico said.

Stevie tried to turn her head to see what they had, but Stone spanked her ass.

"No peeking."

She squealed when he smacked her again, smiling as she pressed her face to the mattress. God, she loved when he did that. She wasn't sure what it said about her that she liked to be spanked, but the man knew how to deliver it in a way that rocketed her lust into the stratosphere.

A hand brushed her thigh as one of them reached for the lubricant. Warm hands began gliding over her ass, her back, down her thighs. She spread her legs wider, silently encouraging them to touch her where she needed it.

"Move toward the headboard," Stone instructed.

Stevie crawled forward.

"More."

She kept going until she couldn't go any further.

The mattress dipped. Someone moved up behind her.

"Fuck, you've got a pretty ass," Nico said, his voice dripping with awe.

Stevie shivered.

"Stone told me you begged him to fuck you here."

So that was what they'd been doing while they made her wait. Gossiping about her.

"I wouldn't say I—" She whimpered when she felt something slick and cool on her asshole. A second later, there was pressure. Two breaths later, something was being pushed inside her ass.

"It's a plug," Stone explained. "Not too big. Not too small. We've got to work up to you takin' a cock there."

Fingers teased between her legs as the toy was pushed in deeper.

"Bear down on it," Nico instructed.

She did, moaning as the thing stretched her to the point of pain. "Nico…"

"Almost there, Stevie. Relax just a little. Let me get it all the way in."

She gritted her teeth, welcoming the discomfort because she trusted they knew what they were doing.

Suddenly, the stretch and burn disappeared, and the result was a feeling of fullness she'd never experienced before.

"Fuck, that's pretty," Stone said, his hand moving over her ass.

She grunted when he tugged on the plug. Thankfully, he didn't pull it out.

"Turn over," Nico commanded.

As gently as she could, she settled onto her back, doing her best not to push that thing any deeper. But no sooner than her back hit the mattress, Nico was on her. He settled between her legs, dragging his cock along the seam of her pussy. She was wet, his dick sliding effortlessly through her slickness.

"Can you take me, too?"

"I don't know," she said honestly.

"We don't have to do this."

His eyes held a wealth of concern, and she knew he was seconds away from changing his mind. So she grabbed him behind the neck and pulled him down. She wiggled her hips, urging him to fuck her while she sealed her lips to his.

Nico pushed in slow and deep. She exhaled in a rush, pulling her mouth from his as he filled her to the point of pain.

"Too much?"

"No," she said, but she nodded her head.

He started to pull out, but she stopped him, slamming her heel into his ass to keep him in place.

"Now it's your turn," Stone said.

Stevie watched as he crawled on the bed behind Nico. She met his stare as she realized what he was doing. Stone was going to fuck Nico while Nico fucked her.

Her pussy clenched around Nico's cock, and her ass spasmed around the toy. Her clit pulsed as the eroticism of the act registered.

"He thought this was about you," Stone said, peering down at her over Nico's shoulder.

She smiled. "Fuck him, Stone. Fuck us both."

His eyes heated, and she watched as his attention shifted.

"You ready for this?" Stevie whispered to Nico.

His mouth opened but slammed shut before any words came out. His eyes widened and his lips parted. Stevie watched every expression register as Stone buried himself to the hilt. He was giving a play-by-play as he did, which only added to the salaciousness of the encounter.

"God*damn*, Nico … fuck, you're tight," Stone said through gritted teeth. "You feel good."

Nico grunted.

Stevie sighed when Stone began to move, which caused Nico's cock to push in deeper before retreating.

"Grab the headboard," Stone said, and a smack reverberated in the air.

Nico gasped, then reached for the headboard behind Stevie's head. She stared up at him as he hovered over her.

A second later, she had her hands planted on the headboard to keep from slamming into it as Stone fucked Nico harder, faster. Every time he drove forward, the momentum pushed Nico inside her.

They rode the wave of ecstasy for the longest time, grunts and groans echoing in the room. She stared up at Nico, watching his face as he accepted every hard thrust.

"Does it feel good?"

"Too good," he groaned. "Fuck. It's too much."

"Not yet," Stone barked.

Stevie cried out when Stone began fucking him harder, driving Nico into her again and again.

She hissed and moaned, trying to hold on until the explosion came, drowning her in sensation as she orgasmed with their names tumbling from her lips.

"Oh, fuck, Stevie! Yes. Come all over me," Nico hissed. "Stone! I'm comin'. Fuck."

Stone roared a moment later as their bodies stilled, all three of them joined.

Stevie was still attempting to catch her breath when Nico pulled out, falling beside her. Stone landed in a heap on her other side, the three of them panting heavily.

"Next time, it's your turn," Stone whispered, kissing her shoulder.

"I'm gonna hold you to it."

And she meant it.

THIRTY-THREE

Monday, February 12, 2024

THE WEEKEND PASSED IN A BLUR.

For the first time since his conversation with his aunt and uncle, Stone didn't spend all his time fretting over the business proposal. Instead, he spent the weekend running errands, spending time with his parents, and hanging out with Stevie and Nico.

He wouldn't go so far as to say he'd established a routine, but he was falling into one that worked for him. Every now and then, he would find himself missing the *go, go, go* that he'd felt on the ranch, but being back in Coyote Ridge gave him a sense of peace he hadn't expected to find.

But it was a new week, and he had a list of things he needed to accomplish before he met with his aunt and uncle next weekend. The first was getting Braydon and Brendon to sign off on his proposal.

So here he was at Moonshiners, waiting for his twin cousins to arrive.

"Is it just me or is this place different than I remember?" Stone asked the bartender as he worked to fill drinks and orders. It wasn't the first time he'd come in here since his return, but it was the first chance he'd had to ask someone about it.

"We gave it an overhaul. Moved the bar to the back and worked our way forward. Plus, we expanded the kitchen, added another bathroom. Increased occupancy to a hundred since we now serve food."

Stone spun on his stool and scanned the room. "Is it bigger?"

"We added on. Really didn't have a choice. Took me a while to convince Rafe it was a good thing."

That was what was different, Stone figured. That and the configuration. Granted, Stone had only been to Moonshiners a few times over the years and only when family suggested it, but he'd frequented the place often before he left town when he was twenty-one.

He didn't remember the walls being quite so ... nice. The structure was still made of wood, but the interior walls were lacquered, with more lighting than he recalled. The bar was still the main focus, but it had been moved to the back of the room versus the side. They still had a couple of pool tables, a jukebox, and bar stools that were hard on the hind quarters.

"And Rafe's got you workin' here?" Stone asked when he turned around.

Stone remembered his dad mentioning that Mack had sold the place to his cousin Rafe.

"The things we do for wedded bliss," the bartender said, holding out his hand. "Holt Callahan. I don't think we've officially met."

Stone shook his hand. "Stone Jameson."

"One of my husband's many cousins," Holt noted, staring at him with a contemplative expression. "You're the lone wolf who ventured out to rule the world from the back of a bull. Am I close?"

He snorted. "Tell me that's not the rumor."

Holt laughed. "Forgive me. I'm a writer. I tend to come up with my own version of events. But it's not too far off, is it? You did win a few championships?"

"A few." Stone took a drink from his beer. "But the bulls won in the long run."

"You were injured, right?"

Stone nodded, but he didn't elaborate.

The door opened, and a chorus of greetings erupted through the room. Stone peered over his shoulder to see Braydon and his identical twin brother, Brendon, walking in. At thirty-nine, they weren't quite so identical anymore. Their features were the same— same nose, same eyebrow ridge, same blue-gray eyes—but not their haircuts or facial hair. Braydon's hair was longer on top, styled with what looked like gel, his jaw clean-shaven, while Brendon's hair was buzzed short, and he sported a beard.

"I'm gonna move this to a table," Stone told Holt. "Can you keep my tab open and put theirs on mine?"

"Will do."

Stone took his beer and went to greet his cousins.

"Damn, boy, you got old," Brendon said with a devilish grin.

"You're one to talk," Stone countered as the man pulled him in for a hug.

"Just better with age."

"And you…" Stone looked at Braydon. "Not a day over fabulous."

Braydon barked a laugh, then jerked him in for a back-slapping hug. "You always were a smooth talker."

"Y'all want a drink? On me."

"I'll take a whiskey sour," Braydon stated.

"Beer works for me."

While they grabbed a table, Stone went to the bar and relayed the order to Holt. On his way to sit down, he shored up his nerve and sent up a silent prayer.

"How's the family life treatin' ya?" Stone asked, directing the question at both of them.

"Keepin' busy," Braydon replied.

"And the kids?" He held up a finger. "Lemme see if I can get this right." He pointed at Braydon. "Rhett, Zach, and Waylon. Seven, six, and five, right?"

Braydon pursed his lips and nodded. "I'm impressed."

Stone looked at Brendon. "Remington and Thad? They're … seven and five?"

"Close," Brendon noted. "Rem's six. He'll be seven in March."

"Six goin' on sixteen," Braydon stated as Holt set their drinks on the table.

"Thanks, man," Brendon said to the bartender. "How's Bailey feelin'?"

Holt's grin amped up a few million watts. "Good. Still has morning sickness, but we're workin' our way through."

Braydon looked at Stone. "Their wife's due in July."

"Congrats," Stone told Holt, making a mental note to check in with Rafe to congratulate him, too.

"What about you?" Braydon said when Holt disappeared. "Got any little ones runnin' around?"

"Not yet."

Brendon and Braydon traded looks.

Stone glanced between them. "What?"

"Rumor is you're spendin' time with Stevie Shepherd."

"And Nico Daugherty," Brendon tacked on.

"Guilty." Stone saw no reason to deny it.

"I stopped in over there last weekend. At D and S," Braydon said. "Jessie's on me to spruce up the yard." He held up his hands. "I tried to tell her these thumbs ain't green, but she won't listen."

"So is it serious?" Brendon asked.

Stone wasn't sure what he was referring to, so he waited.

"You plannin' to put down roots?"

"With Stevie and Nico?" Braydon finished for him.

Stone relaxed. "I'm workin' on it."

They traded another look, this time grinning as though they were pleased by the news.

Braydon picked up his drink and held it up for a toast. "If it means you'll be stickin' around, I hope it works out for you."

Stone clicked his beer bottle against the glass. "Thanks."

"But that's not why you wanted to talk," Brendon stated. "Pop mentioned somethin' about you wantin' to start a business or some shit. Cattle ranch?"

"That was one of my ideas," Stone explained. "But I nixed that one in favor of another."

Both men leaned forward on their elbows, giving Stone their full attention. "Do tell."

He took the cue and laid out his plan, keeping it high-level. They asked more questions than Kaleb and Sawyer, but Stone had answers.

"Wow. Shit, man. That sounds incredible." Braydon looked at Brendon. "Why the hell didn't we think of that?"

"No, shit." Brendon peered at Stone. "You doin' this with Nico and Stevie?"

"That's the plan." He didn't have Nico's buy-in yet, but Stevie had given him a verbal agreement.

"I know Mom and Pop want us to sign off on this shit, but you don't need it," Brendon told him. "As far as I'm concerned, that land's as much yours as it is ours. If you can make somethin' of it, I say go for it."

A weight lifted when Braydon nodded in agreement. "If we can do anything to help, just holler. Between us, we've got five strappin' boys who love to get their hands dirty."

"You mean they love to play in the dirt," Brendon corrected. "Not sure they'd accomplish much, but they'll make a damn fine mess."

Stone laughed, relief swamping him. He fought the urge to ask if they'd talked to Zane. He wanted to, but he figured he would have to confront his cousin on his own.

"How 'bout another round to celebrate," Braydon said. "You're buyin', right?"

"ARE YOU COLD?"

Stevie snuggled closer to Nico, shaking her head.

After dinner, she had curled up on the couch to watch TV. At least, that was what she intended to do, but her mind was elsewhere. Now that Nico had joined her, it was even worse. She couldn't focus on anything except his hard body behind her.

The problem wasn't that she was distracted by him; it was the guilt she felt when she was near him. She'd felt it since Friday night when she barged in on him and Stone. It was selfish on her part. One minute she was telling them to spend some quality time just the two of them. The next, she was planting herself in the middle. Neither one of them had acted as though she'd crashed the party, but she couldn't shake the feeling that she had.

"What's on your mind?" Nico whispered, his warm breath fanning her cheek.

Maybe if she told him, it would reduce some of the guilt.

She shifted, rolling to her back so she could look at him.

God, he was such a beautiful man. It was still hard to believe that this was real. They had somehow moved past being friends/roommates and into … this. She didn't quite know how to define it other than they'd taken a relatively platonic relationship and added some not-so-platonic benefits. Of course, it wouldn't feel real until she broke down and told Niyah. Which she needed to do. Soon. She knew her best friend would support her—that's what they did, even when they disagreed with the other's choice—but what she wanted was to get Niyah's take on it. Was she being impulsive? Reckless? Was she opening herself up to more heartache?

Unfortunately, a convo with her BFF would have to wait.

She met Nico's gaze. "The other night … at Stone's."

His eyebrow quirked. "Yeah?"

She swallowed. "I … um … I need to apologize."

"For?"

"For crashin' your party."

His expression didn't change. It still held a wealth of confusion.

"I showed up after I told you to spend time alone with him. It was … selfish."

Nico's eyebrows hopped, and the corners of his eyes crinkled. "Selfish?"

She nodded. "I told you to spend time with him, and I … interrupted."

More crinkling, but not quite a smile. "In case you don't recall, neither one of us complained."

"No, but that doesn't make it okay. Y'all deserve some alone time."

Nico shifted back, giving her more room. "Alone time?"

"Yeah. You know. The two of you doin' … whatever y'all do together."

He huffed a laugh. "I can't speak for Stone, but I can tell you, I prefer havin' you both there."

Stevie frowned, surprised. "You do?"

"Yeah."

"So you don't want to…" God, she felt her face heating. "You … um…"

"Spit it out, Stevie."

"You don't want to be with just him."

"If you're askin' whether I wanna hang out with him, then yeah. I'd like to. But when you say *be with*, I assume you're talkin' about sex?"

She nodded even as her ears heated to a million degrees.

"Is that what you prefer? Alone time?"

The question caught her off guard, but she answered honestly. "Not really, no. But … it's nice sometimes."

"One on one?"

She nodded again.

"Why?"

Stevie shrugged. "I don't know. It feels more … intimate?"

Nico smiled, and his blue eyes lit up. "Intimate."

She wasn't sure he was understanding her. Especially since he seemed amused by her.

"You think the three of us together isn't intimate?"

"Sex isn't always intimate," she declared, realizing how stupid that sounded. "You know what I mean."

"Actually, I don't."

She couldn't tell if he was fucking with her or genuinely confused. At this point, she wasn't even sure *she* knew what she was trying to say.

"Forget I said anything."

"No. I'm not gonna forget. Let's talk."

Talking was overrated. She should've known better than to address this issue. Or maybe there wasn't an issue, and she was making more of it than she should.

"Did you enjoy spendin' time with him alone?" Nico asked.

She shrugged.

"Be honest."

"Yes," she stated firmly. "But." She touched his cheek, holding his gaze. "But I prefer bein' with both of you."

"But it's more intimate when you're with one of us."

"Not really."

His eyebrows angled into a V. "But you think it is for me and Stone?"

"Yes."

Nico's smile was slow and wicked. "Darlin', I'm not sure you know what you're talkin' about."

"I do, too," she insisted, feeling stupid for bringing it up. She attempted to sit up. "Just forget—"

"Uh-uh," he said, dragging her back down.

His weight shifted, his thigh covering her legs, pinning her in place.

"I'm sorry I said anything," she harrumphed.

"I'm not." Nico leaned down, his lips hovering over hers. "I wanna know how you feel."

"I don't *know* how I feel." It sounded petulant, but she didn't care.

"Do you like spendin' time with me?"

"Yes."

"Do you like spendin' time with Stone?"

"Yes."

"And you like spendin' time with both of us?"

"I prefer it," she said without thinking.

Nico lifted his head and looked her in the eye.

"I know it doesn't make sense." She wanted to explain. "But—"

He put his fingers over her lips. "It makes perfect sense."

In a chaotic, convoluted way, maybe, but she held his stare, wanting him to explain because surely his reasoning was better than hers.

"I prefer bein' with both of you, too."

"You do?"

"Why wouldn't I?"

Stevie shrugged. "I don't know. Maybe because I can't give you what he can."

Nico's eyes warmed. "And he can't give me what you can."

She smiled, her cheeks warming. "Touché."

"With both of you, I have the best of everything."

Okay. So she hadn't looked at it that way.

His lips settled over hers, soft and sweet. She kissed him back, sliding her fingers into the hair at his nape. It was so soft, so silky. She loved that she got to touch him whenever she wanted. It sure beat having to suck down alcohol just to get a moment with him.

The kiss went nuclear within minutes. Probably had something to do with Nico's hands roaming under her sweatshirt. She'd removed her bra earlier, so there was nothing between his callused fingers and her sensitive nipples as he caressed her.

"Take this off," he whispered, lifting up so she could have room to do so.

A second later, her sweatshirt was on the floor. She heard Jäger move, knew he was going to run off with it. At the moment, she didn't care. She wanted Nico to keep touching her the way he was.

Unfortunately, he stopped.

"What're you doin'?"

"Gettin' your phone," he said as he reached over her head.

"What for?" If he thought for one second that they were going to record what he was doing, the man was out of his fucking mind.

He passed her the phone. "I want you to text Stone. Tell him to come over."

"Are you—ahh!" A whimper escaped when his lips circled her nipple, the gentle rasp of his tongue sending electric sparks across her chest.

"Text him," he muttered, licking her nipple before shifting to give attention to the other one.

Holding her phone up, she managed to pull up the text thread. She fumbled a few times, backspaced more than she could count, thanks to Nico's wicked mouth on her breasts. Finally, she hit send.

Before she could set the phone down, it buzzed in her hand.

"He's pullin' up now," she rasped, dragging air into her lungs as her lust skyrocketed.

"Great minds," Nico mumbled between licks. "Is the door unlocked?"

Stevie arched her back, trying to see the door without disrupting his ministrations. "I think so."

"Good."

"Why's that—" Her words were cut off when Nico moved, dragging her sweatpants down her legs, taking her panties with them.

He settled between her legs, grinning wide before he dipped his head.

A knock sounded as pleasure slammed into her.

"It's … open!"

She prayed Stone wasn't with anyone. If so, they were going to get an eyeful because Nico didn't stop licking her pussy when the door opened. Jäger yipped excitedly, but Stevie barely heard it over her pulse thundering in her ears.

"What's up, little guy?" Stone's deep baritone sounded from the front of the house.

Every cell in her body heated at the thought of him walking in to find them like this. She remembered what it was like when she'd walked into Stone's house a few days ago. She'd flashed hot at the sight of Stone sucking Nico's cock.

"Don't mind me," Stone said, his voice still in the distance. "I'm just gonna take off my boots."

Stevie twined her fingers in Nico's hair, holding him to her as he flicked her clit with his tongue.

"And my coat," Stone drawled, amusement ringing in his words.

She was aware of his footsteps getting closer as she was drowning in pleasure.

Then Stone was leaning over the end of the couch, his head above hers. He smiled as he bent down and pressed a soft kiss to her mouth.

"I like walkin' in to find his head between your legs."

His words had sparks igniting on top of sparks. But it was nothing compared to the conflagration that erupted when his work-rough hands caressed her breasts.

Then they were both touching her, and the world somehow seemed brighter. This was what she wanted. No, *this* was what she *needed*. Both of them here. The two of them touching her, kissing her, drawing out her pleasure for blissfully long minutes. Nothing compared.

Nico lifted his head and looked at Stone. "Would you like a taste?"

"Don't mind if I do."

Embarrassment washed over her even though she didn't argue with their suggestion. It was dirty and taboo and so freaking hot, she was sure parts of her body had caught fire already.

The next thing she knew, they were trading places. Stone settled between her legs, the warm rasp of his tongue intensifying the ache that was building inside her. She wanted more, but at the same time, she wanted this to last forever. She whimpered and moaned but resisted the urge to beg them to fuck her. She rode the gentle waves of ecstasy as he licked her pussy.

They traded places two more times, and she realized it was so they could get Jäger settled in his crate and shed their clothes.

"Let's move this to the bedroom," Nico said as he stripped off his sweatpants.

Stevie was boneless, her head swimming from their wicked teasing. She had enough strength to grab Stone when he lifted her into his arms as though she weighed nothing.

"Hi," he greeted with a sexy grin.

"Hi," she whispered, holding onto him as he made his way down the hall.

He set her on the bed, moving over her, his mouth trailing a path of fire up her torso, higher. When they were nose to nose, he sealed his mouth to hers, his tongue dancing past her parted lips. She welcomed his kiss, surprised by how gentle he was being.

She giggled when he rolled, taking her with him so that she was straddling his hips.

He brushed her hair back from her face and smiled.

If it was weird that she resumed their conversation between bouts, she didn't care. "It didn't take you long to get here."

"I was in the neighborhood."

She giggled. "Is that right?"

"Yup. Couldn't stay away. I missed y'all."

"We missed you, too," she admitted as she reached between them to circle his cock with her fingers.

He gasped, his eyes hooded as she guided him right where she needed him.

NICO WALKED INTO THE ROOM TO FIND Stevie sitting astride Stone, sinking down on his cock slowly.

He expected to feel a flash of jealousy, but it didn't come. In fact, he took advantage of the opportunity to watch the two of them together. It wasn't until Stone reached out his hand that Nico realized he was urging him to join them.

The thought of having Stevie between them had his cock throbbing painfully, the need to be inside her stealing his breath.

He had enough sense to grab the lube from the bedside table before moving to the end of the bed. He continued to watch as Stone's cock slid in and out as Stevie lifted and lowered on him. Nico set the lube aside so he could free his hands to touch. And he did, starting with Stone's legs, loving the way the crisp dark hair teased his palms as he gently rubbed, working his way up to his knees. Still, he watched Stone's thick cock, slick with Stevie's juices, as it tunneled in and out of her. His breaths became choppy as the eroticism of the act heated his blood.

Nico didn't stop touching when he crawled up on the bed behind Stevie. He trailed his palms over her ass, higher. His hands spanned the entire width of her back, his thumbs overlapping as he got lost in the softness of her skin.

She gasped when he kissed the small of her back and worked his way up. He felt Stone's fingertips gliding along his sides, drifting high, then low. When his touch disappeared, it was because he was caressing Stevie's ass, spreading her cheeks, groaning as she lifted and lowered her hips, impaling herself on him.

Nico kneeled behind her, watching Stone's big hands move over her soft body. Her pussy glistened, her entrance stretched around Stone's girth. He wasn't sure he could take much more without tipping over the edge, so he got with the program, slicking his cock, stroking himself while he teased her ass with his finger.

"Yes," she hissed. "Fuck me, Nico. Please."

"Here?" He pushed two fingers into her ass. She was tight. So fucking tight.

Stevie lifted up, whimpering as she peered over her shoulder. "Please."

He saw the desire churning in her eyes for that brief moment before she turned back to Stone, pressing her chest to his.

Inching closer, he guided his cock to the tight little rosebud and pressed his hips forward, the head of his cock breaching the tight ring of muscle.

Stevie whimpered.

Stone grunted.

Nico pushed in deeper.

The chorus of grunts and moans filled the room as he sank inside her, stretching her ass. It didn't go unnoticed that he was the one who was taking her anal virginity, but he had to force the thoughts away. He didn't want to come yet and acknowledging that he was her first was a surefire trigger.

Stone gripped Stevie's hips, holding her still as Nico began to rock forward and back, sliding in deeper each time. He could feel the ridge of Stone's cock inside her, and it caused the hair on his neck to stand on end. This had to be the most intense thing he'd ever felt. And he'd thought the same thing the other night when he'd been lodged to the hilt inside Stevie while Stone fucked his ass.

This was somehow different. They were both inside her. Joined as one. All three of them. Together.

"Fuck me," Stevie whimpered. "Please."

Stone rocked his hips, his cock moving against Nico's.

"Please, Nico. Fuck me," Stevie cried.

He wanted to—God, he wanted to—but it felt too good. The urge to slam in deep was too powerful, and he didn't want to hurt her.

"You won't hurt her," Stone said as though he could read Nico's mind.

Nico pulled out, slid in again. The more he did, the more Stevie relaxed, easing the way. He added more lube, drizzling it over her asshole so that it coated his dick.

And then the pleasure took over. Time stood still. The world stopped turning. His entire existence focused on the two people in the bed with him as he and Stone fucked Stevie, alternating until they had a rhythm that worked.

"Yes … yes … don't stop. God, don't stop," Stevie hummed.

Nico's strokes became longer, deeper. He gripped her hips, holding her in place so they could both fuck her.

Perspiration formed on his skin as the heat churned inside him. He was reaching his breaking point, but he didn't want it to end. He wanted to stay like this forever, buried inside her alongside Stone. Nothing had ever felt this good.

"You ready to come for us?" Stone asked Stevie.

Her response was a muted grunt followed by a loud gasp. Nico felt Stone's hand between them, knew he was playing with her clit.

"Yes!"

Nico began pumping his hips with a goal in mind, urging her toward release. He battled the tingling in his spine, gritting his teeth to hold back.

"Nico! Stone! Oh … *goooooddddddd!*"

Stevie's body clamped down, milking his release from him. He slammed into her one final time and felt the pulse of Stone's dick deep inside her. His body splintered, his mind, too. For a brief moment, he was positive his soul had left his body. The pleasure was so intense it was painful.

And then he snapped back into existence, his heart thundering in his chest, his lungs working overtime. He slowly pulled out of Stevie and dropped to his side, gasping for air, wondering how he could still be in one piece after that.

THIRTY-FOUR

Wednesday, February 14, 2024

STEVIE SAT IN HER OFFICE, THE DOOR closed, her phone propped up on her desk so she could see Niyah's face on the screen. The FaceTime call with her best friend had been going on for the past fifteen minutes, during which she had relayed her desperation in a manner she hoped came across as nonchalant. More accurately, she was seeking her best friend's advice on what she should do for Nico and Stone tonight. Being that it was Valentine's Day and all.

"I know it's last minute," she told Niyah. "But it's *Valentine's Day*. I should do *something*, right?"

"We'll get to that, yes. But first, I think we should discuss the fact that you're in a relationship with two men," Niyah countered, her eyebrows shooting toward her hairline. "And you haven't told me about it."

Although Niyah was smiling, Stevie felt guilty because she was right. She'd talked to Niyah several times since she left for California a month ago, but she hadn't yet divulged the details of her budding relationship with Nico and Stone. Or was it relationships? In the plural tense? Her relationships with Nico and Stone. Or maybe it was Nico *or* Stone. If they were separate.

God, her brain was mush, and this conversation wasn't helping.

Yes, she'd known when she placed the call and asked the ridiculous question that Niyah would have questions. That was what best friends did. Problem was, Stevie hadn't given any thought to how she would answer. Or even how she *should* answer. Not because she wasn't eager to talk about it. She was. But she was also nervous. She didn't want to jinx what they had by talking about her feelings.

It was all so confusing. But at the same time, it felt as natural as breathing.

Which she would do now. In, out. Nice and slow.

"Is it serious?" Niyah asked.

That one was easy. "I'm sleepin' in Nico's bed every night, so I'd say yes."

"*Every* night? Wow. That was fast."

"Fast? *Pfft.* You know I've had a thing for him since … forever."

"True."

"And I've been livin' there for … well, a year now."

"Also true."

Stevie felt compelled to come up with more reasons. "We've been … doin' stuff for a year now, too."

"Exactly a year," Niyah agreed.

She sat up straight. "It has been, huh?" She honestly hadn't thought about that. It had been last year on this very day that Stevie had gotten a little tipsy and successfully seduced Nico for the first time.

What a difference a year could make. If someone had told her back then that she'd spend the next romantic holiday wanting to do something to celebrate with Nico *and* Stone, she would've told them they were certifiable.

"What about Stone? Is *he* sleepin' in Nico's bed every night?"

"No."

Niyah laughed. "Disappointed much?"

Stevie laughed. She hadn't meant to say it with so much despair, but it was true. She wished she could wake up to both Stone and Nico every morning. The one-offs were nice, but the more they happened, the more she wanted them to happen again.

"A little," Stevie admitted. "I know it's new, and rushing things is stupid, but I can't help it."

"If you think about it, it's not new, Stevie. You've loved them both for a long time. The heart doesn't understand time references." Niyah tilted her head, her eyes imploring through the little glass screen. "But it does understand someone making promises, then leaving town and never looking back."

Of course she was going to bring that up. Hell, a day rarely passed when Stevie didn't think the same thing. How she'd forgiven Stone so easily when he deserved her wrath.

"How do you feel about that?"

"Well, Dr. Phil," Stevie teased, staring at the phone head-on. "I think I'm crazy, to be honest. I think things are movin' fast because I let them. I think I let Stone off the hook too quickly." She sighed. "And every night when I go to bed, I think about how much I still love him even though I shouldn't."

"No one said that, girl." Niyah's smile grew. "As long as you aren't making this leap into romantic bliss blindfolded, I think you'll be fine."

"My eyes are *wide open*," she huffed. "That doesn't make it any less stupid."

"It's not stupid to want something you've waited your entire life for," Niyah countered, always the optimist. Her best friend grinned. "Plus, you're not gettin' any younger."

Stevie snorted. "Neither are you."

Niyah's face lit up, and her mouth opened, but she closed it quickly.

Stevie knew that look. She'd seen it a million times since the fourth grade. Niyah always did it when she had some kind of news. It was her way of contemplating whether it was the right time to deliver it.

"Tell me," Stevie insisted.

"I ... um..." Niyah giggled, her eyes glittering with what could only be tears. "I'm pregnant."

Stevie jerked back, her chair rolling away from the desk as she clapped her hands together. "For real?"

"For real."

"Oh, my God!" Stevie squealed. "You're gonna be a mommy!"

She couldn't resist the urge to launch to her feet and dance in a circle. When she returned to her seat, Niyah was laughing.

Stevie leaned toward the screen. "That's so great. How far along?"

"Ten weeks."

She did the math in her head. "You were pregnant before you left? And you didn't tell me?"

"I didn't know," Niyah said, still grinning.

"Well, at least you're gonna give birth to a Texan," she teased. "Being conceived here gives him residency. Or is it a girl?"

"We don't know yet."

"Have you told Nico?"

Niyah canted her head. "What do you think? I couldn't tell him before I told you. He sucks at keepin' secrets."

That much was true. "When do you plan to tell him?"

"Since you're gonna go all out tonight, I figure I'll tell him tomorrow."

Stevie huffed, flopping back in her chair. Now that they'd come full circle in the conversation, she realized she still had no idea how to make tonight special.

"Don't look so forlorn. I've got an idea," Niyah said.

Hope flared to life as she sat forward and listened to her best friend map out what she needed to do.

NICO WAS CLIMBING INTO HIS TRUCK WHEN his phone buzzed. He checked the screen to find a text message from Stevie.

💬 I'm officially requesting your presence at home tonight. Seven o'clock. Come hungry.

He responded, smiling as he did.

💬 Does that mean you're cooking?

💬 **I DON'T CARE WHO'S COOKING, I'LL BE THERE.**

💬 Yes, Nico, I'm cooking. And thank you for being so amenable, Stone.

💬 **WHEN IT COMES TO YOU, BABY, I'M EASY. WHAT CAN I SAY?**

💬 What are you making?

💬 Can't you just be easy like Stone? Does it matter?

💬 Just promise not to burn the house down before we get there.

💬 I'll do my best.

💬 **IF YOU SMELL SMOKE, REMEMBER MY BROTHER'S A FIREFIGHTER.**

💬 One more smart remark from either
of you, and I'll go to bed early, and you'll
both miss out.

Nico backspaced quickly, laughing. No way was he going to risk that happening.

Instead, he put his phone in the center console and turned on the truck. It would take him an hour in traffic to get back up north. It was only four, so he had plenty of time, but he had another stop to make before he headed home for the day.

Almost as soon as he put the truck in drive, his phone rang. He tapped the button on the steering wheel to take the call.

"Nico Daugherty," he answered, keeping his eyes on the road.

"What are you doing?"

He grinned as his sister's voice echoed through the truck's speakers.

"Drivin'. What're you doin'?"

"Sitting here with my feet up, enjoying a near-perfect day."

"Only *near* perfect?" he teased. "Sounds to me like Adam's fallin' down on the job."

"No. I don't think he is." She laughed. "Then again, his job's easy. He's only got *me* to take care of, and I'm easy to please."

Nico snorted. "Since when?"

"Why didn't you tell me?" Niyah blurted, her jovial tone disappearing.

He frowned. "Tell you what?"

"That you're with Stevie *and* Stone."

"Define *with*," he said, not sure how much she knew. He wouldn't put it past his sister to ferret out the information by pretending she was in the know. She'd done it to him enough times over the years.

"Stevie's sleepin' in your bed every night."

Well, apparently, she'd been talking to Stevie, which probably meant she knew more than he did. And that was saying something, considering he was the one they were talking about.

"She is," he confirmed.

"And Stone's a frequent overnight guest, from what I hear?"

"He is."

"And you didn't beat him to a pulp for what he did to Stevie?"

Nico sighed, propping his wrist on the steering wheel. Traffic was heavy, so he was going nowhere fast.

"He broke her heart, Nico."

He wasn't sure what he was supposed to say to that. Niyah was right, but it wasn't his place to dole out punishment.

"Stevie's a big girl," Nico reminded her. "She can fight her own battles."

"Not when her heart's been reduced to mush."

He snorted a laugh. "Are we talkin' about the same Stevie? You know good and well her heart's not mush."

"She puts on a good face, Nico. But deep down, she's not over what he did."

"Did she tell you that? Or is that your *Dr. Phil* personality making assessments?"

"Does it matter?"

"Yes. Actually. Did Stevie tell you she put Stone in his place?"

His sister was silent for a moment. "She left that part out."

"Trust her to know what's best for her, Niyah. I do."

Her exasperation was thick in her exhale. "How long's this been goin' on?"

So she didn't know everything. That was good. As much as he loved his sister, there were parts of his life he preferred to keep to himself. It wasn't easy since Stevie was Niyah's best friend, and they shared everything.

"Not long."

"Do you love her?"

"Yes," he said without hesitation.

"Wow. That was fast."

"It's true, though." And he saw no reason to deny it. It was bad enough he spent a good portion of his day thinking about where he'd been a month ago and trying to reconcile it with where he was today. It was pointless to try to rationalize it. It was also pointless to think he would've wanted it any other way.

"And Stone? Do you love him, too?"

"Yes." Granted, that was a new revelation, so there had been a pause before he admitted it.

"Are you sure about that?"

"Yes."

"Does he love you?"

"Niyah. Stop with the third degree."

"I'm askin' out of love, big brother. After all, I had to hear it from my best friend."

He snorted. "You act like *your best friend* isn't who we're talkin' about."

Niyah was silent for a moment, but the screen showed the call was still clocking seconds, so Nico waited.

"I'm happy for you," she finally said.

"Thanks." He took the opening to change the subject. "How's it goin' in California? You ready to come back yet?"

"Nope." Her tone relaxed somewhat. "I heard y'all had snow."

"Ice," he corrected. "Very little."

With any luck, they wouldn't have any more. Since the snowpocalypse a few years ago, when they'd rounded out February beneath a blanket of white that had overloaded the power grid, Nico found himself wishing for warmer temperatures.

"I don't miss that," Niyah said. "And I won't miss the heat this summer either. But I was thinkin' maybe y'all could come out here for a few days. Go to the beach. Jäger would get a kick out of the water."

Nico wasn't sure they were at a point where a vacation was a good idea, but he liked the idea. Plus, he missed Niyah already, and it'd only been a month. By the time summer rolled around, he figured he could be easily talked into a quick trip to see her.

"Or maybe y'all should wait," Niyah said quickly.

"I was about—"

"Until mid-September," his sister continued.

"September?" Nico frowned. "What's there to do in September?"

There was a brief pause followed by, "You could meet your niece or nephew."

Nico felt his chest swell instantly. "You're pregnant?"

"I am."

"That's great, Sis. I'm so happy for you."

"Thanks. Now, don't tell Stevie I told you."

"You haven't told her yet?"

"I have. About an hour ago, actually," Niyah said with a giggle. "But I told her I'd wait to tell you until tomorrow."

"Couldn't hold it in any longer, huh?"

"Nope. But I figure my news won't spoil the surprise she has in store for you and Stone."

"Surprise? What surprise?"

Niyah laughed. "It wouldn't be a surprise if I told you, now would it?"

"You're annoying, you know that?"

"I'm the little sister. It's my job."

AS HE DROVE TO STEVIE'S, STONE'S GAZE continued to dart to the flowers, teddy bears, and chocolates sitting in the passenger seat. He hadn't been sure what to get Stevie for Valentine's Day, so he'd gone the safe route and grabbed as much as he could. And to round it out, he'd grabbed a bottle of bourbon for Nico. He'd noticed the other day that Nico had quite the collection on a bar cart in the dining room, so he wanted to add to it. It was likely overkill, but what was a guy to do?

He'd only celebrated Valentine's once, and that was with Stevie many, many years ago. In fact, she was the only girl he'd ever celebrated significant holidays with. Since he hadn't had a real relationship since then, he was a little rusty.

Plus, this thing with Stevie and Nico was new. Sure, it was moving at warp speed, but that didn't change the fact that he was still treading on unstable ground. The last thing he wanted was to make a wrong move and hurt her feelings or, worse, make her think he expected more than he deserved.

He wished he could give her good news about his business plan, but he didn't have any yet. He still had to meet with Ethan and Beau tomorrow night. If that went well, then it was just a matter of tracking down Zane. Up to this point, his efforts had been wasted, but he wasn't giving up yet. He left a long-winded voicemail yesterday but hadn't heard back from his cousin. He was starting to think he wasn't going to.

But that was a worry for another time, he thought as he pulled into Nico and Stevie's driveway.

Stevie's Bronco was there, but Nico's truck was noticeably absent.

His thoughts drifted back to last night when he'd come over to find Nico and Stevie on the couch. His heart had skipped a few dozen beats when his brain registered the scene. It was as though they'd plucked the fantasy out of his head.

He found himself smiling as he grabbed the loot in the front seat and carried it to the house.

As soon as he knocked, he heard a voice call out from inside the house, telling him to come in.

At least, that was what he thought she said, so he opened the door and peeked inside. "Stevie?"

"In here," she announced.

A yip sounded, and a moment later, Jäger rounded the corner, racing toward the front door.

"What's up, little guy?" he asked the dog as he set his stuff down so he could take off his coat.

Unable to resist, he took a moment to pet Jäger before standing tall and grabbing the gifts. He started toward the kitchen, expecting to smell the aromas of whatever meal Stevie was preparing. Either his olfactory senses were offline, or she wasn't making anything because he got a whiff of nothing.

When he turned the corner, he came to an abrupt stop. "Holy shit."

Stevie turned her head and smiled at him. It was forced, he could tell.

"I want you to know that preparing this was not nearly as easy as it looks."

Stone fumbled to set the flowers and shit on the counter while he continued to stare at the scene literally laid out before him.

"I hope you're hungry," she said, her eyes tracking him as he moved closer.

"God*damn*," he groaned.

This was one gift he would never forget, not for as long as he lived, and he wasn't sure what to say or do. Stevie had turned herself into a human dessert, complete with strawberries, bananas, whipped cream, chocolate syrup, and, yes, even a cherry or two.

His mouth watered with the need to lick his way through the fruit and sugar to get to the best part, which was the very naked woman underneath.

Thankfully, there was noise at the front of the house, followed by Nico's voice echoing through the house.

"In here," Stevie called back, her eyes still on Stone.

A moment later, he felt Nico's presence as he stopped beside him.

"Jesus."

"I know, right," he muttered.

"Seriously?" Stevie huffed. "Y'all choose *this* moment to be speechless?"

"Hey, it's not every day a man comes home to find his woman laid out like a dessert buffet," Stone said, his gaze still skimming her delectable curves.

"Is it *all* edible?" Nico asked, moving closer.

"Yes," Stevie answered.

Stone got with the program, moving around to the end of the island so he could admire her from a different angle.

"*All* of it?" Stone asked, staring at the small pieces of fruit that were piled high, adding what he assumed was supposed to be a discreet element to what could only be described as erotic art.

"How exactly did you do this?" Nico asked, voicing the question that was running through Stone's mind.

"Does it matter?"

No. No, it did not.

"God*damn*," he muttered again, stepping closer so he could touch.

"Is that chocolate syrup?" Nico asked, dragging his finger through a puddle of dark liquid pooling in Stevie's belly button.

She inhaled sharply. "Yes."

Stone touched a mound of white that was steepled over Stevie's nipple. "And whipped cream?"

"Mmm-hmm."

"What were you goin' for?" Nico asked, but even Stone knew the answer didn't matter.

Before he realized what he was doing, Stone was rolling up his sleeves, gearing up to dig in. This was gonna get messy.

Hours later, as the three of them were taking turns in the shower, Stone found himself grinning like an idiot. He never did get a chance to give either of them the gifts he'd gotten them, but he hoped the hours of pleasure and multiple orgasms made up for it.

It was a Valentine's Day that would go down in the history books, that was for damn sure.

THIRTY-FIVE

Thursday, February 15, 2024

"ARE YOU GONNA EAT THAT?"

Reilly peered down to see Tate pointing at the last piece of bacon on her plate.

She pushed it toward him, shaking her head.

They'd met at the diner to discuss at length the real possibility of a double wedding. Since Tate's excited phone call the night he finally agreed to marry Donovan, Reilly had been waiting for this conversation. Up to this point, they'd exchanged bits and pieces but nothing concrete. She wasn't even sure he was serious when he agreed that a double wedding would be cool.

Only now, he seemed to be avoiding the conversation. Every time she tried to ask him something, he shoved more food down his gullet.

"You're avoidin' me," she said, leaning back in her seat and glaring at her best friend.

"What?" His mouth was full, so the word came out muddled.

"You heard me." Her eyes shifted to the plate, then back to his face. "Are you gonna eat that next? Choke down some glass to avoid talkin'? If so, I'm gonna record it. It'll look good on TikTok."

Tate grabbed his napkin and wiped his mouth before reaching for his pineapple juice.

Her nostrils flared when he took a sip. She didn't know how he could even drink that. Eating pineapple was one thing—especially since she'd read somewhere that it made oral sex better because it changed the taste of vaginal fluid, which in turn made it taste... Wow. *Way to go off the rails, Jameson.* She really shouldn't be thinking about Brady licking her pineapple-flavored vagina while Tate was sucking down that juice with a straw. It was weird.

She shook her head and picked up her chocolate milk, forcing away thoughts of what flavor *that* might change it to.

"If you don't want a double wedding, just say so," she snapped, her tone harsher than intended.

Tate slowly set his glass down and sighed. "I do, actually."

Hope bloomed in her heart. "Really?"

He nodded.

Reilly had known Tate all her life, so she had the opportunity to memorize every one of his facial expressions. And he had a lot—like too many. This one ... it was either his constipated face, or he was open to something but knew the cons outweighed the pros.

She wasn't going to like the answer, but she asked anyway. "But?"

His blue eyes looked sad. "But I'm not gettin' married for me. I'm doin' it for Donovan." He leaned forward. "I'm not sure it's what *he* wants."

Reilly crossed her arms over her chest. "Seriously?"

Tate frowned.

"You're tryin' to tell me that not a single part of you, no matter how small, doesn't want to get married?"

He shrugged.

"I call bullshit."

"Hey." Tate glared at her. "It's not—"

"You might be able to make D believe that shit, but I'm not buyin' it. You want to marry him."

"I want to *be* married to him, yeah," Tate defended. "I just wish we didn't have to have a wedding."

"More reason to have a double wedding," she insisted. "At one of those cute little chapels in Vegas. We can walk down the aisle together."

Tate huffed a laugh. "Next, you'll try to fit me for a veil. I'm not walkin' down the aisle, Rye."

"Why not?"

"It's not customary for a gay wedding."

"What *is* customary?"

Another shrug. At this rate, he was gonna pull his neck out.

"We just kinda stand at the altar. There's no fancy way to get there."

Lame. Reilly didn't like it.

"Customary, smushtomary. Who cares?" She leaned forward, resting her elbows on the table. "*Our* wedding. We get to set the precedent."

"I think Donovan would prefer something more traditional," Tate argued.

Reilly rolled her eyes. "I think D would dress up like a dinosaur and wear a tutu on the steps of the capitol building while strangers serenaded 'Wind Beneath My Wings' off-key while dressed up like eggs if you asked him to."

Tate's eyes widened a second before he snorted a laugh.

Yeah, the image of Donovan sporting a tutu made her snort, too.

"He just wants to marry you," Reilly told her best friend. "I heard him talkin' to Brady. He doesn't care when or where. He just. Wants. To be. Your. Husband."

She wasn't surprised when Tate didn't say anything, but Reilly could tell he was processing.

"Plus, we've never been to Vegas. We'll make them spring for fancy hotel rooms, and we can spend a few days pretendin' we're high rollers. We'll make 'em take us to a fancy restaurant, and we can go to one of those clubs the movie stars get into." She took a deep breath. "Think about it, Tate. What better way to—"

"Okay."

Reilly flopped back, shocked. "What?"

"I said okay."

"I know. But did you mean it?"

He reached for his juice. "Yeah."

She watched as he took a sip and kept her thoughts from derailing. "Are you sure?"

Tate closed his eyes for a moment, and when they opened, they were clear, a genuine smile forming on his mouth. "If Donovan's good with it, I'm good with it."

She squealed and clapped her hands together. "It's gonna be amazing, Tate. I swear it."

Now, she just had to figure out how to spring it on her parents.

TATE PARTED WAYS WITH REILLY AT THE diner so she could go to the General Store, and he could go home and shower before his shift.

At least that was his plan, but as soon as he pulled out of the parking lot, he realized he wasn't heading toward the house. Instead, he was driving toward Donovan's office. It was a bit out of the way and meant he wouldn't have time for that shower before he had to be at the station, but he didn't care. He wanted to see Donovan's reaction for himself when he told him about the double wedding. It was the only way he would know whether the man was telling him the truth or simply compromising because that seemed to be what Donovan did.

Tate didn't want Donovan to compromise when it came to his happiness. Although Tate had no desire to stand up in front of a sea of people and exchange vows, he would do it if it would make Donovan happy.

He would hate every second. But he would do it.

Thirty minutes later, Tate was walking into the glass and metal building that housed M-J Architecture & Interiors. He'd only been there once before, and that was on a weekend when they were closed. Tate had been curious and Donovan offered to show him where he worked.

But it wasn't a weekend, and the place wasn't empty the way it had been that day.

He was greeted by a chipper young woman sitting at a glass-top desk.

"Good morning. Welcome to M-J Architecture and Interiors." She flashed a smile. "Do you have an appointment?"

Tate shook his head. "I'm here to see Donovan."

She reached for the phone. "And you are?"

"Umm … Tate."

Her eyebrow lifted, and he could tell she was waiting for his last name.

"Tate Riggs."

Her smile wasn't quite as brilliant, but she pressed a button on the phone and held the receiver to her ear.

"Mr. Jameson. There's a Mr. Riggs here to see you. He said he doesn't have an—"

Tate couldn't hear what was being said on the other end of the line, but the woman's eyes rounded and she was nodding incessantly despite the fact Donovan couldn't see her.

"Yes, sir," she said quickly before hanging up the phone and looking at him. "I'm sorry. I didn't realize who you were."

"Don't apologize. How could you?"

Another smile, this one not quite as uneasy as the last. "Please. Go on back. Mr. Jameson's in his office."

"Thanks."

M-J Architecture & Interiors wasn't as big as Tate had imagined it would be, but it was designed in a way that made it feel huge. Probably had something to do with the fact it was surrounded by walls of tinted glass. Beyond the front reception area, it was completely open on the main floor. Dark, glossy concrete was the base that balanced out the stark white of the steel supporting the second-floor loft space where Donovan and Brady worked. The large staircase was the centerpiece that separated a lounge area surrounded by several desks, most of which were occupied.

Tate made a beeline for the stairs and slowed himself down as he went up.

The second floor contained drafting tables, a large conference area, and two glass-enclosed offices along the back wall. Brady was perched on a stool at one of the drafting tables. He lifted his head as Tate approached.

"Hey, Tate. What's up, man?"

"Hey." Tate felt awkward being there, but he managed a smile.

Before he reached Donovan's office, the man stepped out, his eyes tracking every step he took.

"What's wrong?"

Tate should've expected he would think something was wrong. He wasn't the sort to drop in unannounced or even at all, for that matter.

"Nothing." He forced a smile as he stared at the sinfully beautiful man wearing charcoal slacks and a white button-down shirt with the sleeves rolled up.

"This is a nice surprise then." Donovan's eyes warmed. "Come in here."

Tate followed him into the office and waited while Donovan shut the door. He then flipped a switch, causing the glass walls to go from transparent to opaque in the blink of an eye.

Donovan tucked his hands in his pockets and stared down at him.

The man was gorgeous, but like this, he almost looked dangerous—sexy dangerous, though, not mobster dangerous.

Feeling out of sorts, Tate made his way to the black leather couch and sat, keeping to the edge of the cushion.

"I had breakfast with Reilly."

"Y'all finally come to a decision?"

Tate looked up at him and took a deep breath. "Kinda."

Donovan walked around the black-lacquered coffee table and perched on the arm of the couch. "I hope *kinda* means yes because, Tate, I wanna marry you. And I'd like to do it sooner rather than later."

"And you're okay with gettin' married in Vegas?" Skepticism made the words come out harsh, but Tate couldn't help it. He still didn't believe Donovan was okay with having a quickie wedding in Vegas rather than something traditional where all his family and friends could attend.

Donovan shifted down onto the cushion, moving closer to Tate.

"Baby, I need only two things to make a wedding perfect."

Tate swallowed hard. "What's that?"

"You and someone ordained to perform it, so it's legal."

"What about rings?"

One of his notorious sexy smirks tipped the corner of Donovan's mouth. "I got those before I even asked."

"You did?"

His expression turned serious. "This isn't pretend for me, Tate."

"It's not pretend for me either," he said quickly. "I want to marry you."

Donovan inched closer, gripping Tate's chin between his finger and thumb. His voice was rife with emotion when he said, "Then let's get married. Wherever. Whenever."

"In dinosaur costumes?"

That earned him a look of surprise.

Tate laughed, relaxing somewhat. "I'm kidding."

Donovan leaned in, his lips hovering over Tate's. "If costumes are your thing, I'm in."

Shaking his head adamantly, Tate laughed. "They're not."

"You sure?"

"I'd rather see you in a tux than a tutu."

Donovan's eyebrows popped toward his hairline. "Are you sure? I'd look damn fine in a tutu."

And just like that, relief swamped him. He had known Donovan Jameson for most of his life and the man wasn't the sort to say things to placate people. Tate doubted he would be happy about a tutu, but he got the gist.

"I want to marry you," Tate told Donovan, sliding his hand over his muscular forearm. "The sooner, the better."

"In Vegas?"

He nodded. "With Reilly and Brady."

Donovan kissed him. It was a soft, lingering press of his lips, but Tate swore he could taste Donovan's relief.

When he pulled back, his light green eyes seemed brighter. "Do you have a day in mind?"

"April," he said off the top of his head.

"April. Why April?"

"Because it's between now and June."

Donovan laughed. "So is March and May."

"Yeah, but April gives us time to plan."

"April it is. Do you have a day?"

"The first Saturday."

Donovan's smile grew wider. "I like it. Have you picked out a place?"

"Not yet. But we will. I'll get with Reilly."

Donovan ran a finger down Tate's jawline. "You and Reilly plan the wedding. Brady and I'll take care of the cost, as well as the accommodations."

Tate nodded because he wasn't sure what else to say.

"Now that we've got that outta the way…" Donovan banded his arms around him, pulling him closer as he leaned back. "Let's make out."

Tate laughed, but he didn't argue. He could spend eternity making out with this man and never tire of it.

Donovan's lips pressed against the shell of his ear. "Just make sure you're quiet. You don't want my employees to know I'm doin' wicked things to you in my office."

"Neither do you," Tate said, his cock thickening.

"Baby, you should know by now I don't give a fuck." He brushed a hand over Tate's hair as he peered up at him. "I can't get enough of you, and I don't care who knows."

Tate didn't ask Donovan to prove it.

But the man did anyway.

STONE STOOD ON ETHAN AND BEAU'S FRONT porch, waiting for someone to answer the door.

Beyond the wood, he could hear children laughing and the deep rumble of a male voice. He couldn't make out whether it was Ethan or Beau, but whoever it was sounded happy.

A second later, the door opened, and Beau appeared. He had one kid on his shoulders and one on each foot.

"Hey, man. You're just in time."

Stone looked up at the little boy who was using Beau's hair like reins, holding on tight. "For?"

Beau nudged the door open with his elbow. "We're buildin' a fort."

"A fort?" Stone walked inside, closing the door behind him.

Beau took large steps, keeping the kids on his feet from falling off. Every time he moved, one giant foot thudding on the hardwood, all three of them giggled.

"Tell your cousin Stone what that is," Beau said.

"Blanket fort!" they chimed merrily, two of them bounding up and running away.

Beau lifted the boy on his shoulders over his head and set him on the ground so he could join his brother and sister.

"Wow. They got big," Stone said, watching as Jack, Kiera, and Aiden tossed pillows onto the floor.

"They grow like weeds," Beau said. "Four years old, and they think they're ten."

"Daddy! Get in the fort!" Kiera summoned.

"In a minute, baby girl. Daddy's gotta talk to Stone for a bit." Beau motioned for Stone to follow. "Want a beer?"

"Sure."

Beau led the way deeper into the house, where they found Ethan. He was in the kitchen, oven mitts on his hands, reaching into the oven to pull out a large glass dish.

"Hope you like enchiladas," Ethan said.

"I like pretty much anything," Stone admitted. "Especially if I don't have to make it myself."

"Good answer." Ethan cast an amused look at Beau. "I'm married to someone like that."

"Hey, I'd make it if you'd let me." Beau looked at Stone. "The kitchen's off limits. He's the only one allowed to cook."

"Because the fire department had to come out the last time you did," Ethan countered.

"One time," Beau huffed. "And we needed to remodel the kitchen anyway."

Stone snorted, not sure whether to believe him. "Seriously?"

Ethan's eyes widened, and he nodded.

"It wasn't that bad," Beau said defensively.

"Of course not, baby," Ethan crooned. "The fire only took out one wall. There're plenty more."

Stone choked on a laugh when Ethan rolled his eyes and shook his head.

"The kids were at my mom's," Beau said, as though that needed to be clarified.

"He's not allowed to cook when they're home," Ethan added. "He's limited to sandwiches and the microwave."

Beau opened the refrigerator and pulled out three beers. On his way around the island, he paused in front of Ethan and kissed the man.

Stone had always admired Ethan and Beau's relationship. Although they'd had their share of ups and downs over the years, they'd found true happiness.

"Hey, munchkins!" Beau shouted. "Time to set the table."

An excited "Yay!" was followed by the thud of little footsteps as the triplets raced into the kitchen.

Stone watched in amused disbelief as the three kids did their duty of setting the table—plates, silverware, napkins—before he found himself being herded by three little kids eager to get their dinner on.

The meal reminded him of dinners when he was a kid. He'd done his share of chores alongside Donovan, CJ, and Chelsea. Reilly hadn't been forced to do as much of the work since she'd come along much later.

"The daddies need to talk to Stone," Ethan told the kids when they were finished. "Why don't y'all work on your puzzle for a little while."

"Yay!"

With that, they were off and running again.

"How do y'all keep up?" Stone asked, watching as the triplets raced out of the room, slipping and sliding in their socks.

"I'm younger than you," Beau said straight-faced.

"By a year," Ethan said.

"But he's not." Stone pointed at Ethan.

"By a year," Ethan countered again, reaching for his beer.

Beau winked at Ethan, then looked at Stone. "We've got a routine. Trust me, it takes work to keep them entertained, but we manage."

"One day, you'll know what it's like," Ethan noted.

"I hope so," Stone admitted.

"Yeah?" Beau shifted, giving him his full attention. "Things serious with you and Stevie?"

"And Nico," Stone added.

"Ah. Wow. I did *not* know that." Beau looked at Ethan. "How did I not know that?"

"Cause you spend your days watchin' *SpongeBob SquarePants.*"

"Hey, it's a good time for all ages," Beau said, straight-faced before looking at Ethan. "You knew?"

Ethan nodded.

Stone interrupted their back and forth. "My question is, how did *anyone* know?"

"Small town," they said in unison.

"Touché."

"So they're gonna go into business with you?" Ethan asked. "Farmers' market, right?"

"I take it y'all don't need me to give you my spiel?" he joked.

"We got the rundown from Sawyer. He's got a big mouth," Ethan stated as though that explained it all.

"I heard it from Braydon," Beau noted. "He's got a big mouth, too."

Stone laughed. "To answer your question, yeah, the plan is for them to go into business with me."

"I must admit, I like the idea," Ethan said. "I told Mom I thought it was brilliant."

He was surprised to hear that his aunt already knew about the plan. He probably shouldn't have been because, as they said, it was a small town, and he'd been talking about it with enough people that he knew the rumor had spread.

"So you're okay with it?" Stone asked, watching Ethan's expression closely. "With them giving me the land?"

"I damn sure don't want it," he countered. "Hell, I'm tryin' to convince Autumn to become a partner in the demo company."

"She's suggested more than once for him to take over," Beau explained. "From a management position."

"Nope." Ethan shook his head. "I'm a mechanic. I put in my ten hours and come home to my husband and kids. Where I prefer to be."

"He preferred it when I worked with him," Beau said, his eyes never leaving Ethan's face.

Ethan didn't bother denying it.

"Maybe one day I'll be back there," Beau said, glancing at Stone. "The kids'll start kindergarten soon. I won't know what to do with myself all alone in this house."

Stone was watching Ethan, so he saw the spark of hope that ignited.

He got it because the thought of working alongside Nico and Stevie every day caused warmth to churn in his chest, too.

"We're good with it, by the way," Ethan said. "With you takin' the land. At least it'll be in good hands."

"Thanks. I won't let Aunt Lorrie and Uncle Curtis down."

"They know that; otherwise, they wouldn't've made you the offer. Which is why *we* know that."

Stone took a pull on his beer, hoping it would wash down the lump that formed in his throat. That sentiment meant more to him than he expected.

THIRTY-SIX

Friday, February 16, 2024

"AND THAT'S WHERE I'M AT," STONE FINISHED, watching his parents, waiting for someone to say something.

He'd spent the past half hour laying out the proposal he would present to his aunt and uncle while his mom, dad, CJ, Donovan, Brady, and Reilly listened on with interest. The only person missing from the table was Tate because he was on shift. Or rather, he was the only regular attendee since Chelsea and Paul weren't close enough to have dinner on a weekly basis.

"Sounds to me like you've got it all figured out," his father said. "Now you just need to present it to Curtis and Lorrie."

Stone exhaled heavily. "I still need to talk to Zane."

His mother frowned. "Why haven't you?"

"He won't take my calls."

"Then track him down," Donovan said as though it was that simple.

"Looks like I'm gonna have to," he told his brother in order to avoid an argument. He didn't want to admit that he was frustrated to the point of exhaustion. His two weeks were now up, so he had to sit down with his aunt and uncle, and he was ready to do that without Zane's blessing. As far as he was concerned, his cousin was being a dick.

"Why's he avoidin' you?" Brady asked.

"Hell if I know."

"He has to have a reason," Reilly noted. "Zane's as cool as they come. I think D's right. You need to track him down. Find out what his issue is."

Stone never expected the voice of reason to come from his sister.

"So?" Reilly stared directly at him. "Are we done talkin' about you?"

He choked on a laugh because he should've known she was merely trying to tie his conversation up in a neat little bow so she could move on to more important things.

Stone waved a hand over the table. "The floor's all yours."

She smiled and pretended to take a bow from her chair. "Thank you, kind sir." She cleared her throat and looked at all the faces around the table.

Stone had always thought of Chelsea as the dramatic one. And that made Reilly the theatrical sister. She liked to build up a moment until the air expanded with expectation. Which was what she did, her smile growing wider by the second.

"On with it," CJ grumbled. "Some of us have plans after this."

Reilly laughed. "We're gettin' married."

Everyone looked at each other.

"That's not exactly news," Donovan noted with a grin.

Her next sentence had even more flair. "We're gettin' married … in Vegas!"

"Vegas." Owen stared at his daughter before shifting his gaze to his future son-in-law. "Really?"

Brady nodded, his expression neutral. "It gets better."

Deborah chimed in. "How so?"

"It's gonna be a double wedding," Reilly announced, her eyes locked on their mother.

Stone waited to see how Deborah would react. With her, it was impossible to predict. She was one of the most laid-back people Stone knew, but there were times when she put her foot down.

The pregnant pause from earlier returned. This time, it expanded until Stone thought for sure the walls would blow out from the anticipation.

"Mom?" Donovan frowned.

Deborah sniffled.

Uh-oh.

Stone was prepared to put his arm around her and console her, but it turned out that it wasn't necessary.

"That's wonderful," she sobbed, a tear leaking from her eye.

"Really?" CJ and Stone said at the same time, twice the amount of skepticism dripping from the word.

"Yes. I've always wanted to go to Vegas. Plus, my babies are gettin' married."

For the record, the babies in question were Reilly and Tate. For as long as Stone could remember, Deborah had seen Tate as one of her own.

"And why're *you* cryin'?" CJ asked their father.

Owen pretended to wipe away a tear. "Because I won't have to mortgage the house to pay for it."

Laughter erupted.

"When's this takin' place?" Owen asked when everyone calmed down.

"April sixth," Donovan said. "We'll let you all know when we finalize where."

Stone felt like a bug under a microscope when his mother turned her full attention on him, her eyebrows lifting. "And do you think we'll possibly get to enjoy the celebration with Stevie and Nico by then?"

His mouth opened and closed. He wasn't sure what to say to that.

"Maybe you should let him start with dinner first," Reilly said.

Deborah was still staring, so Stone managed to smile and nod. "Dinner would be better."

"Good. When?"

"I say Sunday," Reilly added cheerfully. "Tate'll be here, too."

Stone huffed a laugh. "You gotta give us a minute. I've only been back for a few weeks."

"Five," Reilly clarified, her smile wide as she glanced at their mother. "And he's only been seein' them for ninety percent of that."

He glared at her and mouthed, "Tattletale."

"What?" She giggled. "Just helpin' things along."

He looked at his mother again. "Soon, Mom. I promise."

She didn't need to say anything for Stone to know his mother was rooting for them. The fact that she didn't question that he was with both of them was a bit awkward. Then again, he wasn't the first in the family to venture into this sort of relationship, and he doubted he would be the last.

Two hours later, Stone was at Nico and Stevie's house, sitting on the couch with Stevie perched on his lap. If it weren't for the fact Jäger was camped out on *her* lap, he would've initiated something more than conversation.

However, he hadn't come over for sex, although he certainly wouldn't turn it down if the opportunity arose.

"When do you meet with Curtis and Lorrie?" Stevie asked, bringing up the subject Stone had been avoiding for the past half hour.

"Supposed to be tomorrow afternoon."

"Supposed to?" Nico asked.

"I haven't talked to Zane yet."

"He still avoidin' you?"

Stone nodded.

"Maybe you should just talk to them anyway," Stevie suggested. "Everything else is in line, right?"

"Almost."

Nico frowned. "What else are you waitin' for?"

"A final answer."

Stevie shifted, staring into his face. "From?"

"The two of you," he said pointedly.

Silence descended for a moment, expanding to the point of discomfort.

Finally, Nico spoke up from where he was leaning back on the other end of the couch. "Maybe I missed somethin', but I didn't realize there *was* a question."

He was partially right because Stone hadn't asked him directly if he would go into business with him. When he'd had the discussion, he'd laid it out with Stevie in mind since he intended to incorporate her dreams into his grand plan.

"Stone?" Stevie tapped his chin. "What's the question?"

He took a deep breath and looked at Nico. "I'd like the three of us to do this together, so I need to know whether you're on board with that."

"I already have a business," Nico stated.

"You do, and I'm not askin' you to turn your back on it. I'm just lookin' for your support. If either of you has a problem with it, I need to know."

"You don't need our approval," Stevie said.

Stone looked at her. "I do, actually."

"Why?"

"Because I'd like to take this"—he waved his hand between the three of them—"to the next level."

More silence. More discomfort.

Again, Nico cut through it. "What *is* the next level?"

Stone heard the confusion in his tone. It matched the expression on Stevie's face.

"Forever," he stated bluntly, then held his breath, waiting for either of them to say something.

They didn't.

And then they still didn't.

"Or maybe I'm jumpin' the gun," he drawled, suddenly self-conscious about bringing it up.

Stevie looked at Nico.

Nico looked at Stevie.

"Okay, now it's just awkward." Stone shifted to move Stevie off his lap, prepared to leave so they could talk about whatever they needed to talk about. Obviously, they weren't on the same page as he was.

Stevie moved quickly, putting Jäger on the cushion between them and Nico. She resisted his efforts to move her off his lap.

"You don't get to run away, Stone."

"I'm not runnin'." He exhaled heavily. "I'm just ... tired."

"Good."

His eyebrows rose. "Good?"

"Mmm-hmm. Because there's nothin' you need to do but sit down."

"Mentally tired," he clarified.

He knew building a business took effort. It took hard work and dedication. Stone had never expected it would be easy. But he also hadn't anticipated that merely getting to the point where he could possibly start a business would be so taxing. He'd spent the past two weeks coming up with a projection for the future. At this point, it was conjecture, and he had nothing to show for it except for a fucking PowerPoint presentation. He'd only had seven boxes to check off and hadn't even completed that task. Perhaps he wasn't cut out for this like he thought he was.

"I can't speak for Nico," Stevie said, her tone soft, almost comforting. "But I'm in this with you. If that's still what you want."

Stone attempted to relax, placing his hands on her hips when she straddled his legs, facing him. "More than anything."

But he wasn't talking about the business plan. "I want it all, Stevie."

Her eyes implored him to continue.

"I want to build a future with the two of you." He glanced at Nico. "I've wasted too much time already. I've missed out on fifteen years because I was too stupid to realize everything I wanted was right in front of me."

Nico continued to stare, not speaking. Hell, Stone wasn't sure the guy was even breathing.

"If it feels too fast"—he looked at Stevie—"you need to tell me."

"It doesn't."

He pressed his fingertips into her hips. "Are you sure?"

It was clear from her expression that she was confused.

"If this business plan doesn't work," he explained, "then I'll find somethin' else. The only thing I know for certain is that I'll be here." He held her stare for a moment. "I need to know you trust me when I say that."

She hesitated, and Stone instantly knew they weren't on the same page yet. Before he could tell her he'd give her some space to think about it, Stevie leaned forward, cupping his face.

"I trust you, Stone."

She didn't. He knew she didn't. She'd said that as much for his benefit as for her own. He hated that she was trying to convince herself he was telling the truth.

At the same time, he wasn't willing to upset the balance of what they were building. It took time. He knew that. And he had a lot to atone for. He was willing to commit to making it up to her if it took the next sixty years.

But right now, he was tired. Too tired to fight, too tired to argue, and too tired to defend himself.

He broke eye contact with her and sighed. "I should probably head home. It's gettin' late. Y'all have to work tomorrow."

"Stay," they said at the same time.

Stevie cut her gaze to Nico. "Jinx, you owe me a cock."

Stone snorted in disbelief. *That* was not how the game was played, but he had to give her points for creativity.

Nico's eyes flashed with lust. "Darlin', you don't even have to ask."

And for a moment—albeit brief—the tension disappeared, and Stone felt at peace.

Nico wasn't sure how they'd gotten onto this subject.

Not the cock part. *That* he expected because Stevie was the sort of woman who went after what she wanted. Her little *faux pas* hadn't surprised him, which said a lot about how well he knew her. Stevie had a way of shifting the difficult conversations to a topic she was more comfortable with. And sex was one of her go-to's.

"I think I'm gonna take a bath," she said now, sitting up straight and stretching. When she put her arms down, she planted her hands on Stone's broad chest. "But only if you promise to stay."

Nico felt Stone's gaze when it swung toward him, so he nodded. "Stay."

"It's settled." Stevie hopped up off the couch. "If I come back to find you gone, I'll hunt you down and kick your ass."

Stone held up his hands in surrender. "Don't wanna risk that."

She flashed a grin at Nico as she pranced out of the room. Jäger trotted along behind her, content to go wherever she went.

Nico knew how the puppy felt. Being with Stevie was a comfort he'd never expected. One he'd gotten used to over the past several months.

When her footsteps receded down the hall, Stone looked his way.

"I do need an answer."

Nico had wondered if they would be having this conversation. Not the business one. He honestly wasn't sure what role he could play in Stone's plan, but he was willing to pitch in however he needed because they were on the same page when it came to the direction their relationship was going. Forever was his end goal, and as long as Stevie and Stone were moving in the same direction, Nico intended to match their pace. Fast or slow, he didn't care. As long as he had forever.

But rather than explain it as it pertained to business terms, Nico pounced on a different one. "I love you."

Stone's eyes slammed into his face and remained there as the seconds ticked by, the rapid thump of his heart the only sound in the room.

The tension ratcheted, growing taut with every breath. Stone didn't say anything, but he didn't look away. Nico wasn't sure what that meant or what to expect. He wished he could read Stone's mind, know what he was thinking.

It felt like an hour, but only a few seconds passed when everything came into focus as Stone moved. Nico's gaze was fixed in portrait mode, blurring out everything in the background except for Stone's face, the hard line of his jaw, the slight slant of his nose, and the desire that burned brilliantly in his hazel eyes.

Before he knew what was happening, he was flat on his back, Stone laid out over him, half his body covering Nico's while the other half lay on the cushion beside him.

Stone's finger pressed firmly into his jaw, urging him to look at him. Nico expected something with a sexual connotation to come out of Stone's mouth. The man was good at spotlighting the moment, drawing it out for long minutes.

Instead, his voice was ragged and soft when he said, "I love you, too."

They remained like that, staring at each other, Stone's warm body heavy on top of him. Nico's chest felt tight, the words—and the sentiment with which they were delivered—surprising in their intensity.

Stone leaned forward, their lips pressing together. Softly, gently. There was no tongue, only a brief moment that stood still as Stone's hand flattened on his cheek, and they shared the same air.

"That's all I need," Stone whispered. "The rest is easy as long as I know where I stand with you."

Nico was shocked to think Stone didn't already know. Maybe they hadn't said the words aloud, but the moments they'd shared these past few weeks had come with their own soundtrack, a ballad that connected past to present to future. Nico had let himself fall into them without reservation because he'd always suspected he could love this man. He did. He knew that as well as he knew the sun would rise in the morning.

"I want to spend the rest of my life with you and Stevie," Stone continued.

Nico touched him, wrapping his arm around Stone simply so he could feel more of him. He put his free hand on Stone's face, his thumb brushing the stubble on his jaw. Neither moved, but the tension, weighted with passion and need, grew thick around them.

"Love me, Stone," Nico whispered.

Stone lifted his head, his eyes dark with arousal and something else. Something more powerful. Nico felt it in the depths of his soul.

A second later, Stone was getting to his feet. He took Nico's hand and pulled him up, then dragged him down the hall to his bedroom. The moment they stepped inside, time sped up. Stone crashed against him, holding him, kissing him. Their mouths sought the other, teeth clashing as their clothes disappeared.

"Nothin' between us," Stone whispered, but Nico could see the question in his eyes: *condom or bareback?*

"No barriers," Nico agreed, desperate to feel Stone.

The only time they paused was so Stone could prepare them both. And then Stone was leaning over him on the bed, his cock pressed right where Nico needed him. Their eyes locked and held as Stone pushed inside him. Inch by inch, Nico accepted everything the man was willing to give him.

It was everything Nico had ever imagined and so much more. The two of them together as one. Rough and dirty, taking a backseat to sweet surrender. The lack of aggression did nothing to lessen the intensity. It was brutally beautiful in its simplicity, and Nico wished it would never end.

"I want to love you like this forever," Stone whispered, his voice rough, his hands gentle even as he manipulated Nico's body, contorting it so his cock went deeper.

Nico knew Stone wasn't referring to the physical act because that was secondary at the moment, a way for them to be connected, but it wasn't what was pulling them together. Sex didn't feel this good. It just didn't. This was far more than their bodies joining.

"Every day," Stone whispered, pushing in slow and deep, retreating just as languidly.

The pleasure consumed him, taking over not only his body but also his mind. It was exquisite torture.

"For the rest of my life, Nico. You and Stevie ... with me ... it's all I want."

Nico felt the same. With the two of them, he was finally complete.

Stone shifted again, lifting up, maneuvering Nico's leg to the side so that his torso was twisted. Then Stone was leaning over him again, his fist planted into the mattress beside Nico's head, the other between his legs, stroking him as he fucked him.

"I wanna wake you up like this." Stone's voice was ragged and choppy, his eyes glittering.

"Yes," Nico rasped, digging his fingers into the hard muscle of Stone's ass, urging him deeper.

"Come for me, Nico," Stone grunted, his breath hot against his face as he drove them both closer to the cliff's edge.

"Tell me again," Nico pleaded, needing to hear the words.

"I ... want ... you," Stone whispered, his words punctuated by the thrust of his hips.

Those weren't the words he wanted to hear.

"I … crave … you."

"Stone…"

"I … need … you."

He was getting warmer.

Nico's spine tingled as Stone drilled inside him, fucking him deeper than he'd ever been fucked before.

"Stone … please…"

"I … love … you."

Nico let go, soaring into the ether as his release shattered him.

"Fuck," Stone growled, his forehead resting on Nico's temple, his cock sinking in one final time. "I love you."

Nico gasped, gripping Stone's arm as he felt the pulse of his cock deep inside him.

"I love you, too."

When oxygen returned to his cells and he could breathe easier again, Nico knew everything had changed in that moment. There was no questioning anymore. He was in love with this man as deeply as he was in love with Stevie. He felt complete for the first time in his life.

And while he was willing to accept it, there was still a niggling of doubt that he couldn't erase. He prayed it wasn't a sign of what was to come but merely an echo of the past that hadn't been erased completely.

Nico slept that night, soundly with Stevie and Stone in his bed, completely oblivious to the invisible hand that gripped the proverbial rug, eager and ready to pull it right out from under them all.

THIRTY-SEVEN

Saturday, February 17, 2024

STONE SPENT THE NEXT MORNING WALKING ON air. His thoughts drifted back to last night over and over, the movie reel in his head on repeat. His connection with Nico solidifying, punctuated by that moment when it had been hard to breathe because he was consumed by a love so intense, it threatened to steal the air from his lungs. Stevie returning to find them crumpled in the bed together, drawing out the moment when she settled between them, content to simply be for a little while.

And when morning came, Stone felt like he could conquer the world.

Unfortunately, the feeling only lasted until mid-afternoon, when he was getting ready to head out to run a few errands. As he was walking out the door, his cell phone rang.

He dragged it out of his pocket and glanced at the screen.

"Hey, Uncle Curtis," he greeted, unable to hide his good mood. "I was about to call you. Thought maybe I could swing by in an hour. I've got the proposal ready for your review."

"So you've talked to Zane?"

Stone hedged momentarily, trying to figure out the correct answer to the question. He opted to be straightforward. "No, actually. I've tried numerous times. He won't return my calls."

Curtis's heavy sigh felt weighted even through the phone.

Stone stood outside his truck, staring up at the brilliant blue sky. "What's wrong?"

"I had a feelin' he wasn't tellin' me everything."

"What does that mean? Who?"

"Zane." Curtis sighed again.

"Is he there? I can come by right now and talk to him."

"No. I haven't seen him in a coupla days. The boy texted me."

"Do you know where he is?" At this point, Stone was willing to track him down if it took all fucking day.

"I don't. He did mention he's meetin' Beau at Moonshiners in a coupla hours."

Stone swallowed because he could hear what his uncle *wasn't* telling him. Zane was the lone holdout. More than likely, his brothers had shared what was going on with him, but he wasn't as open to the idea as the rest of them.

"I can still come by the house," Stone said.

"Stone, I think—"

"I'll talk to Zane," he inserted, refusing to let Curtis shut this down because Zane was being stubborn.

It was one thing for Zane to reject the plan, but since he hadn't heard it for himself, he didn't get to do that. Not yet.

"I'll head over to Moonshiners in a little while," Stone continued. "And I'll call you after. Let you know how it went."

A grunt was his uncle's response.

"I'll talk to you in a bit," Stone told him, disconnecting the call before Curtis could say anything more.

Two hours later, Stone walked into Moonshiners. The lightness he'd felt after last night had dissipated in the face of anxiety. He could feel his opportunity slipping away, and he wasn't even privy to the reason. That was what irked him the most. Almost anytime there'd been a big issue in his life, he could chalk it up to someone—himself included—being too damn stubborn to talk about it.

It was time to rectify that with Zane.

Stone skimmed the dim interior of the bar, searching all the familiar faces and the ones he didn't recognize until he landed on Zane. His cousin was sitting in one of the booths along the side wall, his back to the door. Aside from the beer sitting on the table before him, he was alone.

Not anymore.

Stone took the opportunity to grab a beer at the bar before he walked over.

"Mind if I sit?" he prompted, not waiting for Zane to answer before he slid into the booth.

His cousin's expression remained pleasantly neutral.

"It's been a minute," Stone told him. "How're you doin'?"

"Good. You?" Zane's tone was remarkably dry. Not an ounce of emotion in it.

This was how they were going to play it? Their words cordial, but the underlying frustration simmering like a live wire? No thank you.

"I talked to your dad earlier," Stone explained. "He mentioned you'd be here."

Zane nodded, tilting his beer to his lips. "Congrats. You found me."

"It took me a while."

"You get lost or what?"

Stone heard the animosity but couldn't understand where it was coming from. For the past few days, he'd spent too much time trying to figure out Zane's motivation. No matter how far back he went in his memories, he couldn't recall anything happening that would've triggered anyone to ghost him the way Zane was. Well, maybe Stevie or Nico, but he was directly responsible for what happened between them.

As much as he wanted to pretend it was merely timing that had prevented this conversation from taking place, Stone wasn't in the mood for games. So, he got right to the heart of the matter.

"You've been avoidin' me."

Zane set his beer on the table. "Not really. I just didn't have anything to say to you."

"I don't need you to say anything," Stone countered, trying to keep his frustration from slipping out of his mouth and into his words. "But I'd appreciate you listening."

"Not interested," Zane blurted.

"What the fuck is your problem?"

Zane's eyebrows slammed down, his blue-gray eyes glittering with unleashed anger. "You. You're my fuckin' problem, Stone."

Stone usually expected some sort of weather warning before a tornado like that one blew through. Still, he held his ground. "What the hell did I do?"

Zane snorted and rolled his eyes.

"Tell me," Stone insisted.

Zane leaned forward, his voice low and dangerous. "You want the whole list? Or just the highlights?"

"I want the fuckin' truth," Stone snapped back. "That'd be a good start."

"Why don't we start with how you blew outta town without a fuckin' word."

Stone was shocked by the adamance in his cousin's tone. "Without a fuckin' word to who?"

"Oh, I don't know. Your mom. My mom."

Stone frowned. "What're you talkin' about?"

"Don't play dumb, Stone. It's beneath you."

"I have no fuckin' idea what you're talkin' about."

"Of course you don't because you rewrote history to suit your objective."

Stone set down his beer, staring at Zane, trying to figure out who the fuck ushered him through a door into an alternate universe because seriously? Assuming Zane was referring to when Stone left fifteen years ago, he thought back to the conversation he'd had with his parents before he left. He'd sat down with them and explained what he wanted to do. No, he didn't tell them his full reasons for wanting to leave or what happened between him, Stevie, and Nico, but he did sit down with them. His mother had been upset but understanding. His father had been supportive, reminding him he always had a place to come back to when he was ready.

"So why're you back, Stone? You hear through the grapevine that my parents were lookin' to do somethin' with their land? You thought it would be the perfect opportunity to swoop in? Think this'll be your big break?"

His knee-jerk reaction would've been to tell Zane to go fuck himself. However, Stone knew that wasn't the right thing to do. Stevie was right when she said Zane was as laid-back as they came, so his animosity was out of left field. He obviously had a reason.

"I didn't go to them about the land," he explained, trying to keep his tone calm. "They called me."

"Oh, I know. But you jumped right on it, didn't you?"

Stone frowned, opting for complete honesty. "You're damn right I did. But I'm not expectin' a fuckin' handout. I'm puttin' in the work."

"Sure you are." Zane sucked down the rest of his beer. "Then what? How long will it be before you get bored and leave again?"

"Bored? Is that why you think I left?"

"And hopped from job to job," Zane tacked on. "I've heard my mother talkin' over the years. They call you the wanderer. Always movin' from place to place. Incapable of stayin' put. How long will it last this time? A month? A year? Two?"

"What the fuck do you care?" Stone retorted.

"Because that land belongs to *my* family. Not yours."

Ouch.

Stone exhaled, the wind successfully knocked out of him. "I didn't realize we came from two different ones, Zane."

For the first time, he saw a hint of remorse in Zane's eyes. "You know what I mean."

"Actually, I don't." Stone sighed. "But it doesn't matter to you, does it? You've made up your mind. I'm not a Walker; therefore, I'm just an outsider. Never mind that *my* family's been here as long as yours." Stone squared his shoulders, lowered his voice, and pinned Zane with a stare. "And never mind that you're just as much a Jameson as you are a fuckin' Walker. Or did you forget that part? That your mom is my dad's sister."

Zane's lips pursed, his anger simmering once again. At least it'd come down from a full boil. Problem was, Stone knew there was nothing he could say or do to convince his cousin that his anger was misplaced. If there was anyone more stubborn than a Jameson, it was a Walker.

Stone shifted to the end of the seat, prepared to walk away. "Thanks for nothin', Zane."

He made it several steps before Zane called out, "Wait."

He pivoted, hating himself for hanging on to that single thread of hope that his cousin would somehow recognize he was being a royal douche.

"I'll hear you out," Zane told him, staring at his beer bottle. "But first, I wanna call your previous employer. If they give you a good reference, I'll listen to what you have to say."

Stone rolled his eyes. No way in hell Doug Johnson was going to say anything nice about him. Not after the way things went down. But he figured Zane already knew that. The rumor mill worked fast in this small town. More than likely, Zane had heard the story already.

Since he had nothing left to lose, Stone decided to let it play out.

"Fine." He pulled out his phone and sent the contact information to Zane's phone. "That's the number. Talk to anyone you want."

With that, he turned and walked out.

CURTIS WAS SITTING ON THE FRONT PORCH when Zane's truck pulled down his driveway. He didn't need to talk to the boy to know he was still in a foul mood. He could tell by the way he slammed on the brakes and jumped out that whatever happened between him and Stone hadn't resolved a damn thing.

As astute as he was, though, Curtis had no idea why Zane was hellbent on shutting Stone out. For the past week, he'd listened to one or more of his boys talk excitedly about Stone's plans for the land. They were genuinely looking forward to this farmers' market idea. Everyone except Zane, who'd made his feelings known from the moment he learned that they were planning to part with the land.

"Hey, Pop," Zane grumbled as he stomped up the front steps.

Curtis watched him, silently feeling him out. He knew it was only a matter of time before his pent-up anger spewed out.

"I talked to Stone," Zane said as he flopped into the chair beside him.

"And?"

"I told him I won't support it."

"It?"

Zane waved a hand. "His plan."

"Which is?"

Zane shrugged. "It doesn't matter. It's not a good idea."

"Your brothers think it is."

"Yeah, well. They don't know Stone like I do."

Curtis couldn't keep the wry smile from forming. "And just how well do you know him? He's been gone for fifteen years."

"Exactly." Zane's eyebrows slammed down. "He's not back because he wants to be here. He's back because he has nowhere else to go. I'm not lettin' him leave us holdin' the bag when he slinks outta here again."

"Did he say he was leavin'?"

"It's a given, ain't it? If he wanted to be here, he would've come back a long time ago. Instead, he was out there screwin' up, tryin' to get somethin' for nothin'. It backfired, and now he's crawlin' back lookin' for a handout." Zane shook his head. "Not happenin', Pop. The land belongs to the Walkers. He's not a Walker."

Curtis's shoulders stiffened. "He's a Jameson."

Zane stared out into the distance. "Exactly. *Not* a Walker."

"Your mama's a Jameson."

"Used to be," Zane corrected. "Not anymore."

Curtis snorted a laugh. "You probably shouldn't let her hear you say that."

Zane's gaze cut to him. "Why? It's true. She's been a Walker far longer than she was a Jameson."

He let out a booming laugh. "You honestly believe that, don't you?" He glared at his boy. "Because she took my name, you think she disowned her family?"

Zane stared.

"If you think that's how it works, son, you haven't been payin' attention for the past thirty-four years." Before Zane could argue, Curtis continued. "Your mama took my name, but she's still got five sisters and three brothers."

"Two sisters," Zane corrected.

"Five," Curtis insisted.

"Adele, Celeste, and Katherine are dead, Pop."

"So when I'm gone, you gonna use that little eraser of yours and get rid of me too?"

"Of course not," he snapped.

Curtis raised his eyebrows, waiting for his boy to see how unreasonable he was being. He knew Zane was smarter than that. The problem was he was holding a grudge for a reason, and Curtis suspected it had nothing to do with this ridiculous notion that they were somehow the Hatfields and McCoys. There might've been some animosity between the two families at one point, but that sat squarely on his old man's shoulders. Frank Walker, Sr, hadn't liked anyone and never cared who knew it. Toss Lorrie's father, Phillip Jameson, into the pot, and the two mix like oil and water.

But the feud the Walkers had with this town ended when his old man died. Curtis had spent the better part of his adult life trying to make things right.

"What's really goin' on here, Zane?"

Zane sighed, once again staring out into the distance.

Curtis didn't urge him to answer. He knew he would eventually. Until then, he sipped his coffee and listened to the birds chirping.

"He left, Pop. And he hurt a lotta people when he did."

"Like who?"

"Aunt Deborah, Uncle Owen. Donovan, Reilly, CJ, Chelsea." He paused. "Mom."

"They missed him. Rightfully so. But he made a life for himself."

"Then why's he back?"

"It was time."

"Time for what? To swoop in because there's an opportunity to be had?" Zane huffed again. "How long until he leaves again? Makes Mom and Aunt Deborah cry all over again."

"Why would they cry?"

"They cried the last time."

Curtis chuckled. "Your mama cried last week because some ol' boy died on that TV show she likes. She does that."

"That's different."

"Maybe." Curtis shifted so he could look at Zane. "Stone didn't come back because there was an opportunity. He came back because this is where he belongs."

"And because he's gettin' a handout."

"You think that's what this is? A handout?"

"Yeah, Pop. I do. He's not gonna work for it."

"Why not?"

"He's not reliable."

"Is that somethin' you learned firsthand or another of your many assumptions?"

Zane's cheeks darkened, his anger bubbling up. "I called the Double J Ranch, Pop, so yeah, I know firsthand. They said he up and disappeared on them. Slipped out in the middle of the night."

"Who said?"

"The owner."

"Doug?"

Zane shook his head. "The daughter. Leah. She said Stone's unreliable."

"She happen to mention she wanted to marry him, and he wasn't interested?"

"Marry him?" Zane's shock was obvious. "What?"

"You might wanna talk to Stone a little more. Maybe get both sides of the story first."

Zane huffed and shot to his feet. "It doesn't matter, Pop. My answer's no, and it ain't gonna change."

Curtis didn't try to stop him when he stormed off. He knew his boy. Whatever this was really about would come to light soon enough.

Fifteen minutes later, Curtis strolled into the house.

"Smells good in here. Whatcha makin'?"

"Brownies."

Oh, man. His wife knew that brownies were his favorite. Especially when she made them.

"I heard you two out there," Lorrie said softly as he rinsed his coffee mug in the sink and tucked it into the dishwasher.

"How much of it?" He hoped she hadn't heard the part about—

"I'm still a Jameson," she acknowledged.

Curtis smiled. His beautiful bride's eyesight might be showing the effects of age but not her hearing.

"I told him as much." He leaned against the counter and dried his hands with the towel. "He's usin' this *us against them* mentality as an excuse."

"I know it."

He set the towel on the counter. "Do you also know what's really botherin' him?"

Lorrie looked up, her pretty blue eyes shining with sadness. "Zane always thought Stone and CJ hung the moon."

Curtis gripped the counter, watching her work.

"When they were kids, he followed those boys everywhere."

Maybe he was getting old because he didn't remember that. "They're older than he is."

"Not by much. And not enough that he didn't hang around with 'em when he could."

Since Owen was the youngest of her siblings, Lorrie had always been protective of her baby brother. Because of that, they spent more time with Owen and Deborah than they did with the rest of the Jameson clan, but back in the day, the kids had been close—all of them. It had more to do with living in a small town than their families being tight-knit, though.

"You think that's what this is?" he asked his wife. "Or you think he wants the land and just didn't tell us?"

Lorrie shook her head. "Not that. I asked him if he wanted it. He said no."

"Maybe he lied."

"I don't think so. He's happy at the resort. He gets to work with V every day. I don't think he'd trade it for anything."

That was the impression Curtis had been under, too. And he'd tried to convince the boys the land would be good for a lot of things. None of them wanted it, though. That was the reason they'd offered it to Stone. He knew the boy would do right by it.

It hadn't been an easy decision either. Especially since they knew Donovan was looking to buy more land in town to build more houses. As much as Curtis wanted to support the boy, he didn't want to see Coyote Ridge turn into a housing community like the ones popping up all around them. They had set aside another tract on the outskirts that he intended to give Donovan, but he was holding onto it so he could give it as a wedding present when the time came.

Lorrie's soft hand pressed gently to his chest, pulling him out of his thoughts. He peered down at her.

"It's gonna work itself out. I promise."

"I know, darlin'. I just wish I could do somethin' to move it along."

"How about some brownies and milk in the meantime?"

He smiled at his beautiful bride of sixty years. "I'm thinkin' maybe I should whisk you off to the bedroom while they cool down."

Her smile lit up her face. "I wouldn't say no to a nap."

He chuckled. "Honey, I don't plan to let you sleep."

"You never do."

THIRTY-EIGHT

Tuesday, February 20, 2024

"Have you talked to Stone?"

Nico looked up from his computer when Stevie strolled into his office.

"Not today, no. Why?"

"He's not respondin' to my texts."

"At all?"

She shrugged. "One-word responses don't count."

"Depends on the question."

She rolled her eyes. "I'm serious. That's all I've gotten since Saturday."

Nico didn't want to tell her that was all he'd gotten in the past three days, too. He hadn't seen Stone since he left their house on Saturday morning, but he'd traded a few texts back and forth. Nothing of substance, but he figured that was because they'd said all they needed to say on Friday night. They were in a good place now. Or so he'd thought.

"If it makes you feel better, I'll swing by his place when I go out there this afternoon. I'm meetin' Deborah to get things scheduled. You wanna come with me?"

Stevie shook her head, still leaning against the doorjamb, feigning a nonchalance he could tell she didn't feel. "Can't. I've got meetings all day."

It was that time of year. As they inched closer to spring, things would pick up, especially the design consultations. Stevie met with clients to get an idea of what they wanted before handing the file off to him for the preliminary design. The system was one Stevie set up a long time ago, and it worked for them.

He wondered if they would still do that when she went into business with Stone. Would she have time? Would she even want to do it?

Those were just a couple of the questions that had been running through his mind the past few days. He hoped to sit down with Stevie and Stone in the coming days so they could sort through how this would work. He wanted to ensure they didn't get in over their heads on either side, so he figured it would help to set some guidelines in the beginning.

It was still surreal to think this was happening. That they were going to tackle another enormous endeavor together. This time, the three of them. If he were being honest, he would admit it was terrifying in a sense. It was also exciting, and he was doing his best not to confuse the two things.

"I'll check in with him," Nico promised Stevie. "Want me to invite him to dinner?"

She shrugged, her expression sheepish. "If you want to."

He pushed his chair back from his desk. "That's not what I asked."

Her big brown eyes widened as he stepped around his desk and moved toward her.

"I asked if you wanted me to invite him." Nico stopped directly in front of her, ignoring personal boundaries because he could. And when she looked at him the way she was now—eyes wide, chewing on her bottom lip—he could practically see the X-rated thoughts running through her mind.

He couldn't get enough of her. It didn't matter that they now shared the same bed every night or worked in the same office every day. Nico wanted more. More of her time, more of her touch. He was addicted to her. Probably always had been, but he'd been too stubborn to admit it to himself.

And just like Stone, Nico was ready for the next phase of their relationship. He was ready to jump in with both feet. Not just with Stevie. He wanted the same with Stone. More time. More touch. More everything. He simply didn't know how to broach the subject. They'd been moving fast, or so it seemed. At the same time, it felt like they were wading in quicksand, moving nowhere.

Nico cocked an eyebrow. "Yes or no?"

"Yes," Stevie said, a shiver vibrating her small frame when he put his hands on her hips.

"Yes, what?"

"Invite him to dinner."

"Maybe we should make him invite us," Nico teased, leaning in, aching to fuse his mouth to hers.

"Maybe we should," she whispered, her hands flattening on his chest.

God, he could get lost in her so easily. He could spend hours ignoring what needed to get done simply so he could—

Someone cleared their throat.

Nico glanced over to see Tara standing a few feet away. She was looking at the floor as though that offered them the privacy they'd thought they had.

Stevie giggled, then went up on her toes and kissed him. Softly, quickly.

"Need somethin'?" Nico asked her.

"Rex and Jack are here," Tara explained. "They have an appointment."

"First of many," Stevie said as she slipped out from where he'd caged her against the wall. "Let me know what Stone says."

Nodding, Nico watched as she walked away.

STONE SAT ON THE COUCH, STARING AT the television's black screen. He'd hardly moved for the past three days, choosing to wallow in his frustration rather than tackle it head-on. Whenever he thought about what he needed to do next, he always came back around to the conversation he had with Zane on Saturday. The conversation that felt like the exclamation point on an exhausting journey to nowhere.

Without Zane's support, he had nothing.

Not yet, anyway.

Yeah, it frustrated him to no end that his cousin was being a belligerent asshole, but Stone wasn't giving up. That said, he wasn't beyond feeling sorry for himself for a bit. He'd failed. Epically. What made it worse was that he didn't know what he'd done to piss Zane off so thoroughly. Perhaps his memory was fading around the edges, but he could only remember good times with Zane. They'd been close at one time. Relatively speaking. Zane was two years younger, but not too young that he hadn't spent his fair share of time with the guy when they were kids.

Zane was the youngest of seven, and back then, Stone remembered him as the one seeking attention from anyone who would give it. His brothers had given him a hard time, but that was what they did. Stone remembered stepping in, hanging out with Zane and CJ because they always had a good time when they did, but not enough to warrant the sort of reaction he'd gotten from the guy on Saturday.

Stone wasn't going to let it get him down forever. He merely needed another plan. He had far too much going for him to give up now. Stevie and Nico were the only motivation he needed, and he was determined to prove to them that he was worthy of their love. So what if this plan failed? He could easily come up with another. He just needed to get out there and look around.

"Not gonna get it done from the couch, Jameson," he grumbled, sighing as he shifted to the edge of the cushion, prepared to get to his feet and do … something.

He exhaled and looked around, hoping something would spur him into action.

The sound of an engine coming closer to the barn had him getting to his feet. He had pulled the shades on the front of the barn to block out the world for a few days, so he could only speculate about who might be there. If he were lucky, it would be Donovan. He'd been trading messages with him for the past couple of days, seeking his older brother's input on how to go about course-correcting now that he'd been shot down so thoroughly. Donovan had told him he'd give it some thought and get back to him.

Or maybe Nico was dropping by to check on him. They hadn't talked much because Stone wasn't ready to tell him that his dream was dead before it even got off the ground. He intended to tell them both, but he wanted to have a backup plan before then.

The engine shut off, so Stone headed for the door. At least he'd gotten dressed, so he didn't look quite as pathetic as he felt.

He opened the door and stepped out onto the porch, only to come to a dead stop when he saw the woman strolling toward him. Her golden hair was pulled back into a ponytail, her brown eyes glittering with excitement.

Unfortunately, the brown-eyed blonde wasn't the one he wanted to see. Quite the opposite, actually.

Leah Johnson stopped at the bottom of the steps, presumably for dramatic effect since her beaming smile didn't waver. "Well, well, well. Long time no see, stranger."

"Leah." Stone stared at his former employer's daughter. "What're you doin' here?"

"Hello to you, too." She flashed a smile, her glossy lips glistening in the late afternoon sunlight.

Stone was at a loss for words, so he stared at her as she took the steps one at a time, slowly approaching. Her smile amplified a few megawatts with every thud of her boots on the wood.

"Miss me?" Her voice dropped an octave, taking on that silly rasp she used when she was trying to seduce him.

Because he didn't want to be a complete dick, he avoided telling her the truth and went with, "Why are you here?"

She fluttered her lashes. "Don't play dumb. I know you had that guy call because you were hopin' I'd chase you down and ask you to come back."

"What guy?"

Her pencil-thin eyebrows lifted. "Seriously, Stone? I thought we were past this."

"Past what?" He was sincerely confused. Both by her presence and her reasoning.

Leah leaned in. "Invite me inside, Stone. It's cold out here."

He didn't want to invite her in. Hell, he didn't want to engage in conversation with her. After the stunt she pulled with the shotgun, Stone had left the Double J hoping never to see her again.

"Fine. Be rude," she whispered, her smile widening as she slipped past him and into the barn.

Fuck.

Resigning himself to dealing with this shit show, he turned and followed. He left the door open despite the cold breeze that came in with him.

"Wow. This is ... nice."

Based on her tone, his living space was one level up from a cardboard box on a street corner.

"Leah. Why are you here?" He drawled the words out slowly, trying to rein in his temper.

"Would you mind closin' the door?" She rubbed her arms. "It's cold in here."

His manners prevented him from telling her she wouldn't be there long enough for him to care whether she was cold. He closed the door and shored up his nerve before he turned around.

"That's better. Thank you." Leah sighed, then put her hands on her hips as she turned to face him. Her expression was no longer playful. "I've got a proposition for you, Stone. And I think you're gonna want to sit down for this."

Reilly pulled down her parents' driveway, stopping beside the D & S Landscape truck parked near the walkway leading to the front door.

Her mother had mentioned she had an appointment with Nico this week. Something about finalizing the details for the changes she wanted to make to the front yard. Reilly figured it was more like a ploy to get Nico and/or Stevie over to the house so her mother could interrogate the people Stone was clearly getting cozy with.

Okay, maybe that wasn't her mother's intention, but it certainly was hers, which was why she'd timed this impromptu visit to coincide with that appointment.

As she strolled up the path to the front porch, she checked out the flowerbeds. Her mother's yard—both front and back—had always been the highlight of the neighborhood. Why she thought she needed a designer to help out was beyond her. Between the various water features—her favorite was the wagon wheel that slowly turned as each cup filled and weighed it down—and the variety of flowers and shrubs, there wasn't much that could be done to improve it.

Reilly stopped suddenly, again scanning the area. She thought back to the last time Nico came over. The very same day that Stone came back. And then she'd conveniently gone out of town That sneaky, sneaky woman. Deborah Jameson didn't need landscape design. That sneaky (and brilliant) woman was playing matchmaker.

"I'm on to you, Mom."

She laughed as she hurried up the steps, her smile now firmly rooted on her face.

"Hey, Mom!" she called out as she let herself in.

"In the kitchen!" Deborah hollered back.

Reilly closed the door and forced herself not to skip through the house. "Tell me you're makin' cookies. I—" She cut herself off and feigned surprise when she saw Nico sitting at the kitchen island, an iPad in front of him while Reilly's mom stood beside him.

"Oh, crap," she said. "You have an appointment. I totally forgot."

She silently praised herself for her acting skills.

"Sure you did." Her mother grinned. "Nico, you know my nosy daughter, Reilly."

Nico glanced back over his shoulder. "Hey."

"Hey." Reilly approached, making eyes—*I know what you're doin'*—at her mother when Nico turned back around. "Whatcha doin'?"

"He's walkin' me through the design plan for the front yard."

Not bothering to pretend she wasn't curious, Reilly peeked over his shoulder at the iPad screen. "Oh, wow. That looks nice."

"I was aimin' for awesome, but I'll take nice," Nico teased.

Reilly giggled, walking around the island. As she turned, her gaze snagged on the window over the sink. More specifically, the *view* from the window over the sink. She moved closer, her smile dimming when she saw the big white Ford dually parked beside Stone's truck. She leaned in, reading the decal on the side of the truck.

"What the…?" Reilly turned to look at her mother, crossing her arms over her chest. "Why's there a Double J truck parked at Stone's?"

"I have no idea, honey. That's a question for your brother."

Reilly looked at Nico, wondering whether he had an answer. Based on his expression, he was as surprised by the revelation as she was.

"Good idea," she said, flashing a bright smile. "I'll just head on over and ask him."

Pretending not to hear her mother's words of warning that followed, Reilly slipped out the back door, across the patio, out the back gate, and down the driveway toward the barn. She ignored the urge to pull her keys out of her pocket and drag them down the side of the truck that didn't belong there. Maybe whoever it was had a good reason.

Doubtful. But maybe.

Reilly bounded up the steps and marched straight for the door. She tried the knob, but it was locked. For shits and grins, she pressed her thumb to the biometric lock, only a little surprised when the lock disengaged. She thought for sure her brother would've changed it by now.

Taking that as an invitation to come in whenever she wanted, Reilly opened the door and walked in.

"Hey!" She closed the door, pretending she didn't know he had company. "Just wanted to—" She cut herself off when she turned around, her eyes on the woman sitting on the couch just a few scant inches from her brother. "Oh. Sorry. I didn't realize…"

Stone shot to his feet, his expression rife with … was that guilt? Or maybe he was grateful for the interruption? She hoped for his sake it was the latter. Otherwise, she was going to put the hurt on him.

Either way, she chose to take it as an invitation to introduce herself.

"Hi." Reilly looked between the two of them before focusing on the woman. "I'm Reilly. Stone's sister. And you are?"

The woman stood, her expression one of exasperation for being interrupted. "Leah Johnson."

Reilly frowned, pretending to be searching her memory for the name. She didn't have to search hard. She knew exactly who she was.

Right before her eyes, Leah's countenance shifted from annoyance to downright pleasant as she thrust out her hand.

Reluctantly, Reilly shook it, casting a death glare at her brother.

"It's wonderful to finally meet you," Leah said with a smile. "Stone's told me so much about you."

"Is that right?" Reilly pounced on that opening immediately, using her most eager tone. "What did he say?"

As expected, Leah looked at Stone for help.

She wasn't getting it. Stone stood back, watching the two of them as one might watch a lion approaching a gazelle.

Reilly liked to think of herself as the lion in this scenario.

"You got any beer?" Reilly asked her brother.

"What?"

"Beer? You know. To drink while I get acquainted with your … *friend.*"

Stone frowned. "No. I don't."

"Hmm." Reilly looked at Leah. "He's not big on house guests." She looked back at Stone. "Mom's got some up at the house. Why don't you go on up there and grab a couple? I'll entertain your … friend … while you do."

She could tell her brother wanted to argue, but she cocked an eyebrow and gave him a look that told him she expected full obedience. It rarely worked on anyone she knew, but she'd been perfecting it over the years, so…

Whaddya know. It worked this time.

"I'll be back in a minute."

"Take your time," Reilly told him. "We've got a lot to talk about. Don't we, Leah?"

She got tremendous glee from the confused and possibly terrified expression that flashed on Leah's face.

THIRTY-NINE

STONE WANTED TO TAKE THE OPPORTUNITY TO run far and fast.

It was bad enough he'd spent the past half hour listening to Leah while she attempted—unsuccessfully, he should note—to lure him back to the Double J. She'd gone so far as to offer him his old job back, with a few perks thrown in. Unfortunately, one of those perks was her because her offer included a wedding in the future. According to Leah, she knew it was only a matter of time before he came around, and she'd taken the inquiry from Zane as his cry for help.

The really sad thing was that she'd laid it all out like a business plan—a map of the future designed for profitability.

"She's fuckin' nuts," he muttered as he stomped his way up to his parents' house.

And now the nut job was locked in the barn with Reilly. He wasn't sure who he felt sorry for the most. Reilly was a handful, and if he knew his sister, she was going to tell Leah exactly what she thought. The only problem was Stone didn't know what was rattling around in that brain of hers. Reilly'd been pleasant enough, but underneath that polite facade, he'd seen the heart of a T-rex gearing up to chomp down on its prey.

If lucky, he'd return to find Reilly cleaning her teeth, using Leah's bones as toothpicks.

Okay, maybe that was a morbid visual, but Leah Johnson was the last person Stone wanted to see. Ever. She could take her proposition on back to Houston and shove it where the sun doesn't shine.

He was again thinking about his sister cleaning her T-rex teeth when he opened the door and stepped into his mother's kitchen. He abruptly stopped when he heard Nico's voice coming from deeper inside the house.

That *was* Nico's voice, right? Or maybe Stone was so sleep-deprived that he was hearing things.

The front door opened and closed. Footsteps sounded, and his mother appeared a moment later. Her expression was not what he expected.

"Hey," he greeted. "Everything okay?"

"You tell me." Her eyes shifted to the window over the sink. "Looks like you've got company."

"It's not what you think," he assured her.

"Then what is it?"

Stone had always thought of his mother as beautiful and vibrant. At fifty-six, she liked to tease that she was like wine, getting better with age. He agreed. Only she didn't look young or vibrant at the moment, not with the wary expression or the lack of luster in her eyes as she stared at him.

"Zane called the Double J to get a reference." Stone headed for the refrigerator, fearful he would crumble under the scrutiny. "Leah took that to mean she should swing by and check on me. That's all."

He wasn't going to get into the absurd proposition that Leah had laid out. There was no chance in hell he would ever take her up on it, so it was pointless. Even if she wasn't insisting on marriage down the line, Stone wasn't leaving Coyote Ridge. He was happy right where he was. Maybe not ecstatic at the moment since his career dreams were going up in smoke, but there was a hell of a lot more to life than that.

Stone grabbed two beers from the refrigerator. "Reilly told me to get them," he explained when he turned around to find his mother regarding him carefully. "Was Nico here?"

"He was." She maintained eye contact. "We were going over the remodeling plans for the front yard."

"Did he … uh…?" Stone nodded his head toward the window.

"Did he notice you had a visitor?" Deborah asked, her tone none too pleased. "Yes."

Fuck.

"Did you say anything?"

His mother frowned. "What was I supposed to say, Stone? That it's entirely possible you're gearing up to leave town again?"

"I'm not, Mom."

He could tell she didn't believe him.

"I'm not," he insisted. "I'm right where I wanna be."

Her tone softened, but the fear in her eyes remained. "Are you sure?"

Stone set the beer bottles on the counter and walked around so he could hug her. It was obvious she needed it. And yeah, maybe he needed it, too.

"I'm not goin' anywhere. Not today. Not tomorrow. I'm here to stay."

He wrapped his arms around her, pulling her in for a hug. She returned it with a relieved sigh.

When she finally pulled back, he looked her in the eye. "If I was plannin' to go back to the Double J, do you think I would've left her alone with Reilly?"

Deborah smiled, and it almost reached her eyes. "Good point."

There was a damn good chance Leah would be racing out of the house with tears streaming down her face before Stone ever made it back. Reilly wasn't one for tact. Especially not when it came to defending the people she loved.

Ever hopeful, Stone stood at the sink and watched out the window, waiting for it.

Unfortunately, it didn't happen, and ten minutes later, he was left with no other choice but to have a difficult conversation with Leah.

NICO DIDN'T WANT TO TELL STEVIE WHAT he'd witnessed at the Jamesons' house.

He didn't want her to think what he was thinking. That Stone was reverting to his old ways, and come morning, there was a good chance they'd have nothing more than the tread marks of the man on their souls.

Not only did he not want to tell Stevie, Nico didn't want to believe it was a possibility. But how could it not be? Why else would Stone's former employer drive two hundred miles from Houston? It wouldn't surprise Nico in the least if they'd come to their senses and wanted Stone to come back to work for them. The reason they'd fired him had been petty. So what if he didn't want to get serious with the owner's daughter? No one should be expected to do that.

Or maybe it was the owner's daughter who'd made the long-distance trek, and she was here to convince Stone—

Nico cut off that train of thought. He was not going there.

At least he was trying not to as he headed home. Stevie had texted to ask if Stone had agreed to join them for dinner, but Nico hadn't responded. He didn't want to relay anything in text because it could be misconstrued. Despite Stevie's optimism, he knew there was still a boatload of doubt underneath. She claimed the past was the past—and he believed she was trying to believe that—but with Stevie, it would only take a little choppy water to capsize that boat.

Nico snorted. "If it walks like a duck and quacks like a duck…"

It didn't take much imagination to think that the visit from the Double J was precisely what it looked like.

Despite his best efforts, Nico's anger intensified the closer he got to his house. He should've turned around. Should've gone to Stone's and confronted the man rather than leaving. At least then he would know what he was dealing with. He wasn't prone to jumping to conclusions, but how could he not? Did Stone deserve the benefit of the doubt? After what he'd done fifteen years ago, the simple answer was no. But then that would mean Nico didn't trust him. And without trust, why the fuck was he even considering a future with the guy?

His random thoughts dried up instantly when he pulled down the driveway and found a familiar car parked next to Stevie's Bronco.

"What the fuck?"

Nico prayed he was dreaming and that he was about to wake up and find out that none of this was real. He would open his eyes and find Stone and Stevie sleeping beside him. He could laugh all this off as a nightmare because there was no way the universe was cruel enough to pile all this shit on them at one time.

As he parked, he willed himself awake, figuring surely if this were a dream, that would do the trick.

It didn't work.

And it still didn't work as he opened the front door and walked inside to find Stevie sitting on the couch across from Melanie.

Jäger raced over, slipping on the hardwood as he came to a quick stop at Nico's feet. He considered stalling, but he could feel the tension coming from a few feet away, and the last thing he wanted was to leave Stevie alone with Melanie any longer.

"Hey," he greeted as he shrugged out of his coat.

Melanie smiled.

Stevie frowned.

"What's goin' on here?" he asked, although it was quite possibly the stupidest question ever.

"Melanie dropped by to … see you," Stevie explained from her perch on the couch.

"Well, you've seen me," he said, meeting Melanie's gaze briefly before turning his attention back to Stevie. She looked as though a light breeze would make her crumble.

Not good.

Nico hung his coat on the rack. "About?"

"I was just tellin' Stevie that I missed you," Melanie said sweetly. "I've been thinking about how rashly I behaved and thought maybe we could talk."

It had been over a year since he broke things off with Melanie, and this was the first time she'd *stopped by* for anything. When she left, she'd taken everything she could fit in the moving truck and Nico hadn't stopped her. Not even when she started pilfering his things as punishment. He'd been too wracked with guilt to care at the time.

"I'll leave you two alone," Stevie said, getting to her feet.

Nico wasn't sure what prompted him, but he shook his head and took her hand before she could slip away.

"No need." He guided her back to the couch and sat down beside her.

It was pointless to pretend they were merely roommates. Melanie would find out sooner or later, and he saw no point in delaying the information. And yeah, it was a chickenshit move on his part. Using Stevie as an excuse not to have this or any conversation with Melanie. But hey, survival instinct fed on desperation, not rational thought.

He could feel Melanie's confusion. It filled the empty space, growing heavier every second that Nico didn't release Stevie's hand.

When he conjured enough nerve to look at her, he noticed she was staring at their linked fingers.

"Are you...?" Her gaze shifted to Nico's face.

"Yes," he said simply because the last thing he wanted was any more uncertainty. He was dealing with enough not knowing what was taking place at Stone's right now.

"Oh." She swallowed but didn't move to stand.

Pretending this wasn't completely awkward or that Stevie wasn't doing her best to extract her hand from his grip, Nico asked, "What did you want to talk about?"

A weighted pause lingered while Melanie continued to stare, and Jäger did his best to get everyone's attention.

"How long has this been ... a thing?" Melanie asked, gesturing between him and Stevie.

"A while," he said at the same time Stevie said, "Not long."

Melanie looked both surprised and horrified. "When we were together?"

"God, no," Nico exhaled harshly.

467

She clearly didn't believe him, her eyes swimming with tears when she met his gaze. "Is she the reason you broke up with me?"

"No," he said adamantly.

It was clear from her expression that she wasn't listening. The next words out of her mouth proved it. "You were cheating?"

"No," Stevie said, this time jerking her hand from Nico's grip. "Y'all should talk. Alone."

She didn't give him a chance to call after her before she raced out of the room. A second later, he heard her bedroom door slam shut.

Melanie dabbed at her eyes as though she'd actually been crying. "When did you get a dog?"

Nico stared at the hallway, torn between sitting still and going after Stevie.

"Niyah gave him to me when she moved," he said absently, continuing to stare at the hallway.

"You hate dogs."

Nico's gaze slammed into his ex-girlfriend. "What?"

"You told me you hate dogs."

"No. *You* hate dogs. You decided I did, too."

Melanie had decided a lot of things for him when they were together, and he'd gone along with it because it was easier that way. In his defense, he'd been trying to build a normal life because he hadn't been brave enough to go after what he wanted.

"Why are you here?" he prompted, eager to move this along so he could talk to Stevie.

"I heard a rumor."

That got his attention, plus it made perfect sense, answering the question of why she was there. "Doesn't surprise me. It's a small town. People need shit to talk about."

"Someone mentioned they thought you were gay." Melanie glanced over her shoulder. "But I guess they were wrong since you're playing house with your sister's friend."

One thing he'd always admired about Melanie was how prim and proper she was. She didn't get riled easily, nor did she lose her temper. She buried shit underneath the facade of propriety. Except right now, he didn't admire it. It pissed him off because it was clear she wanted to confront him, but she would simply pick and poke until he erupted, and there was no time for that.

"They weren't wrong," he corrected.

Melanie's head snapped back around, her eyes wide. "What?"

"And I'm not playin' house with Stevie."

Her mouth opened, but nothing came out.

"I'm in love with Stevie," he said, keeping his tone calm.

"How…?" Her forehead creased in confusion. "How does that make you gay?"

"Bisexual, actually." Nico exhaled. "I'm also in love with a man."

Her eyes widened, and he half expected them to pop out of her face and grow bigger, like they did in those cartoons he had watched as a kid.

"Who?"

"Does it matter?"

"Does Stevie know?" she shot back.

"Does she know what?"

"That you're in love with … a man." The distaste practically dripped off her tongue.

"She knows."

Her nostrils flared. "And she's okay with that?"

Nico didn't want to get into this. Explaining it wouldn't change the outcome, and right now, he had far more important things to address than Melanie's confusion over his sexuality.

Forcing himself to stand, he peered down at the woman he'd once asked to marry him. He'd often wondered if he would feel anything if he ever saw her again. At the very least, he expected to be plagued with guilt and remorse. Sadly, he didn't feel a thing. The only reason that disappointed him was that he'd spent so long trying to make a life with this woman but looking back, he knew it had all been a lie he told himself in order to find a sliver of happiness when he doubted there was any to be had.

"I need to talk to Stevie," he told Melanie now.

It took her a moment to realize that was his subtle way of telling her to leave. She stood slowly, swiping her hand down her blouse, her chin tipping up.

"Why did you really break up with me?" she asked when they neared the front door. "Because you wanted to be with her?"

Nico looked her in the eye so she could see his sincerity. "No. And I didn't cheat on you."

She clearly didn't believe him. "Then why? I know it wasn't me," she amended. "I did everything I could to make you happy."

"But I wasn't." He felt his resolve soften. "And neither were you."

"That's not—"

He cut her off. "I was lyin' to myself, Mel. About a lot of things. I couldn't keep doin' it."

Her eyes were glassy. "We were good together, Nico."

He shook his head. She was rewriting history, but part of him understood that. It was easier that way.

"We weren't. Maybe we could've been. In a different life."

That obviously wasn't what she wanted to hear, but in true Melanie fashion, she squared her shoulders and turned toward the door. "If things don't work out…"

Nico exhaled with a sigh.

Melanie turned to look up at him. "I'm just saying."

"I'm in love with two people, Melanie, and I'll do whatever it takes to make it work."

"Too bad you never felt the same about me."

He nodded, just a gentle bob of his head. "I'm sorry."

To his surprise, she didn't blast him with reasons he should be before she turned and walked out the door.

He wasn't sure why she'd felt the need to drop by. Maybe she was hoping for reconciliation. More than likely, she was seeking closure.

Oddly enough, that was what this felt like.

FORTY

"HE CAUGHT Y'ALL IN THE BARN?" REILLY asked Leah, not at all surprised that the woman had spent the past half hour attempting to sway Reilly over to her side by regaling her with details of her time with Stone.

"Yes, he did," she said proudly.

Ever since Stone left, Leah had turned on the charm, and Reilly'd let her think it was working because … well, the truth was, it was entertaining as fuck. Like seriously amusing. The woman was exactly what Reilly had imagined her to be after the conversation she'd had with her brother the first day he was back.

Were you boinkin' the boss's wife again?

Daughter.

Seriously?

Seriously.

Was she hot?

You could say that.

Spoiled, rich-brat hot?

Exactly.

You got caught, huh?

Not on purpose.

Leah Johnson was definitely a spoiled rich bitch. Everything about her screamed oblivious and entitled. Reilly was pretty sure she was sincerely convinced Stone was going to hop in his truck and follow her back to Houston because she batted those fake lashes and thrust out her chest.

In all fairness, Reilly wasn't as certain that he wouldn't, but she would do her part to ensure he didn't have another choice.

It was petty and childish, sure. But who gave a fuck? Stone was where he belonged.

"I might've mentioned I needed his help," Leah continued.

Reilly was lost. "Who's help?"

"My father's."

"Ah." Then it hit her. "Oh. You set it up so your dad would pop in and catch you and Stone in the act?"

Leah's grin was wide and proud. "He would've found out eventually. I was just helpin' things along."

Then it dawned on Reilly what Leah said. They'd been caught having sex in the barn, and Leah had set it up so her dad would catch them. Gross.

Although she wanted to bleach the mental image from her brain, she was too curious to leave it alone. "Why?"

Leah shrugged. "I knew Daddy would insist Stone do right by me. Since Stone wasn't in a hurry to move things along, I added a little incentive."

Reilly nodded as though that made perfect sense when, in reality, she threw up a little in her mouth. "Backfired, huh?"

Leah's gaze shifted to the doors. "Not really. I knew Stone would react the way he did. At first. But I also know I'm the best thing that's happened to him."

"Oh." Reilly choked down a laugh. "Is that right?"

Her voice lowered as though they were sharing state secrets. "He's got big dreams, and I'm his meal ticket."

Wow. Reilly had wanted to be a lot of things growing up—fireman, architect, the door greeter at Walmart—but she'd never wanted to be someone's meal ticket.

"What does that entail?" she asked simply because she knew Leah wanted to share more.

"You can only get so far in life without an education," Leah explained, her perfect nose tilted up in that prissy pose she had perfected. "Stone's good at manual labor, but I don't see him running a ranch."

"He doesn't have the education," Reilly supplied, realizing where Leah was going with this.

"No offense, but there's a big difference between brains and brawn."

"You don't say."

"He's got the brawn, but he needs someone with brains to back him up. He needs me. We'll make a good team."

"So he'll work for you?"

"Eventually, yeah. Daddy says Stone's good with the ranch hands, so I'll let him manage them."

"You'll *let him*. Interesting."

For all the book smarts this bitch had, she was clueless. Her mouth continued to run, and she didn't realize Reilly was baiting her at every turn.

"You know what you *should* do?" Reilly said when Leah stopped talking.

"What's that?"

She leaned in, lowered her voice. "You should make him your house boy. He'd like that."

Leah laughed, her eyes glittering. "That could be fun."

"I know, right? Put a collar and leash on him, parade him around for the whole ranch to see."

Leah's eyebrows lowered.

"Or maybe put one of those things on him. You know." She motioned to her face. "What's it called? That thing that goes over a horse's face? They bite down on that thing. What's it called?" She opened her mouth and mimicked putting her finger sideways. "Anyway. You know what I'm talkin' about. It's used to guide them."

"A bridle?"

Reilly snapped her fingers. "Yes! Exactly. Put a bridle on him. Make him your pet because"—she widened her eyes and thickened her drawl for dramatic effect—"he's uneducated and all."

"I didn't say that."

"Yeah. You did." Reilly stepped toward the island. "And you know what? You're an idiot for thinkin' my brother's an idiot because he doesn't have a degree. He knows what he wants, and he goes after it. He's one of the good ones. He doesn't mind startin' at the bottom and workin' his way up. And the shit he's learned in life doesn't come from a book."

And there it was. The spark she'd been working to ignite. It backlit Leah's eyes and caused her cheeks to turn rosy. Reilly imagined her growing bigger, turning green, and morphing into the Hulk. Unfortunately, she didn't, but she did dial her haughtiness up to twelve.

"I'll have you know that Stone won't ever run my Daddy's ranch. Or any ranch, for that matter. Not without me. He's an outsider. A nobody. If he expects to make it in the cattle business, he needs a name backing him. I'm his best shot at ever makin' somethin' of himself."

"And what exactly do you get out of it?"

Leah's lips pulled back. "I'll have a man who'll do exactly what I tell him to do."

Reilly pretended to be too stupid to live. "That's a thing? Havin' a man for a pet? I *need* one of those. Can I Google man-pet and find one? Or would you call him a show pony? *That's* a thing, right?"

"Call it what you want, but I can give Stone the life he wants."

Reilly twisted her lips and smiled, cutting her eyes toward the door where her brother had been standing for the past few minutes.

Leah slowly turned her head, her eyes widening. "Stone?" Her Hulk impersonation disappeared, and sweet Leah returned. "Hey. You're back. I ... uh ... didn't hear you come in."

Stone looked at Reilly. "You're a T-rex, you know that?"

"And I wear a tutu," she noted, flashing a smile as she leaned back against the counter and crossed her arms over her chest.

Mission accomplished.

474

"TELL ME YOU'RE NOT BUSY," STEVIE SAID when Niyah answered the phone.

"Of course not." Her best friend flashed a grin.

Stevie stared at Niyah's face on the screen, grateful for FaceTime because it meant she didn't have to go without seeing her best friend. It wasn't as good as being in the same room, but it helped. When Niyah lived there, they went to lunch at least once every week, indulged in a girls' night a few times a month, and hung out doing nothing simply because they could. Back before Niyah got engaged to and then married Adam, they spent all their spare time together. So, no, this wasn't the same, but it was better than nothing.

"Melanie's here," she whispered, bringing her phone close to her face.

"What?"

"Meh. Luh. Knee." Stevie pulled the phone back and pointed toward the door. "She's here."

Niyah's eyes widened, her gaze shifting to Stevie's bedroom door. "Nuh-uh."

Stevie bobbed her head up and down. "Yuh-huh."

Niyah frowned. "Why?"

"Dunno."

Her best friend canted her head to the side and cocked one eyebrow. "Don't bullshit me right now, Stevie. What does she want?"

Stevie gave in with a sigh, flopping back on her bed. "She said she misses Nico and wants to talk to him. She showed up before he got here."

"You didn't kick her butt out the door?"

"I felt bad."

"For?"

She shrugged again. She honestly didn't know why she felt bad. She shouldn't. Nico and Melanie were over a long time ago, and unlike Melanie's accusation, it had nothing to do with her.

"He told her we were together," she blurted.

Niyah's eyes widened, and a slow smile formed. "What did she say?"

"She accused him of cheating."

"The cuckoo bird realizes they're not together, right?"

"Back then," Stevie clarified. "She asked him if I was the reason they broke up."

"You tell her no, that your man just so happens to like your other man?"

Stevie smiled. After their conversation the other day about Valentine's surprise ideas, Stevie texted Niyah to let her know that things were looking up. Granted, their text messages would require NSA analysts to decrypt because they spoke mostly in emojis.

She opened her mouth to say something when she heard the front door close.

"Uh-oh." Stevie looked at her bedroom door like that might help her see what was going on outside of her room.

"Uh-oh, what?"

"I think she left."

"Stevie?" Nico called from the hallway.

"Go talk to him," Niyah said firmly. "Then call me later and tell me everything."

"What am I supposed to say? What if he wants to get back with her? What if she went home to get her stuff so she can move back in?"

"Stop it. You're bein' crazy. You said he told her y'all were together."

He had, and that had honestly surprised the shit out of her. Not to mention, it caused an avalanche of guilt to cascade down on her. She had no reason to feel guilty. They'd done nothing wrong. But it still didn't help the awkwardness that had settled like a wet blanket over the room.

"Stevie? I'm comin' in," Nico announced.

Before she could end the call with Niyah, the door opened.

Stevie turned the phone around so Niyah could see her brother. "Say hi."

Nico walked right over and plucked the phone out of her hand. "Hey, Sis. She's gonna have to call you back."

"Be good to her, Nico."

"Always."

"Call me later, Stevie!" Niyah shouted.

Nico ended the call and tossed the phone onto the bed. Jäger popped up, his paws on the bed, his nose sniffing as though Nico had just tossed a treat. Stevie scooped him up and put him on the bed, using him as a distraction.

"Did you know she was comin' over?" Stevie asked because it seemed like a fitting question.

"No." He sat on the edge of the mattress and leaned forward, resting his elbows on his knees. "But it doesn't surprise me."

"Really?"

"The way this day's goin', I'm not sure *anything* could surprise me."

A sense of foreboding swept through like an icy wind. "What happened?"

Nico scrubbed his hands over his face. "I went to the Jamesons' house this afternoon."

"How'd that go?" Not that she really cared, but it was the right question to insert after that statement, so she waited patiently.

"Fine. She officially hired us."

"That's great." However, her happiness injection fell short of the mark. "So what's the problem?"

He sat up, swallowing hard enough that his Adam's apple did a slow bob in his throat.

"Stone was home, and he, uh…" Nico inhaled slowly, then blew it out. "There was a Double J truck parked near the barn."

Stevie frowned. Her brain kicked into high gear, attempting to process what that meant. When it clicked, a vise clamped down on her chest, choking the air from her lungs.

She should've known it was too good to be true.

"Don't jump to conclusions," Nico said, reaching over to put his hand on her leg.

"Are you kiddin' me?" She glared at him. "Like you're not thinkin' the same thing."

She could tell by his expression that she wasn't the only one thinking Stone was already packing his shit to go back where he came from.

"We need to give him the benefit of the doubt, Stevie."

"Fuck that."

Before she could get off the bed, Nico was on his feet, standing directly in front of her.

"Move, Nico."

"No."

She would've scrambled off the other side, but Jäger was laid out on the mattress, snoozing as though it was a lazy afternoon, completely oblivious to the chaos that was making mincemeat of Stevie's heart.

"Let's go over there," Nico said rationally.

"For what? So we can wave at him when he's drivin' down the road?"

"No. So we can talk to him. See what's goin' on."

Stevie clamped her teeth together. She didn't give a shit what was going on. She didn't care if Stone was already halfway to Houston.

Maybe if she repeated it a few thousand times, it would be true.

FORTY-ONE

AFTER HE MANAGED TO USHER REILLY OUT of the house, Stone attempted to do the same with Leah. Unfortunately, she was proving to be a bigger pain in his ass than he remembered.

"Your sister set me up, Stone," Leah insisted. "She twisted my words around."

He huffed a mirthless laugh as he downed one of the beers he'd brought back from his parents' house.

"We were talkin' about you, and she started makin' fun of you for not havin' a degree."

Stone stared at her. "Reilly made fun of me?"

"She did." Leah moved closer. "I was tellin' her how I wanted you to come back to run the ranch, and she said you weren't qualified."

Even if he hadn't heard every word they'd exchanged, Stone wouldn't have believed her. Leah was good at many things, but lying wasn't one of them. She tried. God, she tried. The majority of words that came out of her mouth were fictitious. He didn't know why she resorted to lying, but that was her knee-jerk response.

"It doesn't matter," he told her, exhaling heavily. "I'm not goin' back to the Double J."

"You have to."

"Why?"

"Because..." Her eyes went wild, and he knew she was trying to come up with a reason.

"Come on," he goaded. "Spit it out."

"Daddy ... he's..."

"What? He's sick?"

Stone could tell she was trying to find a way to use that, but her eyes gave her away, and she knew it.

"He's not sick, Leah."

"No. It's ... um ... Not him. It's..."

"You're sick?" he said, hating that he was playing this game with her.

"I ... uh..."

"Leah, it's not gonna—"

"I'm pregnant," she blurted.

Stone stopped, his beer bottle halfway to his mouth. His brain shifted from neutral to fifth gear, racing to figure out how that could be possible. He'd never had sex with her without a condom—they weren't 100%, of course, but he'd still used them. And Leah had assured him she was on birth control. Hell, he still remembered her words when she told him.

You don't have to worry about that, Stone. I'm on birth control. I don't care what my daddy says, I'm not gonna give him another heir unless there's somethin' in it for me.

Because he sensed she was bullshitting him, Stone pushed. "How far along?"

Please, God, let her be bullshitting him.

"I ... uh ... don't know."

"How'd you find out?"

It took her a moment. "I missed a period."

"Just one?"

Her forehead scrunched. "Two?"

"You missed two periods?"

"Yes."

"Did you take a pregnancy test?"

Leah chewed on her bottom lip. "Yes."

"When?"

"I don't know. Does it matter?"

"Yeah. If fuckin' matters, Leah."

"A couple of weeks ago, I guess."

"And you're just now tellin' me?"

"I wanted to tell you in person."

"Don't take offense, but I'm gonna need to see the test for myself."

"I didn't *keep it*. Gross."

Stone rolled his eyes. She truly did think he was an idiot. "I'll run to the store and get another one."

"No," she exclaimed, rushing over. "I ... I wanna wait until I go to the doctor."

"You're in luck. We've got one right here in Coyote Ridge."

He could see the fear in her eyes. "My own doctor. In Houston. I'll go next week sometime."

"Pregnancy test," he insisted. "If it's positive, I'll go to the doctor with you." Because he was convinced she was lying, Stone reached for his truck keys, then walked over to get his coat off the hook by the door. "It'll only take me a few minutes. Twenty tops."

He could feel her eyes on him as he put his coat on. The tension ratcheted tighter and tighter with every breath. He knew it was about to break because that was what Leah did. She was a horrible liar because she couldn't stick with the story long enough to make it believable.

Please, God, don't let it be true.

"Fine," she blurted. "I'm not pregnant. But I could be. One day."

He exhaled heavily, partly from relief, partly from irritation.

"Maybe we could get to work on makin' it a reality," she suggested sweetly.

He shrugged out of his coat and reached to put it back on the hook. "Look, Leah. I'm sorry you drove all this way, but—"

Leah squealed. "Oh, no. I spilled it."

He turned to find her standing beside the island. Beer had poured down her shirt and was dripping onto the floor.

Her gaze cut to him, and he could tell she was making sure he was looking.

"It was an accident, Stone. I was just…"

Accident, my ass.

"I was reaching…"

Stone sighed when she let that sentence die off, too. Leah couldn't even come up with a decent lie. She'd always been that way, and he honestly wasn't sure why. She resorted to bending the truth to get attention. When someone was telling a story, she had to have one of her own—bigger in scale, more dramatic. It was one of the reasons people kept her at a distance. That and she treated most people like they were beneath her.

I'll have you know that Stone won't ever run my Daddy's ranch. Or any ranch, for that matter. Not without me. He's an outsider. A nobody. If he expects to make it in the cattle business, he needs a name backing him. I'm his best shot at ever makin' somethin' of himself.

And what exactly do you get out of it?

I'll have a man who'll do exactly what I tell him to do.

Unlike what Leah told Reilly, Stone had never been under her thumb. At times, he allowed her to think he was, but the truth was, he'd merely looked past her arrogance and haughty indignation, and he'd befriended her despite her irritating need to embellish the truth. She was irritating most of the time, but now and again, she would surprise him. For a little while, he'd even liked her.

"Do you have a shirt I could borrow?" she asked, already unbuttoning hers.

"Go on," he said, pointing toward the hallway. "My bedroom's on the right."

"Thank you." Her voice dripped like honey.

While she sauntered off to change her shirt, Stone grabbed paper towels to clean up the spilled beer.

Too bad Bounty didn't make something to clean up the mess that was his life.

"I HAVE NOTHIN' TO SAY TO HIM," Stevie told Nico, wondering why he wouldn't just listen to her.

She'd told him a dozen iterations of that statement since he insisted on going to Stone's and taking her with him. She didn't want to go. She wanted to sit at home and pout for a little while. She could address the stupidness of this day tomorrow when it was behind her, and she could actually think about it without the red haze that clouded her vision.

"Well, I do."

"What?" She stared at him as he drove toward Stone's. "What do you want to say?"

"I'll know when we get there."

"Meaning you have no idea." She huffed, crossing her arms over her chest. "And what if he's already gone?"

"He's not leavin'."

"You know this for a fact?" she snapped, hating that she was so angry.

"Yes."

"I don't believe you."

"Well, you're gonna—"

Stevie's cell phone rang, cutting him off. She picked the phone up from the cup holder and glanced at the screen.

"It's Reilly," she said, confused as to why Stone's sister would be calling her.

"Answer it."

"I don't want to," she said petulantly.

"Answer. It. Stevie."

"Don't have to be rude," she grumbled as she hit the talk button and put the phone to her ear. "Hello?"

"Hey, Stevie. It's Reilly."

"Uh... hi?"

Reilly chuckled. "I know it's weird that I'm callin', but I wanted to give you a heads up that Stone's crazy ex-employer ... her name's Leah. She's stone-cold nuts, Stevie. I think she believes the shit she says. Anyway, she's at his place, and she's tryin' to convince him to come back. He's not," she added quickly. "But I don't know if she's listenin' to him. She seems like the type to keep pushin'."

"What am I ... uh ... supposed to do about it?"

Another soft laugh. "For starters, you could go over there and kick her ass."

"I don't have a say in who Stone spends his time with."

This time, Reilly's laugh sounded bitter, and her voice softened. "You might not think so, Stevie, but my brother's worth fightin' for. I know he hurt you once, but he's not the same guy anymore. I've never…"

"Never what?" Stevie prompted, needing Reilly to finish that sentence.

"I've never seen Stone so happy. Y'all might not want to admit it, but I'm not an idiot. I know the three of you have somethin' goin' on. So, if you care about him at all, you and Nico should swing by and save him from her. I don't think she's gonna give up. Just beware. I think she's the Hulk in disguise."

"What does that even…" The call ended. "…mean?"

"What did she want?" Nico asked when Stevie set the phone down.

Staring out the window into the night, she gave him a quick rundown of the conversation—at least the parts she understood.

"And then she said somethin' about her bein' the Hulk in disguise?"

Stevie tried to make sense of that as Nico drove faster. She tried to make sense of it all. Melanie showing up to *talk* to Nico. Stone's ex-employer *slash* girlfriend, or whatever she was, coming back. Was the universe out to get her, or what? All on the same day?

It did make her feel better that Reilly had called. It restored some semblance of hope that her world wasn't crashing down around her again.

As easy as it would be to get angry and sulk for the next fifteen years while Stone ran off to do whatever the hell he wanted to do, Stevie knew confronting him was the only real option. And if Reilly was right, Stevie had a few things to say to the crazy bitch who thought she could prance in and take what didn't belong to her.

Speaking of crazy bitches… "What did Melanie say after I left?"

Nico cleared his throat. He did that when he was uncomfortable talking about something.

"I told her I was in love with two people, and I was gonna fight to make it work."

Her heart flipped over to reveal its soft underside.

"It's true, Stevie." He reached for her hand, linking their fingers. "I'll fight for what's mine."

She turned her attention out the window again. Maybe that was what she needed to do, too. Fight for what was hers.

Ten minutes later, Stevie stomped around the Double J truck parked next to Stone's, refusing to let it get to her. She was going to confront this woman if it was the last thing she did. And the only way she was walking out of here was if Stone told her he wanted her to leave. It was interesting what could happen in the span of a few minutes. She'd gone from being full of self-pity to convincing herself that she was now the invincible thing that could take down the Hulk.

If she recalled correctly, the Hulk was invincible, but as God was her witness, she was going to prove Marvel wrong by the end of the day.

As she was banging her fist on the door, some of her courage wavered, but she squared her shoulders, determined to stand her ground.

Stone opened the door, his expression one of ... was that *relief*?

She sure hoped it was; otherwise, he was about to get really angry because she was doing this.

"Hey," he greeted, his gaze shifting past her to Nico.

"Reilly called," Nico explained.

Stone stepped back. "Come in."

"Who's at the door? Oh. Oh, my goodness. I didn't realize we were expectin' company." The woman flashed a smile, pretending to be self-conscious because she was wearing one of Stone's button-downs.

And nothing else.

God. Could she be any more cliché?

"Stevie, it's not what it looks like," Stone said.

She looked at Stone and flashed a smile of her own. "I know."

Before he could launch into an explanation, Stevie marched over to Leah and held out her hand. "I'm Stevie. Stone's girlfriend. And you are?"

"Leah," she said, frowning as she put her limp hand in hers.

Stevie shook it once, then dropped it like it was a hot potato. She glanced down at Leah's bare legs. "We should find you some pants. It's cold. Wouldn't want you to catch a chill." Stevie met her gaze and smiled. "Because you're leavin'."

The woman sputtered, but Stevie didn't give her a chance to spout whatever bullshit that was piling up in that big head of hers.

"We'll be right back," she called out to Stone and Nico, adding more honey than vinegar to her tone as she urged Leah back the way she'd come.

NICO WASN'T SURE WHAT TO SAY OR do. Hell, he wasn't sure he could sputter a word after watching Stevie introduce herself to Leah, then march the woman out of the room like it was her duty.

While contemplating whether to intervene, he held Jäger in his arms as he stood beside Stone, watching Stevie and the half-dressed woman disappear into Stone's bedroom.

"That's Leah, huh?"

"Yeah." Stone huffed, looking as dumbfounded as Nico felt.

"Why's she here?"

"She's insane," he said, his tone lacking any inflection at all.

They stood in silence for another few seconds, staring at the empty space where Stevie had just been. Nico was trying to figure out what to say when Stone turned, gesturing toward the towels on the floor.

"She poured beer down her shirt. On purpose. Then asked to borrow one of mine. She doesn't do anything without an ulterior motive."

Nico glanced at the puddle and then toward the bedroom. "You turned down her offer to go back to Houston."

"More than once." Stone glanced at Jäger as though seeing him for the first time. "Shit. Let me clean that up."

It took Stone only a few seconds to get the spill cleaned up. When he did, Nico set the puppy on the floor, figuring he couldn't possibly cause any more of a ruckus than there already was.

Stone returned to stand beside him. "I was gonna explain everything as soon as I got her out of the house. It's not what it looks like. I didn't—"

Nico silenced him with a kiss, grabbing him behind the neck and crushing their mouths together. He wasn't sure what came over him but he couldn't help himself. During the drive over, he had doubts about how he would feel when he arrived. Trust was a huge part of a relationship, and he knew this would never work if he didn't trust Stone.

But the second he saw him, Nico knew that Stone was as irritated by the situation as Nico had been when Melanie showed up. Neither of them had set these events in motion, but it was their responsibility to deal with them.

Which reminded him...

He pulled back, waiting for Stone to look at him. "Melanie stopped by the house today. Before I got there."

Stone frowned, their gazes colliding as they stood chest to chest, mere inches separating them. "Melanie? The ex-fiancee?"

"Yeah." He spoke softly since they were so close. "She waited with Stevie. Said she wanted to talk to me."

"How'd Stevie handle that?"

"Like she handles everything. With grace and courage." He didn't mention that he saw right through her, though. Nico knew that Melanie's appearance had hurt her, which was why she'd run to her room. He hadn't been surprised to find her on the phone with Niyah, probably trying to make sense of it all and get someone on her side.

What Stevie didn't realize was that Nico was on her side. He would always be.

Stone's gaze implored him as his arm banded around his back, the space between them disappearing fast. "And?"

It was difficult to think when the man was touching him, but he managed. "And nothin'. I sent her on her way. I'm just tellin' you so you know what Stevie's been through already today."

His expression morphed into one of understanding, and he stepped forward, closing the small gap that separated them.

"I don't wanna leave anything to chance this time," Nico told him. "Communication was lacking the last time we were together."

Stone nodded. "I know. And I agree. If we're gonna do this, we've gotta do it the right way."

When Stone leaned in, Nico did, too, meeting him halfway. The press of his lips was gentle, but Nico felt the current underneath—a raging river beating against the ground containing it. Any moment now, it was going to break free and drown them all.

"Oh, my God!"

Nico pulled away, staring at the woman whose eyes were about to pop out of her head.

"What are you…?" Her nose scrunched. "Are you *gay*?"

"Technically, no," Stevie said, her tone flat. "What he is is taken." She marched Leah toward the door. "And you're leavin'."

Nico stood beside Stone as Leah passed, her forehead creased with confusion.

"Don't forget anything," Stevie instructed. "Because you won't be comin' back."

Leah's gaze shifted to Stone, and he could tell she was weighing her options. He realized she wasn't as stupid as she pretended to be because her expression cleared as she realized she didn't have any.

Stevie wasn't backing down, and Nico had never been more in love with her than he was at that moment.

FORTY-TWO

STONE WATCHED AS STEVIE CLOSED THE DOOR behind Leah, preparing himself for whatever tongue-lashing he was about to get. He deserved it, of course, and he could only imagine what was going through her head. If he'd been in her shoes, he would've been livid. Hell, if he found a half-naked man coming out of her bedroom, he would've gone fucking postal.

Stevie turned and leaned against the door. He held his breath, gearing up for her wrath.

Only when she opened her eyes, he didn't see anger glittering in the dark brown depths.

She took a deep breath and lifted her hand, pointing at ... well, he wasn't sure who she was pointing at. Either him or Nico. Maybe both. They were standing side by side, and her gestures weren't animated enough to clarify.

"You are done with her," she said, her index finger stabbing in their direction.

Again, she could've been talking to either of them, but he suspected the "her" in question was Leah.

"It's not—"

"Shh," she hissed sharply.

The sound caused Jäger to bark, drawing all their attention.

"Hey, little guy," Stevie crooned. "It's all good. You're the only boy here right now who's not on my shit list." She cocked an eyebrow. "Keep it that way."

Jäger sat, his tail thumping on the floor.

When Stevie looked at him, Stone opened his mouth.

"No. You don't get to talk right now."

He probably shouldn't get turned on by the fierceness of her tone, but his dick thickened as though her lips were wrapped around it.

"And you," she glanced at Nico. "You're done with Melanie."

"I—"

"Shut it," she snapped, cutting him off. "From this point forward, I don't want excuses from either of you. No more ghosts from the past sneaking up on us."

"That goes for Oscar, too," Nico stated.

"Who's Oscar again?" Stone asked, glancing between them.

"No one," Stevie said at the same time Nico said, "her pain in the ass ex-boyfriend."

"Oh, right." Stone nodded. "I remember now."

"Why bring him up?" Stevie huffed, rolling her eyes.

If he wasn't seeing things, there was the hint of a smile on her mouth.

Her question was clearly rhetorical, but Nico answered anyway. "Only so you know the rules apply to you, too."

"No," she said firmly, walking toward them. "I'm beyond the rules at this point."

"Is that right?"

"From here on out, I get to make them."

Stone grinned. This was the feisty girl he'd fallen in love with all those years ago. The girl who took shit from no one. He could see the fire burning in her eyes, the flames licking at everything in the room.

"No more ex-girlfriends, and—"

"Or ex-boyfriends," Stone and Nico said at the same time.

"Or ex-boyfriends," Stevie amended, although she wasn't happy about it. "We're leavin' it all behind us. Starting anew. Everything that was before isn't."

Stone leaned toward Nico, speaking out the side of his mouth. "Is it me, or does she sound like Yoda?"

Nico snorted.

Stevie marched forward, ignoring them. She stopped directly in front of him, tilting her chin up and meeting his eyes. "I will fight for what's mine, Stone Jameson." She stepped to the side and looked up at Nico. "That goes for you, too, Nico Daugherty."

"Did she just last name us?" Stone asked, glancing at Nico.

"I think she did."

"Make fun if you want," Stevie continued. "But I'm not playin'."

"We're not either," Stone assured her, taking a step toward her.

Nico did the same. "The same goes for us. We'll fight for what belongs to *us.*"

"And you, baby, belong to us," Stone said smoothly. "Don't ever forget that."

Her eyes widened, but there wasn't an ounce of fear in them. "Do you mean that?"

"Of course we do."

"Then prove it."

Stone looked at Nico and saw he was looking at him. In that brief moment, he could practically read Nico's thoughts, and they were on the same page. He gave a slight nod.

"What was that?" Stevie asked, her eyes darting back and forth between them. "That look."

Neither responded as Nico moved, grabbing her before she could slip away. Stone stepped in front of her, crowding her between his body and Nico's.

"I told you the other day that I'm ready for the next phase. Remember that conversation?"

"Briefly." Her breathy tone contradicted her bold lie.

"I think it's time we do somethin' you'll remember forever."

"If you think I'm havin' sex with—"

Stone dropped down to one knee, Nico mimicking the move behind her.

"What are you…?" Stevie gasped, but it turned into a laugh. "Get up. Both of you. Right now."

She tried to dance away, but they grabbed her arms, stopping her before she stepped on Jäger. The puppy joined in the fun, pouncing around her feet.

"Stop!" She laughed, a sound so damn sexy, Stone felt it throughout his entire body. "This is silly. Quit it."

"Not until you agree to spend the rest of your life with us," Nico stated firmly.

"This is dumb. Get up."

"Marry us, Stevie," Stone said softly.

Although they'd turned this into a game, Stone's breath lodged in his chest because he wasn't kidding. He wanted to marry her. Maybe it wouldn't be in the traditional sense, but he wanted forever with them. He didn't care what that looked like as long as they were together.

"You know that's not a thing, right?" she countered.

Stone canted his head. "And how would you know that?"

"I looked it up."

Stone glanced at Nico. "She looked it up."

"Sounds promising to me," Nico added.

"This is crazy," Stevie said, giggling. "Let me go."

"Not until you agree," Stone told her.

"And what?" She snorted. "Become Stevie Jameson-Daugherty?"

Stone looked at Nico again. "Sounds kinda good."

Nico's mouth twisted. "Or, you know, we do it alphabetically. Daugherty-Jameson."

"I like that, too," he acknowledged.

"Hello!" Stevie shouted, drawing their attention back to her. "This is insane."

Stone looked at Nico again. "She's right. Plus, I'm not sure it's workin'."

Nico pursed his lips and nodded. "We should bring out the big guns, huh?"

"Good idea."

"What're the big guns?" Stevie asked, backing up, although they were still holding her arms.

"Don't worry, baby, we'll show you."

"We can't! Jäger's here."

"Did I mention I picked up a kennel for him the other day? Even got him some toys." Stone told her. "Figured he might need it for nights y'all stay over here."

He continued to crowd her toward the bedroom.

"Any more excuses?" Nico asked.

She giggled. "No. No, no. We're not doin' this. We're supposed to be havin' a serious conversation."

"We can be serious when you're naked."

With Nico beside him, Stone took off after her when she made a break for it toward the bedroom.

STEVIE HAD NO IDEA HOW THEY'D GOTTEN to his point. One second, she'd been ready to dress them both down for the shit day she'd had, thanks to the women from their past. Next, she was racing to Stone's bedroom in an attempt to get away from them while at the same time hoping they would catch her and break out the big guns like they promised.

Her head was spinning, and euphoria-induced laughter bubbled out of her. Seeing them on their knees, asking... God, she wasn't sure they'd been serious, but secretly, she hoped they were because the thought of spending the rest of her life with them was the only way to erase images of that bitch coming out of Stone's bedroom wearing only his shirt. Or listening to Melanie go on and on about how she regretted ending things with Nico and how desperate she was for a second chance.

One would've been bad enough. Two was simply cruel.

But she couldn't deny their reactions to those situations had done wonders for her ego.

Stevie squealed when big arms curled around her, lifting her off her feet. She giggled as Stone carried her into his room.

"We're so not done with you, baby," he whispered, his breath warm on her neck.

Before she could say anything, Stone spun around, still holding her up in the air. Nico appeared a few seconds later, his eyes blazing with an emotion she hadn't seen before. It was a mixture of so many things—lust, love, maybe even adoration—and it sent a frisson of heat zinging through her bloodstream.

"Where's Jäger?" she asked, buying time.

"Safe and secure with his new toy," Nico answered.

She giggled and twisted when Nico reached for the button on her jeans, his intentions clear. With Stone holding her the way he was, she was at their mercy. The only sound in the room was her muted grunts and uncontrollable laughter as Nico proceeded to tickle her while he stripped her from the waist down. Only then did Stone lower her so her feet met the hardwood. He didn't release her, holding her still so Nico could eliminate the rest of her clothing.

And then she was naked, and they weren't.

It was a heady feeling, especially when Nico looked at her like she was dessert.

Another squeal bubbled up when Stone grabbed her and tossed her onto his bed, the mattress cushioning her fall. Her brain kicked in, devising a plan to get away because that was the game, but she didn't get far before he was on her, straddling her hips and pinning her arms to the bed.

His smile was wickedly sensual.

"Find somethin' to tie her up with. Check the closet," Stone told Nico while his heated gaze remained locked on her face.

Her clit pulsed with excitement at the thought of them tying her down. He'd never done that before.

Nico's voice sounded far away for a moment but then clearer as he returned to the bedroom. "Do you wear these?"

Stone glanced over his shoulder. "Only if I have to."

"I'm intrigued," Nico said, appearing at the side of the bed, two neckties dangling from his fingers.

"Silk." She looked at Stone. "Nice."

"They'll look much better on you." His eyes heated even more.

Then they were testing that theory, tying her hands to the narrow posts on the headboard, stretching her arms wide. When they were done, Stone got off the bed, standing beside Nico as they ogled her.

Fresh heat crashed over her, sending chills skating across her skin, her nipples pebbling, her pussy growing wetter by the second.

"You have a footboard, don't you?" Stone asked Nico, his tone casual.

"I do."

"Probably better for this. We'll have to keep that in mind for next time. For now, we'll work with what we've got."

494

Stevie expected them to join her, but Stone clearly had other things in mind because he moved, standing behind Nico, his arms coming around him. She lifted her head to watch Stone raise Nico's shirt, revealing all those deliciously defined muscles. She watched every second like this was her own personal strip tease as Stone peeled Nico's clothes from his body.

She was breathing hard, her chest rising and falling like she'd run a marathon, but her cardiovascular system only thought it was in chaos. Her heart rate double-timed it when Stone reached around Nico, curling his big fingers around Nico's cock. He stroked him while he kissed his neck.

Nico moaned and grunted, accepting the pleasure while his eyes caressed her from head to toe again and again.

It was exquisite torture, tied to the bed, forced to endure and not participate.

Stevie was so caught up in the sensual show, she flinched when Nico grunted. She looked up to see Stone fisting Nico's hair roughly, yanking his head back. Nico's neck stretched, his chest muscles bunching.

She didn't hear what Stone whispered in Nico's ear, but when Stone brought Nico's head to level once again, his mouth was open, his eyes wide, his features drawn in what looked to be pain. But Nico didn't pull away, didn't attempt to stop Stone from manhandling him, shoving him forward, bringing him closer to the bed.

Nico's movements were jerky as he put his knees on the bed, not fighting as Stone dragged him closer to her.

"Spread your legs, baby," Stone instructed. "Show me how wet that little pussy is."

Stevie gasped, spreading her legs because she had no resistance when it came to this man's dirty commands.

"Look at that." Stone used his free hand to tease her, dragging his finger through her slickness.

Then he was forcing Nico's head down, down…

Stevie gasped when she felt Nico's heated breath on her sensitive flesh.

"Nice and slow," Stone told Nico. "Don't make her come, but you have my permission to bring her to the edge."

When Nico's tongue lapped at her, she gripped her restraints, holding on for dear life as he tormented her with languid strokes over her clit.

"I could watch that all day," Stone said, standing beside the bed, stripping off his clothes, making it impossible for Stevie to focus.

Between Nico's wicked tongue and the intoxicating sight of Stone's naked body, she was trapped in a blissful state of purgatory, lingering between heaven and hell and never wanting it to end.

STONE HAD NEVER FELT AS ALIVE AS he did in that moment.

Here, with Stevie and Nico. Nothing else mattered except the three of them coming together like this. It allowed him to block out everything else because it paled in comparison.

It didn't matter that Zane held his future in the palm of his hand because *that* took a backseat to this any day of the week. Stone would do what he needed to do to take care of these two people. He would find something else, do something else, *be* something else. It was inconsequential because the whole of his happiness existed right here in this room.

It wasn't even about the sex. That was a bonus, a way to take the edge off their amped-up emotions. It was about connecting on a wavelength that brought them back to where it all began. Rough and dirty was what they all craved, but it was so much more than that. Those things added fun and excitement, but they weren't what bound the three of them together. The only thing powerful enough to do that was love.

"Please!" Stevie hissed, writhing under the onslaught of Nico's ministrations.

"Good girls ask nicely," Stone teased, putting one knee on the bed.

She whimpered. "Please." Her back arched. "Make me come!"

"Still didn't ask nicely." He pinched her nipple, earning a guttural moan. "Is it not enough?"

Stevie shook her head, her eyes closed, mouth in a thin line.

She was beautiful like this. At their mercy, capable of taking only what they were willing to give her. It was how he'd planned it.

"You need more," he said, purposely not phrasing it as a question.

"Yes."

"Hmm." He stretched out on the bed beside her, propping his head on his hand and using the other to pull her leg back, opening her up to Nico's mouth.

Leaning forward, he took her nipple between his lips, lightly teasing the little nub with his tongue. She whimpered, relaxing as he caressed her softly, sweetly. When she began to mewl, he bit her nipple.

Stevie cried out, her back arching. "Again!"

He did it again.

"You think she deserves to come yet?" he asked Nico between intimate nibbles.

Nico lifted his head. "Not yet."

"When?" Stevie cried out. "I can't take it!"

Stone chuckled, releasing her nipple and turning his attention to her face. He pressed his fingertips to her chin, turning her head, forcing her to look at him.

"Say yes."

She frowned. "To what?"

"To marrying us."

Her eyes closed as she shook her head.

"Finger her," Stone instructed Nico.

Stevie cried out when Nico plunged his fingers inside her, his lips wrapped around her clit.

"Don't you dare come," Stone warned Stevie, pinching her nipple again, letting her ride the fine line between pain and ecstasy.

"I … I … oh, God! Please."

"We'll give you everything you want as soon as you say yes."

She shook her head. They tormented her some more.

"Are you ready to say yes?"

Stevie nodded, but she said, "No."

Stone chuckled. She was purposely toying with them, and he loved that she could do that. Loved that she knew they wouldn't give up on her. Saying no meant they would work harder to be what she needed them to be. It wasn't rejection. It was a demand for them to give her everything she deserved.

And this beautiful, sexy woman deserved everything. She deserved the best that life had to offer. Not in the form of money, because Stone had learned a long time ago that money wasn't everything. In fact, it was nothing when you had no one. And he'd spent fifteen years regretting that he'd thrown away the best thing in his life for a dream that was nothing without her.

"Do you love us, Stevie?"

Her head turned, her eyes opened. "Yes."

"Say it."

Nico stopped, lifting his head.

"I do," she whispered, her eyes glittering.

Stone reached for Nico, urging him to move up. He did, propping himself on all fours so he was hovering above her while Stone remained beside her.

"Say it," Nico rasped.

Stevie looked up at him, then back to Stone. "I love you. Both of you."

"Then say yes," Nico's tone was more insistent, but his eyes held a wealth of emotion.

Stevie huffed a laugh. "Fine. Yes."

Stone reached down, thrusting two fingers inside her. "Mean it, and we'll both fuck you."

She giggled. "Then, by all means, yes."

He removed his fingers, reaching for Nico's cock and dragging it along the slick seam of her pussy, teasing her clit.

Stevie arched her back. "Oh, God!"

"Mean it," Nico told her. "Promise to spend the rest of your life with us."

"You promise first," she snapped back.

Stone released Nico's cock, getting to his knees so he could look down into her face. He met her stare, held it for several heartbeats. "I will spend the rest of my life loving you both. That's a promise."

A tear leaked down her cheek.

Nico was there, brushing it away. "This is the only thing I've ever wanted. You. Stone. The three of us. I promise."

More tears streamed, but Stevie nodded. This time, the word was breathless and rife with the same promise. "Yes. A lifetime."

Stone smiled. "You're not sayin' that so you'll get fucked, are you?"

"No," she insisted while nodding her head.

God, he loved her.

"You're a bad little girl. You know what happens to bad little girls, don't you?"

Her eyes flared with heat.

Nico moved, shifting to her other side, giving Stone the room he needed to spank her pussy. She squealed, bucking her hips.

Stone did it again as Nico kissed her, muffling her cries.

The mood shifted then, still sultry and laced with a desperate hunger, but the connection had been made.

Stone spanked her pussy again, but when Nico moved, so did he.

Nico straddled Stevie's chest, his knees under her still restrained arms, gripping the headboard with one hand.

"Open your mouth," Nico groaned. "Let me feed you my cock while Stone fucks your pussy."

"God, yes. Please." Stevie moaned, spreading her legs.

Stone didn't hesitate. He guided his cock into the sweet, hot depths of her body, gripping her ankles and raising them high in the air. The wet sounds of flesh entering slick holes sounded, combined with their grunts, as they drove her to the pinnacle and beyond. Stevie's cry was muffled by Nico's cock, her pussy clamping down on him.

"Fuck. That's it, baby. Come all over my cock."

Nico roared next, his body jerking and twitching.

Stone waited until he moved before dropping her legs so he could lean over her and pound himself into her, holding her gaze, willing her to see everything. His plans hadn't gone as he thought they would, but nothing he could've dreamed up would ever be as good as this.

Stevie. Nico. Stone. Together. Forever.

The mental image sent him soaring as he came.

FORTY-THREE

Friday, February 23, 2024

"ALL RIGHT, MR. WALKER. I THINK IT'S time we had a talk," Reilly said as she approached Zane at the diner.

She'd been sitting in a booth, nursing a milkshake for the past hour, waiting for her cousin to show up. He came into the diner like clockwork every Friday night to pick up dinner for his family, which was the only reason she was waiting. Turned out, stalking people wasn't all that difficult when they had steadfast routines.

Zane glanced over his shoulder, confusion flashing only a moment before recognition set in. "Oh, hey, kiddo."

"Don't, *hey, kiddo,* me," she said, sticking to her duty to be mad at this man. "And don't flash that charming grin, either. I've had my eye on you."

He chuckled. "Is that right?"

"Yup." Reilly smiled at Myrna as the diner owner approached. "You can go ahead and start makin' his order now. I'll just need a few minutes of his time."

"You told them to delay my order?" Again, he laughed. "Sounds serious."

"It is." Reilly pointed toward the booth. "Have a seat."

"Yes, ma'am."

It wasn't easy to remain stern in the face of a man as sweet and charming as Zane Walker. It was a trait she'd always found endearing, especially when it came to this particular cousin of hers.

She would've waited for him to sit down because that was how she'd envisioned this interrogation going, but Zane wouldn't allow it. He was too much of a gentleman to sit down first, so she slid into the booth and moved her milkshake aside.

"All right, officer," he said with a straight face. "What have I done?"

Reilly canted her head and gave him her best *are you serious right now?* look. "Come on, Zane. Don't play dumb with me."

His eyebrows jumped. "I didn't realize I was."

"You're a smart guy. Think about it. I've got you on multiple counts of bein' … mean."

"Mean?" He snorted a laugh and flopped back, relaxing. "What did *I* do?"

Reilly decided it was time to drop the charade. As much fun as it was to pretend, this was serious.

Leaning forward, she rested her elbows on the table and stacked her arms. "Why'd you tell my brother no?"

It took a second, but Zane's eyes cleared, and all amusement disappeared. "How'd you know about that?"

"Everyone knows about it," she huffed. "And I happen to own the General Store. People talk, and they like to talk to me when they're sneakin' in to grab a candy bar."

"Look, Reilly. I know you mean well, but—"

"No," she insisted. "You don't get to shrug me off. Did you know that crazy bitch from the Double J showed up the other day? Tried to sway my brother into comin' back. She said you called and told her he regretted leavin'."

Zane sat up so fast, it was a wonder the table didn't overturn. "I said nothin' of the sort. I asked about his employment history. Not a damn thing else."

Reilly smiled. "I know."

He frowned. "What?"

"I was lyin' about part of it. Not the showin' up part. She did do that." Reilly twisted her lips. "And not the crazy bitch part. She *is* that." She shoved off her amusement. "Your phone call spurred her into drivin' up here and askin' him to come back to the ranch."

"What'd he say?"

"I don't know," she admitted because she had no idea. She hadn't talked to Stone since she left the barn the other night. According to her mother, the Double J truck left early and Nico's truck was parked at the barn all night, but Reilly didn't know for sure what happened.

Zane shifted to get out of the booth. "I think you should talk to your brother."

She reached for his arm, holding firm. "Wait."

Reluctantly, he turned back, facing her once again.

"Just tell me why you don't want him to have that land. And tell the truth. Don't give me some BS about him not bein' a Walker. That's a crap reason, and you know it."

His eyebrows slammed down. "You heard about that?"

"Come on, Zane. You've lived here for thirty-some-odd years. You know this town doesn't allow secrets. And yeah, people are now askin' why there's so much animosity between the Walkers and the Jamesons."

She could tell he was trying to determine whether she was telling the truth.

Reilly decided to prove she wasn't lying. "Bianca came into the store yesterday. Said she heard the Walkers are tryin' to banish the Jamesons. Somethin' about Lorrie bein' on the outs with her brothers and sisters, and since she's been a Walker longer than she's been a Jameson..."

Reilly let the sentence trail off because it hurt her heart just to repeat it. She knew Bianca hadn't been thinking straight when she laid it out like that because the mayor of Coyote Ridge was going through some things, so she wouldn't hold it against her.

"My daddy heard the rumor, too," Reilly admitted. "Told my mom. Broke her heart. She's close to Lorrie."

"I didn't mean it like that," Zane said, his voice rough. "I was ... angry."

"So you *are* the one who said it?"

His shame flashed on his face like a beacon. "I said a lotta things. Wasn't thinkin' about who might overhear."

"When you're at Moonshiners, you might wanna keep the topics general. Sports. News. Those walls have ears."

"Duly noted."

"What is it really?" she prompted.

He sat back, crossing his arms over his chest. His gaze bored into her, but Reilly didn't flinch. She wanted to know because she needed to make some sense of it. Her family was tight-knit. Always had been. The Walkers and the Jamesons were close, had been since her aunt Lorrie married Curtis sixty years ago. They were the ones who brought the families together, and they'd kept them together through the years. Her heart ached to think that something might come between them. Especially something like hurt feelings.

"Did Stone do somethin' to you? Were you two friends or what?" She knew Stone was a couple of years older than Zane, but they'd gone to the same school, so maybe they'd hung out. Someone mentioned Stone's leaving had disrupted family ties. Of course, at this point, the rumor was spreading like wildfire, and God only knows how much it had been twisted.

Zane's gaze shifted to the table. "Not me."

"Not you, what? Y'all weren't friends?"

He lifted his chin. "I was friends with Stevie."

Reilly let that sink in, but before she could ask a question, he continued.

"Technically, I was datin' her best friend."

"Niyah?"

He nodded. "Nothin' serious, but we hung out a few times. I liked her. Then Stone up and left, and Niyah spent all her time takin' care of Stevie because he broke her heart."

Reilly sat up. "So you're sayin' this isn't about Stone? It's about *you*?"

"No."

She cocked an eyebrow because surely she deserved a better explanation.

When he didn't jump to elaborate, she said, "It sure sounds like you're holdin' a grudge because you got dumped by a girl."

"I didn't get dumped," he retorted hotly. "It wasn't serious. Not at that point."

"Then what is it? You're mad because Niyah stopped payin' attention to you?"

"No," he huffed. "I'm pissed because he broke Stevie's heart. She was my friend, too."

His voice carried, causing several of the diners to turn their way. The sounds in the restaurant faded for a moment.

"You realize people get their hearts broken all the time, right? And then they move on."

"Stevie didn't. Not for a long time."

"Maybe not, but she has now." Reilly held his stare. "You realize they're together now, right?"

His surprise registered across his handsome face. "What?"

Reilly nodded. "Stone's with Nico and Stevie now."

Surprise transitioned into confusion. "Since when?"

"Since about the time he rolled into town. They had some … unfinished business. The three of them," she tacked on.

Zane's countenance remained locked in a confused state.

"Apparently, before he left, he spent some time with both of them. It was a thing. Brief, but evidently, it left a lasting impression. They're together now. Or at least they were the last time I talked to him. Then that crazy bitch rolled in, and I don't know what happened after that. She was goin' on about makin' Stone her pet or some shit. I don't know how it ended."

"Her pet?"

Reilly shrugged. "It's a thing. I don't know. What I *do* know is he's home where he belongs, and he's happy." She lowered her voice and leaned in. "He deserves to be happy, Zane. And it pisses me off that you want to interfere with that." She sat up again, crossed her arms over her chest. "All because you got butthurt over a girl in high school."

"I told you—"

"I'm kiddin'." She dropped one arm and fluttered her fingers. "About the last part. The rest, I mean."

Zane sighed. "He hurt a lotta people when he left, Reilly. What's to say he won't do it again?"

"What's to say any of us won't do it?" she countered. "Are you tellin' me he doesn't deserve to be happy because he followed his dream?"

"What dream?" Zane snorted. "He's a wanderer."

Reilly heard something in his tone, something that flipped a switch, the lightbulb burning so bright, she was surprised beams weren't coming out of her eyeballs.

"You considered leavin' here," she said softly, not wanting anyone to overhear. Rumors started quickly.

Zane frowned, but he didn't dispute it.

"That's what it is. You're not mad because that land belongs to the Walkers or because he broke Stevie's heart. You're mad because he left, and you didn't."

His jaw muscles flexed, but he kept his lips tightly closed.

"Tell me you don't still have regrets," she pleaded. "You've got a beautiful wife and four beautiful boys, Zane."

"I don't," he said quickly, then exhaled heavily. "I don't regret it. I'm happy."

He said the words, but Reilly wasn't sure he believed them.

"But you think about what might've been," she deduced.

"There's nothin' wrong with that," Zane defended.

"You're right. There's not. But Stone's not responsible for that. Those are *your* issues."

Zane sat up straight. "Please don't psychoanalyze my life."

"Trust me. I don't plan to." Reilly forced a smile. "But I'm glad we got to the root of it. Maybe now you can give some honest thought to your parents' offer to Stone. If you still don't want him to have the land, at least now you can make the decision with all the facts. Stone's a good guy, Zane."

"You have to say that. He's your brother."

"He is. And considering our age difference and the fact he hasn't lived here for fifteen years, it should speak volumes that I'm so close to him. He's been there for me over the years, even when he hasn't been physically present."

Zane was quiet for a moment before his eyes crinkled, and a smile pulled at his mouth. "You're a good sister, you know that?"

She nodded. "The best. Ask anyone."

He barked a laugh.

Reilly raised a hand, signaling the waitress that it was okay to come over.

Zane saw the move and frowned. "What are you? Like a mafia don or somethin'?"

The waitress set Zane's food on the table, all packaged up in a brown paper sack.

Reilly giggled. "Or somethin'."

FORTY-FOUR

Saturday, February 24, 2024

"Mornin'," Stone said when he walked into the main office of D & S Landscape on Saturday morning.

"Good morning," Tara replied with a smile, her gaze darting to the box he was carrying in one hand, the drill he had in the other, as she reached for the ringing telephone. "Stevie's in her office. Nico's out on a job site."

"Thanks."

Leaving her to her business, Stone headed for Stevie's office. The door was closed, but he'd learned over the past few days that was par for the course. It was the only way to keep Jäger from getting into everything. Stevie wasn't thrilled with it, but she said it was the only option she had.

Hence the reason he was there.

Stone set the box on the floor, leaned it against the wall, and then balanced the drill on top before knocking on the door. He waited until Stevie called out from the other side.

"Careful," she shouted. "Don't let—"

Stone slipped inside, keeping Jäger from sneaking out.

"Oh, hey," she greeted, leaning back in her chair. "I didn't know you were comin' by."

"I brought a gift," he told her as he scooped Jäger up and carried him over to her. He set the puppy in her lap, then leaned in and stole a quick kiss from her utterly kissable lips.

"A gift?"

"Yep." He turned back to the door. "Hold him."

"That's easier said than done," she called from behind him. "He's squirmy and curious and gettin' more so by the day."

"I'm about to solve that problem," he informed her as he stepped out into the short, narrow hall that separated their offices from the rest of the space.

It took less than a minute to open the box and pull out the child gate. With drill in hand, he moved to the outermost point of the hallway before installing it with a few screws.

"What is that?" Tara asked from her desk. "Never mind. I see it now. That's smart. We should put one on the front door."

Stone looked up at her. "I was thinkin' maybe a glass storm door for there. That way, you can see who's comin' in before they get there."

Her eyes widened. "That would be awesome. Then he won't have to be locked up in there all the time."

"And when he has to be, this'll help with that," he told her as he stood up and pulled the retractable gate closed, hooking it so it would keep Jäger in.

Stevie came out of her office, still holding the squirmy puppy in her arms.

"He's good now," Stone assured her. "This way, he can go back and forth between your office and Nico's whenever he wants."

"That's ... wow. I didn't even think of that."

"Tell her about the storm door idea," Tara shouted before answering the phone with, "Good morning. D and S Landscaping Solutions. How can I assist you today?"

"A storm door?" Stevie asked.

"Yeah. The glass kind. That way, Jäger can look out."

Stevie laughed. "You told Tara it was so she could see when someone's comin' in."

"Gotta know your audience to get 'em on your side."

She smiled and it triggered the warmth in his chest as it always did.

For the past few days, Stone had been spending quite a bit of time with Stevie and Nico. Ever since their declarations the other night, they'd taken to spending their nights together. He was bouncing back and forth between his house and theirs since it was easier to sleep at their place because Stevie insisted a girl needed her things.

Stevie had mentioned he should simply move in—though she'd said it in a roundabout way, not an actual invitation—but Stone wasn't ready for that yet. Well, he was, but he wasn't. Until he could figure out what his future held in terms of a job, he refused to become a burden on them. He intended to fully contribute to the relationship when he took that leap. And he also intended for that to happen in the very near future. No more procrastinating for him.

"I'll gladly buy the storm door if you can find someone to install it," Stevie told him as they watched Jäger sniff at the gate.

"I'll pick one up in a little while. I can install it for you."

"You don't have to do that."

His phone rang before he could tell her he didn't have anything else to do at the moment.

Stone pulled his phone from his pocket and glanced at the screen. "It's Zane."

"Answer it," she said urgently.

She was obviously hoping it was good news. The morning after their eventful evening, he'd explained to Nico and Stevie that Zane was refusing to give his approval. They'd taken it in stride and even encouraged him to take some time to figure out what he wanted to do next. But he was through biding time. He'd called the school superintendent that morning and scheduled an appointment to talk about the future of the FFA program and how he could contribute. It might not be his ideal job, but it was something.

"Stone," Stevie hissed as his phone continued to ring. "Answer. It."

He swiped the screen to take the call and put the phone to his ear. "Yeah?"

"Hey. You got some time this mornin' to talk?"

His first instinct was to tell Zane they had nothing to talk about, but he bit back the retort and said, "Yeah. Sure. Where?"

"My parents' house. In half an hour?"

"I'll be there."

"Cool. See you then."

The call disconnected.

"What did he say?"

Stone looked into Stevie's hopeful gaze and relayed the few words they'd exchanged.

"Good thing it'll only take you five minutes to get there."

"Why's that?"

She flashed a grin, and her gaze turned molten. "Because I was thinkin' I needed to pay you for the gate."

"I don't need you to—"

"I wasn't talkin' about money, Stone," she said pointedly, her eyes glittering with mischief.

"Oh." *Ohhhh.* "What'd you have in mind?"

"Follow me and find out."

Twenty-five minutes later, Stone was parking his truck next to Zane's at his aunt and uncle's house. Despite his reservations, he had a spring in his step. That was all Stevie's fault. She'd blown more than his mind right there in her office with her seductive twist on her repayment—which had been completely unnecessary, but he damn sure wasn't complaining.

It didn't matter what Zane had to say because he was pretty sure the smile was firmly rooted to his face. Being back home in Coyote Ridge and having Stevie and Nico in his life was the best of everything as far as he was concerned. The rest would fall into place as it was meant to.

However, he would hear Zane out. It was the least he could do.

He got out of his truck and started toward the front porch but stopped when Zane called out to him.

Spinning around, he watched as Zane hopped out of his truck and made his way over. "Why aren't you inside?"

Zane stuffed his hands in the pocket of his coat. "That conversation doesn't involve me."

Stone was confused. "I don't under—"

"Look, man. I acted like an idiot."

The about-face caught him off guard, but he faced Zane, willing to hear him out.

"I let my personal feelings get in the way. I'm sure Reilly told you, and I'm sorry about that. I fucked up."

"Reilly? What does she have to do with this?"

Zane's eyebrows rose. "You didn't talk to her?"

"Not in a few days, no."

A sheepish grin pulled at his cousin's mouth. "Let's just say that sister of yours is one of a kind."

She was that, though Stone wasn't sure why Zane thought so.

"She dressed me down good. Right in the middle of the diner."

"What?"

Zane laughed. "She missed her calling. That girl could be president one day. Or maybe in charge of the CIA. She's quite the interrogator." He poked the toe of his boot against the ground. "She made me realize I was bein' an idiot. I let my personal bullshit interfere when I shouldn't have."

"What personal bullshit?"

Zane shook his head. "I'll let her give you the lowdown." He cocked his chin toward the house. "Right now, they're waitin' for you, and it's too fuckin' cold to stand out here when the only thing you need to know is that I'm sorry. I know you left because you were chasin' your dream. It's not my place to judge you for that."

"Chasin' my dream, huh?" Stone waited for Zane to look up. "That makes it sound almost noble."

Zane frowned.

"It's true, I wanted to work on a ranch, thought I could make a career out of it, but it wasn't really ever my dream. I lied to myself for a long time, tryin' to make it mine, but it didn't stick."

"Why'd you leave then?"

"Because I was in love with Stevie."

Zane's forehead creased, his confusion evident.

"I was in love with her," Stone clarified, "but confused after … after somethin' happened with Nico. It took one night with the two of them for me to realize what I needed to be complete."

"Two partners?" Zane prompted.

"Yeah. But Stevie was still in high school, and I had nothin' to offer her. When I thought about what I would want from her at that point, what I might ask of her, I knew she deserved more than that. So, no, I wasn't chasin' a dream. I was runnin' from the only thing I've ever loved."

"Wow. That…" Zane inhaled deeply and exhaled slowly. "That makes so much damn sense."

He wasn't being facetious, so Stone waited for him to say more.

"Love makes you do crazy things, huh?" Zane asked. "Your sister tells me you're with Stevie and Nico now."

"I am. And this time around, I won't take it for granted."

"A hard lesson to learn."

That was an understatement.

"I guess I should've heard you out, huh? Would've saved us both some time." Zane stood taller. "I'm sorry for the part I played in this. Like I said, personal bullshit got in the way."

The last thing Stone expected was an apology. He thought for sure he was being summoned so his aunt and uncle could deliver the bad news in person. He'd even come up with a speech of his own because, as far as he was concerned, it was all behind them. Stone wouldn't hold a grudge. In fact, he understood.

"We good?" Zane asked, his eyes glittering with what looked a hell of a lot like hope as he held out his hand.

Stone clapped his palm against Zane's, then pulled him in for a back-slapping hug. "Of course we are, man."

Zane hugged him back. "Maybe you can swing by the house one of these days. The boys would love to see you. And V's eager to hear more cowboy stories. She was pissed that Beau got to hear 'em before she did."

"Just tell me when, and I'll be there."

Zane nodded as he stepped back. "Go on. They've got somethin' to talk about, and you know how my Pop gets when you keep him waitin'."

Stone waited until Zane pulled out of the driveway before he went to the door.

"COME ON IN, BOY!" CURTIS CALLED FROM his place at the kitchen table. "You don't need a chaperone."

Lorrie chuckled. The things her husband came up with. His gruff tone would've scared away a lesser man.

She got to her feet as her nephew came inside, shrugging out of his coat and hanging it on the rack near the door. His heavy steps echoed on the hardwood as he made his way to the kitchen.

"Coffee?" she offered.

"Yes, ma'am. Thank you."

"Sit," Curtis grumbled.

Lorrie rolled her eyes and shook her head as she prepared the coffee. She also smiled because she knew her husband was excited about this meeting. You wouldn't know it to hear him talk, but he'd been going on all morning about it. He was probably looking forward to it more than Stone.

Then again, she wasn't sure her nephew was all that excited. He looked like someone had just kicked his dog.

"Thank you," Stone said when she placed the mug in front of him.

"So?" Curtis prompted. "You bring it with you?"

"What's that, sir?"

A lot of *sirs* and *ma'ams* being thrown around. That usually didn't bode well.

"Your proposal. I got an earful from my boys. I thought for sure you'd bring it for me to take a look at."

Stone glanced her way, then back to Curtis. "I left my computer at home. I thought… I can go get it."

"No need." Curtis pulled a laptop from the empty chair and set it in front of Stone. "Use mine."

"I can't access it from your computer," Stone explained. "It's on my hard drive."

"It's on mine, too." Curtis lifted the lid on the computer. "Go on."

Stone frowned. "I'm confused."

"You shouldn't be."

Lorrie watched as Curtis took a sip of coffee, acting as though it was no big deal. It was a big deal—a huge one, considering the email that had been sent with the proposal.

"My email's open. Pull it up," Curtis instructed.

Stone's finger swiped across the trackpad on the computer, his gaze still lingering on them.

"It's in the email," Curtis said, his tone gruffer than before.

"Yes, sir."

"Now don't go gettin' nosy, boy," Curtis said, and it was clear he was trying to hide his smile. "Just look for the email from Nico Daugherty."

Stone's head snapped up, his eyes wide.

"You look surprised, boy."

"I am."

"Surprised that Nico sent it to me? Or surprised that he sent a novel along with it?"

Lorrie smiled when Curtis looked at her and winked.

Last night, she'd read the email that Nico had sent to Curtis, explaining all the reasons why Stone deserved the opportunity despite Zane's reason. Evidently, they hadn't been aware of their youngest's change of heart.

"Go on and read the email first," Lorrie told Stone because she could see on his face that he was curious.

"Read it out loud," Curtis tacked on.

Stone's gaze swung between them once more before his attention returned to the screen. "Mr. Walker, I'll warn you that I have an extra set of eyes on me as I type this. Those beautiful eyes belong to Stevie Shepherd. As for why I'm writing this and not her, I can't explain. It's simply the way she wants it, and as you probably know, when you love someone, you do their bidding without question."

Lorrie's heart filled with warmth the same way it had the first time she read it.

"I'll also tell you, the only bidding I'm doing is hers because Stone doesn't know about this email. He doesn't know that Stevie and I have spent the better part of two days attempting to figure out how to make his dreams come true because that's what you do when you love someone. You go to bat for them."

Stone inhaled sharply, his eyes looking questionably glassy, but Lorrie didn't mention it.

"Keep readin'," Curtis instructed.

"That's what we're doing. I'm writing this because we want you to know that Zane may have valid reasons for judging Stone based on his history, but Stone is so much more than the mistakes he's made. We've all made our share, and we'll continue to do so because that is the way of life. Stone deserves to be judged on who he is now, and I'll tell you firsthand that he's not the same man he was fifteen years ago. And yes, I'm biased. I love him. Stevie loves him. We only want to give him what he's given us, and that's far more than I can explain in a brief letter."

Curtis snorted, again winking at her. "Brief, he said."

Lorrie smiled. "Hush now. Go on, Stone."

He cleared his throat. "I've attached the business proposal that Stone has worked diligently to prepare. I hope you'll take a few minutes to review it because, sir, it's impressive. I honestly think Stone missed his calling. He's got a head for business, and I think success is inevitable when you allow a man as determined as him the opportunity to pursue his dream. Ultimately, the decision is yours, but we couldn't let you make it without ensuring you had all the facts. Stone is a good man, and you can't go wrong investing in him. I know this for fact … sorry, make that *we*. Can't leave Stevie out. Thank you for your time."

Lorrie didn't attempt to hide the tears that welled in her eyes. The first time she'd read the email, she'd sobbed like a lovesick schoolgirl because that was one of the sweetest things she'd ever read.

"We looked over the proposal," Curtis said when Stone took a gulp of his coffee, clearly biding time before he spoke. "Nico's right. It's rather impressive."

"Thank you, sir."

"Don't thank me, just promise me somethin'."

Stone's eyes locked on his uncle.

"Promise me that you'll keep followin' those dreams. I'm not here to dictate what you can and can't do with that land. It's never been about that. I wanted to see that you were serious and"—he nodded toward the computer—"even without that novel, I knew you were."

"Yes, sir."

Curtis looked at her, and Lorrie's chest warmed from the love she felt for him. It was always like that. Curtis Walker had stolen her heart sixty years ago, and he still held it in the palm of his hand because that's what you do when you find your soulmate. You give it to them because you know they'll take care of it no matter what.

She suspected that Stone had found his soulmates, too.

"This is for you," Curtis told him, producing the envelope he'd hidden in the chair. "I had the papers drawn up and that's a deed to the land. It's yours, free and clear. We only ask that you hold to our original stipulations. If it ever gets too much for you, pass it along to someone in the family who'll do right by it."

Stone's throat worked on a swallow. "Yes, sir."

"Now, if you're done with your coffee, I think you've got work to do, boy."

Stone huffed a laugh, and Lorrie could tell he was holding back the emotion churning inside him.

"Or you could stay for another cup of coffee, and we can talk about your plans to build a garden for the school," she told him. "I love the idea."

Stone smiled. "I'd like that."

"Good," Curtis grumbled. "Go put on another pot, boy, and you can tell us all about it."

Lorrie laughed, shaking her head. That wasn't what she meant, but who was she to intervene?

Curtis somehow knew exactly how to keep the kids from shattering into pieces, even when it was clear they were on the verge.

He was a good man, her husband.

EPILOGUE

Friday, March 15, 2024

"YOU CAN'T TELL ME THAT WASN'T AWKWARD."

Stone glanced in the rearview. "What are we talkin' about again?"

They'd been on the road for almost three hours, during which Stevie had spent the entire time sleeping. Only now, she was awake and apparently starting a conversation he was supposed to be a part of. Only he had no idea what she was talking about.

"Are we already home?"

"Two minutes out," Nico told her. "I need to stop by the office before we go home. Tara's meetin' us there with Jäger."

"I miss him," Stevie said, yawning.

Stone did, too.

"I still can't believe your sister interrogated you about your intentions," Stevie said.

Ah. So they were back on that.

Stone had invited Stevie and Nico to go with him to Dallas after Chelsea gave birth to a healthy baby boy. While Stone's parents had been up there for a week, arriving in time for the birth and intending to stay for at least another week, Stone had planned to slip in and out, making an appearance, greeting the newest Jameson, and then getting out of the way. Donovan, Tate, Reilly, and Brady all had the same plan. CJ had gone up before they did, but he'd left as soon as they arrived, not wanting to overcrowd, or so he claimed.

The visit qualified as good for the most part. Stevie, Reilly, and Deborah had spent all their time cooing over the baby. The men had sat around, congratulating Paul and giving him shit about all the sleep he was about to miss out on.

It had been quite entertaining right up until Chelsea started interrogating him about his intentions with Stevie and Nico. Mostly Nico. She was rather protective of her ex-boyfriend despite the fact they'd all reminded her that things hadn't been quite rainbows and unicorns back when they broke up. Chelsea was trying to see the good in everything, so they hadn't argued too much about it.

"And she wasn't mad," Stevie noted. "What was up with that?"

"Why would she be?" he asked.

"You're her brother. Nico's her ex-boyfriend." She didn't add the *duh,* but Stone could tell it was implied.

"And she's married with a kid," he retorted.

"Plus, it's been fifteen years," Nico tacked on.

"And that," Stone agreed.

"I wouldn't've been okay with it."

"Really?"

"Probably not," she said. "Could you maybe speed it up a little? I've gotta pee."

Stone chuckled as he pulled down the driveway leading to D & S Landscaping Solutions.

"Brace yourself," Nico warned.

Stevie grunted at the first pothole they hit. "Oh, God. Hurry."

Stone laughed, dodging as many potholes as he could, trying to help her out.

"Oh, good. She's already here," Nico said.

"Yes. Very good," Stevie said through gritted teeth. "I'm not sure I can hold out long enough to unlock the door."

Stone parked the truck beside Tara's car. Stevie didn't wait for anyone, launching herself out and racing up the steps. He was almost on the steps when he heard Stevie shout.

"Oh, my God! What the—"

Stone glanced at Nico, both of them bounding up the rest of the steps and racing after her. He came to an abrupt stop, barely avoiding a collision with Stevie.

"What the hell?" Stone asked, staring at his brother. "CJ?"

"It's not what it looks like," CJ declared.

Oh, Stone was pretty sure he was wrong about that. His hair was disheveled, his shirt partially unbuttoned. Behind him, Tara had her back to them as she tried to put her shirt on. They'd clearly been getting busy or about to be until they were interrupted.

Stevie squealed, then darted toward the bathroom. "Don't move!" she shouted. "We're gonna talk about this in a minute."

"She's gotta pee," Nico told them, trying to be helpful. "Where's Jäger?"

Tara pointed toward their offices.

Jäger barked from his spot on the other side of the child gate. He barked again before Nico could make his way over.

Stone stared at his brother, confused. Just two days ago, he'd sat down to a family meal with CJ and Jamie, his girlfriend. A girlfriend who *wasn't* the redhead standing behind him.

He wanted to call CJ out on it. To ask him if he broke up with Jamie, the girl he'd been seeing for *years*. However, he was cognizant of Tara's feelings, and if she wasn't aware of CJ's relationship status, Stone figured it wasn't his place to inform her. Yet.

"Could y'all maybe give us a minute?" CJ asked, his eyes pleading.

"Sure." He turned and headed outside, Nico right behind him, Jäger trotting along.

"Tell me I was seein' things," Nico said when they were outside, the glass door closed behind them.

Jäger made a beeline for a patch of grass.

"No. Definitely not seein' things."

"What about Jamie?"

"Question of the hour," Stone said, walking over to the deck rail and propping a hip against it.

The door opened behind them. Stone turned to see CJ walking out, planting his Stetson on his head.

"Can we talk?" his brother asked, glancing between him and Nico.

"I'll be inside. It won't take me a minute to get what I need, so just let me know when y'all are done."

Stone nodded, then turned his attention to CJ.

CJ glanced behind him, waiting for the door to close. When it did, he turned back. "You're probably thinkin' I'm a shithead."

"It had crossed my mind, yeah." Stone crossed his arms over his chest. "You and Jamie call it quits?"

CJ swallowed, his gaze shifting to his feet. "Not exactly."

"Fuck," Stone huffed. "What the hell're you thinkin', man?"

"It's not what it looks like, Stone. I swear—"

"Then what is it?"

"Me and Jamie … it's…" He exhaled roughly and tipped his head back, staring up at the sky. "It's not what it appears."

Stone tried to process what he was saying, but it didn't make sense.

"Okay," he drawled when CJ didn't explain.

But that wasn't enough to prompt his brother.

"CJ?"

"I wish I could tell you, but I can't."

"Does Tara know?"

"Yes."

Well, that made him feel a little better. Not much, but a little. He didn't want to think his brother was a cheater. There were a lot of things he could tolerate, but he'd always been of the mind that you love the one you're with. And if you want to be with someone else, end things. It was the only fair thing to do. For all parties.

"All right then," Stone said, standing tall. "I guess it's your life to do with as you see fit. Just…" He looked at the building. "Just don't break any hearts, okay?"

"Trust me when I tell you, that's not gonna happen."

Stone did trust CJ. He was a stand-up guy. Always had been. He was a giant pain in Stone's ass a lot of the time, but he was a good guy.

"Maybe next weekend we could get together," Stone told him, turning around when he heard the soft rumble of an engine.

"For?" CJ stared out at the car approaching.

"I've ordered supplies to build the first greenhouse. Thought maybe you'd help out. If you don't have a shift."

"I can do that." CJ nodded his chin toward the car as it parked. "You know this person?"

"I do not." Since it was Friday, Stone knew the office wasn't open. Didn't mean they didn't get people who stumbled across the place and pulled in to check them out.

"I think I'm gonna head out," CJ noted. "I'll see you next weekend."

"If not before," Stone threatened, watching as his brother walked toward his truck.

"Y'all get that straightened out?" Nico asked, coming out to join him on the deck. Hearing Nico's voice, Jäger raced up the steps, nearly nose-planting into Nico's leg for attention.

Before Stone could respond, Nico mumbled something under his breath.

"Are y'all ready to get—" Stevie's words cut off abruptly. "Oh, my God."

"You sure are sayin' that a lot today," Stone told her. "And not in the way I like to hear."

Stevie planted her hands on her hips and marched past them, down the steps, and right up to the car where a guy was getting out. He had a huge grin plastered on his face as she approached.

"Hey," the guy greeted. "You look good, baby."

"Do *not* call me that," Stevie snapped, stabbing a finger in the guy's direction.

Stone cocked an eyebrow and looked at Nico. "Who the fuck is that?"

"Oscar," Nico growled.

"*That's* Oscar?" Stone couldn't help it, he laughed. "Wow. I was expectin' some big, burly cowboy or somethin'."

Nico frowned, his tone reflecting his surprise. "Really?"

He damn sure hadn't expected some scrawny teenager. Granted, it was obvious Oscar wasn't actually a teenager, but someone hadn't told his wardrobe that yet.

"He never gives up," Nico muttered under his breath.

Stone grinned. "I know a way to help him along."

Nico's eyes lit up with curiosity. "Yeah?"

"Yep. And after we scare him straight, I think we should take our girl home and remind her why she's got no time for other guys in her life."

"I like where you're goin' with this."

Several hours later, after they'd set their girl straight and worn themselves out in the process, Stone sat on the back porch of the home he now shared with a damn cute dog and the two people he loved more than life.

His life had come full circle, and he knew he would never have to waste another minute searching for anything. It wasn't necessary when he already had everything he could possibly need.

ACKNOWLEDGMENTS

When I first sat down to write Stone's book, I knew minimal details about him. I knew he had left town for bigger things, and I knew he was coming back. As the story came together and I met Stevie and Nico, I knew this was going to be one of my absolute favorites. I hope you enjoyed reading their story as much as I enjoyed writing it.

Now for my thanks…

My husband, my rock, is always at the top of the list. He not only allows me to live my dream but also shares it with me. He has dinner with me every night, even if he thinks I might spend too much time talking to imaginary people. I'm okay with that as long as I don't have to cook.

Chancy, Jenna … as usual, I couldn't do it without your feedback.

Nicole Nation 2.0, thank you for your constant support and love and for those of you who have my back. You've been there for me from almost the beginning. This group of ladies has kept me going for so long that I'm not sure I'd know what to do without them.

And, of course, YOU, the reader. Your emails, messages, posts, comments … they mean more to me than you can imagine. I thrive on hearing from you; knowing that my characters and stories have touched you somehow keeps me going. I've been known to shed a tear or two when reading an email because your support brings so much joy to my life. I thank you for that.

ABOUT NICOLE EDWARDS

New York Times and *USA TODAY* bestselling author Nicole Edwards lives in the suburbs of Austin, Texas, with her husband, their three fur babies, and the youngest of their three children, who has threatened never to leave home. When Nicole is not writing about sexy alpha males and sassy, independent women, she can often be found with a book in hand or attempting to keep the dogs happy. You can find her hanging out on social media and interacting with her readers - even when she's supposed to be writing.

Connect With Nicole

I hope you're as eager to get the information as I am to give it. Any of these things is worth signing up for, or feel free to sign up for all. I do my best to keep each one unique and interesting.

NIC NEWS: If you haven't signed up for my newsletter and want notifications regarding preorders, new releases, giveaways, sales, etc., then you'll want to sign up. I promise not to spam your email, just get you the most important updates.

RAMBLINGS OF A WRITER BLOG: My blog is used for writer ramblings, which I am known to do from time to time.

NICOLE NATION: Visit my website to get exclusive content you won't find anywhere else, including sneak peeks, A Day in the Life character stories, exclusive giveaways, cards from Nicole, or join Nicole's review team.

NICOLE NATION ON FACEBOOK: Join my reader group to interact with other readers, ask me questions, play fun weekly games, celebrate during release week, and enter exclusive giveaways!

INSTAGRAM: Basically, Instagram is where I post pictures of my dogs, so if you want to see epic cuteness, you should follow me.

NAUGHTY & NICE SHOP: Not only does the shop have signed books, but there's fun merchandise, too—plenty of naughty and nice options to go around. Find the shop on my website.

Website:	www.NicoleEdwards.me
Facebook:	/Author.Nicole.Edwards
Instagram:	/NicoleEdwardsAuthor
TikTok:	/@nicoleedwardsauthor
BookBub:	/NicoleEdwardsAuthor
Goodreads:	/nicole_edwards

THE JAMESONS OF COYOTE RIDGE

Hot Chocolate Wishes
Rough & Dirty

AUSTIN ARROWS

Rush
Kaufman

CLUB DESTINY

Conviction
Temptation
Addicted
Seduction
Infatuation
Captivated
Devotion
Perception
Entrusted
Adored
Distraction
Forevermore

DEAD HEAT RANCH

Boots Optional
Betting on Grace
Overnight Love
Jared *(a crossover novel)*

DEVIL'S BEND

Chasing Dreams
Vanishing Dreams

MISPLACED HALOS

Protected in Darkness
Salvation in Darkness
Bound in Darkness

OFFICE INTRIGUE

Office Intrigue
Intrigued Out of The Office
Their Rebellious Submissive
Their Famous Dominant
Their Ruthless Sadist
Their Naughty Student
Their Fairy Princess
Owned

PIER 70

Reckless
Fearless
Speechless
Harmless
Clueless

PRIMAL INSTINCTS

Chase (Volume 1-3)
Capture (Volume 4-6)
Claim (Volume 7-9)

HEROES & HAVOC

(Sniper 1 Security, Devil's Playground, Southern Boy Mafia)

Wait for Morning
Beautifully Brutal
Without Regret
Never Say Never
Beautifully Loyal
Without Restraint
Tomorrow's Too Late

STANDALONE NOVELS

Unhinged Trilogy
A Million Tiny Pieces
Inked on Paper
Bad Reputation
Bad Business
Filthy Hot Billionaire
RULE

NAUGHTY HOLIDAY EDITIONS
2015
2016
2021